IDAHO

Emily Ruskovich grew up in the Idaho Panhandle, on Hoodoo Mountain. Her fiction has appeared in *Zoetrope*, *One Story* and the *Virginia Quarterly Review*. A winner of a 2015 O. Henry Award and a graduate of the Iowa Writers' Workshop, she now teaches creative writing at the University of Colorado Denver. *Idaho* is her first novel.

IDAHO

EMILY RUSKOVICH

Chatto & Windus

LONDON

1 3 5 7 9 10 8 6 4 2

Chatto & Windus, an imprint of Vintage,
20 Vauxhall Bridge Road,
London SW1V 2SA

Chatto & Windus is part of the Penguin Random House group of companies
whose addresses can be found at global.penguinrandomhouse.com.

Copyright © Emily Ruskovich 2017

First published in the UK by Chatto & Windus in 2017
First published in the US by Random House in 2017

penguin.co.uk/vintage

A CIP catalogue record for this book is available from the British Library

HB ISBN 9780701189082
TPB ISBN 9780701189099

Printed and bound by Clays Ltd, St Ives plc

Penguin Random House is committed to a sustainable future
for our business, our readers and our planet. This book is made from
Forest Stewardship Council® certified paper.

For Dearest and Fa

2004

They never drove the truck, except once or twice a year to get fire-wood. It was parked just up the hill in front of the woodshed, where it collected rain in the deep dents on the hood and mosquito larvae in the rainwater. That was the way it was when Wade was married to Jenny, and that's the way it is now that he is married to Ann.

Ann goes up there sometimes to sit in the truck. She waits until Wade is busy, so that he won't notice that she's gone. Today, she comes here under the pretense of getting firewood, dragging a blue sled over the mud and grass and patches of snow. The wood-shed isn't far from the house, but it's hidden from view by a stand of ponderosa pines. She feels like she is trespassing, like none of this is hers to see.

The truck is parked on a rare space of flat land, an unlikely shelf carved into the mountainside. In front of the woodshed, around the truck, a few loose bricks lie here and there in the grass and snow. Spindles of mangled wire lean against the trees. Hanging from a long larch limb are two thick ropes that sway opposite each other now, but look as if they might have once been connected by a flat board—a child's swing.

It is March, sunny and cold. Ann gets into the driver's seat and shuts the door quietly. She pulls the seatbelt across her body, then rolls the window down so that several droplets splatter on her lap. She touches the wet spots with her fingertip, connecting them with lines in her mind to make a picture on her thigh. The picture reminds her of a mouse, or at least a child's drawing of a mouse, with a triangle face and a long, curlicued tail. Nine years ago, when Wade was still married to Jenny and both of his daughters were still alive, a mouse had crawled along the top of the truck's exhaust pipe into the engine compartment, and built its nest on the manifold. She thinks of how strange it is that Wade probably remembers that mouse, remembers the sound of it skittering under the hood, and yet he's forgotten his first wife's name. Or so it seems sometimes. But the mouse—the mouse is still very much alive in his memory.

A few years after Ann and Wade married, Ann found a pair of deerskin gloves in a toolbox high on a shelf in a closet. They were much nicer than the work gloves Wade usually wore, and seemed to be brand new except for the odor of something burned. That was how she learned about the mouse in the first place. She asked why he kept the gloves stored in their closet instead of using them. Wade told her that he wanted to preserve the smell.

What smell is that?

The smell of a rodent's nest that caught on fire.

The last smell in his daughter's hair.

It was a long time ago now that he said things like that. He stopped talking about the details of his daughter's death once he saw how much Ann held on to them. He probably thinks she's forgotten about the gloves, it's been so many years. But she hasn't. He keeps them in the filing cabinet with his papers, in his office upstairs. She has opened the drawer just enough to see them.

That mouse had probably been in the truck the whole winter, during that last year that Wade was married to Jenny, that last year that May was alive and June was safe. Ann thinks of the mouse going back and forth in the snow between the truck and the barn, hauling mouthfuls of hay or insulation or tufts of stuffing from the dogs' beds, making its nest bigger and having babies in it once spring arrived. Some of the babies probably died early on and were absorbed by the nest, their tiny bones like shards of straw themselves. And other mice came, too; you could hear them moving under the hood if you put your ear against it. The little girls liked doing that.

Well, at least Ann imagines they did.

One day in August, the whole family got into the truck. Wade at the steering wheel, where Ann is sitting now, Jenny next to him, their daughters, June and May, nine and six, crammed in back with a jug of lemonade and Styrofoam cups, which they carved pictures into with their fingernails. The girls probably wanted to ride in the truck bed, but their mother would have said it was not safe on the highway. So they sat facing each other in the cab with their backs against the windows, bumping their knees, probably fighting.

They forgot all about the mice. They didn't notice anything at first, driving slowly over the dirt roads. But once they reached the highway in their town of Ponderosa, a smell like decay and burning hair, skin and seeds sizzling on a hot engine, entered through the vent and filled the whole cab of the truck until the little girls were gagging and laughing and pushing their freckled noses out their windows.

They had to drive on with their windows down, tolerating the smell, for the hour drive through the Nez Valley, past Athol and Careywood, then up the long road nearly to the top of Loeil, the mountain where the birch wood was already cut and piled, ready to be loaded. Their hair and clothes, and Wade's gloves, held the burned smell in their fibers. Ann pictures June and May. They wait in the sun while their mother rolls the birch logs onto the truck bed and their father stacks them there. The girls lean against the tires, slapping horseflies on their legs, pouring lemonade into the dust.

The smell would have been there on the way back, too. It is the one constant. It connects two things in Ann's mind that she can't manage to connect otherwise—the drive up the mountain and the drive back down. The drive back down is the part Ann comes here to try to understand.

There would have been things Wade had to consider, before he could take control and go for help. Practical things. Shutting the tailgate, for example, so the logs wouldn't roll out. He would have had to remember to hold the handle up and then push in—there was a trick to it—in order to lock the tailgate. That he would re-member, that his fingers could do what they were supposed to do even in the midst of his horror, has something to do with the rea-son Ann loves him. One day, perhaps, everything will be gone from his mind except the trick of the tailgate latch, and Ann will love him still.

She thinks of how easy it would have been to get lost on the way back down, since they'd gotten lost so badly on the way up. How could anything have looked familiar? The narrow, grassy roads. The crudely made road signs nailed to trees: That he had read them an hour before seemed impossible to her. All of it seemed impossible. The summer sky, the snapping of twigs under the truck's tires. The smell of grease and honeysuckle. Jenny's breath fogging the window.

Ann has had to imagine most of it, everything beyond the facts Wade told her or she heard on TV. She did try very hard during those early days to keep the radio and TV off, so that everything she knew she knew from Wade. What Wade wanted to tell her, she would keep. But she wouldn't let herself go searching; she wouldn't let herself ask.

But all of that is different now that Wade is forgetting. She wants to ask him if he and Jenny spoke, before his memory is lost for good. Did Jenny look out the side window or straight ahead? Or did she look at him?

At what point did he rip down the rearview mirror?

No, Ann thinks, it isn't even the drive back. It is his getting into the truck at all. Opening the door and getting in. Jenny there with the cup of lemonade shaking in her hand—or maybe not shaking, maybe perfectly still. Maybe the cup empty. Maybe the droplets of lemonade spilled on her lap like the droplets of water now on Ann's thigh, in the shape of something harmless, something that the child in the backseat might have drawn.

Ann runs her hand over the dashboard and the soft, moist pollen of last summer sticks to her palm. It is all put together for her, here. The rearview mirror is up again, glued in place, and there's a dream catcher thrown around it, with two fluorescent feathers hanging down. The carpet has been shampooed, the right backseat replaced entirely, with one that looks like the original on the left, only a brighter shade of blue and missing the little holes where the stuffing came out and where the girls might have once stuck their fingers.

Ann turns the key to let the engine run while she sits here. She breathes deeply. Nine years and the smell of the mouse's nest is gone, but every now and then, when she shifts in the driver's seat and the dust rises from the cushions, she catches what might be the hint of that old smell, distant and thinly sweet, leather and burning grass.

Though of course it could also be the controlled spring fires down in the valley fields, far away.

■

Ann and Wade have been married for eight years. She is thirty-eight now, and Wade is fifty.

Last year, Ann found a box of Wade's old shirts in the attic. She brought the box downstairs and sat on her knees in a warm square of sunlight on the floor. She unfolded the shirts one at a time, held each one up, and placed some in a pile for the Salvation Army and some in a pile to keep.

Wade walked into the bedroom and saw her doing this.

"Is this too small?" she said. She didn't turn around because she was trying to decide about an oil stain. She was holding the shirt up above her, to see the light shine through it.

Wade didn't answer. She thought he hadn't heard. She folded the shirt and moved on.

But the next thing she knew, Wade was pushing her head down, pushing it hard, into the box of clothes. She was so shocked that at first she laughed. But he didn't stop. The cardboard edge rubbed against her throat, and her laugh became a gasp for air and then a scream. She clawed at his legs, thrashing blindly. She pounded her fists on his shoes, jammed her elbows into his knees. He was speaking to her in a voice she recognized—she couldn't think from where—but it was not a voice he'd ever used with her. "No! No!"—almost a growl.

His dogs. He used that voice to train the dogs.

Then he let her go. He stepped back. She lifted her head, slowly, with caution. He sighed deeply, then he touched her shoulder as if to ask for her forgiveness, or—this occurred to her even in her shock—to offer forgiveness to her. After a minute, he asked her if she'd seen his mowing shoes.

"No," she said, staring into the box of clothes. She sat on her knees, shaking, smoothing down the static in her hair, over and over again, as if that would make a difference. Wade found his shoes, put them on, went outside. In a few minutes, she heard the tractor. Wade was clearing the knapweed from the pasture.

In the year leading up to the strange episode with the box of clothes, he had done other things that alarmed her. He made phone calls to his customers, accusing them of sending bad checks, even as Ann proved to him with bank statements that he was wrong. He threaded his bootlaces so that they tied at the bottom instead of the top. He purchased the same pair of pliers three times in one week. He threw her fresh loaf of bread, still sinking in its warmth, into the mulch bucket to feed the hens as if she had baked it for them. Once, in the last week of January, he cut a beautiful white pine and dragged it a mile through the new snow. When he arrived in the yard where Ann was, he motioned to it, smiling. "You think this is too tall?"

A Christmas tree.

"But Christmas— Wade, it was a month ago."

"What?"

"You don't remember?" She laughed, horrified. "Where do you think you got that coat you're wearing?"

But the day he pushed her into the box of clothes was something very different; it was the only time his disease manifested itself in violence, violence so far removed from the man he was that Ann couldn't fathom such a thing happening even in the moments that immediately followed.

But after it happened once, it happened again. A few months later, he pushed her against the refrigerator, so that her cheek pressed against a coupon she'd hung there, for a diner called Panhandler Pies. She fought him, but just like the first time, fighting only hurt her more. When he let her go, she pushed him away from her and screamed at him, but he just stood there sadly, as if disappointed in her.

Another day, not too long after that, Ann poured a bucket of pinecones onto the kitchen table. She intended to decorate them with peanut butter and birdseed, to hang on the tree limbs for the finches. But as soon as she sat down to work, she felt his hand on her head, and he pushed her down into the pinecones. The pinecones left a rash of tiny cuts on her left cheek.

Later still, the wind blew open the door of one of his daughters' old rooms. He thought it was Ann who had opened it. He pressed her forehead against the door once it was closed again, and told her, "No, no, no," until she said, in her fear and shock, "Okay."

She did not understand these things, but knew that Wade didn't understand them, either, and so she found no way to express her anger. No way to stop these episodes from happening again. The pain and the shock of them wore off the more they happened, and she began to bear the assaults because she didn't know what else she could do. She took note of what provoked him, and made sure never to do those things again. No more pinecones, no Panhandler Pies, no boxes of old clothes, no going in his daughters' rooms. Simple enough. These things were a kind of collection she began to keep, a list she would run down in her mind, eventually not out of pain anymore but out of wonder, as if something were right there on the edge of her life, waiting for her to discover it. At night, when he was asleep, she thought about these things as she studied the face she loved. His pale eyelids stark on his sun-roughed face. His lips chapped, his cheeks unshaven. Such inherent kindness in his body that it was impossible to picture this man doing the things he had certainly done. She touched her lips to his thick hair, and she closed her eyes, too.

Wade has been training dogs since he was a boy. Hunting hounds, rescue dogs, seeing-eyes, service dogs for veterans. Now he raises bluetick coonhounds from pups, just a few of them at a time, and he trains them to tree animals he never shoots, because killing doesn't interest him. What interests him is the training itself. And now it's what interests Ann. She watches this training as if she is learning something about their marriage. When she sees him teach a lesson to a dog, pushing its snout down hard into the feathers and blood of a hen it killed, and then into the freshly dug soil under the chicken fence, she sees that he does it with love. Love and disappointment and a sense of duty to teach it something for its own good, as if the only way the dog will remember its mistakes is if those mistakes have a texture and a smell and taste. It isn't punishment, exactly; it's a way to remember. And maybe it's the same with her. It's as if he now acts upon what he's always felt, that there is a language barrier between him and Ann that can be broken only with force and brute love and a few hard, repeated words. *No, Bad, Not Yours.* At least he wanted her to hear him.

Sometimes, of course, it breaks her heart.

Once, a commercial for fabric softener came on TV. It showed a mother and two girls taking clothes down from the line after a sudden thundershower, snapping the dresses from the pins. The line sprang up; the droplets flew and splattered them. The scene on the TV upset him. He couldn't remember why, or whom to blame, but just like the time with the pinecones on the table, Ann saw this special panic on his face. She touched his hand as if to say, as if to make it easier, "*I'm* doing this to you." His eyes fell on her. She got down on her knees in front of the television. He pushed one side of her face hard against the TV screen, saying in his practiced voice, "No! No!"

This was the way she loved him now.

She felt his rough hand against her head, the static in her hair and the small shocks of the screen on her temple. She felt in those moments that she was finally doing something for him, something that mattered, as if this were a part of her vow she'd only just now learned how to keep. She nodded her head between his hand and the screen ("I'm sorry, Wade, I'm so sorry") and promised him it would never happen again.

◼

Ann has seen two pictures of his younger daughter, May. The first was on TV. The second, a Polaroid, she brought out from under the refrigerator with her broom five years ago. She picked it up out of the dust and hair, and there was something sticky on its surface that when she scratched it came off in tiny red peels, like dry jam. In the picture, May held a cloth doll that looked just like her:

blond, straight bangs, hair cut to her chin, Popsicle-bright lips. She wore a swimming suit top and skirted bloomers, and there were cat scratches across her round, white belly. She sat on a tall stump in a clearing in the woods, with her chubby legs crossed in a perfect mimicry of maturity, her pink sandals fallen in the dust.

May wasn't smiling, though she was well aware that the picture was being taken. Instead, she looked down dramatically with her eyes fluttered closed, holding her doll loosely away from her but also against, as if she were about to passionately kiss its dirty cloth face. Her head was tilted to the side and her lips were parted, her bangs swept just slightly over her eye, and she faced the doll and not the camera, touching the little pink thread of a mouth with her cautious finger, like a lover. She looked maybe five or six years old, full of passion and feeling beautiful.

It is this May whom Ann pictures sitting in the backseat of the truck nine years ago on that August day.

In the scene Ann sees in her mind, May feels personally slighted by the horseflies that bite her arms. She has crawled into the backseat of the truck but the flies have followed her from the outside. Her mom and dad are still loading wood. Her older sister is in the forest somewhere. May is pouting, her lips kissing the small bites on her white skin, murmuring as they kiss, as if they're the lips of someone else, consoling her, touching her, telling the bites to go away.

As the flies land, she slaps them. Her handprints are bright on her skin. At first she tries to capture the flies in the Styrofoam cup she has for lemonade, but there are too many. The flies learn her rhythms and try to trick her, landing in places that are difficult to slap, like the back of her neck, where she can hardly feel them on her downy hair. The buzzing around her head is as infuriating as the stings themselves. They are equally in peril: the flies of her vicious little hands, and she of their bites, each one a surprising pinprick of pain that makes the skin on her whole body tighten. It is a maddening game that they are playing, full of anticipation, tension, dares.

Ann sees May, sitting with her hand perfectly still in midair, waiting for the fly to trust her so she can kill it, and then there is a black stop in Ann's mind. As if her eyes have shut suddenly after looking at the sun and the last outlines of color are swimming in the darkness under her lids. The buzz of the flies, the sound of someone running, the halfhearted clucks of bored crows in the mountain woods: All of it reduces to a crackling static and a darkness.

When Ann's mind opens up again like an eye, what is most startling is how peaceful the scene has become. May, in the backseat, sits with her head down on her knees, perfectly still. The horseflies land on her arms, now that her hands aren't slapping anymore. Her blood is sticky and warm in her hair. The buzzing quiets and the flies settle on her arms, almost tenderly, like children sick of fighting and ready for sleep. Some of them are not sure the game is over, that it isn't a childish trick and her hands, so quiet now, won't suddenly tense and fly to life. These flies rise again and buzz and bounce against the window and then land somewhere else. But eventually they settle down, too, settle down so much that they stop biting, and rest on her still arms like those arms are home, washing their antennae, letting the hundreds of facets of their eyes go out of focus for a while, as the dense yellow light through the window penetrates the fractured panels of their wings and warms them in these moments when everything is safe.

∎

There was one time a few years ago that Ann didn't return home to Ponderosa until very late. She'd been out running errands when the car broke down. She called Wade to let him know, then waited in town for the car to be repaired.

Driving home that night up the steep dirt driveway, she saw

their house in the distance. It was dark except for the window in Wade's office upstairs on the left side, and then, strangely, two glowing rectangles of light at the bottom of the front door. His workshop, which was a separate building on the other side of the garden, also had two glowing lights on the door. The lights perplexed her. She didn't know what they could possibly be. Lanterns? But why? It was only when she was standing right at the door of the house that she understood the rectangles of light were holes that had been cut into the wood, through which the inside lights were shining.

It made no sense. Frightened, Ann went inside, grocery bags in her arms. In the dim light from the floor lamp, she saw that there were many holes cut into the knotty-pine walls, leading to the outside. Each hole was a rectangle, about a foot tall and a half-foot wide. The books were cleared away from one of the shelves so that holes could be cut into the wall behind them. There was one hole above the kitchen counter, so that the moonlight spread out on the Formica.

Her heart raced. "Wade?"

Through the holes, the wind entered the house. On the wall above the lamp, five or six silk moths, some of them as large as her palm, opened and closed their eye-spotted wings. A giant beetle was dragging itself across the hardwood floor, gleaming like a knife. In the sawdust, which was everywhere, were cat prints.

She turned on the main light, and saw that the insulation had been pulled out in perfectly cut cubes and these cubes were stacked neatly by the sliding glass doors. There were other holes on the inside walls of the house, between rooms. Some of the holes led nowhere but deeper into the walls. One hole in the bathroom door.

"Wade—" But her voice caught. A cat meowed.

She turned around. A cat rubbed his side happily against a chair leg and purred up at her, slowly blinking his green eyes. He wasn't a cat she knew, but she picked him up. His heavy, warm body calmed her down. He rubbed his face vigorously against her jaw as she held him.

She took the purring cat upstairs, walked quickly past the two closed and empty rooms, each with a perfect rectangle cut into the bottom of the door, then opened the third door and looked at Wade.

He was sitting on a stool in his office, wearing a coat, looking down at some blue and yellow receipts on the desk. The wood burner was on the desk, too. There was pine smoke in the air.

"You're home," he said, turning around on his stool, reaching for her hand. She saw the blisters between his thumb and forefinger, where he would have held the saw. "I'm sorry you had to wait in town so long." He pulled her gently down onto his lap, while she held the cat in her arms. When she saw his face, she felt like crying. The weariness in his eyes was gone. Strangely, against all reason, he looked younger. He looked like the man he'd been when they first met—he looked like Jenny's husband.

He smiled, looking down at the cat. "He's a stray," he said, shaking his head. "But he hasn't always been one. He meowed right at the door of the workshop when I was out there, so I let him in. Then I thought why not let him in the house, too?" He laughed.

She touched the sawdust on his sleeve with her thumb, a gesture that took the concentration of her whole body. The sawdust was in his hair, too. "What happened to the house?" she said in a low, careful voice. He looked at her, confused. "The holes," she said.

"They're doors," he said, as if he were surprised that she didn't know. "He can come and go as he pleases."

"Oh," was all she said. The cat leapt off her lap. She stood. "Doors." She heard the violence in her voice, and only then did she know that what she felt was anger. "You were cutting cat doors, dozens of cat doors." She felt what he must have felt the time he shoved her face against the TV, a frustration and pain so deep and hopeless and long-standing, having nothing to do with him but which she blamed him for entirely.

She thought she might say something else, but she didn't. She turned around, walked down the hallway, past the two empty rooms, and went downstairs. He did not seem to understand she was upset, so he didn't follow her. Good. She found a flashlight. Outside, the stars shone and the wind was strangely warm and it tossed her hair. The dogs, sniffing her pockets, excited that some-one was out in the night, followed her down the hill to the larger of their two barns, which was empty except for some lumber and tools. She thought of nothing but the task before her. She climbed the ladder to the loft, where she found some plywood and several sheets of siding, left over from when Wade and Jenny had built the house. She threw the scraps down to the floor of the barn. Up in the loft, there were mouse and dove droppings everywhere. The pollen and dust stuck to her face. She started to cry, throwing down the lumber. Eventually, still crying, she climbed down the ladder and plugged in the chop saw and quickly made a stack of little rectangles out of the siding and plywood, which she then loaded into a wheelbarrow.

She pushed the wheelbarrow up the steep road in the darkness. Ahead of her, in the clearing, the house, with all its lights on now, glowed through the windows and holes. It was a house that a child would draw, with its dozens of crooked, too-small windows. She lost her breath pushing the wheelbarrow, but she didn't stop. The flashlight in her pocket, still on, shot straight up out of her coat, diffused in the sky.

She worked for over an hour, nailing the squares of siding over the holes, pushing the chunks of insulation back into the empty squares on the inside, so that only their paper backs were showing. She did not fix the holes between rooms. She fixed only those that led to the outside. The cat went inside through one of the holes and then back out, as if making a display of how well the doors were working.

When she was finished with her work, she put the tools away, swept up the sawdust from the floor, and then took a shower and got into bed.

Eventually, she heard Wade coming down from the second floor. His steps were slow, as if he were realizing something. She heard him stop and stand for a long time in the middle of the stairs. She could almost hear his fingertip outlining one of the cat doors, as if he couldn't believe that it existed.

She lay in bed staring at the wall. When he got into bed with her, she felt the change in his body as soon as he touched her. He was himself again.

"I didn't realize," he said. She did not turn to face him. She could hardly contain the relief that rushed through her, so she trapped it inside of her by shutting her eyes. Her whole body began to shake with it. She was crying again. He wrapped himself around her. "I'm so sorry."

She turned around to face him when she heard that he was crying, too. She touched his face over and over again, tenderly, running her finger down his cheek and across his forehead like she would a child's. "It's okay," she said, smiling through her tears. After a while they closed their eyes, held each other for a long time.

When it felt like he had fallen asleep against her, she turned around in his arms, holding his hand against her chest. He woke when she moved. "Can I ask you something?" he said after a moment. She could tell already, from the innocence in his voice, the trust that there were still things he'd never asked her, that a piece of him was gone again.

"Yes," she said.

"Have you ever loved someone else?"

"No," she said. "Of course not."

"Did you sleep with other people, before me?"

She shut her eyes tight and swallowed. Of course he once knew

17

that she'd been with others, but now she said, "No." She said, "Just you."

He sighed like he was relieved.

In the darkness, she lay thinking how strange it was that suddenly her history was gone, too. Everything in her life that had happened before him, everything that had brought them together, was gone. The school. Her childhood. All of England.

For a moment, the lightness of this absence was almost a relief, and his hand at her heart was its own beginning and end, a story that included only them, that began with the touch of their hands and ended with the same. She could live in this moment for a while, if she had to.

For all she knew, Jenny was gone, too, from his memory. His life with her, with May and June, the sounds of his daughters' voices and the last smell of their clothes, bled out of the house through its many wounds, bled out into the night, gone now from this story of him and her.

The moment had passed, but she decided to ask him anyway. "Did you?" Barely a whisper.

"No," he said softly. "Just you."

She turned around and kissed him. And just like that, they became each other's first love.

The following morning, Wade understood the damage he had done to the house and to his workshop, and he felt ashamed. But Ann did not let him see how much the event affected her. She remained cheerful as she swept the beetles out with the leaves, and hung the fly tape in the kitchen. They caught the large moths in jars and set them free. He set traps for the spiders and the mice. The cat left again, as if he had come only for the prospect of a hundred doors.

Ann and Wade had made plans that year to visit her father in Scotland, but she canceled after this happened. She was sad not to visit him, especially since she felt him drifting away from her. He was awkward on the phone, wanting only to joke, and sometimes he handed the phone to his brother, her uncle, so she could talk to him instead. It pained her that he never once mentioned her letters to him, though it was not in her father's nature to talk about personal things. She made a promise to herself to be more lighthearted in her letters, as a way of bringing him closer to her.

It turned out to be a beautiful fall on Mount Iris, maybe the most beautiful of her life. She and Wade went on long walks together through the changing woods, chilly in their sweaters, kicking leaves. They put leashes on their goats, and fed them apples that they picked from haggard, wild trees. The goats chewed with difficulty. Ann watched the green froth fall from the leathery lips.

Wade's memory went in little ways, mostly. One time, he made the bed inside out, with the comforter underneath and the sheets on top. But what was more surprising to her was that he'd made the bed at all. She'd always been the one to do it, and it was nice, this change.

She found her hairbrush in the freezer and sometimes he got calls from concerned customers who said their orders had been filled twice. But nothing really mattered, the way most things don't, even the things done right.

She learned how to deal with the moments when his memory lapsed. Sometimes, she felt it happen even without him saying a word. On a sunny fall day, she lay next to him on the ground, and as he dozed she felt his old life, his memories, radiate off his skin. She felt everything leave him but her. She shed her own life, too, to match him. They lay there together like a point in time. A cloud drifted in front of the sun and things shifted inside of him, and when she sensed this, she allowed things to shift inside of her, too. They became their regular selves again, still warm from the lost memory of a minute ago.

But underneath her happiness was a dread that one day this would be all they had. All associations would be lost: the smell of the gloves, the sound of the truck door slamming shut. All the details she still wanted to know. Everything reduced to nothing more than itself.

They burned some rotten furniture one afternoon, way out in a clearing in the woods on the edge of their property. Surely it had been brought there by some distant, unknown neighbors. Often, on their walks together through the forest, they made a game of searching for these corrupted places that needed their attention. "Let's go on a date," Ann would say, laughing, taking off her clean clothes and putting on her filthy, torn jeans, smelling of past garbage fires.

Sometimes, among the garbage, they found useful things. Once, for example, Wade found a wrecked truck, and he tore the leaf springs from the axle. It was a special kind of metal he could find only on older trucks; he used it in his work. He heated the metal with a forge until it glowed red, then he pounded it down, shaped it.

On the day they found the rotten furniture, they threw branches over a mattress, then poured diesel on the pile. They stood back, watching their fire crackle and blaze. He slipped his arm around her waist. There was a heaviness in his touch, a sorrow in his smile, even in his laugh, and an understanding that they had arrived here together from somewhere else, that the story was longer than just each other.

She will miss that awareness in him once it's gone. She leaned into him, smelled the fire in his clothes. She looked at his handsome face turned toward the flames, then she looked at the flames, too. The air above the smoke burned invisibly, wavering like reflections on water, making the mountains far behind it seem to tremble in their heat.

"Here we are," she said, not knowing what she meant.

"Here we are," he agreed, and pulled her closer.

When Ann first moved to the mountain, there were horses here, not goats, Appaloosas grown so mean after a year without Jenny and June to ride them that Ann was afraid to go near them, even to brush the burrs from their matted manes. The smaller barn, which was close to the house, was where Jenny stored the hay, stacked to the roof. Not long after Ann moved here, she and Wade sold the horses and the hay with them, all but a few bales.

It was a different building after the hay was sold; it was empty and full of possibility. There was a window that looked out on the forest. Ann had a vision then of turning the barn into an office, where she planned to put a piano keyboard and a desk.

The dust rose around her as she swept. She used a broom to remove the spiderwebs and abandoned hornet nests in all the corners. It was exhausting and good, and when the room was all swept, she lay on one of the few remaining bales in the corner, and her hand fell down in the crack between the bale and the wall.

There was a book on the ground, fallen so that the spine was up and the pages were bent and splayed against the floor. She felt it at her fingertips, softened from mildew and grainy with dust, a large paperback.

It was called *Drawing Faces*. It was an instructional book that showed various methods for sketching expressions, beginning with ovals and grids and un-melded shapes. Each page showed one further step in the evolution of the sketch, and ended with a detailed generic face, all the grid lines erased, the hair filled out. It was a book for adults, the sketches too precise and difficult for children. Near the end, on the first sheet of practice paper bound into the book, was a half-finished pencil sketch of a woman's face. In the bottom right corner, a signature.

Jenny.

Ann saw the erased lines of the face. She saw how carefully the instructions had been followed. The face was turned a little to the side. The nose looked confidently drawn—rectangle and circle erased—but one eye remained unshaded, blank, caught in the lines of the previous step like an eye seen through the scope of a gun, the pupil at the crosshairs. But the hair that fell on either side of the face was bold and detailed.

Ann shut the book.

The barn wasn't the same after that. She tried to ignore it. She moved her things in. A desk, a piano keyboard, and even an old computer with a program on it for writing and recording music. The little studio was beautiful.

But the woman in the corner thought so, too. Ann could feel her there, thinking how nice it was to have a moment to herself, away from her daughters and husband, to sprawl out on the hay bales with her drawing book on her chest and her bare toes curled over the tight red twine, her arm slung lazily over her eyes to shield them from the light, her pencil sharpened. Ann imagined the old spotted horses chomping their hay nearby. The hornets in the corners buzzed, and outside somewhere, under the clothesline where rose-colored shirts were starched with sunshine, two girls were filling miniature blue teacups with sand.

Because Wade had thrown everything away—drawings, clothes, toys—each accidental remnant loomed in Ann's mind with unspeakable importance. Four moldy dolls buried in the sawdust of a rotten stump. A high-heeled Barbie shoe that fell from the drainpipe. A neon toothbrush in a doghouse. Then, finally, the half-finished drawing in a book. Artifacts heavy with importance they didn't deserve, but which they took on because of their frightening scarcity; they built up against her, making stories of themselves, memories inside her head that should have remained in Wade's.

Even the raspberry bushes that Ann didn't plant. For a long time they came back every year to haunt her, came back with pure perennial will to snag her sleeves and scratch her legs and pull her in. Jenny had put them there. Ann deprived them of water but they lived on rain, the berries shriveled and dry and sour, crumbly as chalk. Each year they announced their future selves with stubborn reddish-brown shoots of new cane alongside the green ones. For a while, she did everything she could to kill them passively, but then one winter, when she saw them leafless and without power, she hacked them away with a machete, the fine snow flying up around her.

It was confusing, not knowing if what she needed was more of his family or less. Those four moldy stump dolls had made her cry out of love; the teacups by the clothesline, each one small enough to cap a fingertip, overwhelmed her with disbelief; the bluebird embroidery on a tea towel, which surely Jenny had done herself, made her feel guilty; the empty rooms made her feel nothing but their emptiness. Once, waiting in line at the post office, she saw a little girl in the parking lot beating her fallen bicycle with a stick. Ann laughed. But then, very suddenly, her eyes filled with tears.

She kept the drawing book for a full year, moving it from place to place, trying to lessen its meaning by shoving it here and there on the bookshelf, mistreating it ever so slightly. Then one day, in anger at herself, she sealed the book with the drawing still inside of it in a manila envelope and addressed it to the Sage Hill Women's Correctional Center. She did not put her return address in the corner. She wrote on the outside of the envelope, "Attn.: Prison Library. A donation for your stacks." The postwoman made no comment, though surely she saw the address. She smoothed a postage sticker onto the corner, then dropped the envelope into the pile with one intimate and protective glance.

Now, this March day, Ann stops at the barn on her way back from the woodshed. The truck exhaust hangs in her hair. Her blue sled is full of birch logs she doesn't need but which she will use to make a fire anyway, the logs an excuse for visiting the truck, the fire an excuse for the logs. The more fires she makes, the more she can go up to the truck and try to understand.

Sensing that Ann is near, the goats call out from inside the barn. She drapes the sled's rope over the birch wood, then pushes open the barn door.

Inside, the air is chilly and stale. The goats rush toward her. She squeezes their ears, pats their hides. They shiver gladly at her touch. She speaks cheerfully to them, though she feels Jenny's presence here as strongly as she ever has. Through the barn window, she can see the ponderosa grove from which she has just emerged, and she feels suddenly the presence not only of Jenny, but of a life she herself nearly led. A life without Wade.

Breaking with a stick the skin of ice that's formed on the goats' water trough, she struggles to understand what she knows is a simple fact, *I am here because you are not here.*

The goats clamor; she feeds them hay.

"You are not here," she says, softly, to the presence in the barn. "You are not here."

But the reassurance is its own admission. Its own pain.

She leaves the barn quickly, closes the door behind her, resumes her dragging of the sled down the hill.

When she's nearly to the house, she sees Wade in the garden. He is kneeling in the mud and snow, untangling the wire the beans will climb. She stops to watch him, stands in the threshold of pale grass between the house and garden.

"I love you," she says.

Startled that she's there, he looks up from his work, his face both tired and innocent, his dark-blue eyes expressing gladness.

■ ■ ■

Ann grew up in Poole on the south coast of England. But she was born here, in Idaho, not in Ponderosa but in the small mining town of Kellogg in the Silver Valley of the Panhandle.

She does not have a single memory of those three early years in

Idaho. When she was nine years old, her mother mentioned having come from America, and Ann didn't know what she was talking about. She had forgotten the journey across the Atlantic altogether. The only thing her parents could think to tell her about Idaho was that her father had worked in the Sunshine Mine and had escaped the famous fire three years before it started.

After that, Ann could close her eyes and let Idaho become not a place but a feeling, entirely separate from America, without borders or a history except for that which belonged to her: the silver mine. One hundred miles of tunnels one mile deep below the ground. She couldn't believe that she had come from such a place. When she thought of it, she felt that those three forgotten years in Idaho had settled deep inside of her and unsettled all those beautiful years that followed. Idaho was the mine and England the unsteady surface of her life.

So she moved back. She was twenty-eight years old. Her mother had passed away a few years before, and her father had recently moved to Scotland to live with his brother. So Ann left England, too. She got a job teaching choir at a small school in Hayden Lake in northern Idaho, less than an hour's drive from where she was born.

The school sat near the lake on two acres of treed and unmanicured land at the end of a newly paved road. It was a small charter school for high-achieving students interested in the humanities. The students at her school, about two hundred total, spanning ages six to eighteen, seemed as a whole very sweet and devoted not only to their studies but to one another. Though it was nearly an all-white school, the curriculum stressed culture and international studies. Ann couldn't decide whether it was very strange or very natural to find this adamant broad-mindedness in a rural school so close to the headquarters of the Aryan Nations, the white-supremacist group, which at that time still held its World Congress every year and marched in the Fourth of July parade. Every day on her way to work, Ann passed the long dirt driveway that led to the compound in the woods, and she felt sickened and bewildered that it was real.

Ann's classroom was a portable set apart from the rest of the school. She could open the window and listen to the waves on the lake just down the hill, or to the sound of chainsaws somewhere far away that carried over the water. The school grounds did not include the lake, but the students liked to go down there in the afternoon to wait for their parents. One evening during the first year that the school opened, the year before Ann came, a boy looking for his backpack fell through a half-sunken dock that was almost entirely hidden by cattails. His right leg went all the way through. Thick splinters of treated wood cut into him. The piling below, which had once held the dock in place, speared his leg. No one heard him calling out for help, and his parents, believing he was at a friend's house, didn't think to go looking for him. It was a windy night, and in the morning, the janitor found him unconscious, lying on the dock, his leg still caught. The doctors had to amputate his leg at the thigh to save his life.

His name was Eliot. He was sixteen when he enrolled in Ann's choir class. She remembers how she felt when he sang behind her as she played the piano. That such a voice could come from a high school boy, a careless, clowning boy, never seemed real to her. Underneath her effusive praise was an impossible suspicion that he was cheating. He made her uneasy with how at ease he was. All the special attention she gave him, extra help after school, every major solo in their concerts, he accepted as if he didn't notice, without embarrassment or gratitude. He had large brown eyes and matted hair, and behind his ear he wore a sharpened pencil that he never used. The way he leaned on his crutch when he talked to her, one leg of his khakis pinned up loosely against his thigh, made him seem so casual and cool that she felt herself trying to lean with him, holding out her hand to touch a wall or desk that wasn't there, as if she were the awkward one because she had an extra leg. When he spoke to Ann in those practices after school, at the very end, when he was no longer singing but telling her about the other things in his life, she felt so disoriented by her joy at being near him that it was like half of herself was about to fall, only without his crutch to catch her.

It didn't occur to her then that she felt differently about him than about any of her other students. There was a group of girls and boys who liked to linger and talk to her after class, fooling around with the piano and looking through her music. She loved them all, treated them in a sisterly way, but there always came the time when she had to send them home because Eliot needed to practice. When it was just the two of them, when he leaned over her, singing, to turn the page as she played, she smelled his warm, sweet breath near her neck, and that was when she felt most keenly her dread of their daily parting.

Ann didn't like the apartment she was renting at the time, and her roommates were friendly to the point of intrusion, so she found herself spending a great deal of her free time in her portable classroom, which was furnished with an old piano, a small rising stage, a desk, a green couch beneath the window, and the musical posters left by the previous teacher. She spent so much time in her classroom that it came to feel to her like her real home, and the rented room a place she merely visited. Often, she spent the night on the green couch with the classroom window open above her, so that the night sounds of the school and lake, unknown to anyone else, even the janitor, fell over her and carried her away into sleep. She rose early and showered in the teachers' lounge, brushed her teeth and hair at her desk, in whose drawers she also kept a few pairs of clean clothes. When her students came each day, they seemed to her more like visitors than students, and the things they touched seemed like *her* things. She noticed where on her door Eliot's shoulder leaned, to hold it open for the person behind him. She did not wash off the mess of fingerprints he left on the windowpane when he opened it in order to shout at another boy in the parking lot. She did not tell him to stop picking at a hole in the green cushions, where he would never in his life guess his young teacher had slept the night before.

The black crescent scuffs that Eliot's crutch left on the risers were touching to her, marks of his life on hers. When he went home for the day, and she was left alone with these traces, she found in his absence something close to the desolation she had expected to find in her new landscape but never did. A vastness that confused her, even humiliated her slightly. And meanwhile, the boy was as indifferent as a continent. There was a coldness in his unwavering ease, his constant and impersonal joy.

She clung to this loneliness a little. On weekends, she even found herself feeling homesick for her classroom. Even when she was there inside it, she felt vaguely sickened by the lovely things she saw out the window—the feathery frost on the weeds in the winter, or, much later, the lilies in bloom down on the water, muddled by his fingerprints on the glass.

Once, after Eliot's practice, his dad was late to pick him up. He lived about fifteen minutes from school, and Ann offered to drive him home.

"Teachers don't drive," he said, rolling his eyes in disgust at her naïveté about her own species. It was the same joke he always made to her, but she had not found any other way to respond than to laugh. Over and over again—"Teachers don't get cold"; "Teachers don't get thirsty"; "Teachers don't eat." Over and over again, Ann laughed.

That day, they drove to his house in near silence. He looked at her skeptically from his seat, the window down and his hair blowing. She expected him to say something gently mocking, but he didn't. His silence was rare. And rarer still was the way he looked at her when he got out of the car. He just stood there in his driveway, leaning forward a little to see her. "Thanks," he said finally, then smiled and shook his head, as if he knew something that he didn't believe.

The following day, Eliot's little brother came in to school early and emptied the contents of Eliot's locker into a big plastic bag, including the prosthetic leg he never wore.

The principal informed Ann that Eliot had withdrawn. His parents had split up and he'd moved with his mother to Oregon. His brother, the principal said, was staying with the father.

"But it's the middle of the year," Ann said to the principal, thinking that the boy had been forced to move against his will. "How will he catch up?"

He was failing most of his classes anyway, he told her, so catching up wasn't really an issue. It was his choice. The parents let them choose.

She didn't know how to go on teaching after such a loss. She was irritable with the other students, and during her break, she put her elbows on her desk and tried uselessly to cry into her hands. Most shocking of all was the cruelty she felt he had shown to her personally by attending on his last day in Idaho an after-school rehearsal for a concert he had no intention of singing in. Ann couldn't accept it, couldn't believe it.

At the end of that day, she wandered through the empty school and thought she might go look in Eliot's locker. Maybe something would be left there, maybe pictures still taped to the locker's door. She knew where it was because she had often seen him there, talking to his friends with the locker door wide open, no doubt showing off the astonishing mess he cultivated there. Inside the locker, she'd seen the prosthetic leg bent up against the books and his wild disarray of papers.

But when she entered the hallway, she saw a little girl standing in front of his locker, alone. The girl was holding a small gift in her hands, wrapped in tissue paper.

The girl didn't see Ann. She was very young, maybe eight or nine. The elementary children were kept separate from the high

29

school most of the day, so the girl might not have had a chance to notice that Eliot wasn't there. She had short, dark hair and bangs. She had already changed out of her uniform, and wore jean shorts over white tights with grass stains on the knees. She also wore a ratty rose-colored sweater and rose-colored shoes that had faded to gray. She closed the locker halfway to check the number on the front. Ann could see her trying to think what this empty locker meant. The girl looked down at the carefully wrapped present in her hands and then at the locker. Quite suddenly, as if she thought someone was going to catch her, she placed the gift in the locker, shut the green metal door, and hurried away.

Ann waited until she was gone and then she opened the locker herself. She picked up the package, a rectangular box wrapped in pink tissue paper. She guessed it held some nice pens or a watch. There was a card that said, *Happy Birthday Eliot, With All Of My Deepest Love In My Heart, June Mitchell.*

The card touched Ann. She felt both warmth and pity for the little girl. She took the package to her portable and unwrapped the paper carefully.

Inside the box was a knife. It had a shining blade about six inches long. Ann gasped, out of surprise at seeing such a weapon wrapped so tenderly in paper, and also at how beautiful it was. The handle was made of bone, and scrimshawed on the bone was a cottage. On either side of the cottage was a rose with a heart in its center. The knife was lying on top of its leather sheath, which was decorated with cat's-eye stones. She picked it up. It was so sharp that just by touching the blade to examine it, she accidentally cut herself. A very small, fine cut, which did not hurt and bled only a drop.

She didn't know what to do with the package. She certainly couldn't return it to the locker now that she knew what was inside. But she didn't want to get the girl in trouble with the school, either. So she put the knife in her desk.

Two days later, she looked up June Mitchell's information and called her parents. On the answering machine was a man's gruff voice. She left a message but didn't mention the knife. She simply asked if one of June's parents would stop by her classroom to discuss their daughter's behavior at school. She also didn't mention that she was merely the choir teacher and didn't know June personally. She just left the number of her room.

Three days later, June's father knocked politely on the doorframe with his knuckle, even though the door was open to let in the sunlight. When Ann looked up, he took off his baseball hat, as if out of respect for her, or maybe the school. His hair stuck up in a vulnerable way, and his eyes were squinting. He wiped his boots on the mat outside before stepping in.

"I've come about the knife?" he said.

She stood. "Oh, I wasn't sure you knew."

"I saw it was missing and thought June might have taken it. We've already punished her enough at home. She was never going to use it in a violent way. She's very gentle."

"I'm sure she is."

"You're one of her teachers?"

"No, I'm just the one who found it. I teach music."

"You must be from England?"

"Yes."

"Neat accent," he said, and she laughed at the awkwardness of the compliment. He didn't seem to notice. He looked around the room then, and at the piano. "It would be a real shame to suspend her," he said. "School is the best place for her right now. I don't know what we'd do if we had to take her out." All of this he said without meeting Ann's eyes.

"No, it's nothing like that. Just as long as she knows now it's not okay."

He nodded. "She knows now. I apologize." He looked at Ann. It seemed that he expected her to have more to say. Her desk was behind her, and she was almost sitting on it, her hands holding on to the edge of its surface. "I made it for my wife originally, before June took it," he said.

She did not hide her surprise. "You made it?"

He laughed gently. "You liked it?"

"It's beautiful."

"Well, maybe she did right to take it here. Maybe she was advertising." Ann smiled. "Anyway," he said, "is it possible for me to get it back?"

But the knife was now in the pocket of her coat, and this seemed an admission of some kind. So she fumbled around in her desk drawers, pretending to have misplaced it.

He waited. In the end, she took it out of her jacket pocket and handed it to him with a shrug. He smiled. Then he slid the knife from its leather sheath and examined it in the light.

"We had to take June out of the normal school," he said. "We were lucky this place opened up so we could put her somewhere new. I don't know what we'll do now that she's at it again."

"She's done this before? I thought—"

"I mean she's boy crazy. In a pretty serious way. She gets her heart broken all the time and it hurts her like she really loves them. It's hard to see her like that. We don't know what to do, really. She's stolen things before to give boys, nothing like this, though. Always older boys, too." Ann didn't say anything. After a moment he nodded to the piano. "My daughter plays," he said.

"Well, she should join my class. We could use her."

He smoothed off the side of the blade with his hand. "Not June," he said. "May, the younger one. She still goes to the normal school. June gets ballet." He put the knife back in its sheath, and rubbed one of the stones with his thumb, as if to polish it. "I wondered, do you only teach in a big group or do you give lessons?"

"I would like to do both eventually. I just moved here."

"How much would they cost?" He squinted at her. A ray of sunlight from the open door lay between them, at their feet.

"You mean singing, or piano?"

"Piano."

"Well, if she'd be willing to play for the choir when she got good enough, I'd teach her for free. I'm always here after school."

He nodded. "I was thinking of myself, actually," he said.

"Oh?"

"I heard about these studies, that it's good for your brain?"

She laughed. "Is there something wrong with yours?"

But he looked at her seriously, and she regretted the question, which she had meant as a joke. "I don't know yet," he said. "But it runs in my family. I'm just seeing what your prices are, is all," he said quickly. "I've been looking around a bit."

"Well," she said, "let's say twenty dollars for a lesson every week."

He walked over to the piano and set his hand on top of it, then knocked on it with his knuckles, as if somehow to test the quality of its wood. "All right," he said finally. "That sounds fair."

She went to her desk and looked through her appointment book, and after a long time she told him when she would be free.

He put the knife in his pocket. He shook her hand.

At first, he was very embarrassed by the lessons, the beginner books he had to learn from, with their childish covers. But he treated the lessons formally, and paid attention to everything she said about how to sit at the piano bench and how to curve his hands above the keys like he was holding a baseball. She could see him imagine that baseball in his palm every time he was about to play. He was apologetic for his mistakes and he tried hard. She could see in his books that at home he wrote the names of the notes above the notes themselves, then erased them before his lesson. She would have him tap one of his hands on his knee while he played a simple rhythm with his other hand. He was not naturally musical. He rubbed his hands often between songs, as if playing strained them. She felt warm and puzzled by him, watching his large, clumsy hands with their scars and calluses, playing tunes like "Oh My Darling Clementine."

He did not seem to derive much pleasure from the music. As he played, he wore the expression of a man at work, as if music were something he could load into his mind like wood into a shed. Store it up, for winter use.

So she tried to find something he would like. One evening she went through some of the books she had brought from England, and found some folk music that was very simple and easy to play, for adults. One of these books she had ordered specially when she was a teenager, because it contained a song written by a man in Idaho. She decided to sing this song as he played. He was so startled by her singing that he had to stop.

"Do you not want me to sing?" she said.

"No," he said, very seriously. "Let's try again."

But he could not do it with her singing. They tried again and again, and soon she laughed and slapped his hands out of the way and said, "Get up." She sat down and played it for him.

He practiced this song harder than the others after that. Soon he was able to play with the right hand while she sang the words. She sang slowly but gladly, though the song itself was mournful.

> *Take your picture off the wall*
> *And carry it away*
> *Dye your hair the shades of fall*
> *Don't let time turn it to gray*
>
> *Don't think of me, I'll be all right*
> *Seems I've always done okay*
> *Just give me one more kiss good night*
> *For the last time, turn away*

Each time he made a mistake, he insisted he had not made that mistake at home, which was something children who hadn't practiced had said to her often in the private lessons she used to give in England. She wanted to laugh, but he never broke in his earnest attempts and so she never laughed.

They made small talk before and after every lesson, but the only personal question she ever asked him was about what he had meant about something running in his family.

He told her that his father began losing his memory in his early fifties due to early-onset dementia. When his father was only fifty-five, he walked out of the house in the middle of the night, not knowing where he was going, or how to get back. He froze to death overnight, only a mile from his house.

"It was like that with my father's father, too," said Mr. Mitchell, which was what she called him. "Only with him it wasn't freezing."

He came once a week for several months. When school let out, he kept coming through the summer. She led a summer choir one morning a week, and he came on those afternoons, after the students had gone home. The days were hot and so she left the door and window open, but still his fingers left dark smudges on her keys, which she wiped up with a white cloth damp with vinegar. If after the lesson he planned to deliver a knife somewhere, or he was on his way to a trade show, he would invite her outside to see his work. He seemed more comfortable when they were outside at his car. He seemed to like how carefully she examined his work, the handles embedded with brass or copper pins perfectly flush with the wood, the fine and perfect blades with no line separating the cutting edge from the rest of it. He told her the names: Osage Bow, Cliff, Nessmuk. These knives were different from the one June stole, more brutal but in a way more beautiful, meant for skinning. No scrimshawed cottages, no cat's-eyes on the sleeves. Those had been touches he had added for his wife. These handles were made of antlers or mammoth ivory or ironwood. The only decoration, besides the embedded pins on the handles, was his signature at the top of the blade. The letter *M,* engraved to look like two mountains, for his last name.

Sometimes she asked questions about his materials. He told her about the stores of armadillo tails in his freezer, which he used on knife handles. He baked the tail in the oven, then tapped it with a hammer to shatter the bone inside, then cleaned out all the meat and shards of bone with a special tool so that only the shell remained.

"Believe it or not," he said once, showing her the detail on a knife handle, "this is a piece of a whale oosik."

"A piece of what?"

He laughed. "Never mind. It's expensive, that's all I'll say."

One day in August of that year, she was sitting in the living room while her roommates were playing cards in the kitchen. She was reading a book, but the television was on with the volume turned all the way down. When she looked up, she saw a photograph of a family on the screen. A mother, father, and two girls. The smiling mother was bending down to put her cheek against her daughter's for the picture. The woman's long dark hair hung over the little blond girl's shoulder. The other girl, older, with straight brown hair, was off to the side, looking a little surprised that the photo was already being taken, as if she were still preparing the expression on her face for it.

The father in the picture, leaning on a fence at a fair or theme park—there was a Ferris wheel in the distance and both girls had glowing green bracelets on—was Wade Mitchell.

■ ■ ■

The Sage Hill Women's Correctional Center in southwestern Idaho has a small library of donated books. The librarian is named Claire. Ann has spoken to her on the phone five times in the last six years. Claire's voice is like her name, which is like a knife blade: sharp, competent, and shining.

The temptation to call the prison library is always at its worst when Ann has just been inside the truck. Her two secrets—sitting in the truck, calling the prison—are so closely tied to each other in her mind that now, when she is back in the house sitting in front of the fire she's just made with logs she's gathered from the woodshed, she feels once again that familiar beckoning.

No. What is there to gain?

She must be careful not to call too often, not to draw attention to herself. But perhaps by this time, Claire has forgotten. So Ann brushes the sawdust off her jeans, goes to the bedroom, and shuts the door. She lifts the phone off the nightstand, sits on the floor, her back against the bed, the phone on her lap and the receiver at her ear. She knows the extension for the library. It is not too long before Claire's voice is there on the other end of the line. Ann clears her throat, doing her best to hide what remains of her accent.

"Yes, hello, I'm calling to find out about the popularity of a certain book," says Ann.

"What inmates check out is confidential," says Claire.

Ann shifts the phone to the other ear. She has been through all of this before. "Of course. I'm not interested in knowing individual inmates. I was thinking of sending another donation. I know there's no computerized log, but I wondered if you could have a look at the book for me, and just let me know, very generally, if there is some demand for another like it."

"Have you called here before?"

"No," says Ann. "Why?"

Claire sighs. "Give me the author and title. I can go check on the shelf. But there's a line forming. Do you mind waiting?"

"Not at all. The author's name is Jacobs." She pauses, hoping Claire does not remember. "The book is *Drawing Faces*."

"Okay, please hold on."

Ann takes a deep breath, shifts on the bedroom floor.

For some six years, the drawing book she found in the barn has waited on the prison shelves, untouched. Each time she calls, and each time she asks for information in a similarly roundabout way, she has found out that the card inside the book is blank. Not a single name. Why, in a place where there is so very little to do, has no one ever sought out drawing lessons? Do the prisoners not see the book when they run their fingers along the spines?

But it is not the book itself that is the secret. It is Jenny's unfinished sketch in the practice pages at the back. She is waiting for Jenny to find it, so that finally, after all this time, they will have to share an acknowledgment of their connection, which is something Ann needs more and more as Wade's memory fails.

Ann knows, of course, that if she wanted to communicate with Jenny, she could. She could write a letter. She could go visit. But such directness is unthinkable. She wants Jenny to have to meet her halfway. She wants them to find each other, like strangers on common ground.

It's late afternoon, and feeling the warmth of the phone against her ear as she strains to hear the prisoner's voice checking out a book on the other end, Ann looks down at her legs and shoes and the pinkish stain on the bedroom carpet.

She has never thought about this stain before. But for some reason, in this moment, the phone at her ear, she knows with impossible certainty that it is medicine. Cough syrup. Spilled from a teaspoon that a woman held to the mouth of a dark-haired child.

She feels almost dizzy with the suddenness of Jenny's presence in the room, as if she can almost touch her. Moments like this never feel like her inventions (though she knows that's what they are), but like waves of memory that come at her so suddenly and with such force that it seems they must be her own. Ann lets herself be taken by them. Always. That they aren't real is the impossible thing—a Wednesday morning, the TV on in the other room and the sound of cereal poured into a bowl, the young girl, June, drowsy and petulant with fever, saying she *has* to go to school, she *can't* stay home—

Shhh, Junebug, drink this down. Then I'll tuck you back in bed.

But the girl shakes her head. The boy she loves is waiting in the schoolyard, and if she doesn't go today he might start loving someone else, Becky C. or Amy R., and besides, she's drawn a picture just for him—

Bring it tomorrow. Please drink this.

And Ann can almost see the picture for the loved boy, the softly pressed crayons and white cats—

"Hello?" Claire.

"Yes?" Ann says.

"I found it."

"And?"

"Someone checked it out about a month ago, but that's all. Just one person."

"Who?" Ann says, without meaning to.

"I told you I can't tell you that. Is there anything else I can do for you?"

Ann closes her eyes. She puts her hand up to her heart, as if to quiet it. "Is there anything drawn on the practice pages in the back?"

"Is there supposed to be?" But already Ann can hear the flipping of pages in Claire's hands. "No," says Claire. "There's nothing here. All blank."

■　■　■

After Ann saw Wade's picture on TV all those years ago, he did not come for a piano lesson for six months. The last time Ann had seen him was early August, just a few days before the accident. Accident? She catches herself thinking that word sometimes. Murder is too difficult to believe.

In all that time, her life might have moved on. She might have quit her job, fallen in love, left the state or even the country, and never heard or thought of him again except in that distant way a person might think of a near-stranger associated with tragedy.

But she didn't leave. Ann was still in the choir room by the now-frozen lake, listening to the ice fishermen yelling in the distance in the evenings. She made copies of sheet music and read novels at her desk and sometimes fell asleep there.

She still sprayed vinegar on the piano keys and wiped them with a white cloth, but when she turned on the news and heard his last name, she felt a horrible sadness wash through her and leave her empty of everything except a strange feeling that it all had something to do with her life, some mystery that was meant for her.

Then one evening in the middle of February, there was a knock at the choir room door. The snow was falling outside the portable in a swift, swirling wind lit up by the single streetlight in the small parking lot. The cold wind, and the dimness of her classroom, made her squint, and all she saw at first was a tall bearded man in a heavy coat. He took off a large glove, and then raised his hand to take off his winter hat.

"Wade." It was the first time she ever called him that.

Still standing in the cold, he said, "I would like to start my lessons again, if I could."

They did not talk about his unthinkable loss. Once or twice a week for three months he came with his colorful books under his arm. He had forgotten most of what he had learned before, but it didn't matter. They started over. They spoke only of the music he was learning, or of the songs her choir was singing, or sometimes of his knives. His demeanor was the same, earnest and very formal, apologetic and serious. They never referred to Jenny or June or May, or to the life sentence Jenny received following her confession. Every now and then, at home, one of Ann's roommates would turn on the TV, and Ann would hear Wade's voice, desperate and yet somehow heavy with patience, very briefly asking for help in the search for his still-missing child. It was the same few seconds of tape the news played over and over again, six months after May's death and June's disappearance.

What was Wade doing during those days between lessons? It felt vulgar, like a violation of him, to try to imagine. He implied nothing during his lesson, not even with a heavy look. They both acted as if Ann had been confined to the classroom since the day he left, never turning on a TV and never seeing that picture of his family at the fairgrounds.

But she'd seen the picture several times. It aired more frequently than Wade's plea for help in finding June. When the picture came on the screen, first showing all of them and then zooming in on the face of June Mitchell, the missing daughter, Ann tried to look away. How strange to see that little girl caught there in that instant, that little girl whom Ann had seen not so very long ago, standing in front of the locker. It was the most intimate thing she could imagine, this photograph of his family as they had once been, caught off-guard in their happiness. She wondered who gave the reporters that picture. Sometimes, as Wade played the piano, she wanted to put her hand on his and say, "I always looked away," as if that meant anything at all.

But they never touched. She gave him a few new songs but mostly he relearned the old ones. The first time she sang along since he'd come back, he seemed amazed that a thing like that could still happen. This time the song she sang was a children's song, called "Symbols of the Land." There were lyrics in the back for every state. She sang the words for Idaho.

Mountain bluebird, fly away
Appaloosa, spotted gray
Western white pine, clothed in snow
The mock orange blooms in I-da-ho

Then he asked her, "Do you remember that one song we did before? 'Take Your Picture Off the Wall'?"

"Yes," she said, then added with caution, "but it's very sad."

"Do you have it here?"

She found it in the bottom drawer of her desk. She bent the spine open against her knee, then placed it on the piano. "Let's see how much you remember."

He remembered it better than he did the others. He began to play, then stopped. "Aren't you going to sing?" he asked.

"All right."

And so she sang.

Sometime in the spring, as Wade was preparing to leave after his lesson, she saw him studying something in his hand, a serious expression on his face. He tilted his hand as if to examine the object he held. "Huh," he said.

"What is it?" she asked.

"I'm trying to remember why this was in my pocket."

It was a saltshaker.

"Oh," she said slowly.

He looked up at her, a little surprised. Then he laughed. "I guess this is what I'd figured I'd start my car with."

"You lost your keys?"

"They're not in my pocket. *This* is in my pocket."

"But you drove here. You must have them."

"They're not here."

"You're sure?"

"I'm sure."

There was a long pause. Then she pointed to the saltshaker in his palm, and said in a mock-serious voice, "I guess you'll have to make it work with the salt, then."

He laughed. "I guess so."

"Should we go try?"

He smiled. She feigned seriousness and threw on her scarf and went out the door of the choir room. When they got to his car, he tapped the saltshaker against the keyhole. He smiled at her, and shook his head. "No use."

"Here, let me try," she said. She took the shaker from his hand and shook it at the car. The salt fell against the door and then down onto the pavement. She tried the handle again. "Well, a saltshaker is not so different from a key. It's just the wrong shaker, that's all."

She found his keys on the top of the car. The sun was out and warmed her hair. They both leaned against the car, their shoulders a few inches apart. They looked off into the distance, where the road disappeared into the trees.

"I could take care of you," she said softly. She was very surprised to hear herself say this, but even so her voice was calm, as if she had been intending to say it all along. But really it was the only time that such a thing had occurred to her, and the words escaped her so quietly that she wondered at first if he had even heard. As she waited to find out, dozens of blackbirds, startled at nothing, rose off the telephone wire at once. Ann and Wade watched them converge and scatter like a handful of black sand thrown against the sky.

After a long time he said, "It wouldn't be right."

"I know," she said, almost as quietly as before. "I would want to, though, if we could." She did not know where her own calmness came from. "I could come live with you," she said, "where you live. I don't mind anything. It doesn't matter."

He nodded his head once, then looked the other way, as if he heard a sound over by the school. "Sometimes for a second I forget," he said, "and I think May and June are still alive, and that it's Jenny who's dead. Like we're struggling to manage without her, and we'd give anything just to talk to her for a while, ask her questions like where things are kept that we can't find, just to hear her give us instructions so we'll get by. And then I remember I could talk to her. I could send her a letter. Or go see her in prison. It makes me almost sick that it's possible."

They stood side by side, leaning against the car. She was careful not to look at him, but to stare straight ahead, not moving.

"You might still find your daughter," said Ann, unable to say June's name. "You shouldn't talk about them as if they're both—"

"I shouldn't talk about them at all," he said, with some reproach in his voice. It seemed to Ann that he was suddenly angry at both himself and her. She stepped away from the car, and he unlocked it. He got inside, shut the door, then sat at the steering wheel for a moment before turning the key. She stood a few feet away, waiting for him to look at her. He did, but only to nod goodbye, his expression distant and even cold. She was sure then that he wouldn't be back.

■ ■ ■

As soon as school was out, they were married. She quit her job. He held her and she breathed in the smell of his coat, moving her cheek against him in disbelief that this was what they felt. But it was; it had been all along. She moved into his small house on the mountain an hour north of the school, where he—they—raised goats for meat and milk, he trained dogs and made knives, and she gave piano lessons in their home. Adult students only, no children. She boiled the chickens she raised and ate soup with Wade at night. They made love under the scratchy wool blanket, found surprise in each other's ordinariness, safety in each other's pleasure.

She pounded her own boots against a post to get the mud off, and set them down on the porch beside his.

She dragged the firewood down the hill in a blue sled.

Sometimes, she sang.

She loved him so much that there was never anything else she might have done.

■ ■ ■

The August day that left the smell in his gloves: Ann has lived it so many times that it feels like something she has seen and not imagined, something unchangeable even by truth.

Wade and Jenny and June and May.

They are far away on Mount Loeil, loading wood onto the truck. Why not cut wood on their own mountain, on their own land?

Because they want birch, which doesn't grow on Mount Iris. Birch is better wood, denser, more energy per cord. Wade saw the ad for cheap, good birch in the *Nickel's Worth*. Whoever had cut the wood didn't know its value, but Wade knew.

He stands now in the truck bed, stacking the wood in front of the back window, careful to leave a gap between the wood and glass. Jenny picks each log up from the ground, whacking off the small limbs with a hatchet before rolling the logs onto the truck for him to stack. Hers is the harder job, but her stacking is lopsided, and she is sick of Wade correcting her, so they have traded places.

It is a hot, dry day. Ticks crawl all over the brush and Wade crushes them between his thumbnails and wipes the blood—deer blood, coyote—in smears on his jeans. The heat is oppressive, and draws into the dense air a sweet fragrance from the papery birch bark. The flies rise and fall in thin spirals, everywhere. Wade and Jenny can hear the katydids, which sound at times like the popping of a fire.

The wilderness goes on and on, ranges and ranges of mountains, ordered and powerful, layered against the sky. It is a vast danger they can sense all around, even if they can't see it from where they stand. They have driven so long up the narrow, rutted road that their lives feel far away.

The girls discover a deer's antler in the brush. They talk about how their dad might want it to make a handle for a knife. They argue about who will be the one to give it to him. Then they forget about their dad's knives, and instead take turns holding the antler on top of their heads, pretending to be reindeer. June chases May, using a long weed to whip her, and May bucks from side to side with both her fists tight around the antler, holding it in place on her blond, neighing head.

Where could this memory have come from? It astonishes Ann

45

that it came from anywhere, that it's not something she has seen or been told. She has conjured a vision out of a single, unrelated detail: Long ago, on Mount Iris, shortly after she married Wade, she found an antler, colored red and green with crayons. She knew the little girls had played with it. That antler caught in her imagination, the Christmas colors, too, and both were given to that August day on a different mountain, which the real antler had nothing to do with.

Soon the antler is lopsided and held up by one hand. The prancing has ceased, though the whipping continues. All of May's attention now is on the flies, which have come out of nowhere and from everywhere to bite her, fat black flies with bluish wings. She slaps them with her free hand, and when that's not enough, she frees the other by dropping the antler into the weeds. June abandons her whip. They stand in a clearing in the woods hitting each other and themselves. The brush crackles and buzzes all around them, and May begins to run.

The flies, too: no mention of them in the papers, no mention of them from Wade. But Ann remembers in her rented house on the old TV: A reporter stood in the clearing, the pale logs in the distance. "So far no evidence that the murder was premeditated . . ." At that moment, Ann saw a fly settle on the reporter's arm, and then another and a third, and he spoke in a hurried, distracted way that had less to do, it seemed to her, with the burden of narrating such facts than with the concentration it took to keep his arm so still.

Ann thinks, Now that May has run out of the clearing, June suddenly doesn't mind the flies so much; her swatting is half-hearted. She drags a stick as she walks. She follows the sound of rushing water and finds a clear mountain stream along which Indian paintbrushes grow. She feels a surge of something between anguish and ecstasy at the thought the stream has just given her, of Eliot, and she throws herself down by the stream to feel it even more, her arms wrapped tight around her legs. The mullein weed grows like cabbages all around, and she rips off a single, pale green, fuzzy leaf and lays it over the tops of her knees, so that she can bow her head and rub her face across it, thinking of the boy's lips. How soft the lips are. How much like the mullein leaf they would feel against her forehead. Not the leaf itself. No, she and the leaf are separated by the soft fuzz of hairs that grows from all its veins. She only *seems* to touch it, but she does not press down hard enough to bend the hairs, to feel the leaf itself. It is only a graze. That is as close as she can come. Any farther and she loses this in-between place that she imagines, where a leaf becomes the nearness of a boy's skin. Always nearness, never contact itself. What she knows of her own longing she knows only by these impressions, which she can get to anytime, if she's alone, mullein leaf or not.

Ann opens her eyes, lost in her imagining: June hears the truck door slam shut in the distance and knows that May has climbed inside.

Outside, Jenny says, "I have to stop."

He asks, "Are you okay?"

His voice is so clear. He rolls another log. The sweat in his hair drips down. Jenny sees it sting his eyes.

"I want to sit down a minute," she manages.

"Take your time," Wade says, and he walks past her, cheerful and indifferent. He walks over to the boulder in the clearing. He climbs to the top of it, to see over the trees, his posture confident. He stands there, arms crossed, looking out.

Jenny opens the truck door. On the dashboard is a Styrofoam cup filled with lemonade. She gets into the passenger seat. She takes the cup in her left hand and gulps. Cool, sharp on the roof of her mouth. She waits for the sugar to push through her veins. She sees the forest beyond the white rim of her cup. She closes her eyes. The hatchet is still in her right hand, hanging out the door.

She hears someone behind her. It is her daughter May.

Jenny doesn't put the lemonade down. Through the front side window, out of the corner of her eye, there is a sudden sputter of light, revealed by a branch falling away from the sun it had hidden. Jenny moves her arm, not the one holding the lemonade or it would spill, but her right arm, which a moment ago hung limply out the open door.

It is a sound not so different from all the others and now it's not a sound at all. There are a few flies bashing themselves against the windowpane. The leaves outside are shaking and the bough that fell is caught and held by other boughs.

Wade on his boulder, looking out.

This is the best that Ann can do. This is as far as she can go.

■

Sometimes now, Ann feels surprised that she and Wade didn't wait longer than they did. He lost his daughters in early August. In late August, Jenny waived her right to a trial, entered a plea of guilty, and, in a hearing that lasted twenty minutes, was sentenced to life in prison with the possibility of parole after thirty years. During this hearing, the judge seemed to find her lack of self-regard unsettling, her adamant plea of guilt unusual. He pressured her to give an explanation, but she said only that she had committed the murder of her child and that she wished to die for it.

The divorce was finalized in October. In February, Wade entered Ann's life again, and in June, they were married.

June—two months shy of a year since his unthinkable loss. But it felt much longer than that. If they had been aware then that only ten months had passed, she thinks they would have waited longer. But it hadn't occurred to her to keep track, to count. The world had changed so fundamentally since May's death that to measure time in months seemed senseless, cruel.

They spent their brief honeymoon at the ocean, but they didn't call it a honeymoon. In the shadow of May's death and June's disappearance, the word felt inappropriate, even crass.

The day after their wedding, when they were walking down a

seaside street, the rain began to pour and they were caught in it without umbrellas. It was early afternoon and they found a house that was empty and just recently sold, on a wealthy street. How had they known to look for a key, taped under the porch? The feel of it at her fingertips, like magic.

Because of a travel delay that resulted in an overbooked train, they had spent their wedding night in regular seats, not a sleeper as they had planned. It had been her doing, not pushing for a cabin. She could tell that Wade had wanted to, and she knew all she had to do was mention to the conductor that it was their wedding night, and arrangements would be made, no matter what they said about the sleepers being full.

But their love had been delayed between them for so long, she didn't mind this one last night of waiting.

So at the time they found the empty house, on the day after their wedding, they had done nothing more than hold hands, and kiss once in the courthouse before the justice. That kiss had been, to Ann's astonishment, their first.

What their lives had looked like until that day in the courthouse, to the outside world and even to them, was a man taking piano lessons from a woman. The only change elicited by their engagement—their engagement being merely the weeks that followed Ann's offer to take care of him, on the day the saltshaker appeared in his coat pocket—was their long hugs goodbye after the lessons. During these hugs, she rubbed her face against his chest. She stood on her toes and he rubbed his nose across the top of her forehead. They breathed deeply, holding on. Sometimes this went on for several minutes, both of them standing together in the middle of her classroom, the door already open for him to leave, sometimes propped open by their bodies.

The restraint felt natural. They both simply knew how the other felt: that it was necessary to delay everything, even a declaration of love, until they were legally bound in it.

Rain pounded on the roof of the empty house they found them-selves inside of that day after their wedding. The wood floors shone with streaming light-shadows of the rain, reflected on wood by the sliding glass doors. Clean counters, empty rooms, nothing but a box of baking soda in the cupboards.

They let go of each other for the sake of coming back again. He went downstairs and she wandered the main floor, their separate hands trailing along separate walls, feeling for light switches.

On the wall, about a foot above the floor, there was a small silver handle. A laundry chute. Ann pulled on the handle, opened the little door, and looked down. She saw the top of his head; his hand was still touching the light chain he had pulled, illuminating the basement below her while she stood above him in the dimness. His head seemed so vulnerable to her down there, because he didn't know she was seeing it.

She threw her jacket down the chute, and it landed on his shoul-der. He touched it, surprised, looked up. Then she dropped her shoes, both at once. One of them hit him on the head. Their laughs met each other inside the laundry chute, one going up, the other down.

She dropped her socks, which fell onto the floor, then her sweater, her watch, the band in her hair, her earrings (which she lost for good that day, two pearls), her T-shirt.

Then, after a moment struggling to get them off, soaked from the rain, her jeans.

He stopped laughing when those fell. She could see his arms and his chest and the top of his head and the bridge of his nose. He looked at her clothes draped across his arms and he waited. She saw his chest expand in a deep, expectant breath. And the moment he looked up at her, as if to say, "Come on now, this isn't really all," her bra fell right onto his face. The strap stung him in the eye. Then, looking up again, his eye watering, her underwear.

He laid her clothes down on the basement floor, below the laun-dry chute. He tugged the chain again. The light went off.

Part of her wanted to hide herself in the bathroom as she heard him approach, an exciting nervousness overtaking her. But she stood there, waiting.

I won't take even one step away from the wall, she thought. Her shoulders were leaning against the wall, and her bare calves brushed against the cold handle of the laundry chute. It will be all his doing, coming to me.

She waited. Covering her smile with her hand and then not covering it anymore, and then not smiling anymore, she listened to his footsteps on the stairs. And in a moment, there was Wade, standing at the end of the hallway in the half-light, his face sad and earnest and beautiful, his lips parted as if there were something he needed to say but decided he could not.

He came toward her, and then put his mouth on hers.

∎

On the last day of what they did not call their honeymoon, in the cabin they rented that week on the ocean, Wade told Ann the full story of what happened, for the first and the last time in their marriage.

His recall of the events was disjointed. The conversation began without her knowing it began, just as the sun was setting. Ann asked Wade about his childhood. He told her that he had grown up on the northern Camas Prairie, near Grangeville. Then he said, as if it followed naturally, "I didn't tell my mom until a week later that her granddaughters were gone. They lived a full week longer in her mind."

Ann said nothing, sensing an incredible danger in his heart. They were both silent for what felt like minutes. He was sitting in a wooden chair by the window, she on the floor in front of the fire.

When he did finally speak, it was distant, as if it were not himself speaking, his eyes wide.

He told her that the only logical thought he had access to through his shock and despair was the necessity of putting distance between his wife and his only living child. He had to leave June in the woods in order to keep her safe. What else could he have done?

"I was going to come back for her." Then he paused. "It was an old couple at a farmhouse who called the police. They helped us," Wade said. Ann took note of the "us." Jenny and Wade, still together, still bound up with each other in his mind in that moment. She thought about the sound of the sirens far away on the dirt road, thought of what Jenny must have seen before her: birds, maybe, rising from a field. Scattering and converging the way Ann and Wade would see them do only nine months later, standing in the parking lot of the school. "The old man wrote me a letter a few months after. I didn't read it. But I do know it was some kind of apology. I don't know what for." He choked. "May was so alive, she was—" He held his head in his hands. She wanted to reach out and touch him, but she was afraid that her touch would break the feeling that had fallen over him in the cabin on this last day of their trip. He was saying what she had never believed he could. He lifted his face again, became stoic. "I was in the back of the truck stacking the logs, and May walked right past her mother and me without waving to either of us, without saying hello. She just opened the truck door and got inside. She slammed it like she was mad at me. Or at June. And I thought June would be following close behind, telling us what happened, what May had done and how they were fighting, and I thought, Why do they have to fight like this, when this could be such a nice day?" He stopped. He looked right at Ann. "But then I heard May singing inside the truck, and I thought, Well, she isn't mad at all. She's in there singing. And none of this had happened yet. I went on stacking logs. And we didn't— There just wasn't— It hadn't happened yet."

"Where was your other daughter?" She was careful not to say their names.

"Out playing. There was nothing at all wrong, nothing. Then Jenny told me she was thirsty, so we took a break. I stood over in the shade. I heard her get in the truck for something to drink. She must have still had it in her hand. I don't know how much time passed. Not much. I heard June running behind me, and I looked at her. She was running toward the truck, too. She smiled and waved to me, because I must have waved to her. She went to the truck, to the driver's side."

He leaned forward, put his palms over his knees. This time she did touch him. She put both her hands on the backs of his.

Ann felt about to cry. "I don't understand why— I don't understand."

"Because there is nothing to understand," he said, taking away his hands, darkening, perhaps scared of Ann's tears. He stood, picked up his chair, and set it a few feet from where it had been before. It was a meaningless gesture because he did not sit down again. He just stood there, swaying slightly. Then he looked out the window. The ocean wasn't visible, just the white sand and the beach grass and the fog. His voice was soft but angry. "It wasn't an accident, it wasn't a thing that she did on purpose. It was a thing that happened. To her and by her, and that's it."

He paused, looking out the window. Ann controlled her tears, pulled the blanket more tightly around herself, and felt for the first time the pain of the unspoken logic that she would carry with her forever: His longing for his daughters was a longing for Ann not to be his wife.

A warm evening light fell over the room. He picked up their dinner plates from the table, put them in the sink. Then he poured the bucket of clamshells that had been sitting in the sink out in the sand in front of their door. While he was out there, he stood with his back to her, listening to the waves.

■

From then on, Ann asked only softened questions, made only vague allusions, and sometimes she got answers. She learned at some point that the last time Wade ever saw Jenny's mother was at the hearing. Jenny's father had died when May and June were still small, so her mother came alone. She and Wade did not speak when they saw each other, but she did phone Wade a few months later, just to tell him that she had gone to the prison to visit Jenny, but that Jenny had refused to see her. Wade didn't know what to say. He didn't know how to be of comfort to his former mother-in-law, and he didn't know how to let her be of comfort to him. She must have felt the same, because it was the last time they ever spoke.

Other details came, slowly, but Wade never did tell Ann the whole story again. Why would he, after the air was cleared that once, after he felt he had said all that he was obligated to say? But she felt the story living on all around her, felt herself collecting meaning even from the glances of strangers.

For years after she moved to Mount Iris, she bought her groceries in Sandpoint, a town that was more than an hour away from their house, because she couldn't bear to wander down the aisles in Miller's Grocery only twenty minutes from home, where all the people she saw wore the same unasked question on their faces. Five years passed, six, seven, but the people in Ponderosa were no less baffled. Their fascination had fallen on Ann. They could not conceive of her. It wasn't a specific question they asked with their eyes. Not *What is it like?* Not *What are we supposed to do with you?* Not *Why have you married into this?* The question was vague, oppressive, everywhere.

It wasn't a question at all, but a statement of fact declared in the eyes of strangers.

I know you.

That's your question?

I heard about it.

Yes.

Even now, all these years later, the question takes the form of fear. Teenagers who were small children when May was killed avoid meeting Ann's eyes.

Or the question takes the form of politeness. A door held open at the feed store in Spirit Lake, by some old man who otherwise doesn't hold doors open for strangers. It takes the form of conceit. The postwoman in Ponderosa feels entitled; she moves with confidence and knowing, as if because her fingertips have had the privilege of sorting out Ann's envelopes, she has glimpsed what she thinks is inside them all—lies, pleas, false trails, dirty news, licked closed by the tongues of the past.

But in Sandpoint, when Ann went there during those early years, no one knew her. She shopped slowly, anonymous. And after shopping, she wandered down to the water and watched the sun set on Lake Pend Oreille. Like its shape and name implied, the lake seemed to listen. An ear. At its top curve Ann stood, listening back to the Ice Age silence of the water, and in this silence she dreamed. She felt June treading through unlikely futures—some horrifying, some hopeful—none of them taking place inside that house carved on the handle of the knife.

Why, still, of all that's happened, is that little house the most painful thing to picture? To think of that girl standing still in the hallway at the school, watching for Eliot, listening for his laughter in the halls, touching her fingertips to the engraved hearts inside the roses on a knife?

Eliot moved back to Idaho after high school. Seven years after he left, when he was twenty-four, Ann saw him from her car. He was with a young woman, near a fireworks stand along the highway that ran past Ponderosa. The young woman wore a green plaid summer dress and her black hair was back in a fashionably haphazard braid. She looked younger than him, but it was hard to tell. The moment Ann saw really was a moment, like a photograph. The girl was bent over, looking into a cardboard box whose side flap advertised ROTTWEILER PUPPIES $25. Ann did not see the dogs; she did not see the girl's hand dip into the box to bring one out. What she saw was the moment right before, when, on her way down, to include Eliot in her excitement, the girl had pressed her fingers on the knuckles of his hand on the crutch. And that was all. The loose hair at the girl's temples flew up when Ann drove by, catching the wind.

Ann drove past the Texaco and the post office, then past the gravel and rock yard and laundromat, and after that the road curved and there was forest along the highway. She pulled over on the shoulder and turned the engine off.

That other girl's hand on Eliot's crutch—there was something final in that. June would have known it, too. If June, as a young woman, had been the one driving by, she would have thought about that girl, thought about her hand on Eliot's, maybe for a long time, not necessarily with real pain because she would have long been over him (June would be sixteen if she were alive; she had been nine when she loved him), but certainly with some sadness for all the futures she had once imagined for herself, some of which took place alongside a one-legged boy.

She had loved him. They both had. June and Ann herself. That was the one piece of information Ann knew about June on her own, separate from what Wade had told her or what she had learned from the news. It was only Ann who had seen June at Eliot's locker in the school after hours, fingering the package in her hands, her rose-colored sweater tight on her shoulders. And then that stubborn jolt of her body when she dropped the package into the locker, deciding to believe it would be found.

Which, of course, it was.

Ann remained there, parked on the side of the highway, forcing herself to sit in one position: hands on the steering wheel, her back straight and tense, her eyes locked on her lap. When her body began to ache, she made herself sit a little bit longer, and a little longer still, to make sure enough weight was given to that moment the girl touched Eliot's hand, a moment that contained the only thing Ann was ever sure June wanted for herself.

It was the first time Ann had ever allowed herself to feel the possibility, the very present likelihood, that June was dead.

■　■　■

As soon as Ann hangs up the phone in her bedroom, she feels overcome with guilt. This happened the other five times she called the prison, and each of those times, it was hard to look Wade in the eyes for a long time afterward. Calling the prison library, and mailing the book there in the first place, are the only times that her imagination has ever reached into real life, has ever conjured real danger.

Trying to escape her guilt, Ann gets up from the bedroom floor and goes to the piano. Hardly breathing, she plays from memory, trying to quiet the accusations now rising in herself.

But Wade's voice is a memory, too. It hovers on the edges of the notes like a pedal tone, an ache: *Sometimes for a second I forget, and I think May and June are still alive, and that it's Jenny who's dead. Like we're struggling to manage without her.*

And they are. They are struggling to understand, to find the missing piece that is each other. Ann has reached out from the mystery she's caught inside of, has meddled in his past love, touched the forbidden places. She has put herself where she doesn't belong. In a book in a prison. A prison where the other half of Wade's life is being led.

Then I remember I could send her a letter. It makes me almost sick that it's possible.

She feels sick, too, pressing these piano keys that May once pressed. Even after all this time, even after all of her imagining, she can't truly feel how very real May's death is.

But it is very real to Wade. He feels what she could never dream of feeling. And what would he feel if he knew what she had done? How would he react if he thought of Jenny touching her finger to that spine in the library, pulling it off the shelf, discovering some piece of her past?

Ann closes her eyes and leans forward as she plays, trying to push herself beyond this terrible afternoon. The song is one from her days at university in Durham. She has forgotten parts of it, but skips over those parts seamlessly, as if they never existed. She replaces them with variations of the melody.

But the music doesn't hide her, so she stops. The piano's hush fills the room. Through the window, she sees her husband, walking through the snowy, muddy garden, toward his workshop. Then she sees him open the door and disappear inside.

Wanting to absolve herself in his presence, not by confessing, just by standing beside him, allowing him to love her in his unknowing way, she goes outside, walks through the garden. Through the door of his workshop, she hears him humming, softly, hears a clatter of metal things. She sees him standing over several trays on a counter, looking through them. There is something clenched in his hand.

She comes up behind him and touches his back. At that moment, he turns around, smiles sadly and with surprise, and opens his hand for her to see what he is holding. A wooden knife handle without the blade. He rubs his finger over the handle to get the sawdust out of the ridges he's carved, and she sees where he's wood-burned the outline of two mountains, his trademark.

"Beautiful," she manages.

"You like it?"

"I do."

"It's for you when it's finished," he says. "The blade is the one I made out of that old truck we found together."

"Really?"

She takes the smooth piece of wood in her hand.

"It's yours," he says again. "I was just looking for the blade. I don't remember where I put it. It's not in my office, either."

"Wade," she says. "Thank you."

The simplicity of his gift, the innocent surprise of it. All at once Ann feels touched by a misery she is not sure she's ever known before. She feels it sharply, like love. This man has burned these mountains into wood for her.

He smiles at her expression, misunderstanding it. To hide inside of his misunderstanding, she gets up on her toes and she hugs him. He kisses her shoulder, and she imagines he is touched by what must seem in this moment like her gratitude for the piece of wood still in her hand.

But it is not gratitude that she is feeling. It is her betrayal in its light. Even as he holds her in his arms, she holds her secrets away from him. Even as he carves these flowers in his workshop, she holds the telephone in their bedroom.

It makes me almost sick that it's possible.

He begins to kiss her, all over her face. She wants to confess, but it is impossible to know where to begin. It is impossible to know the least selfish thing to do.

He buries his face in her hair and he breathes deeply. But he cuts his breath short and pulls his head away. "Ann," he says, "did you go somewhere?"

"No, I'm here," she insists, kissing him roughly on his mouth now, kissing him through what are tears just barely held back.

He laughs gently. "No, there's exhaust in your hair." He buries his face in her hair again. Then he looks at her, carefully this time. "It's really strong. You don't smell it?"

She is cautious. "I don't smell anything."

"It wasn't there a few hours ago."

"It wasn't?"

"Really," he says, looking into her eyes now, "did you go some-where?" There's a strain in his voice, underneath the lightness of the question. And there is a strain in Ann's silence. "Why were you running the truck?" he says softly.

She could tell him now. She could.

She looks up at him, and crosses a line she's never dared cross. "Sometimes I go up there and sit."

"Why do you do that?"

"Why do you think?" His face isn't angry, but he doesn't know where to look. He can't look at her. "Wade. Why do you think I go up there?" Her voice is gentle, though she knows that this will bring him pain, and she feels something not gentle growing inside of her. She says, "I want to hear what you remember." He opens his empty palm and shakes his head. She steps forward. "The rear-view mirror. It's glued back on now, I know. But you ripped it off, didn't you? You ripped the mirror down that day." He shakes his head, his eyes wide. Then she says, tears in her voice, "It was because you saw May in it."

He turns away from her.

"You're my husband," she says then, firmly. She is crying now. She is sorry for her frustration, her cruelty, and she reaches for his hand to try to lessen it, but even as she touches it, she can't stop. "You know you don't like me going up there, but you don't know why. You're so angry at me and you don't remember why."

He has taken a few steps away. He is looking for something to distract himself, to focus on. He looks out the window at their garden. There is a spot of dried mud on the window. He touches it. He moves his finger against it gently, as if to rub it off, but it's on the other side of the glass.

That spot of mud is a universe away. Aware of her futility and his, exhausted by this awareness, she leans back against the counter but, in doing so, bumps the tray of blades at the edge. She tries to catch it, but it falls. The blades clang loudly on the floor, so much falling that she puts her hands over her ears. She looks down at them. Almost relieved for this distraction, she kneels down to pick them up.

She hears Wade step toward her. Still kneeling, she looks over her shoulder and she is horrified to see that he's relieved by the fallen blades, too, desperate for this distraction. Now there is something physical, something he has heard and can see. A mess she's made. Before she can think, before she can stop him, he grabs her shoulders. He forces her head down onto the floor and holds her face against the fallen blades.

"No, no!" she cries into the wood floor. She tastes the blood from the cut on her lip. She struggles, but that hurts her more.

He holds her down.

"Please!" she whispers, her eyes shut against all that metal.

And then he releases her, suddenly. He staggers backward, as if he's the one who's hurt.

She touches her lip to see how badly it is cut. First she looks at the drop of blood on her fingertip, and then she looks up at him.

He seems terrified: "Oh, Ann."

Her tears stream down her face. He tries to help her up, and she sees his shaking hands. But she doesn't let him help her up. She stands on her own. She turns her back to him, leaves the workshop, and runs as fast as she can past the house and down the road.

░ ░ ░

At the mountain stream, after the flies have made her sister run back to the truck, June is alone in the quiet of the afternoon. She makes a hole in the mud with her finger, squatting among the mullein cabbages, and into this hole she drops some spit from her mouth. When the spit has fallen in, she covers the hole back up and wipes her muddy finger on her pants. She presses her foot firmly on the place where the hole was.

Of course it was Ann who used to do that, not June, and Ann was much younger than nine. But it doesn't matter. She imagines June playing out Ann's own ritual there by the stream on Mount Loeil that August afternoon, in the private place by the birch trees that June has found for herself to hide from the flies. Ann imagines the spit falling from the thin lips of the dark-haired girl, the dirty pink sleeve she wipes her mouth on, that pink-faded-nearly-to-gray shoe she presses down on the damp earth. Ann is so sure of that step that if she went there now—though, of course, she does not know the exact place—she knows she would see the small footprint still there, hardened among the nettles, like the cast the police later made of it.

May has probably just gulped down the last of the lemonade. June picks up a stick and swats a tree branch with it, annoyed at the thought of her sister. As she approaches the clearing where her mom and dad are working, she realizes she doesn't hear their work anymore. No more logs banging against the truck bed. They must be on a break. June feels a little jolt of excitement. There will be snacks in the glove compartment. May will be complaining about the fly bites and Mom will put some calamine lotion on her, and then May will get Mom's neck all sticky putting her gummy little face there like she always does.

Gummy little face: dry jam scratched off a Polaroid.

June sees her dad standing on a boulder looking at the mountains. Her mom is standing near him, very still, looking not at the mountains but at the pile of wood that seems to June undiminished even after all their work, that endless little pile that will keep them here in the hot woods all day. Then her mom moves toward the passenger side of the truck. So June hurries; she is not sure about the snacks in the glove compartment, whether they are the same or whether she will have to fight with May about who gets which flavor. She breaks into a run, her fastest run, but just before she reaches the truck, she stops to tie her shoes. They are muddy, so she kicks them against a stump once they are tied.

When she kicks her foot the final time, she hears a sound. For an instant, she thinks it is a sound that she has made herself, with her foot. But then she looks up into the treetops. A loose branch has just fallen high in the trees and been caught by the other branches. The leaves shake all around.

She looks down from the treetops. She goes to the truck, to the driver's side.

She sees through the window.

There is a vision of her mom in the kitchen, doing many things at once but wanting to do only one of them. Read a book, maybe. But so much is happening. Maybe she's washing a pan in the sink and she's propped the book up on the counter so she can read it while she washes. Maybe there is a pot boiling on the stove behind her. And maybe it starts boiling over, but then at the very last second, very calmly, her mother turns away from the sink and the book, turns the stove off, and goes back to reading and washing again. The pot does not boil over, but just barely.

That is how familiar a gesture it seems to June, the motion of her mother's arm. Turning off a stove mid-sentence. Then finishing the sentence.

Her right hand moves with a quick, practical grace, first in front of her, gliding by the dashboard, and then, with only a slight turn of her body, through the space between the two front seats, and then behind her. A fast arc of life, and swiftly the hatchet comes down on May.

There is the peaceful slump of her sister.

Just as there is no transition between what has just been and what is now, there is no moment of wonder in the girl, no decision to be made. She turns and runs without thinking, terrified of what is possible now. The dry twigs snap under her faded rose-colored shoes, and her father yells at her first in the old way. Then, after a moment in which he must have seen inside the truck the flashing blood, he yells at her in a voice that isn't his, a sickening voice, a clogged drain, yelling, inexplicably, her name. But she hardly hears him, and the thick woods lash at her. Invisible webs cling to her arms as she runs.

■   ■   ■

VIOLATORS WILL BE SHOT. Even without the signs posted on her neighbor's trees, Ann feels this threat as a border of air as she runs past them, down the mountain. She feels the threat more than ever now that her own home is a place of danger. These acreages she's trespassing upon now, these acreages she is crossing in her desperation, are unloved, never touched except every few years to repost these awful signs. Great reaches of cheap land on which people huddle in the corners closest to the dirt road in the valley, because to live any farther up would mean trouble in the winter. Acres and acres of land, and yet entire lives are spent within a twenty-foot radius around some trailer. But ownership reaches out from the filthy beds, where bodies are sleeping in the flickers of afternoon TV; it reaches out, a sweeping arm, across every tree and rock contained within its legal—and nevertheless rightful—border, and those trees and rocks become something other than themselves, a history that is the history of the people who claim them; the dark trees are exclusive, conspiratorial. Running as fast as she can down the gulches, through the cold, grasping at branches to keep from falling, her hands burning on the bark they touch, Ann sees that this land they're all so proud of is worthless. Steep, parched, dusty, and susceptible to fire in the summers, and the summers a reprieve from the winters that define these mountains.

She stops to catch her breath, holds some snow up to her cut lip. Her feet are cold and wet. The air is damp. She drops the red snow. She looks down at her freezing hands, and when she looks up again, she sees a different sign, this one hand-painted and posted on a gate between two pines: EMU OIL, SOAP, EGGS.

She dabs some snow to her face again, then goes to the gate and opens it. The emu pen runs along the side of a trailer, and back partially into a meadow. One of the tall birds tilts its head and eyes her as she approaches. It lifts its leg and curls its large claw up against its body, as if to ask a question. She sees other emus, off in the trees, moving in their prehistoric way, squalid and regal.

Her cut might be deep enough that she needs stitches. Someone will have to take her. She doesn't know her story yet; she doesn't know how much she'll tell. But she's too cold, too exhausted to think.

Already, not even to the porch, she can smell the inside of the trailer. It is a warm, humid smell that hangs around the door, heavy even in the cold. Trailer skirting has been used to form a lean-to against the house, inside of which she sees a bath mat and a dog bowl.

She knocks. Almost immediately, a gray-haired woman answers.

"I need . . ." says Ann. But because the face of the woman is not at all alarmed at the sight of the cut on Ann's face, because she says nothing about it, and instead stands there calmly, all Ann can say is, "I saw the sign on the fence."

The woman nods and motions into her trailer. "Wait here," she says, then disappears for a moment into another room, and reappears with a handful of toilet paper. She hands it to Ann, and Ann thanks her, as she dabs it to her lip. She does not cry, but feels as if she might, because she is so relieved to have her pain acknowledged by another person, even if the only acknowledgment is a handful of toilet paper.

But the woman says nothing about the cut. Instead, she leads Ann through a small kitchen and into the living room. A large man is sitting on a couch watching a television that has been set atop two columns of magazines. There are spots on the wall from water damage and a sick-looking lapdog beats its tail against the ground, lying with its face on the floor, looking up.

"Wepshin," the man scolds, and the little tail stops thumping.

The man doesn't say anything about her face, either, even as she holds the toilet paper against it and feels the paper grow damp as the blood soaks through.

At the back of the room, there is a shelf with all of the emu products, and small handwritten signs taped underneath them.

"You want jelly you'll have to come back in the summer. Lots of people come looking for jelly," says the woman.

"No, no, nothing like that," says Ann. "I really need to— If you wouldn't mind—"

But the dog has come to the woman's feet and is whining. The woman kneels down and cups its snout with her hands and says, affectionately, "Oh, I know, I know, you're getting old." Then she stands. "The top shelf is the soaps, made with the fat of the bird, lavender grown right outside," she says, pointing to a window box. "Next shelf is some jerky we smoked ourselves; here are the massage oils, hair oils, bath oils. Well, you can just read the tags. Take your time. My name is Gina."

Gina goes into the kitchen, where it sounds like she is frying giant eggs in bacon fat.

Ann feels her hands shaking. She feels something sinister here in this trailer, something that silences her. She doesn't know what it is. She wants to get out of this place, but she has to think. Where can she go? Holding the toilet paper to her lip, she uses her other hand to pick up a package of soap and looks at the price: ten dollars. Ten dollars? A bottle of bath oil is fifteen. She looks over her shoulder and sees Gina in the other room, hears the crackle and pop of the eggs. The man is still watching sports, the dog's tail is thumping at Ann's feet, and she feels that the dog is panting too loudly, so loudly she can smell its breath. The moisture, the filth of the air settles down on her skin, and she wants to get away.

She realizes the feeling of chaos is coming from a constant buzzing sound. It grows loud, then quiets.

The shelf that holds the emu products, she notices, is placed in such a way that it creates a very small room behind it. Ann steps around the shelf and looks into this dim space the size of a closet. And there, in a strange glow of light, is a boy.

He is about ten years old. He leans forward over a table. The buzzing is coming from something in his hand. She looks more closely. It is a kind of pen with a vibrating needle at its tip. The pen is attached to a cord that disappears into a small black box with many dials, which in turn is plugged into the wall. She sees the back of the boy's head, the white scar in his short hair, the hole in his thin red shirt, just below his neck.

On the table in front of him is a giant eggshell, green and teal and white, lying on top of a thin light box on the table. He is using the pen to carve a picture. She can't see what the picture is, just the light caught in the threadlike lines. All around him are other eggs with pictures carved into them, elaborate forest scenes, mountain lions, bears. They are beautiful, astonishingly so. The boy sees Ann but does not turn to look at her. He focuses on his shell and the buzzing goes on, as if Ann isn't there at all.

"Hello?" she whispers.

He mumbles something she can't hear over the buzzing of his pen.

He is carving a girl's face. This face is surrounded by an elaborate mosaic of trees, so that the tangles of the girl's hair become the branches, the sharp moon in the sky a trinket in her hair. The trees are dark and teal, and the girl is white. His needle is shaping the delicate curves of her jaw.

"Is that the one you want?" Suddenly Gina is behind her, her arms crossed, a black spatula in her hand.

"I hadn't thought. I don't know," says Ann.

"Buzzy's prices, not mine. Tell her."

The boy turns off the pen, gives Ann a long, bored look, his jaw hanging open. "Faces are eighty, flowers sixty, mountains seventy," he says quickly, as if the effort of saying it is too much.

Ann shakes her head.

"Out of your range?" says Gina coldly.

"I don't have enough. It's not why I'm here."

"You don't have anything. Nothing but some cold feet and a cut on your face."

Ann begins to cry. "No," she says, but she feels dizzy. The dark room tilts ever so slightly in her vision. "My husband is in trouble," she manages.

But the boy turns his pen back on. He drills through the hard shell to make the pupil of the girl's eye, her pupil the absence of a pupil, a hole in the center of her teal iris through which the light box shines out its yellow light.

He wipes the shell dust away with his dirty hand.

"I have to go," Ann says, "I have to go." She hurries out of the trailer, nearly tripping on the sick dog, and then nearly tripping again on the rotten porch. It is snowing now. Gina yells after her, "Shut the gate!" but Ann doesn't comprehend these words until long after she is through that gate. She doesn't know what she is frightened of, but she doesn't stop running, feeling as she goes that her limbs are not her own, that she is missing from her body, that she is caught here in the snow and the confusion of someone else's life.

■   ■   ■

Wade had told her once, not the day on the ocean, but a different day, when he hardly meant to tell her at all, that he was the one the officers arrested.

He said that he stopped at the first farmhouse he came to. He didn't pull up the driveway; he stopped in the middle of the main road, and he got out and ran. But there had been so much confusion when the police arrived that they did not know who to question. They pushed him against the truck and put handcuffs on him, and he didn't fight it. They did this even though Jenny was down on her knees on the gravel road, blood on her clothes. The old woman from the farmhouse was kneeling beside her, hugging her, trying to get her to calm down. The officers didn't know what to do with the truck where May was. Nobody thought to move the truck, so it stayed there in the middle of the road. It was Wade's protests that he had to return to his little girl, the one who had lived, that delayed everything. The police could not understand. They thought he had lost his mind, that he was pleading to get back not to a place but to a time, to where his daughter was still alive, as if May herself were waiting up there in the moments before the hatchet came down.

When Jenny confessed, softly (Ann imagines), after trying to get their attention, for no one had noticed her much at first, with the child in the backseat and the man pleading to "get back" to his daughter on the mountain, all she said was, "I did this." They still did not take the handcuffs off Wade. Maybe because he didn't ask them to; he asked for only one thing, to go back for his other daughter, and they didn't, they couldn't, understand.

When they finally realized he was talking about a second girl, two police officers drove up Mount Loeil with Wade in the backseat. He said nothing the whole way except where to turn. They did not know then that June was lost. It had not occurred to Wade that she would not want to be found by him, and so they did not call for the bloodhounds or the search team until a full hour later, when they arrived in the clearing where a few crows were sunning themselves on the halfhearted pile of birch, and found June gone.

They searched everywhere, calling June's name, crushing the white Styrofoam cups with their black boots. And when the search team finally arrived, the bloodhounds sniffed Wade's deerskin glove.

Why, if it was your glove, not hers? asked Ann.

Because June had put it on earlier that day, as a joke. How funny her little hands looked in her father's giant gloves. That was the hardest thing for him to tell her; Ann could see that in his face, grief-stricken, but no tears. June's joke about her hand in his gloves. But he remembered it because he needed to. Because there was no article of June's clothing in the truck. Because the bloodhounds needed something to sniff and so he found something for them on the edge of his memory.

But maybe his own hands had covered up her smell already, because the hounds chased false trails down steep gulches and through streams.

And later, when pictures of June's face appeared on flyers in grocery stores and gas stations, no one seemed to see her even when they looked. Only Ann and Wade, for whom the faces of other children took on, for a flash, the shape of June's. Pictures in magazines, library flyers, advertisements. Any indistinct resemblance, any slight hint at the curve of a nose, and there she was: in a passing car, in a commercial, or in the webs of light shining through the fissures in a carving on an egg.

■　■　■

The sun is setting now, and Ann is lost and out of breath, unable to orient herself in these woods. Her cut has stopped bleeding, but it throbs in the cold. She feels a flicker of true panic, a wild fear not of freezing to death, but of never being found after she has.

But then she sees something close by. An armchair. For a moment, there in the woods in the winter light, the panic subsides. She forgets her pain and the horror of the emu farm and of what Wade did to her, and she stares at the armchair, as if its mere association with a living room and fireplace can warm her. The bottom cushion is gone, torn to shreds and scattered around on the shrunken snow.

There is also a wooden picture frame with no glass and no back, and, she sees now, a lamp. No shade or bulb or cord, but the base of a lamp fallen on its side.

She bends to pick up the shadeless lamp, encased in the soil beneath the snow. The porcelain is blue like the chair. She turns it around and brushes the caked soil off of its front, and there on the porcelain is a white oval and inside of the oval is a house of the same blue color as the lamp itself.

She had an idea as a very small child of what it meant to be grown up, and what it meant was having a house that you filled with things like this. Things that, individually, you had no feeling about and couldn't ever remember choosing or paying for, but that the years of your life had collected for you and that therefore spoke on your behalf. Such things, in Ann's child mind, were necessary and boring and beautiful, and they matched. Whatever hateful things happened to you when you grew up could be diminished by the power of the certainty of these *things,* which were a protection, as if they held collectively a magic of their own, a scattered shield.

Holding the lamp now, she recalls the empty house they found on their honeymoon.

Chilled, bare-skinned, happy, shy, she had stood there in the hallway, waiting for Wade, and looked in the room across from her and filled it in a moment with her eyes. With chairs and a bed and pictures on the walls, and a lamp like this one. Blue. Between two of his footsteps on the stairs, maybe, she had filled the house with their futures.

And when they made love in the hallway on the clean, cool floor, she had felt these things around her, had felt the bed and its new pillows just out of sight, tucked into the corner of the empty room. Her body was chilled in every place he wasn't touching her. Her back pressed down on the hardwood floor. Her clothes, fallen down the laundry chute, lay in a pile far below them.

The expression on his face as he finished was of half-hidden relief. When he left her body, he began to cover it with quick, light kisses. Her breasts. Her stomach. As if to warm her. Such fast kisses, as if he did not want one to dry before she felt the next.

She had shivered, in the cold and in the shock of her joy.

She shivers now, standing over the ruined armchair in these darkening woods.

"I love you, Ann."

"I know, and I love you," she had said.

"I have loved you since I first saw you—"

"Don't say it, please don't."

"—in the classroom."

"Please." And she pulled him down against her. She cupped the back of his head in her strange, new hands.

As she stands over the armchair in the darkening woods, she can almost hear him humming all those years ago, all the way from that August day. It's a song from an old book. A song about a photograph.

> *Take your picture off the wall*
> *And carry it away*

From this tall boulder, he can see down into the bowl of the valley. Over the trees, he can see the road that brought them here.

Where are the mountain bluebirds? He is looking for them already. The dry air smells like September. Soon school will start. Her quiet, sunny classroom will be filled with children. The piano teacher will open her windows so the choir's practicing voices will fall over the parking lot and mix with the sounds of motorboats in the distance, of the lake swelling against the old docks.

The smell of vinegar on a cloth, to clean the ivory keys. The sound of her voice. Over the same keys his clumsy hands have labored, her own will move with ease.

Somewhere close behind him, twigs are snapping under little shoes. His older daughter, June, is coming toward him. In a moment he will turn to see her there. Knowing this, this beautiful thing, he listens a moment longer to the mountains, and hears, somewhere in the trees, the crackle and snap of dry branches, in some breeze too high for him to feel.

Wade has told Ann none of this. She knows it on her own. She knows it only now, in the cold and in the dark.

Boy crazy. In a pretty serious way. It hurts her like she really loves them.

When Jenny gets inside the truck to wash down the dust in her throat, Ann is only an idea to her, a voice she can hear in her husband's heart, humming as quietly and persistently as a fly at a window. She has felt this voice all along but has not been able to put her finger on the source—what is that residue on his laughter? And is it true that he listens now with an unusually rapt attention to June's idle talk of school, as if trying to glean from her recounting of a thousand school-day glances some singular glance from someone in passing?

But these thoughts aren't formed yet. To Jenny, Ann has no name; the feeling has no name. Not jealousy, not suspicion, not even unhappiness.

Until—

I heard May singing inside the truck, and I thought, Well, she isn't mad at all. She's in there singing. And none of this had happened yet.

In her husband's heart, and now in her daughter's. An inherited trace of music. The choir teacher in the hallway, in her family, in the truck. May sings—

> *Take your picture off the wall*
> *And carry it away*

In a girl's voice, she hears a woman's.
She hears Ann's.

■   ■   ■

In the darkness, Ann stumbles onto the road, sick with revelation. The mystery that was meant for her all those years ago. *I was there—I was there inside the truck. And he doesn't know, he doesn't know.*

Her feet numb, the cut on her lip sealed against the cold. She rubs her hands over her arms to warm herself. In the distance, there is a soft glow from beyond the road's bend, and for just an instant there appear the silhouettes of several emus, trotting as a confused flock down the middle of the road. In perfect symmetry, they divide, half into the woods on one side, half into the woods on the other. So quickly she can hardly believe what she has seen. The headlights have split them apart.

Headlights.

She waves her arms. She stands in the road and waves them again and again.

The truck slows down and stops for her. The door opens.

Wade.

"I didn't mean to do this," he starts, so desperately, coming toward her, his voice strained, frightened.

"I know, I know."

"I looked everywhere. I drove up and down this road four times. I called the police." He chokes on his words. "I told them what I did to you."

"I only ran to clear my head. I wasn't running from you."

"You should have run from me," he said. "I was so scared of what I did to you."

"I'm glad you found me."

"That cut will need stitches—" he says.

"I'm so cold," she says.

"I've got the heater on." He takes her arm, cups her elbow in his palm, and leads her to the passenger door. "This can't happen," he says. "Nothing like this. Never again."

"It won't," she says, and she believes it. She puts her palm against his cheek. She makes him look into her eyes.

"I'm so sorry." Tears in his eyes.

She climbs in, and he closes her door. For only a moment she is alone there, in the truck. Everything is very calm and strange. Her door closed, his open. The dream catcher swings from the rear-view mirror. Somewhere in the darkness, emus run in the woods on either side of the road.

Now he is beside her, in the driver's seat, his door shut.

The vent blows hot air on them. He puts his hand on top of hers. "I took the mirror down because I didn't want Jenny to have to see May as we were driving. I knew I wouldn't look but I thought she would. I didn't want her to have to see."

"You don't have to do that," whispers Ann. There are tears streaming down her face, too.

"I need to tell you things," he says.

"That's not what I mean." She leans all the way across to his seat and rests her forehead on his shoulder.

He leans his head on top of hers. "What do you mean?"

For a long time they sit that way. He takes one of her hands between both of his.

"Me," she answers after a long while, softly crying. "Don't do anything like that for me."

2008

Plastic flowers in a plastic vase. A nightstand bolted to the floor.

Elizabeth's awake.

Hatred, forgotten in her sleep, arrives in her stomach at the sight of those flowers, which are not for her but are striving to seem to be. They've been placed here in the prison infirmary in order to create the illusion of a worried family as a way of coaxing a patient back into the world, even though their petals are cobwebbed, and God knows how many prisoners have died in this bed after suicides that didn't take until hours later, right at the moment suicide was no longer necessary because, Look, someone sent flowers.

The flowers reek with all that stale time and pretense. She might throw up.

She has been in the infirmary for almost a week for stomach cramps, the result of grief. She hasn't been able to hold down her food ever since the guards informed her she wouldn't be allowed, not ever in the two lifetimes she owed, to attend the prison school that has been her only sanctuary here these sixteen years.

A month in Lock should have sufficed for her infraction, but no—that hideous month, where she crouched in the agony of unremitting light, where she sucked, now and then, the leather corner of a Bible, wasn't enough, so they took away her education, too. Elizabeth will pay for her one offense forever, all the rest of her two trapped lives. The classroom, forbidden to her now, is the only tolerable place in this whole prison, the only place that actually resembles her old life, unlike those flowers, those pathetic intimations—

A footstep.

Elizabeth lies dead still with her eyes shut. Rigid in the bed, she hopes she hasn't already been caught awake. She has a new cellmate now, Jenny, and she knows that's who it is, that's who's shifting in this room. They lived together for only a week before Elizabeth collapsed, but she can picture Jenny perfectly now: hands clasped, her patience like a sickness the way it encompasses her, hair ragged and graying, hands ruined by chemicals, her face eerily pretty. Why does she keep coming? Their sentences have overlapped by thirteen years in this small prison, and yet the only words that have ever passed between them are: "You live here now" and "Yes," spoken in the cell two weeks ago, the day that Elizabeth was released from Lock to find that Jenny had moved in. Elizabeth had heard about Jenny's long-suffering silence, and she had seen the way Jenny scrubbed the hallways, making a display of her submission to misery. What a thing to look forward to living with. But why has she come here to visit? Why, when they are nothing to each other but bodies forced to share a space?

Another footstep, another. It's only a nurse walking by. Elizabeth opens her eyes. No one's here.

She rolls over, clutches her stomach.

She would almost rather Jenny's vacant presence than her hovering absence here in this half-room with curtained walls. Jenny's absence seems to describe her better than her presence does; she is a looming vessel of her own withholding. Elizabeth had noticed that quality in her long before they were cellmates. She wants nothing. She prefers nothing. She's never complained. She's hardly said anything at all, to anyone, in all these years. So why hover here when she's not here? Sleep, Elizabeth, go to sleep. It doesn't matter. Sickness can spin the trivial in nauseating spirals; the most intolerable boredoms become infected with importance when you are sick. Like the flowers. Why direct such fury at them? They are pieces of plastic; they have no intention of their own. And Jenny is only silent because she has nothing to say, and she came to visit you in the infirmary only because it was something to do, and besides, it was only once. Once while you were pretending to sleep days ago.

No, Jenny is not a mystery. There was a time early on when Elizabeth might have watched her with a secret fascination because of what she'd done. She might have even pictured Jenny in the front seat of that truck. Would have seen, every time she looked at her ordinary face, a different face. The same face, but right before, and then right after. Elizabeth would have sought out her own disgust by doing so, and the disgust would have meant something promising about who she was.

But that was long ago. She has long since lost interest in motives, in the details of other women's crimes. Even the hatchet makes its usual sense. A mother who loves her child with all her self is only so far from the hatchet anyway; one casual swing and it's done. Hatred, love, all muddled up in that space inside a whisper, when the words don't matter anymore, when the baby's half asleep and you can carry it all the way there if you want, on nothing but the tone of your voice. *When the bough breaks, the cradle will fall.* Sing it as softly as you like—the words clench their own teeth. The child still falls.

—but then again (Elizabeth thinks, in some conscious place inside her dreams, inside her sedative and the dusty smell of plastic flowers), there was something, once, that Jenny wanted.

Three or four years ago, there was a vote. One of the prisoners had a brother who wanted to donate a piano. The warden showed the prisoners the space in the common room the piano would occupy.

Is this what you want? the warden asked. A rare thing, to see the warden, a stocky woman with a square, pleasant face. But an even rarer thing to vote. Elizabeth wondered why this of all things was a question worth asking. Why wouldn't they take what they could get?

The warden said, "All in favor," and every hand but one went up.

The warden said, "All against," and there was Jenny's hand.

Strange—so very strange to remember it now. Jenny's hand in the air seemed then the first and only word that she had ever spoken, hovering above them all, out of place, absurd. She had lived alone for so long that speaking seemed to hurt her body. So it was strange to think there could be anything that Jenny wanted or didn't want. Strange to see in her after all those years some semblance of opinion, a quiet but active will.

Her hand, the only one, rising as if astonished at its rising.

■

Beautiful Elizabeth!
She wakes suddenly, as if someone has shouted at her. Her mouth is parched. She has dreamed about her school, about Mr. Abram and Mr. Damiani, her teachers, those two free people who

79

volunteer their Thursday evenings week after week to teach fourteen inmates anything they know enough to teach. Humanities, history, music appreciation, poetry. Their happy voices, so adamant about poetics. Their self-conscious, joyful, professorial selves. They wrote comments all over Elizabeth's poems, just like her real professors used to do in college. Not just checkmarks and corrections. Real words.

Stronger verbs, Elizabeth.

Too many syllables in this line. Read it aloud. Clap it out.

Beautiful, Elizabeth!

It was Mr. Abram who wrote that last one, next to a stanza in a sonnet she wrote. She still has that sonnet with his note in the margin. She used to lie in her bed and remove the punctuation in her mind, removing the comma so that the *beautiful* was not addressed to her but described her, and removing the exclamation point because it was distant, no gravity at all. His handwriting was boyish, the letters far apart enough that she could cover up that comma and exclamation point with her fingertips—index and middle—and still see everything else.

Beautiful Elizabeth

Beautiful Elizabeth

Beautiful Elizabeth

It wasn't his voice that she heard in her head. It had nothing to do with the man who wrote it. It wasn't even a sound, just a feeling. Something that belonged to her. Something she could strive to make true— *Beautiful*—

"Elizabeth."

The chaplain is sitting in a chair beside her bed. When did he get here?

"Leave me alone," she says. She's surprised to hear in her voice that she's on the verge of tears.

The chaplain smiles at her as if she has not just said what she has said, as if his being here is a marvelous surprise. He is a slight man in his fifties, with large eyes and a bald head. He holds up a foil-topped cup of pears. He shakes it side to side, as if to entice and also scold her, as if she is a picky child and her starvation is by her own choosing.

She decides to pretend it is. "I hate pears," she says.

He says, softly, with a sad smile, "I know this isn't about losing your poetry class."

She says, "Oh, really."

"You're sick because of what you did to Sylvia."

"I'm sick because they took my class away."

He shakes his head. "We've been through this."

"Tell me who took my place in class," she demands. "Tell me who gets to go."

"What you really want to know is can you forgive yourself."

"What I really want to know is her fucking name."

He sighs. By this time, they are merely enacting the same old scene. She can tell that he knows already he'll make no progress with her today. He sets the cup of pears on the nightstand beside the flowers. "I'll come back when you're ready to talk about what you did," he says, standing, and he leaves her staring at the flowers.

Those flowers. Not trivial at all. They act like they're sitting on a farmhouse kitchen table. They act like they've been recently un-wrapped from cellophane. They act like it's water they're sucking from that glass instead of air.

But she's no longer amazed to find herself so angry. She under-stands her rage at them: The flowers remind her of Sylvia. Sylvia, her old cellmate, her old best friend. Sylvia, the reason that school is no more, and the reason, therefore, for this sickness.

It is Sylvia's bed that Jenny sleeps in now. Sylvia's air that Jenny breathes.

Elizabeth and Sylvia were cellmates until only one month ago, for nearly sixteen years, both incarcerated the same year, when they were in their twenties, Sylvia for setting fire to a house she believed her aunt was inside of, though she wasn't—only her uncle, who died in the fire—and Elizabeth for shooting her boyfriend and then her neighbor, who had seen.

That very first year, almost immediately, almost without discussion, the two women began to make a collage on the cell wall.

The collage had no end. It was always shifting, morphing, the wall becoming thick with papers taped over other papers. No other cell looked like theirs. A work of art. Everything from their lives, they put up there: drawings, photographs, magazine spreads, letters they wrote to each other. Tape was scarce, so they stuck some of their scraps to the wall with dots of toothpaste.

It was Sylvia's idea to pretend that they had always known each other. She said they should pretend they chose each other long before they were locked up. It was not hard to do. Elizabeth would stare at the collage, trying to be hypnotized by it, blending her memories with Sylvia's. "Remember when?" They each had several childhood photos, and Sylvia arranged them in the very center of the collage, overlapping, so that it looked like the yard Elizabeth stood in when she was ten years old was the same yard that held the swimming pool nine-year-old Sylvia was splashing in. In that pool, Sylvia's skinny face looked eager. Her red bangs were cut short at the top of her tall forehead, a hairstyle that in all the other photos never changed above an eager little face that barely did. Elizabeth, by contrast, saw someone different in every picture of herself, her hair bleached and then darkened, her eyes narrowing with the years. Her hair is short now, dirty-blond. She doesn't change it anymore. She used to let Sylvia run a brush through it. The brush was a gift to Sylvia from her aunt, the same aunt she had intended to kill in the fire. It was heavy and wide, and there was, until recently, a mirror embedded in the back of it. Sometimes, as Sylvia brushed, Elizabeth would stare at the wall, let her eyes go out of focus. They would speak to each other with nostalgia about things that had never happened, because speaking that way made their cell less claustrophobic, turned their confinement with each other into a sisterhood.

But then, one night two years ago, Elizabeth had a dream about the yellow line.

In waking life, the yellow line was painted in the hallways and over the sidewalks in the prison yard, and inmates going from place to place were required to walk on it. But in Elizabeth's dream, the line ran through her childhood home, right through the center of her house, so she couldn't stop in the kitchen and hug her mother, who stood at the oven where the yellow didn't reach. She could move through her landscape but only to see it on either side of her. The only other person walking along the line was another little girl, wearing water wings. She had red hair and she was pretending to play hopscotch, but she only hopped with her feet together so that the soles of her shoes never touched the tile floor, only the terrible yellow. Nine-year-old Sylvia.

It was a hideous dream, and when she woke she could not fathom having ever loved that ugly collage or the ugly girl with whom she made it. When she looked at the wall and at Sylvia, she felt an intense violation, as if she'd been swindled out of her own past, manipulated out of her own childhood. She had the same dream night after night, so, after fourteen years of intense friendship, she began to keep her distance. She closed her ears to Sylvia's timid declarations of friendship, didn't care at all when Sylvia wept with bewilderment at her cruelty. Elizabeth spent her free time curled up by her icy window in the top bunk, looking out at the yard instead of at the picture-plastered wall where their two pathetic lives had mingled. She poured herself into her schoolwork. Sylvia didn't go to the prison school, so that was the only part of Elizabeth's life that Sylvia couldn't reach into with those pale, freckled, too-cold hands. How had Elizabeth not seen what those hands were like before? Her fingers were long, their intelligence disturbing. In her dreams, Elizabeth had the impression that Sylvia's fingers were responsible for the yellow line, as if they had drawn it out of the ground like a dirty child would a root or worm.

One night, Sylvia was down in her bunk, and Elizabeth was in the bunk above, reading. Elizabeth heard Sylvia pulling the hair out of her brush to clean it. An effervescent sound—the fizzing of the hair ripped out of the metal teeth. Elizabeth, not long ago, had allowed those silver teeth to run through her hair. Her hair, breaking in Sylvia's hand, rolled around on those dry fingers. It made her sick to think how freely she gave up some part of herself.

So she climbed down the ladder and grabbed Sylvia's face.

Both of them were shocked, but Elizabeth didn't let go, and Sylvia didn't scream. Elizabeth's fingernails bit into the pale skin, three into the forehead, and one on either cheek. Because Sylvia remained silent, Elizabeth dug harder.

But it was as if Sylvia expected this abuse, and she bore it out of love. For Elizabeth? That's what it looked like, and yet Elizabeth knew it was something else, something Sylvia was building secretly in herself that wasn't Elizabeth but contained her as an ingredient. She let go of Sylvia's face and watched her cry there on the bed. Then, with what felt like a radiance in her whole body, Elizabeth turned around and tore down the picture of the swimming pool. She ripped it into many pieces. Seeing her cellmate diminished there on the bed, seeing that piece of their made-up childhood shredded on that disgusting concrete, she felt elated, already addicted. So she ripped down a Christmas card, a drawing, a page of music they both knew Sylvia had never really played but had claimed to in the delusion of their childhood together. Through all of this, Sylvia lay on her bed, weeping, watching, not resisting. Elizabeth ripped down everything. She tore up every one of Sylvia's scraps. Her own scraps she put into a cardboard box with her other things, then shoved the box below the bunks. All that remained was a paper-link chain, drooping along the ceiling in uneven smiles, and the spots of dried toothpaste on the wall.

Pieces of ripped photographs stuck to the bottoms of her damp bare feet, and after she climbed up the ladder to her bunk, she picked these pieces off her skin and dropped them, also, to the floor.

From her bunk, she stared at the wall she had dismantled, shock pulsing through her body like pleasure. The next several days, she felt revived. Her every movement was a statement, eloquent and vicious. For a few nights, the dreams went away, and she was glad. She did not look directly at Sylvia for nearly a week.

But as sudden as her change of heart was, it couldn't compare to the suddenness of her heart's second reversal. She was on her way up the ladder one night after using the toilet, and she accidentally saw Sylvia's sleeping face and the tiny scabs on her cheeks. She was surprised by how they moved her, how they seemed to catch her in an act. She saw clearly now what she had done, and was sickened by her own cruelty. This was an ugly spasm of feeling, as confusing and as powerful as the initial impulse to hurt her, but even more urgent. Her body felt seized by guilt that she would do anything to get rid of. She thought that maybe all she needed was Sylvia's forgiveness, which would be easy enough to achieve. So once she was up in her bunk, she dropped her hand down between her bed and her wall, and she waited. She had to lie on her side against the wall for her arm to fit. When Sylvia turned over in the bottom bunk and saw the ghostly hand above her, she lifted her hand and took it. By that time, Elizabeth's arm was asleep, but the gravity, the strength of Sylvia's hand woke it, sent tingles running up her arm.

Sylvia's thumb stroked hers. Under the firmness of that hypnotic thumb, Elizabeth knew that the next day Sylvia would brush Elizabeth's hair, and give her stale coconut cakes from Concessions, and flash her pathetic, ingratiating smiles, and they would fall into their old game again, "Remember when? Remember when?" And the cake would taste good, her brush would feel nice, and if she tried hard enough, she could get numb to what it meant.

And if she couldn't get numb, well, then she would strike her. She would bite her. She would claw at her eyes, then plead for forgiveness—another hand dropped in the night.

Such was the pattern between them for nearly two years after that night. The pattern was what they called their friendship.

But a few months ago, on one of the very rare days that Elizabeth found herself both alone and outside in the daylight, she made a decision. It was the first week of May. She was carrying buckets of slop out to the pigs, whose feeding and cleaning and general care were all among her duties. That day, there were free men spraying knapweed on the other side of the fence. They moved the hose back and forth as if watering a garden.

The pleasant hissing sound of the poison coming out of that hose, and the sight of those small, flashing rainbows in the spray, brought her back to some summer of a childhood that must have been her own—a sprinkler in the yard of a run-down neighborhood house, and Elizabeth, naked, running through it. It was a warm memory, beautiful and untouched. She remembered that yard, she remembered the feeling of the sun on her skin, she remembered the sound of her mother's voice, heard distantly, in particles and flashes, through the spraying water. And that's when she realized that she still had something to protect; she still had a childhood. It was there; it was her own. This realization came at the same time, or maybe was the same, as the realization that she would stab Sylvia.

But as sudden as this thought was, she did not feel surprised. She merely thought, *With what?*

And at this new problem, the day took on an even more rare quality. The air felt fresh on her face. With relish, the pigs ate the slop she poured into their troughs, their curly tails springing around just like any other pigs' tails anywhere else in the world. She felt more peaceful than she had in a long time. She felt focused and alert, like the planner of a party, giving herself over to the urgency of tedium, the salvation of detail. When, where, what part of the body? She would have to figure out a weapon that would hurt Sylvia enough to get her transferred to a different cell but not enough to cripple her. Glass, a knife, that rusty piece of the pig trough? She dreaded the blood and ugliness of the event itself, because it wasn't the violence she desired. It was the practical effect the violence would bring about: Sylvia's removal from her cell, and therefore from her life.

But in all Elizabeth's planning, a full month of planning before she carried it out, she did not take into account everything she stood to lose. She was prepared for her time in Lock, that closet-size hole; she was prepared for the cold shoulders of the other inmates; she was even prepared to share her cell with a woman who had killed her child. But the loss of her poetry class—she was not prepared for that.

In the infirmary, grief-stricken, she thinks of her class. Her mouth fills up with chunks of phrases she'd like to spit at anyone, sharp fragments of her love. What did she love? The photocopies, the smell of them, the feel of them in her arms as she walked those hundred and four steps on the yellow line through the evening, right to the classroom door only fourteen women were permitted to open. Fourteen—of which she is no longer one. That one certain spot of toothpaste on the cell wall, which she used to lick just before she left for class, a superstitious habit, the closest she has ever come to prayer. That little spark of peppermint on her tongue, which became a shock of light in her mouth that she would speak out in the hour that followed, when the instructors called on her to answer questions or to recite the poems memorized inside her mouth. Her instructors: the two kindhearted men, high school teachers, who avoided looking at the yellow line because they were ashamed that they didn't have to walk it, too. They seemed ashamed also of the alarms on their belts. Black strings hanging from little black boxes they need only pull, and then all the things that Elizabeth felt would ring through the prison loud enough to hurt her ears, a screaming pulse toward which the guards would begin to run. How embarrassed the two teachers were of that power hanging from their belts, the potential of their betrayal, of their ability to deafen her at any moment with her own contraband illusions.

And she did have illusions. She knows that now. She lived as though school were a part of her self, as if her self could not be taken.

There is not space in this ugly curtained room to say any of this, even though the chaplain has asked. The chaplain is here again. Another day has passed, perhaps, and he is looking down at her. He is waiting for her to speak, but there is not space in his bald head for all her anger and her love.

She says only: "Fuck Sylvia."

"That's a start," he says, sadly. He is sitting in a chair beside the bed. "Tell me what you feel."

"I feel sick. I feel like throwing up."

"I mean about what you did."

She feels a very old fatigue come over her at this request. She closes her eyes. The previous chaplain used to try to get her to talk about the men she killed, and he wouldn't leave her alone until she announced that her crimes were a living torment, that it hurt her to speak of them. A lie. Of course she wishes she hadn't committed murder. Of course she feels guilty. But to speak about it in those terms feels strange and false, even disrespectful. Her murders are the given of her life; they are the premise. She can go an entire day and not think of them once, the way she wouldn't think about her own birth. Like her birth, they have delivered her into a new realm: the afterlife that is prison. Murder, the moment it was committed, became less an action she'd performed than a reality that she had always, suddenly, been inside of. The families of the people she killed, they are out there, living themselves out, and she is sorry for them, but they also have very little to do with her. It's shocking to think that people are still treading along in their grief, in hatred of her. It's almost unseemly when she thinks of it. Almost like she's ashamed of them and not of herself.

But she will talk to the chaplain if it will get her what she wants, if it will get her any closer to the classroom she longs for, that premise of its own, that life inside an afterlife. She'll say anything he wants her to. So she stifles her fatigue, and pictures the mirror she pried from the back of that heavy red brush, a glass as thin as puddle ice. What had it felt like to plunge it into Sylvia's leg, to see those fast streams of blood? It felt like salvation, like a shudder of life from within that secret childhood, outward to the surface of her own skin.

She says, "It's fitting that I stabbed her with her own mirror. That's what they call in my poetry class 'dramatic irony.'"

He says, in a dull tone to mock her, "You mean because she was stealing your childhood."

"Childhood, soul, whatever you want to call it."

"A person can't steal someone else's childhood."

"She was making me cruel."

"You could have asked for a room transfer if that's true."

"You don't have a clue."

They go on like that, stupidly, for a long time.

But then, to her surprise, the chaplain gives up. Suddenly. So suddenly, she doesn't comprehend at first what he is saying: "You want to know who's sitting in your seat?"

"Leave me alone."

"You want to know who, come Thursday, will be there in the classroom instead of you?"

"What are you telling me?"

"Her name."

"You're not going to tell me her name."

"She tried to tell you herself."

Elizabeth sits up. "What? When?"

The chaplain looks resigned, even a little disgusted. "She came here to tell you. You're going to find out anyway. She didn't want you to have to waste your energy looking out the window on Thursdays, watching for who's walking that line. She wants to help you. And if you try to get revenge on her the way you did on your last cellmate, I promise you—"

Elizabeth laughs in his face.

"What about this is funny?" he says, with more fatigue than anger.

She laughs even harder, then catches her breath. "Because it sounds like what you're about to say to me—"

"What?"

"You said 'my last cellmate' as if the person we're talking about is my *new*—"

"It is," says the chaplain. "It's your new cellmate. And I don't agree with what they did, but I think it's part of your punishment to live with your replacement. She wanted me to tell you, and I'm also going to tell you this: If you try anything, you will end up in Lock for the rest of your life."

"Jenny Mitchell," she says, still laughing, disbelieving, thinking of the woman who never asks for anything at all, not even a piece of tape to keep her box closed so that when it falls during searches, the school portraits of her dead daughters won't splatter all over the floor. Jenny would never want to go to a class, would never accept the offer, would never say yes to anything at all.

But then Elizabeth remembers, somewhere inside of her, something else: the expression on Jenny's face as she raised her hand in order to vote against the piano. And at this memory, she feels a falling inside of herself. She says to the chaplain again, her body hot, an ache in her voice, "Jenny Mitchell? You're telling me it's Jenny Mitchell?"

■

There is nowhere for her mind to wander after that. Now that she has her answer, she can no longer indulge in the dream that the

90

prison officials are bluffing, that she will get to go to class again, that all will be forgiven.

She thinks of Jenny in the classroom, Jenny who has killed her child, Jenny smelling of the solution she scrubs on the shower floors in an unnatural and perfect rhythm at a constant speed, as if something beyond this prison requires her to.

What will the teachers write on her unpracticed poems?

The question hurts her. She thinks again of her own poetry, thinks of all that was possible then. She feels pain even at the memory of the long chains that Sylvia used to make out of loops of paper. As if they were in elementary school, counting down to Christmas. Sylvia didn't seem to know that counting down was what such chains were for. She just made them for decoration, stuck them up with toothpaste in lazy, drooping *w*'s along the ceiling, and because she never ripped off links as the days went by, the chains came to represent for Elizabeth a very accurate depiction of their time.

The paper-link chain was the only thing Elizabeth hadn't ripped down when she destroyed the collage. For years, at night, she would touch each loop with her eyes and say for one "Beautiful" and for the next "Elizabeth," and follow the chain back and forth, the drooping smiles, loop by loop, touching each momentarily with one of her teacher's words and then the next, until she was able, finally, to fall asleep.

She wakes, and there is Jenny, sitting on the corner of the infirmary bed.

Elizabeth is enraged at the sight of her, but also paralyzed. Jenny's face is flushed, her bangs are pushed to the side, revealing the white hair usually hidden at her temples, hair gleaming either from sweat or the vapors rising from the buckets she leans over all day long.

Elizabeth writhes away, seizes the bedsheet and pulls with all her strength. "Get out!"

Only the second thing that Elizabeth has ever said to her.

"I came to see you," Jenny says, surprised, getting up from the bed.

"Get out," Elizabeth screams, but her voice is hoarse, burned with the acid of her anger.

"Are you feeling bad again?" Jenny asks, looking at Elizabeth with concerned eyebrows, looking at her with all the pity in the world. "Did you eat?" Jenny tries again. Who knew that she could speak so normally? Who knew she was capable of small talk?

Then Jenny says, as if they are sisters, as if she has the power to settle Elizabeth down, as if there could be some secret for the two of them to share, "I have an idea you might like."

Elizabeth closes her eyes because there is nowhere she can look besides at Jenny or the flowers. She's exhausted, too exhausted to try any harder to get Jenny out of this room. They are both quiet for a moment. Then she hears Jenny take a step. Elizabeth opens her eyes and sees Jenny picking out the cobwebs from the flowers in the vase, gathering them in her hand absentmindedly, like a mother would. She rolls the webs darkly in her hand until they look like a single bead. She throws the bead into the trash can placed beside the bed for Elizabeth to throw up in.

"Don't you want to hear my idea?" Jenny asks, shyly now, raising her eyebrows to let Elizabeth know she's really trying.

"Here's an idea," Elizabeth says, and even Elizabeth is surprised by the violence in her voice. She hears in her voice what she has just this moment become capable of. "Why don't you go get a hatchet and we'll make believe I'm your—

Daughter, daughter, daughter, daughter
Elizabeth can't believe this word has left her mouth. For the rest of that terrible day it echoes on the walls of her sleep, white and billowing, the word and the curtained walls themselves, in and

out, cruelty, like breath. It is the only thing she hears. Jenny does not come to the infirmary again. Elizabeth does not eat.

When the chaplain comes later, she is crying. He gives her no smile this time. He just says, "Hey." There is nothing more unpleasant than a chaplain resigned to disappointment.

"Hey, Chap," she manages, and hopes to perk him up with how pleasant she is being, even through her tears. She needs him here, for once. He sits down in the chair.

"You've got to eat," he says. He sets a foil-covered cup of peaches on top of her covers, along with a tiny plastic spoon.

She feels touched that he brought peaches instead of pears. There was a little bit of hope in that, as if he'd thought, *What if the problem really is that she doesn't like pears?* She wants to reward him for still thinking about her with hope, so she takes the cup and peels off the foil, but she knows when she smells the thick, clear syrup that it's no use.

"I brought you something else," he says finally, with hesitation he wants her to hear, so that she knows whatever it is he's brought her, she doesn't deserve it. She notices for the first time he has some papers rolled up and tucked under his arm. He unrolls them, tosses them on her bed.

"What are these?"

"It's something you want," he says, sounding very tired. "Why don't you look."

She sets the peaches down and looks, but she is so frightened by what he could possibly think she wants that she can't see what it is. Her eyes are filled with tears again.

"Well? What do you think?" he asks.

"I don't know."

"Read it to me."

Swallowing, she picks up the papers. There is poetry typed there, and all around the poetry minuscule handwriting in blue ink.

She reads aloud the printed part, "The Two Trees by W. B. Yeats." She looks at the chaplain, then down again. Narrow columns of poetry running down the page, photocopied from a book.

"Read in the margins," he says.

She squints to decipher the writing all around, in blue. At first all that she can make out is the *A*'s and *D*'s. *A says. D says.*

Abram and Damiani, her instructors.

A says what do you think the bitter glass is? Sarah says but God was never sleeping. D says, Sarah, read that line out loud for us.

Elizabeth stops. She looks at the chaplain, who leans forward then, resting his elbows on his knees, his chin on his folded hands. "Where did this come from?" she asks.

"It's everything they said in the poetry class on Thursday. Every line they went over. Every question that anybody asked or tried to answer."

"Are you saying I get to go?"

His disgust at her misinterpretation makes him laugh, unkindly. "No, you don't get to go." He stands, shaking his head.

"I'm not trying to be ungrateful," she says. "I just don't know what it means."

"Jenny Mitchell's taking notes for you. That's her copy. She wants you to have it. There's some extra paper you can write your questions on, and she will ask them for you in class. She said you can write poems and she'll turn them in so you can get help with them. She'll do it under her own name. Not that I agree with that, but I'm willing to turn a blind eye because she's doing it for you. She's not looking to advance herself falsely. She just said yes for you."

"Oh," is all that Elizabeth says, but too quietly to hear, and the chaplain tells her to eat her peaches, and then he leaves.

She does eat the peaches. When her body tries to throw them up, she concentrates so hard on holding them down that she gives herself a headache, but succeeds. Later that night, she manages several spoonfuls of oatmeal, and the following day a mush of saltines and broth. She chokes down gummy buttered noodles, leans back her head so that the cornmeal mush can slide down her throat without her body knowing what is happening to it. It is an agony to eat, but a worse agony to taste that word inside her mouth, its soft, floating first syllable followed by the sharp, metallic second, that little lick, a flicker.

Daugh-ter.

She tries not to think of it. All she does for three full days is hold down a bit of food. Then, when she is weak with her sadness but no longer throwing up, they send her back to her cell.

■

It is evening and Elizabeth is lying on her bunk. She is looking out the single window at the gravel and the sage, the spooled shadows of barbed wire. The sun is setting. Even with nothing worthwhile to land on, the light lands. It is copper. Its brief lingering on the ground is worth the pain Elizabeth feels at the sight of it.

She has also noticed that her fingernails are very clean and evenly cut. She remembers, faintly, in the infirmary, telling a nurse that she vomited because her hands were never far enough away from her face that she couldn't smell them. She remembers trying to explain about the burned oatmeal she had to scratch out of the bottoms of pots to feed the pigs, those sour, jiggling ribbons of oatmeal and soap. She herself knew her sickness had nothing to do with the smell and the nurse knew, too. But now she remembers, very faintly, that same nurse holding her hand as she lay mostly asleep. She can't remember the nurse's face, just the feel of her hands. They were older hands, rough and warm. She clipped Elizabeth's nails, setting each clipping on the bedside table in the shadow of the flowers. Then she cleaned her fingers with a Q-tip and some alcohol.

The revelation of kindness hurts worse than cruelty. There is no way to equal it. Nowhere to put her gratitude, and so it thrashes in her body.

Silence is something she can bear a little better than a failed attempt at saying what she means. Down below her, in silence, Jenny lies on her bunk. In the mornings, when they stand side by side for the first count, they are close enough that their shoulders touch, but neither one says anything. And when, randomly one day, the guards come to search them, and Jenny and Elizabeth are on their knees side by side, with their pants down, and Elizabeth sees in Jenny's face that even after all this time, she is tortured at the affront of this, that she does not bear it any better than if it were her first time, that in fact it only gets worse and worse the longer it goes on; and when Jenny goes to wash her hands after the search is over, because her fingertips have been where they have been, and she stands at their numbered sink and the cold water runs over her fingers while she bows her head so that Elizabeth can't see that she is crying; and when Elizabeth sees that the reason she is washing her hands is because she's about to pick up the photographs that have spilled once again from her little flat box beneath her pillow because she can't think, after all this time, where else she could possibly keep it where the guards won't make it fall; and when her hands are dried off and she does bend down and pick the pictures up, always in the same order, chronological so that her daughters at their oldest existing state stare up at her, and the younger photos are somewhere at the bottom, where she doesn't have to see—even then Elizabeth says nothing and the nothing aches inside of her.

■

The following Thursday, Jenny makes no show of getting ready for class. She gathers up the photocopies without looking at Elizabeth, and leaves as if she is merely on her way to scrub the showers and hallways.

It is common hour, when everyone usually gathers in the common room to watch television while the chosen fourteen go off to class. But Elizabeth doesn't move. She lies up in her bunk, staring out the window, and she sees Jenny walking through the evening on the yellow line.

The vision awakens in Elizabeth a memory. She hasn't thought of this in a very long time, though at one point in her life, the vision had been important to her, a disturbing mystery. She hasn't made the connection until now that this Jenny is the same Jenny from the memory.

The memory is from a day long ago, ten years ago, maybe. Elizabeth was sitting in the classroom by the only window, with her history book open on her desk. She remembers how glad she was to get the window seat that day, because she was working as a scrubber then, and had spilled chemicals on her clothes, and hadn't had time to get rid of the strong smell before class. She sat close to the open window, hoping her teachers wouldn't smell her, and she saw Jenny in the yard.

She didn't know Jenny then. No one did. It was the first time that Elizabeth had ever seen her, and Jenny had seemed, through that classroom window, on the brink of death. She was so weak she wasn't able to walk on her own; two guards held her up and she staggered between them. Her hair was matted at the back of her head in a dreadlock pillow. The loose strands frizzed around her pasty face. She looked as if the sunshine hurt not just her eyes but her whole emaciated body.

It must have been sometime within Jenny's first five years, when she lived in a cell by herself because the prison authorities didn't know at first if she was dangerous. Hers would have looked the same as the other cells, only smaller. It would have had a television and a bed. But what was different was that she took her meals there and she wasn't allowed to go out in the yard at the same time as everyone else. There were a few other women who lived alone, and Elizabeth had often seen them walking around the yard on their own time, watched by the guards. But she had never seen

97

Jenny go outside, which is why this one glimpse caught in her memory.

Somehow, she's divorced that memory from the Jenny she now knows, and it's only now, seeing Jenny walking toward the classroom, that she remembers. But many years ago, the scene had been important enough to Elizabeth to inquire. She found out from some other girl, she doesn't remember who, that during Jenny's five years alone, she declined to walk outside every single day but one. That was the day Elizabeth saw her.

She thinks of this scene for a long time in the bed, trying to figure out what it means. It's strange that it would be possible, if words were possible, to ask Jenny about that day and that Jenny would probably remember it, might even remember Elizabeth's gaze through the window, if she'd seen.

But, an hour later, when Elizabeth hears Jenny return from class, she does not move, does not speak, does not breathe, pretends even to herself that she's not there.

Then she feels something on her bed. She turns around. On the very edge of her thin mattress is a stack of papers Jenny has just put there. Elizabeth stares at the papers for a long time before gathering them up, pulling them close. At the very top of the first page, Jenny has written in tiny blue handwriting, *A poem is due next Thursday. Some extra paper at the back for you.*

Elizabeth reads the photocopies the rest of the night, in the dim glow of her bed lamp. It is a compilation of poetry, mostly by Byron and Keats, which Mr. Abram and Mr. Damiani have put together, along with some essays on the time period. Elizabeth does not read the poetry. Instead, she studies every word the woman sleeping below her has written in the margins, trying to picture these words coming from the hand of the woman she saw all those years ago staggering on the yellow line, half dead in the arms of guards. Not a trace of Jenny anywhere, even in her own handwriting, just thin blue trails of other people's words.

D says this poem in I-ams almost whole way through. Where meter breaks (see where I circled the phrases he pointed out) imagine a voice breaking too. Form and content intertwined. (People seem to know what I-am means. I assume "first person point of view.")

Elizabeth closes her eyes. She tries to revive some energy in herself, some passion for the poetry she's supposed to be reading, but she feels nothing at all about it. Her only feeling is about the words that Jenny's written.

A says more than 10 syll. in this line but still pentameter because the extra syll. is soft not hard. Pentameter measures beats not syllables per se. He says clap it out. They are clapping now.

After much agonized deliberation, the only thing Elizabeth writes on the paper Jenny's given her is this: *Ask A and D what an I-am is because I don't know either.*

Of course she knows. She could have written instead, *An iamb is a rhythm like a heartbeat. Short, then long.* But there is too much silence to wade through, and this can't be the one thing she says. So the teachers can tell Jenny what Elizabeth doesn't have the strength to. Jenny will ask the question only if she thinks it's Elizabeth she's asking it for.

■

The months pass. A new routine begins. While Jenny is in class on Thursday evenings, Elizabeth goes to the common room to sit with all the others because she can't bear her thoughts when she's alone. She sits at the back on the piano bench, and watches everyone except those chosen fourteen in class watch TV. There are two broken keys on the piano, side by side, a C and D, and Elizabeth likes to lift and drop them as she pretends to watch the show. Nobody sees her doing this; nobody cares. For as much as everyone had wanted the piano, hardly anyone has ever played. The keys feel good to lift and drop. She is surprised to discover in their falling a very small sound. A wooden sound, incredibly faint, but also with a hint of some string nearly but not quite struck. It makes her feel something sweeping and secret, and she lets her fingertips lift and drop, over and over again, those two broken keys, smooth, heavy, yellow-white, and she likes to feel the trapped music getting out.

But every evening that isn't a Thursday, she takes her common time in the cell. There, she writes poetry that does not feel like her own, about someone who is not herself. What comes out of her pen is strained, a slight variation of her usual style, characterized perhaps by nothing more than a great restraint between the words. She finds no pleasure in her poems. Because these poems do not feel like her own, it is not so difficult to write *By Jenny Mitchell* underneath their titles.

Jenny turns in these poems as her own, and they come back covered in Mr. Damiani's and Mr. Abram's teacherly praise and gentle critiques. At the top of one of Elizabeth's poems there is only one small note: *Beautiful, Jenny!*

Mr. Abram's handwriting. Haphazard, self-conscious, as if every stroke of every letter has fallen there by accident.

Beautiful Jenny.

Elizabeth can barely sleep at night. The strangeness of being bound to this silent woman in the margins of those photocopies is more like being locked up with her than actually being locked up with her. Elizabeth speaks to Jenny only in the questions she writes down for Jenny to ask the instructors, and Jenny responds only with answers the instructors provide for her in class. What kind of a language is this? What kind of a prison? *Here's an idea.* The photocopies, with their minuscule handwriting all over them, reveal too much. The very letters seem to ache at her because they make her think of Jenny's hands, writing without stopping for an hour straight, on Elizabeth's behalf. Elizabeth can bear the loss of school better than she can Jenny's struggle to give it back. But how can she stop? How can she say, *Beautiful Jenny, you don't need to do this anymore, I don't want you to do this anymore?*

Every day, Elizabeth is aware of all the sounds that are not words. Jenny breathing in the night, Jenny not breathing when the guards search her body, Jenny using the toilet, running water over her hands, shaking out her sheet, murmuring in her sleep.

Jenny writes more in the margins than is printed on the pages.

Today we arranged the desks in a circle. Everyone quiet, writing. The assignment is to describe a place we knew in childhood. A different desk this time. A phone number carved on it, I assume from when these desks were at a college. 208 area code. I don't know which desk was yours. I would sit there if I knew.

At night, in silence, in the glow of her bed light, Elizabeth follows these elaborate trails of handwriting up and down the paper. Each time Jenny abbreviates a word—*p* for poem, *cr* for classroom, *ws* for window seat—Elizabeth feels a pressing intimacy, a language Jenny is teaching her to understand. And all the while, Jenny lies still below her. Not sleeping, Elizabeth knows, but listening to the rustling of these pages, the dragging of Elizabeth's fingertip across her words.

D brought old grammar book to show 1852. What students used to learn back then, difficult. D said be v careful when we hold it. I held it for you. Cover chipped, binding smelled like pipe smoke & mildew. An inscription, To Mardell, With love, Larry Gene. Thought that sounded like something you could use in poem. Such an old name, Mardell.

It is too much. Elizabeth trades the rubber sole of one of her shoes for four pieces of tape, which, when Jenny is out of the room, she puts over the lid of the picture box under Jenny's pillow. Then she is afraid. She worries Jenny will think that the tape means she has looked inside the box. So, in a panic just before Jenny returns, Elizabeth removes the four pieces of tape, crumples them up, and throws them into the toilet.

One Thursday, in the common room, as Elizabeth sits in the very back at the silent piano, lifting and dropping its broken keys, she notices Sylvia watching her.

Elizabeth hasn't spoken to Sylvia since the stabbing, but she has seen her body in the shower: a pink pucker in her left leg, a sucked-in, smoothed-out gash. Nearly nothing at all. It's amazing how little Elizabeth has thought of her since all of this occurred. She has wondered once or twice what Sylvia thinks of her. Would a hand dropped in the night be all that was needed to get back a taste of that mindless, dogged devotion? It might be, and that's sickening. Now, seeing Sylvia's stare, Elizabeth looks at her directly for the first time since she stabbed her with her mirror. Her red bangs have grown long. She has lost the look of alertness, the readiness for connection. Who is she now, without Elizabeth?

But Sylvia doesn't look away, as Elizabeth thought she would. They stare at each other, and for a moment the two women are locked together once again. There is something new and startling in Sylvia's gaze, an expression Elizabeth has never seen on her, as if she has a secret. Perhaps all it is is a lack of love.

Elizabeth, suddenly uneasy, is the first to look away. But when she does, she sees, in her periphery, Sylvia stand. Sylvia crosses the room, walks slowly toward Elizabeth.

Her heart races. For that instant, it feels like the old days, as if Sylvia's bra holds some little packaged cake. But cake is not the thing that she reveals. Instead, she puts her hands on the piano. Still standing, her shoulder very close to Elizabeth's face, Sylvia begins to play.

Music—she plays music.

Sylvia's hands move so fast over the keys it is like they aren't her hands, not the hands Elizabeth knows, not the pale, skinny hands that she had clasped in the night through her disgust. They are fresh hands, capable of strangling, capable of taking for herself, capable of—sound.

Sylvia sits down on the bench, and then uses the pedals, too.

She is good. She is very good. Elizabeth had no idea. Something about it disturbs her, and she leaves the common room, feeling on the verge of tears. She can hear the music playing down the hall, the sound of Sylvia's past life, still alive in those fingers, and she feels defeated. She climbs up the ladder to her bunk, stares at the blank concrete wall marked with dots of crusted toothpaste. But still she can hear her playing. How strange it is that at one time, not very long ago, this room is where Sylvia lived. The music playing down the hall was in her fingers all those years, those fingers that ripped hair from the red brush, those fingers that pressed photographs to the wall, that stroked Elizabeth's offered hand. If music can live in Sylvia's fingers for sixteen years without ever revealing itself, are there things that live in Elizabeth that time won't touch, that nobody can take away?

It isn't until she hears Jenny enter the room that she remembers: Jenny once wanted this music not to play.

Elizabeth sits up. A string of helpless words, pleas and admissions and declarations, enter her mind, but somehow she can't say them. She looks down at Jenny, expecting to see some pain on her face at the sound of the music, some anger or shock, but instead what Elizabeth sees is the absence of any expression at all, adamant neutrality. The melody courses through the open door of the common room, down the hall, all the way to Jenny, where the music seems to stop. Halted, like an animal at a gate, a child at a word it doesn't know.

Later, deep in the night, Elizabeth finds something Jenny wrote weeks ago that she never noticed:

I asked your question. An I-am is a pair of syllables. The first one soft, the second loud. It's the rhythm of the human heart, which is also the natural rhythm of human speech.

The first snow falls. It is evening, not a Thursday, about a month since Sylvia began to play the piano. Elizabeth is in the library, trying to find one book on all these shelves that she hasn't checked out before, but there is nothing, not one new book. She can't distract herself. The library opens up to the common room, where someone is playing the piano. In the last few weeks, Sylvia has been giving lessons to a few of the girls. Not with much passion or interest, just as a thing to do.

In the library, Elizabeth can hear some of the things Sylvia says to her pupils.

"Sit up straight." "Are you counting? You're not counting." "Curve your hand like you're holding a ball." "B's are flat. Flat. Flat. Flat!"

Whose voice comes from that small mouth? Elizabeth hears in it no ingratiation, no pleasure in the sharing of her skill, no satisfaction at the novelty of being needed, no Sylvia at all. Is Elizabeth the thing that's happened to this woman?

More perplexing than the change in Sylvia is the change in Jenny. Every now and then, somewhere in her school notes, Jenny writes something very personal, a note inside of the notes, as if accidental, as if not meant for Elizabeth at all. Such breaches never happened early on. There are not many of these accidents. But, for example, beside a line in "Tintern Abbey"—"A presence that disturbs me with the joy"—Jenny has written, then erased but not well, *Music.* And, farther down, beside the lines "If I should be where I no more can hear / Thy voice, nor catch from thy wild eyes these gleams," she has written, *But wouldn't it be torture to seek out this lovely place even if*—the *even if* crossed out—*because*—underlined—*nothing there has changed?*

These two notes, written on the same poem, have helped Elizabeth understand. The sound of a piano doesn't change, no matter where it's played, a living room, a prison, just as a river remains the same even if once you walked beside it with your sister and now you walk there by yourself. The piano hurts Jenny because of its connection to some beautiful memory of someone she loved, someone who played the piano for her in her old life. Elizabeth has felt that pain, too. To be confronted with something so humane in such a place hurts. It's like Jenny herself, taking these notes. If only

Elizabeth could stop her from this awful kindness, if only she could stop the music, too, if only they could acknowledge, the two of them, that what Jenny feels for the piano is what Elizabeth feels for her—an affront of the most unlikely gift. It has been nearly six months that they've been cellmates, and still no "Thank you." No "I'm sorry." No "Hello."

But Jenny doesn't know that it is Elizabeth who has brought that piano to life. She dared it into music, dared Sylvia's hands into playing. Would Jenny stop writing on those photocopies if she knew what Elizabeth has done? Would that revelation be enough to break them of their silence?

In the common room, some of the other girls are singing along to the piano lessons. Children's songs, mostly, and badly played by Sylvia's students, so that the singing, to keep in time with the music, is so slow and filled with hesitation, with waiting for the notes to catch up, that it is mournful.

And then it happens: a break in the silence, though not with words. With tears.

It is a Friday at common hour, the snow is falling outside, and down the hall, Sylvia plays something new on the piano.

It is a melody Elizabeth recognizes, but only faintly. She doesn't know the words but senses that there are words, can almost hear the shape of them in the piano's tones, a circus melody. In this music, there is a calm, generic joy. It is like a song played out of a music box or carousel, or sung, lips unmoving, from the mouth of a doll, in whose plastic head the melody is there on some spool, ready to be wound with the silver key and then let go, that key spinning slowly at the back of a baby's head.

Elizabeth is in her bunk, reading the blue handwriting she would like never to read again, studying her cellmate's face by studying these letters, staring so hard her vision blurs them into a hazy streak of blue, and Jenny, below her, begins to cry.

The crying is almost silent, too. Elizabeth hears it only in the breath Sylvia's hands take on that piano. In that moment of silence, a jagged exhale, carried out on tears.

Later, she wishes she'd gone down to the bunk and sat beside Jenny. She wishes she had placed her hands over Jenny's ears, looked into her eyes, and said that she was sorry for all of it—for the piano dared to life, for the burden of bringing the classroom into the cell, for the terrible thing she said all those months ago when Jenny visited in the infirmary and Elizabeth became someone she wishes she were not.

She doesn't say those things, or anything at all. But the tears open up something inside of her, and she knows all at once what she will do.

The following Thursday, Elizabeth can barely breathe with her anticipation. As soon as Jenny leaves for class, Elizabeth climbs down the ladder. Her body feels heavy, magnetized, dangerous. Stepping off the ladder onto firm ground, she must pause to get her balance. She closes her eyes and takes a breath. She leans her forehead against the ladder rung, feels the hot and ringing cold.

She has been waiting for this hour all week long, looking at the clock every few minutes in the dark laundry room where she's been transferred, having lost the privileges of sunshine and fresh air the pig farm job allowed. She has sweated through her clothes as she folded the endless clothes identical to those she has on. Her nerves have caused her to throw up, once at lunch, and once again at work. It has been a long time since she's lost control like this; she's been holding food down a long while. But an answer provokes as much anxiety as the question once did.

There is not a lot of time. In spite of her nausea, in spite of the cold, leaping clamminess of her skin, she rummages under her mattress and finds the half-roll of Scotch tape she has been hiding for three days. It cost her the only pair of socks she owned without holes. She rips off pieces of the tape and lines them up, ready to be used, on the rungs of the ladder. Her hands are shaking now. The smell of torn Scotch tape is a smell from another life.

She gets down on her hands and knees and reaches far under Jenny's bed. At her fingertips, she feels her own cardboard box, which she put there two years ago. She holds it on her lap.

Ragged edges, smudged gloss, the glare of accidental creases. This is all she sees at first. Streaks of crumpled color. A wonder she has kept any of it at all. But even so, she begins to tape these scraps onto her wall. Quickly, blindly, as if they are her very life:

Birthday cards that used to sing, tattered book covers fallen off their spines, pencil sketches, comics, perfume advertisements still laden with scent, a failed still life of peaches, a tiger mask on a paper plate, a queen of hearts, a label from a bottle of sparkling cider, the sleeve of a sweater she once loved from which a paper hand emerges, all the fingers but the middle folded down—she folds them up—postcards her mother sent, poems written on the cheeks of celebrities, scraps of material, jokes and fortunes, a glossy photo torn from an archaeology book of a mummy holding her mummy cat, a horoscope chart, a dried sprig of larkspur, a brochure from her college, two chocolate wrappers, each with pictures of frogs, a book of used stamps, *National Geographic* spreads of ancient trees, waterwheels, Amish men, Mars.

A picture of herself at twenty, a picture of herself at seventeen, a picture of herself at ten, a picture of her pregnant mom.

She does not know how much time has passed, but it feels like her hour is more than expired. The piano plays on and on down the hall. She wipes the sweat off her hands onto her pants. Her ears are ringing, and she steps back, feels the cold of the metal door through her now-damp shirt, against her spine. She looks at what she's done for the first time.

In that instant, the vision of the walls is like a vision of a dark street through a rain-glazed window. Bloated and magnified color, blots of shine, falling rivers of light and dark. Then the individual pieces open up their faces, whose colors are connected somehow loosely to the ringing in her ears. She has hung up her scraps in off-center splotches, with gaping bare wall between them. The splotches themselves are lurid. She sees the ten pieces of tape just barely holding up the sweater sleeve and the paper hand on which she notices now that she once drew five garish emerald rings on one finger. The *National Geographic* spreads hold light only in their soft crumples, so that from this angle she can hardly see the photos, just the evidence of two years spent inside a cardboard box.

But she is not dissatisfied. Perhaps because she is exhausted, perhaps because there is nothing more holding her up than the cool door behind her, she feels in this moment that it is enough. That she has said to Jenny, after all this time, everything that she meant to say:

I am the woman in your room.

And just as the walls seem to echo this very statement, she feels the door behind her open. She steps aside. There is Jenny, holding the photocopies, standing in the hallway, looking, for once, surprised.

"I'd like to be your friend," Elizabeth says bluntly. Her tone of voice suggests she has said the opposite of what she has. It is the first thing she has said to Jenny since the day in the infirmary, months ago. *Why don't you go get a hatchet and we'll make believe I'm your—* "Friend," she chokes again, dizzy with amazement at finally breaking through the thick, hot screen that she's been living behind. She sits down on Jenny's bed, her legs weak. She feels the slick sweat on her forehead stinging her pores. She has a vague awareness of her own smell, bright and sour, leaves in mud.

Jenny says nothing.

"If you hate it," says Elizabeth, again in her strange, blunt voice, "I'll take it down. Or if you find any of it offensive, I'll throw it away. The sweater is going to fall off anyway. I know the whole thing is ugly."

Jenny hands the photocopies to Elizabeth, without looking at her. She is looking at the walls.

"I left space for you," Elizabeth says, not blunt anymore, but slightly pleading, a little desperate, hugging the photocopies to her chest. "There can be something of you up here, too—that's the point. Something from your life."

But Jenny does not seem to have heard. She says nothing. She just stares. Elizabeth does not know, in the face of her own desperation, what to make of Jenny's silence.

"This is something you want, too, right?" says Elizabeth, her voice strained, pleading.

"Yes," is all that Jenny says. A whisper.

But that, too, is enough.

At the sound of the word, Elizabeth closes her eyes. Two tears fall at once at their closing. She has never known such relief. The tears drop right to the ground. There is nothing to wipe away. Elizabeth holds the photocopies close to her chest, as hard as she can, so hard she can't breathe. And then she does; she takes a breath.

1985–1986

In the small town of Spirit Lake, which is five miles north of Ponderosa, the early-evening snow holds a faint pink light. Wade, thirty-one years old, walks through the snow along the highway, wearing his winter coat. He drags a sled full of supplies: candles, food, vitamins, a new chain for the saw.

It's very quiet and cold, too cold for the children in the town to make snowmen in the park, and the shops are closing for the evening. The snow falling on the grocery sacks in his sled makes the smallest sound when it lands on the plastic, a sound like brushstrokes.

Wade passes the elementary school, closed for Christmas. A truck slows down behind him, stops. An old man leans across the cab to roll down the passenger window, and then he calls, over the head of his dog next to him, over the sound of the engine and the Christmas music playing inside the cab, "Ponderosa?"

"Thanks."

Wade loads his groceries into the snow-filled bed of the truck, then he lays his sled upside down over them. He gets in beside the old border collie, holds his hands against the heating vents to warm them. The old man wears a fur hat and large black gloves. Wade tells the man to drop him off at the base of Mount Iris, and the man looks surprised at this request, but doesn't say anything. They drive on in silence, and every now and then, self-consciously, the old man taps his large gloved hand on the steering wheel in time to the Christmas melody. The heater blows on their faces. Wade smells the melted snow in the dog's matted fur.

Wade says, "I used to have a border collie."

"They're good dogs," says the old man, peering into the snow flying at his windshield now.

"I stole her from an old boss," says Wade.

The old man chuckles, distracted by the icy roads. He does not ask for the whole story or seem to notice a story has been implied. Wade doesn't mind. The warmth and the Christmas music and the pipe-smoke smell of the old man's coat have calmed him. What an unexpected reprieve from the cold. Seven months have passed since he and Jenny left their home on the northern Camas Prairie to live on the mountain whose base they're driving toward, and this is one of only a few times since the winter began that Wade has felt so calm.

Here, of all places. In the presence of a stranger.

"We don't own a plow," Wade says. "The man who sold us our land in the spring told us there was a school bus driver who lived at the very top of Iris. He told us the county plowed the road all winter long so the school bus could get to all the kids."

"Well, that's two lies in one," says the old man.

"What's the other?"

He laughs. "That there are kids up there at all."

True—Wade has seen no children. Up there, in fact, he has seen no one at all. When he walked down the mountain this morning, dragging the empty sled, he saw only the prints of animals, scatters of rabbit panic, traces of blood, NO TRESPASSING signs nailed to trees on hostile-looking land he can't imagine wanting to trespass upon.

Out the windows, the snow flies fast. The sun is setting. What's strange is that at this point, the old man beside him knows more than Wade's own mother does. He and Jenny have lied to Jenny's parents, too. They've said the plows have come. They've said that their jobs can be driven to and therefore aren't lost. But the truth is that neither he nor Jenny has been to work all winter long.

The truck passes the Texaco, the rock yard, and the laundromat. Wade sees the sign for Ponderosa, announcing THE LITTLE TOWN THAT THOUGHT IT COULD. Thought, but was mistaken? He wonders that each time. It must be a joke; he isn't sure. In a few miles, Wade will be left there at the edge of those woods, at the edge of the darkness, and he will have to begin the long walk up. The tape cassette sings on and on. Wade lets the dog lick his hand, and he considers that this might be the time to tell the whole story, to hear the words from his own mouth, here in this truck with a stranger who already knows more than anyone else but still stares ahead without judgment.

Wade takes a breath. "We have a baby on the way," he says. The old man only nods. "Due in March."

"What are you going to do if it comes before the snow melts?"

"We have a plan," says Wade, hoping the old man won't ask what it is, so that no doubt can be cast on his precarious hope. The new chain for his saw is a part of this plan. He has cut eleven trees already—nine still to go. What little money they had left they spent on helicopter insurance. Very slowly, but as fast as he can, Wade is clearing a space of one hundred feet in diameter, creating the only clearing on all forty acres, so that a helicopter can land should they need to call for one.

But the old man doesn't ask what the plan is. He peers with concentration at the road ahead. Wade looks out the window at the dark pines, and the old man's knowing of the facts seems to diminish the facts themselves. He is glad to be inside this familiar music. The hot, blowing air chaps his lips. Wade removes his hat, feels calm in the presence of the old man, who adjusts to the heat, too, but does not turn it down. The snow blurs over the windshield, and the old man watches it closely as he drives, pulling off first his left glove, then his right, with his teeth.

There is a swastika tattooed on the back of his right hand.

"You'll make it through," the old man says. "The spring usually comes when it's supposed to. Even up there."

Looking away from the hand, looking out the window, Wade manages to say, "I hope so," but the regret he feels is like the road he will soon be walking up through the wilderness, a road that is only a road because he remembers it being one. How could he ever have guessed this kind of danger, this quiet danger all around, even inside of winter gloves?

Wade and Jenny are prairie people. Prairie people living on a mountain they had not noticed was so much larger than themselves. An acreage purchased in a hurry because it was cheap, because it was nothing like a prairie. Such arrogance and childishness —an avalanche of a dream. But what kind of person would tell them they wouldn't be trapped on a snowy mountain when surely, without a tractor or a plow, they would? Still, they should have questioned it. They should have made sure. And now the only other person in the world who knows the truth of their desperation has tattooed his hatred to his hand.

There are plastic children's toys broken at Wade's feet. He notices them for the first time as the truck slows down. They clatter against one another when the old man makes the turn onto Clagstone. Wade is careful not to break them further, shifts in his seat to give them room.

"My granddaughter," the old man says, nodding to the toys. He smiles. "She's ten, but she's outgrown all of these things. It's not that I don't like a clean truck. I leave those there, because whenever she rides with me," he says, laughing, "I get a kick out of the way she picks those things up and acts like she can't even believe in them. She acts like they're fossils. 'Look at this one, Grampa.'" The truck comes to a stop. Wade opens his door. The cold wind brings up the powder snow. The old man looks at Wade, his eyes gleaming. "Could she ever have been so young?"

When they purchased these forty steep acres in the spring, there were buttercups in the wild grass. Winter was far away, a mere superstition, already defeated in their minds by the county's plows, which they had been promised would come. They built a barn to-gether quickly, and they lived in it, sleeping in the loft. Wade worked on building a house up the hill, and Jenny worked as a vet assistant in Priest River. They were thirty-one years old and des-perate for a baby.

For ten years, they'd tried to conceive. It was a decade spent among family and friends on the prairie, a decade of stability and safety and qualified happiness that at a certain point they couldn't bear. The move to the mountain was a part of their longing, a great distraction from it.

But one month after moving here, Jenny became pregnant.

They attributed this miracle to the mountain. They chose names in its honor. "Aaron," meaning "mountain," if it was a boy, and Lily, a companion to Iris, and a name Jenny had loved since child-hood, if it was a girl. They lay up in the barn loft at night and their plans rose out of their mouths and hovered there in the pine rafters like a dream of owls. The fall was warm. They boiled water on a campfire for washing. They could see their house up the hill, half built.

One hot fall day, they went on a drive to the very top of the mountain, and there, in the weeds in a meadow, just down from the radio tower, they saw an abandoned school bus. "Hey, look," Jenny said. "The bus driver must live around here. That must be the old one."

That was the strangest part about it all; the abandoned school bus had seemed such casual proof of what they had no reason ever to question: the existence of the bus driver, who was the reason the plows would come.

They finished their house in early November. In that week before the first snow fell, they had their furniture shipped from Grangeville. But of all the things that were supposed to be delivered—their kitchen table, couch, rocking chair, and Wade's old crib—eight cardboard boxes and a new bed were the only things that arrived before the snow and therefore arrived at all, because, of course, no plow ever came. The delivery truck couldn't get there. And by the time they understood this, by the time they finally accepted that they had made a terrible mistake, it was too late. They tried to hire someone from town to clear the roads, but no one could. They were too far away, the road too steep. It was an eight-mile walk to the valley, where the town of Ponderosa was, and Jenny was six months pregnant. Wade thought at first that maybe they could walk down together, slowly, so that her parents could pick them up at the base of the mountain and take them both back to Grangeville until the baby was born. But Jenny refused. She was angry that he had even considered taking such a risk: their unborn baby, their one chance in a decade of trying, out in those woods, out in that bitter cold.

So they came to terms with their predicament. They assessed what they had. And it was only then, in the shock of their new lives, that they thought about that abandoned bus again, how it was parked in a strange place among shattered glass and bullet shells, how there didn't seem to be any house nearby, any house at all on that whole drive to the top. Why hadn't they thought about the fact that a school bus would be kept at a lot, not at a residence? Now, when Wade tries to picture that bus up there in all the snow, he wonders why it didn't occur to them to investigate, to question.

But it was too late. They surveyed their nearly empty house. Wade got a knife, tore into the eight boxes that had arrived. But all that was inside were papers that had once belonged to his dad, papers no one ever sorted through in the nearly thirteen years that he'd been dead. Wade's mother, just remarried, had finally packed them up, sent them from the prairie to the mountain because she could not bear to throw them out herself.

Wade and Jenny glanced at the mess inside, then sealed the boxes back up. Closed, the boxes became a strange feature in the otherwise empty house; they became the chairs, the tables, the nightstands. Each stoic address gleamed under too much tape: 7846 FOREST SERVICE ROAD, PONDEROSA.

When Wade returns to the house with the sledful of food and supplies, his feet frozen in his boots, he finds Jenny sitting on a box by the fire. She looks tired. Her hair is tangled, and she wears the same clothes she did the day before. But she smiles at him. She says she's glad he's home. Remembering the swastika, remembering the woods he's just trudged through, the steep and slippery hill, he is struck by her warmth. She seems to him right now like the only safe place. He sits on the box beside hers, and they watch the flying snow with their backs to the fire, a blanket over their shoulders, her hand on his, his hand on their unborn child, who is kicking inside of Jenny. Out the windows, whose glass is filled mostly with their reflection, the boughs of ponderosa, white, and lodgepole pines drop the snow, then rise again, freed, to gather more.

Outside, the coyotes' howls bore tunnels through the frozen silence. The ravens in the trees anticipate the spring, when they will nudge their weakest from their nests, this act already in their hearts, as if already committed. The garter snakes, deep in the ground, hibernate alert. Bodies cold, unmoving; minds twitching, hot. So many secret, coiled wills, a million centers spiraling out, colliding into a clap of silence that is this very moment in the house, this beautiful oblivion in which they love each other.

The twelfth tree falls. One absence closer. The morning sky is a singing blue. The valley shimmers in the frost.

Soon this near-clearing in the woods will be a circle of nothing but snow. This is the hardest he's ever worked in his life, shaping this small vastness where he and his wife might one day come to be lifted away, carried right out of this dream that they are living, delivered into safety so that they can deliver their baby. This is where the helicopter will meet them, will summon the snow up into the last storm of the winter they will have to survive.

When he returns to the house for some food, Jenny is sitting on a cardboard box filled with papers, her back against the wall, the telephone on her lap, swollen ankles crossed, the receiver at her ear. She is talking to her mother. Her voice is strained and cheerful, every word carried on false eddies of laughter. She tells her mother she spent all day yesterday shopping for baby clothes in town. "You'll just love them. Some little yellow shoes," Jenny says, staring out the window at the gray fog and the tall, dark pines and endless snow that keeps her trapped miles and miles from any store, from any yellow baby shoes.

Her desperation pains him. She is more trapped than he is because she can't work in the cold, for fear of hurting the baby. What she seems to feel, though, isn't boredom but its opposite. A constant rush of adrenaline. She is nervous, teary, quick to accuse. She has dropped three plates in the last three days and wept over the loss of each as she bent down to clean up the porcelain. She eats cold, solid soup right out of the can. Sitting on the box by the fire, in a bored panic, she makes lists of things that babies need, estimates what each will cost. She calculates how long it will take to save enough for a tractor to plow the roads the following winter.

The next morning is cold, but much warmer than the day before. A fog hangs over the valley. They can't see the mountains across from them or the roads below. A bull moose appears out of this fog, rips gray lichen off a tree with his teeth. The top of the snow is disrupted only by his hooves and bobcat prints. From the

porch, Jenny throws sunflower seeds on the snow and the chicka-
dees appear out of nowhere in a cheeping frenzy, then, as soon as
the seeds are gone, disappear back into the white.

The yellow shoes wait in the closet only when the closet doors
are closed.

◼

One night in bed, in the dark, Jenny whispers, "Do you think we
missed Christmas?"

"I don't think so," he whispers back.

"You don't think that it was yesterday?"

"No."

"I have a feeling it was."

He laughs.

"I'm *sure* it was," she says. "Wade, let's celebrate."

He turns over in the bed, feels around for her face, then brushes
her nose with his fingertip. "It's not going to be much of a celebra-
tion. I have only one thing for you, and it's edible."

"It's not like I've been shopping. Go get your gift. Please? It's
almost midnight. Let's celebrate before we're two days late instead
of one."

So he finds the cold flashlight in the covers, the electricity out yet
again from another storm, gets out of bed, fumbles on the wall for
his coat hanging from a nail. He reaches into the pocket and lifts
out a chocolate orange. She sits up. "Is that what I think it is?" He
comes back to the bed, then holds it out to her. She takes it in her
hand. "It is!" The golden foil flashes in the light.

"Knock it open," he says, getting back under the covers, wrap-
ping his arms around her.

She knocks it on the windowsill. She peels open the wrapper.
The dark chocolate slices fall open, brittle crescents smelling not of
chocolate but of flowers. They each eat one.

"Merry Christmas," he says, crumpling the foil. Then he presses
his still-chocolate-tasting lips to her bare belly.

"We have all these packages," she says. "All these huge presents your mother sent."

"Yeah, right."

She says, "Well, they're something to open. That's what you do on Christmas, you open things. It doesn't matter what's inside."

"What will we sit on if not our boxes?"

"We have to go through them sometime."

"Do we?"

"It's your dad's things! I'll go get a knife."

"I have one in my coat in here."

"Let's pretend," she says, "that the packages are presents for each other."

"Should I make a fire?"

"I don't think it's all the way out. I think we'll get it going again."

So they sneak into the living room as if they are children and they sit in the glow of the embers. She pulls one of the boxes they've been sitting on close to her, and she rips the tape with his knife. Then, with ceremony, she opens the four flaps one at a time, looks up at Wade with exaggerated gratitude in her eyes. She looks down at the papers. "Wade," she says, "you break my heart."

"And you break mine."

They lift out his father's scraps one at a time. Coupons, receipts, torn envelopes, subscription renewals more than two decades old. They take turns throwing the scraps onto the embers, which soon become a fire. There is nothing to keep in this box. It is all expired offers and paid bills. They move through it quickly. Neither of them says what a terrible waste of postage it was for his mother to send expired junk mail by UPS. They stomp the boxes down, throw the flaps into the fire, whose heat has made them drowsy enough that they crawl into bed before they know they are doing it. They have left the flashlight on accidentally in the bed. In the commotion they make in the covers, its beam rolls over the wall clock, where Wade sees that they are already forty minutes into tomorrow.

After his dad died, when Wade was only nineteen, he began to believe that the prairie, the open space and the sameness, had something to do with his dad's early dementia, with his death. And maybe with his grandfather's and great-grandfather's, too. Three generations of early dementia in that same house on the same flat land that looked the same as everyone else's. The land there had varied only in color. Brown roads, black, tilled earth, a checker-board of distant farms, green alfalfa, red wheat. Even the farm-houses looked about the same, chimneys of whitewashed brick, old-fashioned gables half hidden in the clusters of cottonwoods that were the only trees for miles and miles. But in the winter, in the snow, there had been no sign of these distinctions, no lines to separate one acreage, one history, from another. The wind would blow so evenly over the prairie that footprints, as soon as they were made, were filled again with snow.

How easy it must have been for his dad to get lost.

But already there is a story on this mountain. Fifteen felled trees: the story of his child's birth before it's even happened. That is a difference he or she has made already, a difference that could be seen from the sky looking down. Even when his memory is gone, he will still be able to see this clearing with his eyes. A change in a landscape, all because of his baby. He has cut into this mountain a parcel like that of the old prairie—a history, a back door to memory.

He shoves cotton in his ears. He starts the chainsaw. This ponderosa will take him all day to cut and drag and haul. He pushes the blade through the wood, and the sound of the saw rises, but then he sees in the corner of his eye a flash of dark red in all that black and white.

Jenny. He turns off the chainsaw, takes the cotton out of his ears. She is standing right at the edge of the clearing, her hands over her ears to protect them from the roaring saw, her wool scarf, the color of bricks, wrapped around her mouth and nose. When she sees him looking at her, she drops her hands from her ears.

"What is it?" he calls, setting the chainsaw on the branches and moving toward her, his heart racing. It's not an easy walk from the house in all this snow. Only in an emergency would he ever take Jenny here, and then only to be lifted away, saved.

"Jenny, what is it?" he calls, but she doesn't answer. She pulls the scarf down from her mouth and holds it at her neck with her hand, as if about to speak. He reaches her. "Is everything all right?"

"Yes."

"The baby?"

"I'm sorry, yes, we're fine."

"Why are you out here?"

"Yesterday was Christmas," she says, her voice distant. He can't believe this is what she's come to say. He waits for the real reason. "My mom just asked how our Christmas was. If we'd waited only ten more minutes," she says, out of breath, and in a kind of daze, "we would have missed it."

He's angry. "You're not wearing gloves."

"I needed to say . . ." She dips her reddened hand into the pocket of her enormous coat, and takes out a photograph. "Look."

The photograph shows Wade's father, Adam, as a boy.

He glances at it, hands it back. "What are you doing out here?"

"I've been going through the other boxes since you left," she says. "I found . . ." She stops, shakes her head as if disbelieving what she has come to say.

Confused, angry at her for scaring him, he looks again at the photograph in her hand. His father as a boy smiles, the prairie spreading out behind him. There is a girl in the background, right at the edge of the photo.

"Do you know who she is?" Jenny asks, and she touches her fingertip to the girl's face.

"Why?"

"Just look at her for a minute." So he studies the girl. She wears a filthy dress. She looks about the same age as Wade's father, ten or eleven. Two long, thin braids hang over her shoulders. Her hands grip the fence behind her, and she leans forward and smiles so hard it is not like a smile but like the baring of her teeth. Her eyes are shut from the force of this smile, her face tilted to the sky in an aggressive assertion of joy, her throat stretched and gleaming.

"You've never seen this girl before?" asks Jenny.

"She's probably a neighbor girl or a cousin," Wade says. "It's a picture of my dad, not me. Why would I know her? Did you think this was a picture of me?" There is still anger in his voice that he hopes she hears.

Jenny turns the photograph over. There, in a shaky handwriting, are two names written below a date: August 1928.

"Her name is June Bailey Roe," Jenny says. "She owes us almost ten thousand dollars."

The days are different after that. The snow falls as hard as it ever has. Wade shovels it off the roof. He hacks the icicles from the eaves. He stands in the center of the clearing he has cut. He looks up at the sky, and he imagines the helicopter approaching. He imagines that, in the midst of all this white, he would look to the pilot like the pupil of an eye.

But the last tree cut down does not make the difference it might have before. It is the same mountain it always was. Vast, dense, deadly, alive. The only other difference is the whispers. Rushed whispers, as if always under the covers of a bed, a secret held aloft by the shaking beams of flashlights. They are Jenny's whispers, mostly. She falls into these loud hushes without noticing, and sometimes the whispers are enraged beyond whispers and that is when she realizes the conspiratorial way she has been speaking and that is when she laughs. He laughs, too, sometimes. But it is strained laughter. He feels as if there is someone who can hear them, as if the winter is no longer the prevailing secret (though they keep it, still, from their families), but rather the winter is the thing they keep their secret from.

June Bailey Roe was eleven years old when Wade's father, Adam, was ten.

There is no record of their childhood together except the single photograph that now rests at the top of a small pile of papers in the center of the otherwise empty living room. The eight boxes from the prairie have been fed to the fire. There is nowhere to sit except the bed where they eat their meals, their plates on their laps. The small stack of papers is all that remains of the contents of those boxes. To keep them from flying away when the door is open, Jenny has placed one of Wade's knives on top of the stack.

There is not much to go on, but there is enough.

Wade's father sent June Bailey Roe the first check, for two thousand dollars, in 1968, when he was fifty years old, and when she was fifty-one. The check was a gift for what Adam believed, in the confusion of his disease, was her fourteenth birthday.

The letters Jenny has found are all Adam's rough drafts, the same phrases written again and again, the wording tweaked, wildly sentimental in places, the handwriting often illegible. Most of these letters are paper-clipped to nothing. Many are scribbled out. Who knows which phrases survived into the final draft? Only June Bailey Roe does. What Jenny has gathered from these scraps is the guilty promises, the half-formed delusions of love: Adam believed, inside the solitude of his illness, that the little girl in the photograph was his secret daughter, Wade's half sister, still fourteen years old.

Where had this notion come from? Wade has no idea. When Jenny shows him the evidence, he nods but tries to look past it, tries not to see the tender words, the guilty proclamations. Had Adam believed the picture of himself at ten was really a picture of Wade? And was the photograph therefore proof, in his mind, of his unfair preference for his son and his poor treatment of his lost daughter, who, even in the moment the photograph captured, has had to strain, to fight, to be included? That stretched throat, that growling smile.

The photograph hurts Wade. And more than the content of the letters, he is hurt by the endless attempts at them, that none of the letters were good enough for her.

Eight checks of varying amounts. That's how many they have record of. Nearly ten thousand dollars in total.

He feels the pain of his father's death sharply. That this little girl had managed to cling so fiercely in Wade's father's mind unsettles him, because he, Adam's son, had not managed to do the same, had not managed to be remembered by his own father.

But he doesn't tell Jenny this. He lets her go on in her strange excitement. Sometimes, instead of whispering, she falls into long silences that he can't break until he persuades her to come outside, to walk around. The cold air gets her talking. He knows her body is flashing hot and her hands ice cold inside her gloves. Her breath freezes to her hair, streaks of white in the middle of her two dark French braids. She has brushed and braided her hair every day since the day she burned all those boxes in the fire. The winter diminishes in her eyes in light of her new project, her scheme to get the money back. She is furious. Glad. She thinks that they are saved. Not by the clearing Wade has labored to cut, but by the ten thousand dollars she plans to extract from the thief, from the heartless old woman that is that little girl. He even catches her using the words "that little girl," as if that woman, now almost seventy, one year older than Adam would be, could really be Adam's secret child.

Walking, they startle grouse from snowy, tangled bushes heavy with rotten white berries. They smell stale lichen on the frozen air. Jenny talks excitedly, pointing out the places around the house, telling him her plans for their land now that they'll have money.

"We'll buy a tractor as soon as the snow melts. I want to clear out paths. I want to put benches way out at the edges of the property line. I was thinking where you're making the helicopter clearing we could build a gazebo, not anytime soon, but at some point, it could be this secret wedding place."

"Whose secret wedding are we talking about?"

She laughs, touching her belly. "Crazy! I'm crazy!" Her eyes blaze.

In the night, Wade sits on the bed and he writes out the threatening letters that Jenny dictates as she paces the room, constantly revising, her hands at all times consulting the mountain their child has become on her body, the mountain she coddles and fears and seems to draw the words from: *Give the money back.*

Another son who lost his father might move on, given enough time. Another son's grief might diffuse into something vague and settled out like wisdom, expand like the beam of a flashlight in the fog.

But Wade, having long since moved past his grief, finds himself now inside of that fog, unable to see past it. For years, Wade had been able to ignore his fear that he, too, would suffer from dementia. This fear would surface in him in moments of great emotion, but usually he could overcome it. But now, seeing these letters his father wrote to June Bailey Roe, seeing his father's painful devotion to someone who simply wasn't real—a daughter he never had—Wade is unable to suppress his dread. All that love, all those feelings, all that pain, fastened to nothing, a terrible, drifting chaos. His future loss of mind becomes the new premise of his life, and he feels, already, the loss of the things that he loves, feels himself trying to find some other way to hold on to them.

He doesn't tell this to Jenny, either. Maybe he will someday, but not now, not when she needs something to hope for. He lets her feel relieved, revived, nourished by her indignation, satiated by her own exciting threats. A month passes, and all through it, in the midst of other conversations, Jenny's accusations against "that lit-tle girl" rise.

"Who accepts money from a demented old man? One year older than he is! His illegitimate child! I know you think the money should go to your mom, but it would only hurt her to find this out. She's got her new husband now. We're going to have a baby."

That last is the most frequent refrain, the best proof she has to offer of what they deserve and June Bailey Roe does not. The baby—the dream they feed the vitamins to, the mountain on her body.

Wade cannot contest these things. And so he takes dictation, signs his name at the end of each letter. But his hand writes for him; he hardly pays attention to the words themselves. Instead, he pictures all the places June Bailey Roe might be, sixty-eight now, a survivor of his father's dementia.

How could he ever admit to Jenny the strange way that he has come to feel?

At the very center of his pain, he feels respect for June Bailey Roe. She is like a sliver in Adam's memory, fresh and tender to the day he died, long after Wade was forgotten, having healed inside of him without leaving so much as a scar.

June Bailey Roe deserves that money, because she has found a way not to disappear.

But Wade carries a letter in his pocket once a week when he hikes down through the snow to Miller's Grocery in Spirit Lake. He drops the letter in the mailbox there. Some of the letters are threats, Jenny's words in his handwriting. Some are desperate ap-peals to June Bailey Roe's sympathy. All contain instructions for where to mail the money she owes them.

They have only her Ketchum address of some sixteen years be-fore.

Jenny proceeds as if it's a kind of game.

"Write, 'We have a lawyer now.'"

He looks up from the notepad at her.

"Really, do." She nods, excited. Then she looks at the snow as if her eyes can stop it from falling. "Write, 'This is your last chance.'"

She has seen a vision of their lives.

■　■　■

But no letter, no check, arrives. Spring does, though. It comes just when it should, just when it was promised. Everywhere, there is the sound of dripping trees. Streams run far beneath the snow, and emerge on the muddy road, cutting gashes through it. Wade and Jenny climb into the truck together. Jenny sits in the passenger seat. Her dark-red scarf covers her hair, which is tangled again, longer than he's ever seen it. Her lips are chapped, her eyes soft, and her expression open, willing, waiting. Wade revs the engine. The muddy snow spits up from the tires, splatters the branches he's laid beneath them to mitigate the mud, and the exhaust hangs in the air along with the mossy smell of melting. With enough rocking, enough cajoling, they pry the truck free.

Their baby girl, Lily, is born safely in a hospital the following week. No helicopter needed. The twenty trees might as well have been left standing.

■　■　■

Months pass, and the mountain now is as it was when they bought it just over a year ago. There are buttercups in the grass. The birds' song enters through the open windows of the nursery, where Jenny holds Lily, their astonishing happiness, in her arms.

The furniture has arrived, and they have work again. Jenny is back at the vet's office, and now that the road is clear, Wade is able to get the materials he needs to finish his workshop so that he can continue making and selling knives, as he had done in Grangeville.

Jenny seems almost to forget the winter altogether. She pours all of her energy into the baby. She buys the yellow shoes that were once a dream that got her through the winter, which itself has become a dream again, a distant one, cleared by phantom, future plows. The letters stop. All of that passion with which she wrote those letters, all of those agonizing trips Wade took to the post office, their whole stressful scheme, has vanished. It is a great weight off his shoulders.

But they still do need some extra money to save for a tractor, and so he starts working in the fields of the Rathdrum Prairie, moving irrigation pipes. It is work he hasn't done in a long time, not since just after high school, but he doesn't mind it. It was what he was doing when he first met Jenny thirteen years ago, when they were both nineteen. Now, he lifts the pipes with their baby on his back. On Jenny's days off, she joins Wade working in the fields, and they take turns carrying the baby, singing to her as they work.

One mild summer day, their bodies sore from carrying pipes, but their hearts light, Wade and Jenny decide to drive to the top of the mountain. During this drive, Lily is quiet in Jenny's arms.

They don't really expect to find the school bus. But there it is in the distance, in the weeds.

They park the truck, and walk toward it on no trail, over lumps of ground disturbed by dirt bikes and four-wheelers. The knapweed grows purple and silver, snaps with katydids clinging to the stems.

All four of the bus's tires are flat and shot through with bullets. The side mirrors are ripped off, the metal that connected them gleaming in the sun. Carefully, Wade and Jenny climb the stairs, and the bus creaks with their weight. There is the sound of panicked wings, and then no sound at all.

They do not climb all the way in. Jenny stands at the top of the steps, holding Lily. Wade stands just behind her. The windshield is shattered on the driver's seat and across the dash, the shards sparkling on the aisle. Jenny doesn't want to risk walking over them, so they both look over the guard rail at the seats, many slashed open, a few removed. Grasshoppers bask on the hot canvas. From a hole in the driver's seat, several gray feathers are bursting, still fluttering as if recently disturbed.

"Jenny," he says, looking over these seats, smelling the hot canvas and the dust and the dry flowers outside. "I want to talk about her name."

The specks of dust and small feathers rise in the slant of sun through the broken windshield.

Jenny turns her head, looks at him. "What do you mean?"

"I want to change it."

Jenny looks at him with a blank expression, then turns back to face the bus, all those empty seats. She says nothing, stares as if mesmerized by the twinkling dust. After a long time, Wade touches her arm, turns her toward him. He says quietly, "I want to give her everything the rest of my life. I never want to forget that she's the one I love."

"You're talking about June," Jenny says, her voice far away. He's startled to discover in her no surprise.

"Yes, for her name."

Neither says anything for a long time. Then, as if she has broken free of a trance, she shakes her head, says clearly, "Don't you think it'll mess a child up, changing her name like this?"

He laughs softly. "Lots of things can mess kids up. This won't. She won't even remember."

"I don't even know if I like the name June."

"I don't like the woman we're naming her after. But I admire her. There's something in her that survives."

"June," she says. "Of all the people to name a child after . . ." Her voice drifts, lost. They both look down at the baby in Jenny's arms, who is sucking on her own knuckles, while looking with detached curiosity at the sparkling glass. Wade and Jenny stand that way for a moment longer, feeling the evening settle down inside the bus. Outside, the crickets are singing. After a moment, the song fills the school bus, too. Crickets they did not know were all around them sing first with mistrust, and then as if there is no one there at all.

1995

June's door is closed. Jenny senses what it means: May's broken heart.

"Someday you'll want that, too," Jenny says to May. "A closed door." She makes sure that her tone is light and sensible, meant to comfort her daughter, but May, six years old, hardens her face against her mother's consolation—her mother's accusation.

The two of them are sitting at the kitchen table, rolling pinecones around on plates of peanut butter, Jenny working quickly, brightly, humming as if she's got a song stuck in her head (she doesn't), every now and then sticking her fingers in her mouth and sucking off the peanut butter with what is surely—Jenny knows that May knows—a falsely oblivious delight.

And because May knows, she works in silence, barely moving her hands, studying her mother with suspicion as she rolls the pinecone absentmindedly across the plate, not even noticing the peanut butter is all used up. Jenny knows that May is searching her face for an admission—that all of this, even the pinecones, even the birdseed and the pretend song dancing around in her mother's head, is a lie. How could such things be real when her sister has shut her out by shutting that door? How could her mother not feel it?

Jenny would like to take her younger daughter in her arms and mutter into her sweet blond head that she does, she feels it, it is like the breaking open of her heart. But it would not be fair to June, who has just turned nine and should be allowed to break free of their ideas of her. And though Jenny tries to make it up to May— the pinecone bird feeders, for example, a project she does not really have time for today—May resists.

So Jenny sprinkles birdseed and fastens the wire to the pine-cone's top, and twists it for a hook. She holds it up. She smiles. "There."

"Nice," May says. When had May become capable of sarcasm? Both her daughters have surprised her in the past few weeks. June, hot-tempered, quick to tattle, jealous little June; how softly she's responded lately to her sister's attempts at provocation. Looks of sympathy and bewilderment at her mother, over May's shoulder, as May slings her inarticulate accusations. How unlike June not to fight back, not to hit and claw. It's Jenny who has to intervene.

But what June has said to May is much sharper than fingernails. Jenny can picture the sympathetic shrug of June's shoulders when June told her sister, "It was just a phase, May. I'm sorry."

This in response to May's bitter shouts about June's indifference toward their dolls.

"Phase." Playing with dolls, she means. The last nine years of her nine-year-old life, she means. Such an adult word she has now tacked onto her childhood. All of what they know of June, June herself has dismissed as naïve and temporary, her whole life a fleeting infatuation. *Phase*. May, for some reason, had thought the word meant "static." She had pictured television snow. Jenny didn't know at first what May was talking about through her kicking and her screaming and her tears. *What do you mean, static? What do you mean it doesn't work? June broke the TV?* Until finally May got through to her. What May couldn't handle was her sister's blotting out with white noise May's very self and their very life together as sisters. May bashed the soft plastic head of her most beloved doll on the corner of the piano bench, until Jenny picked May up, smoothed down her thrashing limbs with the same gestures she would use to smooth down the static in her hair, and said, "No, a phase is sort of like a place. You're in it for a while, but then you leave."

"Like her room?" the girl had lashed, her face blotchy and insane.

Outside the rain pours down. In the new stove, Wade builds a fire. It is spring, but the smell and sounds of the fire combined with the storm outside cast the wrong season over the house. It feels like fall, like the long winter they've just endured is coming at them from the wrong direction, will plow them over, back in time. Even the bird feeders they are making remind Jenny of Christmas instead of spring. It's the green wires, she supposes, the little hooks. All of this has put Wade, too, in a melancholy mood. Jenny glances over at him. He does not seem to hear what's happening at the table, but he, too, is affected by the loss of the doll world. While he worked in his office, he used to listen, with an almost academic interest, to his daughters play. Both he and Jenny knew the names of the more important dolls, and who was dating whom. Wade could hear from his office both girls in June's room, the door of which was always open. May and June performed voices for the dolls, the men and women both. The men spoke more slowly. And because May and June couldn't deepen their voices enough for each other to believe, they compensated with a deepening of volume: The men's voices, strangely, were the whispered ones.

Sometimes Jenny and Wade joked about the games in bed.
Did you hear Veronica is paralyzed?
What do you mean, paralyzed?

She can't move her legs. It's a rare disease. Joe found her just lying there in bed.

Joe? What was Joe doing in her bed?

Knowing laughter. Raised eyebrows. A pretended smugness. Wade and Jenny shook their heads in pity at what the other didn't know.

Boy, are you out of the loop.

The dolls are like Barbie dolls, but less expensive, smaller, made of softer plastic. Their limbs are pliable, their faces neutral, their eyes far apart. They come dressed for winter: removable boots, plain sweaters. The special ones come with cotton dogs or cats or bodiless babies rolled in white felt as tight as Tootsie Rolls. There are twenty-two dolls in total, and June and May used to start their games by counting them, taking attendance, making sure no one was missing from their respective lives.

Until very recently, all the playing took place in June's room, in her closet. None of June's clothes were in there, just four wooden shelves, which May and June had divided into different rooms with pieces of cardboard that had doorways cut into them, to form a five-story house through which the dolls moved, guided by the girls' hands. The men and women pressed their faces against one another for kisses. Mothers dropped babies, and rushed them to hospitals on the other side of the room. They told lies; they declared forbidden loves; they made shocking confessions. Sometimes they fell victim to robberies or kidnappings.

Inside of the cardboard rooms were pieces of furniture, also made of cardboard, and real Polaroids taken by Jenny of the dolls arranged in families or couples, taped to the cardboard walls. These pictures had to be updated when families were broken, or wives remarried, or when people died. Which they did—die— elaborately, and not because a doll was lost somewhere and May and June needed an excuse, but because sometimes the twists in the story were worth the sacrifice. They were never resurrected, either, as far as Jenny knew.

May has tried to play alone since June quit the games. Four of the dolls are hers. She is too proud to ask June for the rest, even though June's dolls are all just sitting there in the closet going to waste. Jenny has seen them in there, the same man leaning over the same stove for weeks now. Husbands and wives still sleeping on their flaps of cardboard. Children arranged in nurseries, unmoving.

Lately, May has been carrying her coveted four around the house, trying out new settings to no avail, doing all of the talking and whispering herself. But she is self-conscious; she doesn't know what they say to one another without June there to guide her through the narratives. She is only pretending to pretend. Twice May has caught her mother listening to her sad little games, and twice May has flown into an embarrassed rage. She is not at all her usual self; she is prone to shocking tantrums, completely outside of her character. For days she has sulked around the house, finding excuses to knock on June's door. Usually the excuses are mean; she used a stick to fish out a pair of June's dirty socks that had fallen behind a bathroom cabinet, just so she could open June's door and throw them in. "Here's your dirty old disgusting socks!"

But even June knows what all of it means. She knows that May is lost without her. And perhaps she is sorry. Jenny thinks she probably is.

"She's probably just reading, you know," Jenny says to May. "I bet she wouldn't care if you went in there and read, too."

"I hate reading," says May, and Jenny has to smile.

They have cleaned up the pinecones and the peanut butter. Wade has gone out to his workshop, and Jenny puts on a movie, even though it is the middle of the day. When she does, May gives in a little. This broken rule of movies in the daytime is admission enough for her. She acknowledges her mother's attempts, finally, with a softened look but nothing more. She holds her arms very tight around her legs, and watches as if she isn't watching, by lifting her eyes just barely above her kneecaps, in order to see the screen.

Before long, May falls asleep, as Jenny knew she would. Jenny has been waiting for a chance to go to June's room without May knowing. Jenny remembers what it was like, all those years ago. It was never dolls for her, nothing so tangible as that. It was more of a feeling. As if, for the first several years of her life, everything held over her a sort of knowledge and insistence. Fence posts, wallpaper, the lawn at certain hours of the day. These things glowered at her, or smiled. Even something as ordinary as the blue rolling chair in her father's office had some hold on her, some whisper of a new dimension in its puffs of dust sent upward by her fists against its cushions. There was an intensity inherent in everything until, one day, there wasn't. The blue chair rolled on its wheels to the window when she pushed it. The rising dust was rising dust. And when it was gone, there was only a knot of longing somewhere deep inside of her, a vacant ache: adolescence. Boredom.

It's why we fall in love, Jenny will tell June.

We fall in love to get back to that dimension, that wonder.

She goes to the laundry room, where, from the pile of clean clothes, she picks out a few articles of June's, folds them, then goes upstairs to knock on her daughter's door and tell her that this, this lost doll world, is the reason there is love.

But when she comes to June's door, she doesn't have to knock. The door is open. Just barely open, and surely by accident, but Jenny can see through the crack.

June is sitting on the floor. Jenny can see most of her face, turned toward the closet. She sees the small, rigid back. June's hands are clasped tight on her lap. Her shoulders move in minuscule jerks, as if she's dreaming. But she isn't dreaming. Jenny looks closer, nearly afraid: June's eyes are wide open, staring into her closet. Her lips part for a moment, then close.

In the doorway, Jenny is unable to move, though she knows she is not meant to see what's happening in June's room. She holds the cool, folded clothes close to her. Speak, speak or go! she urges herself, but she can't. She's held there. She opens her mouth to say

June's name, but something happens. Something happens to June's face. It lights up in a way that isn't her own face, but someone else's, someone else's happy face. And Jenny recognizes it instantly as the face of one of the people on the shelves. A girl doll. Katie. It is an expression June used to wear every time she made that one particular girl doll, her very favorite, talk. A twitching, thoughtful expression.

She is *playing* with them. Jenny can't believe it. June is moving the dolls around in her mind. She is making them talk to one another. She just has to look at the house in order to concentrate. So the man leaning over the stove is not really at the stove anymore, though that's where his body is. He has moved so far beyond Jenny's image of him that he himself has likely forgotten ever having stood there at all, cooking dinner likely for a wife now long his ex. All of them walking from room to room, having their dramas, getting dressed and undressed, the men no longer having to whisper, but speaking loudly in June's head. Laughing, yelling men. All of this without her touching them. Because touching would mean playing and you don't play with dolls when you are nine.

Jenny turns away. Her eyes are filled with tears. Not meaning to, not thinking, she hurries down the stairs, hugging the small pile of clothes. She isn't sure what she is feeling—relief, yes, but also something else. Fear. Fear that such exclusion from her daughter's life could be possible. Cardboard walls have sprung up in her daughter's mind, and childhood is the space between them. June's childhood lives on in its vivid paralysis. The whole doll world is now closed off to everyone but June. Jenny is hurt. Yes, that's what it is. Tightening in her chest is grief.

When Jenny reaches the bottom of the stairs, and sees the back of the couch, and the flickering TV, and May's arm hanging over the side of the couch, she is touched by how safe the girl is inside her sleep, how safe from what she thinks is loss, but is really just the fact of a world spinning on without her.

Jenny goes to her, wakes her. Takes her in her arms and holds her close.

■   ■   ■

The guards are women, too. They might be mothers. They un-make the beds, shake the pillows from their cases, empty Jenny's box all over the floor, all over her crouching body.

The floor, in the palms of Jenny's hands, is cool. Three other women are on their knees beside her, holding the same floor, all of them new to Sage Hill. This is a holding cell, a temporary place where they've kept Jenny since her transfer here a week ago fol-lowing her sentencing. Her real cell isn't ready yet. But tomorrow it will be. Her real sentence will begin, tomorrow, in a place called Lock.

Tomorrow.

Strange how time was once a thing to measure—hours, days, weeks. How impossible to remember what it must have been like to know a day as a thing that passed.

The four prisoners stare at the door in front of them. The door is solid, painted green, the color of asylums. Green, the antidote for insanity.

"Stand up," says one of the guards.

So Jenny and the others raise their arms, put their hands behind their heads, their elbows so close that Jenny can feel her cellmates' heat, their sharp, radiant anger. Sisters, now.

They follow the same commands. They hear the same voice.

The guards are looking for something.

"No," Jenny and the others say, together, in response to a ques-tion Jenny isn't sure they have been asked.

And the guards seem to believe this, but only after swiping their arms over the shelf, to hear the crash of their few belongings; only after sticking their fingers inside the little sewn holes on the bottoms of the mattresses; only after lifting the lid on the back of the toilet, and sticking their fingers in the water, feeling around for the lie.

The guards wipe their fingers off on the pillowcases, then drop them, again, to the floor.

"Clean up this mess," they say, and leave.

And so they do. Numbly. As if their limbs are lifted up by someone else's eyes, they move through this holding cell without speaking. They stuff the pillows back into their cases, spread the harsh, scratchy blankets evenly over the thin mattresses.

And when they are done, a girl's voice, surprisingly young, enters their cell through the intercom, her voice edged with static. "Count Four begins in two."

Whose voice is it? It is nearly like a child's, the way it rings out orders like a sort of game, Mother-May-I, Simon Says. In this voice—does she imagine it?—a hint of innocence, of some surprise that anyone would listen to a voice so small.

"First count begins in one. Inmates, stand ready at doors."

Then the lock slides open on its own; the door floats open on its own. They step out to stand in front of it, in the hallway cage. She sees, across from her, and on both sides, the lines of the other prisoners, arms hanging down, slight nods of recognition at one another, but faces neutral, smiles slight.

All of them are waiting to be released by this voice, this strange intercom's voice of a child. She feels now as she felt inside that courtroom one week ago. Her legs had lifted her not just at the judge's command, but at the simultaneous command of a voice she did not know the source of, a girl's voice that felt both within her and without, and whose words were less a command than a creation.

The judge's voice was not much louder than a whisper. The sentence was delivered from his mouth but was somehow separate from the man, as if the child voice spoke for him, too. *Life,* he said, as if it was a gift he was bestowing, *life.*

As if the word could make it so.

The names of women called, again by the voice of the girl, the static voice on the intercom, the echo across the green concrete.

It is as if her life is miniature now, and some child looks down at her through the window of the sky, and, without moving her own lips, opens Jenny's. Jenny's lips make the shape of someone else's words.

She is counted. From somewhere in the wilderness, June is staring in.

"Mitchell."

When her name is called by the girl, whose voice trembles in the static, it is a shape that Jenny returns, a shape without a sound, the shape of the space between four walls.

"Here."

Here. She is here.

1995

When May reaches the shade near the clothesline on the hottest day of the year, she lifts the lid off a garbage can. The garbage can is as tall as she is, and filled with water. Still holding the lid with one hand, she moves her free fingertips back and forth on the water's surface, to test it. Warm. She slings the lid away with what she hopes resembles fury, to indicate to anyone who might be watching how committed she is now to her purpose here, how finished she is now with lids of any kind. It spins in the dust, upside down like a saucer, then stops.

She wears a thin, striped dress and no shoes, her sandals kicked off down the hill. She steps onto a hot cinder block by the garbage can, then brushes the dust off each foot with her hand. The garbage can is blue, as are the shaking reflections its water throws on her arms as she stands over it now, smelling the warm plastic, moving her finger across the water's surface, breaking here and there a delicate sheen of oil she knows to be from her own skin. She climbs into the water one leg at a time, sucking in her breath as if the water is cold. It is not cold. It has sat here, under the hot lid, since yesterday afternoon, when she filled the can with the hose and shivered in it for a while. Now she feels the water crawl up the backs of her legs, under her dress, up her whole body, even to the tips of her hair; it engulfs her. She snaps her dress down and it drifts. She finds herself at eye level with the water's surface, her sunburned shoulders submerged. Her knees are bent, and in a moment she is holding them, making herself compact so she is floating, no part of her touching the garbage can at all. She rises and sinks in the blue circle. Occasionally she pushes off the bottom with the tips of her toes and springs up into the air, her arms open wide, the droplets flying and splattering the ground with force enough that they bring up puffs of dust like pebbles would. That is how fine the dust is.

From here, she can see the back of her pale-yellow house, down the hill. She can see, close by, the pasture and the horses chomping on the hot weeds. She can see her sister's garbage can a few feet from her own, the lid still on. There is also June's bike, propped up against the same tree since Easter, its chain rusted, the seat chewed open by a squirrel.

May has been looking for Rocket, her orange tabby cat. She lost him today sometime around eleven o'clock. She has trudged through the heat to each of Rocket's usual places, twice, calling his name in a whisper because calling out loud would make the loss official. She whispers, "Rocket," now, barely a sound, looking up at the sky and the ragged, hideous tops of the pine trees. The more she whispers it, the more the name becomes a movement of her body, the "rock" being the motion she is making in the water, the "it" being herself. The water spills over the rim of the garbage can.

Now she sees June, who is nine, marching up the hill. June is wearing dusty white shorts over her blue swimming suit, and their mother's sun hat. It is a straw hat that ties under her chin. Its shadow obscures the expression on June's face, which May strains to see. She wants to predict her. But June's head is down; she is looking at the ground and has a towel wadded under her arm.

May climbs out quickly, retrieves the lid from the dust. She has an idea. Forgetting to brush off her feet, which are covered now in dirt and pinecone petals, she sinks into the water and lets the lid fall over her so it seems like she isn't there at all. She leans her head back, so that only her lips and her nose and her eyes are above water. She floats there, listening. Nobody can see her. She can't hear June, only herself, the wild drumming of her heart inside her ears inside the water.

Not her heart—the drumming of June's fingertips against the plastic.

"I know you're in there," says June flatly.

May pushes the lid off with her head. She sees that June has already taken off her shorts and placed them carefully on a stump. With her sandals still on, June removes the lid of her own garbage can, tests the water with her fingers. June likes the water cold. Immediately, she dips a coffee can, placed there for this purpose, into the water and begins dumping it out.

May sinks back down into the water, which she is annoyed to find is now filthy due to her failure to brush off her feet. Pinecone petals float on the surface. She blows them away from her, across the water.

June turns on the faucet and the cold water sprays out of the hose. She fills her garbage can, which now is a quarter empty, to the top. Finally she finds her book, wrapped up in her towel, and gets into the water with it, sucking in her breath so much her ribs poke out.

When she's in as far as she will go, she exhales a slow, glad sigh, to indicate, it seems to May, how much better it is when the water is cold. She hangs both elbows over the sides to keep her book dry, and rests her chin on the rim of the garbage can, and begins to read, her face hidden by the brim of the ugly hat.

"What's that about?" says May.

"A girl today whose spirit is linked to a girl on the Oregon Trail," says June quickly, turning the page.

"Is it good?"

"Very."

Both are quiet, then. May looks away from her sister, down at the house and the mountains behind the house.

It seems to May there are two Junes now, and who they are to each other, the two Junes, is unclear. Who they are to May is not: She loves one, she hates the other. The one she loves she rarely thinks about. That is the old June, the one who played with dolls. When the old June is around, May simply feels that things *are;* she does not admire the old June, or seek her approval, or yearn for her.

But this other one, the one she hates—entire days of May's life have been lost, trying to get under this new June's skin. May wants both to please her and to irritate her; she wants to surrender and rebel; she wants to be this June and to worship her and to claw her down to the old June's level all at once, claw her down with her fingernails, which are sharp. Like a fox's teeth. Just last week she plunged them into the new June's arm.

May dips down low so that her mouth is underwater, and there, in secret, she smiles a little smile. New June or old, there is always her smell; there is always her *self.* May smells it now, a current running under the tang of the heated-plastic water, under the smell of the trees and the sun-dried towel and the other, more common odors of her sister.

The smell is *June.*

June's boundaries seem beyond her; she herself hovers in the air above her skin in the form of that almost electric smell. It is not the smell of her dirty skin, or lake hair, or sweat, or the boiled milk on her breath at night. But something underneath. A hint. That is a good word for it, *hint,* thinks May, because the smell seems to be only a clue. May has encountered it just one other time. They were all at the house of her father's friend, after a dull dinner. There was lightning outside. The windows were open. Her father's friend had set the fan up on the floor so that it blew over everybody's legs under the table, where a tense, old dog was crouched, afraid of the thunder. May was sitting on the floor near the table with her sister, unaware of the dog, until the fan threw the air of the dog into her face, and May looked up. She felt suddenly overcome with the nearness of discovery, and she asked loudly, ferociously, nearly shaking, "What is that smell?" so that it seemed she was making an announcement rather than asking a question. Her voice was loud enough that everyone stopped talking and looked down at her.

"It's a scared animal, May," her father had said, gently, apologizing with his eyes to the man whose story May had interrupted. But May did not care. She widened her eyes at the shamed dog, then widened her eyes at June.

Did June know she had a smell? May has never said a word about it to her. Not ever, not once. She suspects that June suspects, because June is very particular about her baths. She begs in the store for bottles of scented lotion. She scrubs herself so hard she leaves a rash. She seems to leave soap on her body on purpose, and there is the soap smell, too, above the hint.

May does not have this smell. She knows this. She once brought the subject up to her mother. "Do I smell like June?" Her mother, looking quickly over her shoulder to make sure that June hadn't heard, said in a hushed voice, "No. It's just nerves. It will pass. I had something like it, too. She can't help it, so please, May, there's no reason to tell her. It would only make it worse."

Nerves. A sort of odor in the word itself.

Such a request, when May had known already to keep it secret, aged her a little. She became aware of something deep inside of herself, trapped underneath her ordinary love, stale and pungent and faintly sweet and quickly disappearing, like the opening of a forgotten jar inside of which a pet grasshopper has days ago died among its wilted grasses. Disgust: It is a feeling older than she is.

Not disgust itself, but her rising above it, her keeping it a secret. And therefore she loves June more because June has made possible May's capacity for holding back, for never using the one weapon she's been given, for restraining herself and leaning in closer, leaning in to whisper in her sister's ear and taste the round, musty odor of a scared animal. She does not hold her breath against the smell; it is something she nearly likes. And her sister, if in fact she does not know, if in fact she lives in that kind of ignorance, is made younger—younger, even, than May.

June turns another page. The sound of her dry fingers on the book's dry paper makes May shiver.

"Have you seen Rocket?" May asks as casually as she can, her arms hanging limply over the side.

"Nope," says June. But there is something about the way she says it that makes May want to look at her more closely. She is confronted suddenly with suspicion. But June's face is hidden still. It is hidden by the hat and by the face of the girl on the front of her book. May is only about a foot from this girl on the book. They are at eye level. May leans in closer. The girl looks a little like June, May thinks, only the gleam in her eyes is shaped like a covered wagon. All of June's books are about the same thing. The girls differ only in hair color and the shape of the gleam.

"What happened to the book with the other girl? The one with ships in her eyes?" asks May.

June's eyes move impossibly fast. She is only pretending to read. "Her spirit was entwined with a girl in the past captured by pirates." She is making a show of her patience, by answering.

"Yeah, but what happened?" May says it with force enough that June should look up. But she does not.

"What happened is I finished it."

"Oh," says May. And her temper takes form: She feels the secret of June's smell curl up out of her throat and into her mouth, and she needs only open it and the question would come out, "Do you know that you smell like a nervous dog?" And the new June would cower inside herself to be hugged by the old one, to be told by the old June that it isn't true, but the old June, who is sensible, who thinks not much of herself, would know that it is true, and she would emerge, there in the water, holding her arms around herself, trembling, weak. "May, do I really?"

"No," May could say, "I only made that up."

But it would be done, lost. She could not use it again. Not only that, but her sister would be wrecked. May treasures too much her only power, so when the secret comes into her mouth, like now, she must do something to keep it in. She clenches her teeth. Then she grabs June's book and throws it against a tree.

June shrieks in surprise. May is already climbing out of the garbage can. She is using June's towel to dry off. She drops the towel down in the dust and wipes her feet on it.

"Stop it!" yells June, clawing out of her can, the water spilling everywhere. And now there is that familiar old June in her voice. That radiant, shaking anger that the new June is too composed for. Her words rise out of her as if boiled in tears.

This is all that May was looking for. She is not sorry, but she does not get any pleasure out of it, either. She has done this out of necessity, to protect them both from the spoken knowledge of the smell. Having done so, she instantly forgets the incident altogether, even though June is in the background, lurching around, shaking her book, crying out her same old threats. May leaves the clothesline shade, once again with the whisper of her cat's name trailing gently down from her barely moving lips.

Rocket.

2006

On a dark, rainy afternoon in September, Ann pulls into the parking lot of a shop in Kennewick, Washington. It's Sunday; the shop is closed. The warm wind has swept the leaves into the pools held by the sloped pavement. Ann tries the locked door. She peers through the window above the CLOSED sign at a dark room.

She knocks on the window, waits, but no one comes.

Not knowing what else to do, exhausted with her nerves, she leans her back against the glass to stay dry under the overhanging roof, and she closes her eyes. She is a half hour late, and Tom has probably decided she isn't coming, just like the half dozen other times this past year when she tried coming with Wade and something came over him and they had to turn back. Now Wade is at home alone. Twice on the long drive here, she turned around to go back to him, but then she turned around again. That's what made her late, all her indecision and her fear.

There is a knock on the glass. She turns around, and Tom opens the door. It is the first time she's ever seen him. He is maybe a little older than she is, early forties, tall, with a long, thin face and dark-blond hair tied back in a ponytail. "I'm so sorry I'm late," she says.

"It's good to meet you." His voice gentle, calm.

She says, "I'm glad you changed your mind."

"I changed it years ago, but I couldn't tell you. I wasn't sure if it was right. Wade's okay at home?"

"Yes, he'll be okay." He helps her remove her dripping raincoat, hangs it up. "I don't know what help I can possibly be," she adds. "You know I never knew them."

"But you saw her."

"Only once."

"That might be more helpful than a hundred times," he says.

He leads Ann through the narrow shop, a bicycle shop, to the very back, where there is a door framed by the light inside the room it opens to. Before he opens the door, he pauses. "I should tell you that I have my doubts. I was good for a high school kid, but I think I peaked back then. I'll keep going, but I'm not accepting any money for it, anything beyond the cost of printing and postage."

"No," she says. "We're paying you. That's not up for debate."

He shakes his head, and looks like he might say something more, but he doesn't.

The room is cluttered and smells like old coffee, pencil shavings, bicycle grease. The walls are mostly bare, one of them water-stained. A bookshelf too large for the room holds jars of colored pencils, plaster casts of different faces cluttered around the jars of paintbrushes. Stacked on the floor are papers as large as blueprints, penciled fragments—a shoulder, a hand. And another stack of something else, covered in a sheet.

"It's the only place I have to do this," he apologizes.

But the desk is tidy. A glass of water rests on a closed sketch pad. Above the desk, thumbtacked to the wall, are three lines of photographs, each above the other. The first photograph in the top line shows a little boy she almost knows, a freckled boy, sitting in tall golden grass. The same boy grows up a little in each subsequent photograph, his freckles disappearing, and it isn't until Ann's eyes land on the shy-looking teenager leaning against a car that she understands what should have been obvious: The little boy is Wade. All these little boys are Wade at different points in time. Ann is taken aback to find him here—him, and his childhood.

Just below Wade, Jenny grows up in snapshots, too.

These are photographs Ann's never seen, but has been looking for, it seems, all of her married life. For so long, she has searched the mountain for traces of Jenny—ponytail holders shaken years ago from Jenny's hair, Chapstick fallen from jacket pockets. To see her like this, out of the dust, her chronological life laid out plainly on the wall, Ann feels alarmed by the dark simplicity of all that occurred. Jenny. She is a smiling little girl missing her front teeth. She grows new teeth in a flash, and in another flash hides her teeth altogether in a serene, close-lipped smile. Her hair is long, then short again. Her shoulder sunburned, then blinding white. In one photograph, labeled "16," Jenny wears a blue sleeveless blouse, stares into the camera with such honesty in her eyes that Ann has to look away.

Just below Jenny, in another, much shorter line, are photographs of June.

"You've never seen any of these," says Tom, not quite a question.

"What are they doing here?"

"Wade brought them to me years ago. They help me understand her genetics, like which features are late to show. She looks more like her dad when he was little, right?" Ann doesn't answer. She's too mystified. So much detail at once: the duct-taped buckle shoe Jenny as a little girl wears, the spotted horse nibbling her hair, the way she folds her hands on her lap, sitting by a pond. Never has Jenny been less real, less comprehensible, than she is now. So much more can be divined in the tattered label of a Chapstick tube. "But I think she might come to look more like her mom. She is twenty now," Tom says. "I'll show you what I have, but I can't promise they're any good."

"You said *is*," says Ann, softly.

"What do you mean?"

"Not *would be* twenty—*is*. Not even Wade has ever talked that way."

Nine years ago, in 1997, one year after Ann married Wade, she walked into the post office in Ponderosa, and she saw the first age-progressed image of June, produced by the National Center for Missing & Exploited Children. The flyer showed two pictures side by side. June at nine—the age she was when she went missing—and June at eleven, the age she would be if she had lived.

The first image, which was a photograph of June at nine, was taken professionally at Hayden Charter, the school where Ann taught choir. Sitting on the stool in front of an emerald backdrop Ann remembers once sitting in front of, too, June smiled weakly, her shoulders pushed up ever so slightly as if she had been caught there on that stool when she was supposed to have been elsewhere. There was a certain uneasiness about her gentle face, too, as if she were afraid of the camera flash. Even so, she was prepared enough for the school photograph to tilt her head a little to the side, something a lot of little girls did on picture day, as if a tilted head meant "pretty." Her dark, straight hair looked freshly trimmed. She wore a plain white collared shirt.

In the portrait beside it, which was produced on a computer but appeared to be a photograph, eleven-year-old June wore the same shirt, and nearly the same expression, except that her eyes were opened a little wider, and she seemed, in spite of these wide eyes, to be asleep. There was something absent, or nearly absent, in her expression, but it was also true that she looked, at first glance, like the girl the nine-year-old would have grown into. Only she did not lean forward or tilt her head. She did not look afraid. She looked like she was waiting, calmly, for something she had known all her life would arrive sometime soon. There was no anxiety in that face. Her hair, which in the first photograph fell at her jawline, had grown down to the middle of her chest, and was layered. There was a realistic flush on her cheeks, a resolve in her smile. All of her, so very real.

Ann had been unsettled when she saw the computer-generated image on the post office bulletin board. As real as it was, it was also a projection, a guess of life, a face manufactured out of the faces of those who had loved her.

No one but the missing are ever estimated in this way, Ann had thought. No one but the missing are granted, with such deliberate generosity, their grandmother's smiles, their father's chins, every trace of someone else a cry to believe in, a test of faith and a testament of family; these traits are the layers of pixels overlaid on a screen. A mother will emerge on a daughter's face long after mother and daughter are lost to each other. Even a mother who killed: Her features are given their due; the resemblance isn't softened because of what the mother's done. The daughter isn't spared, even in this afterlife, her mother's nose. The particulars of that nose are what might save her, after all, bring her out of the darkness these pretend photographs reveal, make her real again, make her, against all odds, recognized. Found.

Ann and Wade have received an age-progressed photo every two years. But now that June would be twenty, they will receive one every five. June will be caught in these instants smiling peacefully from her hypothetical future. Reluctant and grateful, June will stare out from the walls of department stores, from the back pages of real estate pamphlets rolled up in mailboxes. Revealed, patient, tired, her expression trying to hide the weight of the grace she's been saddled with, to go on living, aging, beyond the scope of her real life.

Bones in the wild grass, brought up by rain: a much better guess, but too obvious to believe.

Ann and Wade did not talk about that first flyer on the Ponderosa post office bulletin board, but she sensed in Wade, in those weeks that followed, a discontent, a restless focus. One morning she woke up and Wade was gone. It was a few months since the age-progressed photo had appeared. On the table, Wade had left an unsealed envelope with Ann's name on it.

Inside the envelope was a photocopy of a newspaper article, dated almost sixteen years prior, September 1981.

> Alana Onbrook, who ran away from her home on the Nez Perce Reservation in 1978 at age 14, was reunited with her family Tuesday morning at the age of 17 following a stranger's recognition of her at a motel in Spokane.
>
> Seattle resident Jim Lee, who recognized Onbrook and called the police, says that he saw a "Missing Persons" flyer on a window at a Seattle gas station. He says the flyer caught his eye because it was not computer-generated, like the usual government-issued flyers depicting the age progression of a missing child, but was rather a full-color photograph of a painting.
>
> Also unusual, Lee says, is that the flyer showed more than Onbrook's face. It depicted her whole body, and included such details as a band T-shirt, a cigarette between her fingers, recognizable Seattle graffiti on the wall behind her, and leaves and trash blowing across the sidewalk, over her bare feet. "There was even a toe ring," Lee recalls.
>
> Authorities learned Wednesday that the portrait artist, Onbrook's cousin Tom Clark, is 18. He was 17 at the time he made the flyers and distributed them to major cities across the country.

"It was my senior project in high school," Clark said Wednesday. "I'm as shocked as everyone."

For his senior project at Kennewick High, Clark painted 20 different scenes depicting his would-be-16-year-old missing cousin in various places across the country. He drew her working in an apple orchard; on a street corner, homeless; on a country road, petting a llama, among many other scenes, he says.

Clark says he got the idea for the project when he first saw his cousin's age-progressed picture, produced by the National Center for Missing & Exploited Children (NCMEC), on the bulletin board at a Kennewick post office. Clark used the facial structure the NCMEC predicted, but added his own flourishes.

His art teacher and mentor, Diana Siegal, who supervised the project, says she was so moved by the paintings that she gave Clark $300 for printing and postage. Clark used the money to mail the flyers to businesses he'd never been to in more than 15 American cities.

The NCMEC reports that the odds of finding a missing child decrease significantly every hour during the first three days a child is missing. "We are very aware of how lucky we are," says Onbrook's mother, Tracy. "Because of Tom, our family can finally begin to heal."

In the bicycle shop in Kennewick, twenty-year-old June stands in a watercolor painting, the yard all around her littered with children's toys, junked bicycles, a tattered American flag.

In the bicycle shop in Kennewick, twenty-year-old June puts gas in her dented blue Nissan at a filling station whose dirty window advertises beer and fishing tackle.

In the bicycle shop in Kennewick, twenty-year-old June leans against a brick wall, holding a cardboard sign—DO YOU SEE ME?—her enormous coat patched with duct tape, her hair in dreadlocks, her feet wrapped in a scarf, a scratch of snow across the sidewalk.

In the bicycle shop in Kennewick, twenty-year-old June stands in a highway ditch, reaches over a barbed-wire fence to pet a red horse.

In the bicycle shop in Kennewick, twenty-year-old June wears a short dress and too much makeup on a city street; on a park bench, she wears reading glasses, a yellow blouse; on a dock on a river, she holds a blond-haired child whose face is hidden in her shoulder; she sits on a twin bed in a run-down motel, her face frightened and resigned, her eyes black.

Ann closes her eyes. She is sitting on a wooden stool. Tom sits on a chair beside her. The sound of the rain pounding on the roof has ceased. A fresh yellow light enters the storefront, reaches all the way to the back room where they are, and Ann can feel this light on her closed eyelids. She opens them. "How long did it take you to paint all these?"

Tom, sitting in the office chair, with the canvases spread all across the desk, says, "I couldn't get your husband out of my head. Even though I told him I wouldn't do it when he came to me in '97, almost right away I started painting her. I've painted her off and on for the last nine years, until I finally decided to call him."

"Why now?"

"Because I saw the most recent flyer of June. And it just didn't seem right to me."

"Nine years," Ann repeats, looking at the paintings. She does see what Tom means about his abilities; there is something untrained about his art, something slightly immature. He is talented, but the perspective is strange; or maybe it's the shadows that are not quite right. And yet, he has captured something in June's face that cameras and computers have failed to capture, something Ann had seen in June the one time she ever saw her.

She picks up one of the canvasses. June's eyes are lit up, like she's just been laughing. She sits on the edge of a trampoline in a trashy yard, in a yellow bikini top and jean shorts, a shining magazine on her lap. There are dark freckles on her chest.

"Others must have come to you for help?" says Ann.

"Twenty-three other families, most of them in the early eighties, right after Alana was found. I told them finding my cousin was a fluke. I couldn't handle it."

"Maybe it wasn't a fluke."

"My aunt thought I was exploiting Alana, using her for an art project. She was right. I didn't know it then, but when someone spotted her, I was so shocked that I knew that I'd never actually believed this could work." He shakes his head. "The article about me was picked up by the Associated Press. And soon there was a man at my door telling me that his son was abducted ten years before from a street fair in Iowa. He forced money into my hands and I forced it back into his. One woman had a baby stolen eight years before out of a carseat. She wanted me to draw her infant as an eight-year-old. She kept shaking this picture at me, until I practically slammed the door in her face." He looks down at the paintings. "Your husband, when he came to me nine years ago, I hadn't had someone come in a long time. It took me by surprise." He points to the wall above the desk, at the old photographs of Jenny and Wade and June. "Your husband left these pictures in my mailbox."

For a moment, they study the photographs of Wade and Jenny and June. Ann looks into the eyes of the little boy, Wade, standing in the grass. She thinks of all the things he doesn't know yet.

Then, as if Tom has been debating whether or not to mention it, he says, "He left a knife in my mailbox, too." Ann feels her heart catch. "At first I thought it was a threat. Then I didn't know what I thought. If he'd left money, I would have given it away, I would have been so mad. But I kept the knife."

Tom opens the desk drawer, where Ann can see now the small

parcel, wrapped in loose, thin leather. Tom hands this parcel to Ann. She unravels the leather, drops it to the floor.

The knife is the very same knife she herself once kept in her own desk drawer, the one June left for Eliot.

A carved house. A handle of bone.

When Wade came home from Kennewick nine years ago, he told Ann only, "I did what I could. But he said no." She helped him take off his coat. They sat down on the bed together.

Both were quiet for a while. Then she said, "How did you find that article?"

"One of June's old teachers sent it."

"Did I know her?"

"No, not at your school, her first-grade teacher. He's been in touch a few times. He saw the new picture of June in the post office and he remembered reading about Tom."

"How do you feel?"

"It would have been a long shot," he said.

She sensed some of the old danger subside, and she said, without her usual caution, "You don't like the flyer in the post office."

"I don't dislike it. It does seem like what she would look like now."

"But you feel something else, too."

He looked down at his hands holding hers on his lap. Then he said, "She looks tired."

"Yes."

"She looks too young to be that tired."

"Yes."

"It lacks hope. I want to hope."

Two years after that, in 1999, the National Center for Missing & Exploited Children sent another flyer, which Ann saw, again, on the Ponderosa bulletin board. June, age hypothetical thirteen. Her face slightly more mature, her smile touched with lip gloss. A hint of breasts inside her polo shirt. But still the same calm expression, the same unsettling peace in her eyes.

Again the official updated pictures came, in 2001, then in 2003. Age fifteen, age seventeen. Her expression growing farther and farther away, almost vacant now, the face of a ghost. Only a few days after the 2005 portrait appeared on the bulletin board—age nineteen, green polo shirt, sky-blue backdrop, lipstick instead of gloss—Tom Clark finally called Wade.

But by that time, Wade, only fifty-one, had begun to change. Much of his concentration was taken up hiding the fact of his failing memory, pretending he knew what was going on. But it became clear to Ann that he did not remember the Kennewick artist, and maybe periodically did not remember his daughter was lost, just that she was somewhere else, out of touch.

Four different times over that year, she tried driving him to Kennewick to meet the artist she had spoken to on the phone. But each time, somewhere around Medical Lake, Wade became angry with her. He accused her of not looking hard enough.

"Not looking hard enough for what?" she asked.

But he did not know what he felt beyond that, just that she was tricking him, that she was pretending to search for something she didn't want to find.

His anxiety was such that she worried he'd have a heart attack if they drove on, or else that he would become so upset as to cause an accident by grabbing her like he had before, which is why, today, after a year of trying to get here with Wade, she drove here, to Kennewick, alone.

∎

The knife allows Ann to access something she nearly doesn't have, a whole and unwavering impression of the little girl who had stolen it, a new knowledge of June that is not new at all but has for so long been the center of all other impressions that paring it down to itself makes it seem new.

Because of the object on the table, Ann is able to tell Tom, with shocking confidence, what he needs to know. This is the reason she came, to help him understand enough to paint her. "She looks too resigned here," she says, holding a canvas away from her to better see it. "What if her eyebrows were raised a little, like she's afraid she's missing something?" Tom nods. He makes a note. "Something about her hands here is right. Those are her hands. Not just how they look, but how she held them, how she would hold a baby if she had one."

Then, about a different picture: "I wonder if she should look a little more confident here on the trampoline, like finally she has something she has wanted badly for a really long time."

"Like what?" Tom asks, and Ann sees that he's bewildered by her confidence, that he never believed she could offer this much.

"Womanhood," says Ann.

He looks at her, unsure.

"Her new body," says Ann, embarrassed.

At some point in their talk, Tom opened the shop door to let in the fresh, after-rain air. It's evening and the birds are singing outside, and their song is carried through the shop.

"She's wearing yellow," says Ann, realizing this for the first time. "In all of these pictures. I didn't see that before. Even the yellow scarf around her feet."

"Yes, I— Yes," says Tom, and there is something strange about his expression.

"She liked pink as a little girl," says Ann, remembering the wild-rose-colored shoes and the ragged petally sweater, and the tissue paper she once wrapped around the box that held the knife now gleaming on the desk before them. Tom does not say anything more about the color, but writes something down.

They continue on like this for quite a while, deciding which of the paintings should be sent to which cities, how many copies to make.

"I like this one for the bulletin board in Ponderosa, where we live," says Ann, pointing to the picture of June reaching out to pet a horse over a barbed-wire fence. "It has the most hope. I want Wade to see this one when we go to get the mail."

"I agree," says Tom. "I don't think it would do any good to show him all of them. Some of them are hard to see."

"They all are," says Ann.

"Yes," says Tom. "They are."

Later, in the dark parking lot with its rich smell of leaves and rain, she pauses for a moment beside her car. Tom has walked her out to say goodbye. She is filled with a reluctance to leave. She says, "I know it doesn't seem like they're my family, but they are. And I want them all to be together here." From her purse, she takes out the Polaroid she has kept there all these years, the picture her broom found underneath the refrigerator, of May sitting on a stump with her doll.

She hands it to Tom. She knows that face so well, she doesn't need to look at it again. She says, "Will you put it up on your wall? It's the only one I have."

"Are you sure?"

"She belongs with them. With all of them."

"I'll put her there."

She nods, then she gets into her car.

Driving the three hours home through the darkness, Ann thinks of the two sisters, the one she saw for a moment, and the one she never saw and whose photograph she's just put into the hands of someone she will likely never see again. June's life on Tom Clark's wall will get longer and longer; it will go on and on in endless speculation, painting after painting, all the years of her hypothetical life. But May's life stops at that Polaroid. No one is guessing for her. No one asks what she would look like at seventeen. *Would*—when her sister is *might*. There is no understanding such a discrepancy. The suddenness of that stopped life, the shocking end of all imagery. May, at the moment she died, became something she had never been before and that her sister will never be—absolute.

Ann drives on and on; the little towns are scarce lights in the dark. She knows that what she and Wade and Tom are doing is futile. The whole project is an act of desperation. Each scene Tom paints becomes, by virtue of his having painted it, the most unlikely scene of all because it is the one that he has guessed. June on a trampoline. June petting that horse. Those possibilities vanish as soon as they are thought of. The world doesn't work that way.

And yet—and yet—Alana was found. How can it be that Alana was found?

Ann's life, for ten years now, ever since she married Wade, has followed this secret trail of lost images, real and imagined. A Polaroid under a refrigerator, into her purse, into the hand of a stranger, onto the wall of a bicycle shop. Ann never showed Wade that Polaroid of May, and she never told him about June at Eliot's locker. Her impressions and connections are so fragile, even though, somehow, her marriage isn't. Her marriage to Wade is a sound and solid thing, composed of so many shattered flashes overlaid by shattered flashes that there is no way to slip between them anymore. She loves him. Oh, how much she loves him. And she's afraid that one day he will ask himself again why Jenny did what she did. Ann is afraid that he will discover herself in the answer; she is afraid, too, that there is no answer; and she is also afraid that there is and that he will lose that answer soon, will lose what he doesn't know is the connection that would kill him.

Please let him never ask, please let him never wonder, please never let him implicate his heart in what occurred, as she has had to implicate her own. Ann will never ask Wade her one last question.

What was May singing that day? Could you hear, through the truck windows, the words of that song?

This question returns to her at moments like these, moments when she's alone. It's been two years now since she found herself standing in the snow in the middle of the woods looking down at an armchair and a lamp that one and only time she ever ran from her life with Wade. It was there in the woods two years ago that the question took form in her mind: Not to have the answer—that is why she can return to those woods forever, can work through the logic and the likelihood again and again, can give images to a phantom possibility just as Tom gives images to June. First she might tell herself, *How can you go on, knowing you were there in that truck, knowing you were the reason for all of this?* And then she will see how self-centered that is, how pointlessly destructive. A person knows thousands of songs and can access tens of thousands of strands of other songs she doesn't quite know. Even a child. Why, of all those thousands, and of all the infinite possible songs made up in a moment, songs made of nonsense, of objects in proximity to the singer, does May have to sing the song that Ann taught Wade?

Senseless speculations.

It is the most unlikely thing of all because it is the thing she's guessed.

And yet—and yet.

The way Tom had looked at her, it was as if he could see plainly the connection she's afraid of. It pains her to think of someone else now following the path that she is making. She has taken Wade's past and she's laid it out in front of her, her future a backward trail, even as it disappears. That slow erasure, that white line through all that darkness in his memory, is what she will follow through her life. And surely it will lead her to her own secret prison, will take her right up to its doors.

1999

A knock on the door—a kindness so foreign at Sage Hill that Jenny doesn't comprehend it. She does not say, "Come in." The knock has been transformed already in her mind to a memory of a different sound, the *thunk* of her forehead against her window earlier today, when she hit it on purpose just hard enough to make a lavender bruise, which is something new to look at in the window's reflection. Otherwise, out the window there is only another nauseating wall, whose cracks she has followed so intricately they have become the hairline fractures in her vision, through which the dark migraine seeps. Her inch-thick mattress smells like urine and tears. The television, always off, high in the corner of the room, makes her feel uneasy, as if it is watching her. The blanket is as rough as burlap, and in this moment she rubs it on her thighs to ease the itch of the rash spreading there and on the small of her back.

She is forty-five years old. She has been in this cell, alone, since she was forty-one.

Another knock. This time, she turns around.

The door opens, and a woman guard about her age steps inside. "I received a message that you're needed. I have the phone number for you to call."

"Who?" She tastes blood.

"I don't know."

"My husband?"

"I don't know."

"I can't."

"You won't come?"

"I don't know."

The woman comes to the bed, touches Jenny's arm gently. "Sit up." Jenny sees her face, brusque and practical eyes. "Follow me."

Jenny's bare feet are blackened from the cell floor, toenails eaten by an infection she hides because she doesn't care about healing it. The loose clothes hang on her body. She wants Wade to see her suffering so he'll be at peace. She wants him to smell her suffering so he'll turn away. She feels such scenes approaching. But in the room where the woman leads her, there is only a metal chair bolted into the floor and a telephone sitting on a counter in front of the chair. The woman hands her the slip of paper. Jenny doesn't recognize the phone number. It isn't an Idaho area code. Has Wade moved? It's been four years. So much might have changed.

Even the uncertainty of his phone number hurts her; it opens up the opportunity for visualizing what she's been so careful all these years not to visualize. Wade's life. His physical form. His clothes. His movements. Where is he?

Jenny coughs hard into her hand to clear her throat. She feels dizzy, but still she lifts the receiver to her ear. She dials the number. It rings twice. An operator asks her to say her name.

"Jenny Mitchell," she manages.

After a moment, a man's voice says, "Mrs. Mitchell?"

But the man on the other end is not Wade. She's so relieved and simultaneously so disappointed that she begins to cry, silently, holding that receiver to her ear.

"Is this Mrs. Mitchell?"

"I'm divorced." Her voice raw.

"But your husband was Wade Mitchell?"

Her whole body trembles. Tears fall from her eyes, burn the cracks of her lips. "What happened?"

"My name is Tom. I'm—"

"Wade's okay?"

"I think so. I saw him two years ago."

"Where?" Her head buzzes.

He speaks quickly. "I'm an artist working on age-progressed pictures of your daughter."

"You're from the Center for Missing Children?"

"No. Please don't tell Wade that I'm doing this," he says.

"But he asked you to?"

"But I said no. I said very emphatically no. But I can't get her out of my head. I want to try to help, but I have to see first what I'm capable of."

"No one ever sent me any of those flyers. I don't know what you're asking."

"It's hard to know, really," he says, then tries a soft laugh, but it sounds strange. "It might not even be real. I read something about age-progressed pictures, about how they're made. I read that some mothers know things they can't."

She feels her heart race.

"And I wonder," he continues, "I wonder what you know. About June. For my picture. Something about June."

It takes the strength of her whole hand to hold the phone up to her ear. Her hands are strange in the yellow light, like an old woman's hands. There are things she knows, yes, June used to read books—books with faces on the front, little girls—June let an apple rot in a raincoat pocket an entire summer, her room smelled like cider. The apple turned to mush, brown putrid cold sweet mush. Jenny, looking for a knife June stole, dipped her hand in that pocket and screamed with surprise at the mush—June sitting in front of the closet, those twitching hands—the tangled mat in June's hair the size of a kitten when they cut it off of her, a kitten on the floor May played with, tied it to a string, set out a bowl of milk—she once had a different name—put it in your picture what she used to be named—

"Mrs. Mitchell?"

"I'm divorced," she says, angry. The tears still streaming down. How to put it in a photograph, the smell of the moldered apple, the twitching imagination of those hands?

She feels panicked, dizzy. "I have something," she says. But she doesn't know what it is she has, and she begins crying, freely now.

"Do you want to call me back? Why don't you call me back, after you have some time to think."

"Tomorrow," she says. "I will call you tomorrow."

Back in her cell, out of breath, she stares out the window at the wall, her whole body shaking, wanting desperately to see past those gray cracked stones.

But the sameness of that prison wall is like a winter spent in a wilderness you can't hope to matter to. And there is never anything to see. Now it is the gray wall that blocks her vision. Back then, it was snow and trees and animals with expressions like the winter itself, impersonal and honest and cruel. Everything sees past her and saw past her then. No sign from the mountain or the prison that she is anything at all.

If only the winter could have opened up to show her it was vulnerable, too. The sound of running water far below the ice. Secrets sleeping, waiting. Shocking. Like the features of a newborn face where she had expected to find only softness, only some muddled promise of a person, not those wide-open eyes with their fierce assertions of life.

Her missing daughter. June.

The greatest torture of these walls is that they stop her from searching. If she could, she would trudge through the wilderness without resting, calling her daughter's name until her voice was burned and gone. She would walk without sleeping, walk until she collapsed on that mountain she made terrible. Then she would fold herself up inside a half-believed footprint, and she would die there. Searching. Coyotes would eat her daughter's name right out of her.

She goes on thinking this way for hours, straining her eyes to see past the gray wall, through those cracks into this other future, where her daughter runs, where she chases. Her head aches. She doesn't eat the food offered to her at one, inserted through the drawer. She seldom eats it, but scrapes it into the garbage so they think she has.

At five o'clock, there are two men at the door, just like always. They are here to offer her an hour of exercise. And just like always, staring out her window, she opens her dry mouth.

But this time, she says, "Yes."

She is as surprised as they are. It is the only time that she has ever said yes to a walk outside. They don't ask why. They open the door.

Outside, the air is smooth. Her skin hasn't felt the sun in four years. The pavement is wet—has it rained? She walks on the yellow line, the painted path she isn't allowed to stray from. The sunlight chills her, the surprise of heat, buttery light on her arms.

Down the hill, outside the fence, she sees the town of Sage. She sees the smear of sunlight on the face of a clock gleaming on a tower and the McDonald's *M*. All of it hurts her eyes. The two men hold her up so easily, she is like a child. What must she look like? Pale, bruised, her clothes too large on her body. Sometimes she can't move her feet, and so the men nearly drag her. Each man has an arm hooked in hers.

The pools of wet sun are like the cool, spotted sounds of stethoscopes. Smudges of footsteps, the wounds their unborn feet once tread in her. How dark and bright at once, their kicking in the night.

She sucks the hot, smooth air. Dandelions bloom in clusters all along the bottom of the fence, their heads poking through the loops. She closes her eyes. The summer evening sun presses on her eyelids.

She's in a kitchen. She's making a lemon meringue. June and May fighting in the kitchen. Not play-fighting. May hitting June on her temple with a spoon. June screaming she will kill May. Neither one will stop because neither one will stop. Jenny is in the middle of all of this trying to measure the sugar. May bumps her leg and she drops the cup of sugar all over the top of June's head. None left in the bag, both girls yelling. She is about to lose her temper, about to scream. Her hands reach for the closest thing. The closest thing. Her hands lift up two eggs from the open carton on the counter. "Here," she says. "Go hatch these. Both of you."

Silence.

Each girl holds out both her hands, cups each egg between them, already whispering through the shell, proclaiming devotion, *Little baby, little chick.* They hurry out two different doors, over two different lawns, out to different corners of the land. And for hours after that, for days, they are careful, flushed, quietly agonized. They know about the hens, about heat. They make nests in the hay. Nests in the drawers. They hold the eggs up to their bellies. They find each other, put their two eggs close, breathe hot air on them. Lay them in the sunlight on top of a pillow.

Jenny opens her eyes. Tell him, put it in the picture, the color, the white pillowcase with that egg in the center and the egg's oval shadow overlapping the shadow of the curved hand so close to it, a

167

dark and yellow crescent shadow because something in that room is believed in—

Even though it's all a trick. Nothing but cold yolk inside.

A trick. The dandelions. *Momma had a baby and her head popped off!* What had it meant, Momma's head or baby's? She must not remember right. The grass along the fence smells sweet. The pop of those joyful blossoms up into the air, sudden death, the children laugh. Or another game, a test for love. Rub the blossom on the wrist and does it leave a mark? Or—hold a buttercup under someone's chin, see if it makes a yellow glow. It's supposed to mean something about the person, supposed to tell a secret she doesn't want told.

The chins always glow yellow. That's the trick: There's always a secret. Everyone has something she doesn't want told. The yellow shadow under June's chin. She's terrified that someone will see it. She's terrified that someone won't. She's afraid the trick won't work on her, just her in all the world, just on her the yellow won't show. She is terrified of being different even if it keeps her safe.

Put that yellow shadow on her throat. Put it in the picture.

That is all that she can manage. Fifteen minutes have gone by. The two men nearly have to carry her back, and in her cell she crawls onto the pad half asleep, relieved, feeling as if she has already told the artist what to do, what to put into his picture to save her daughter: Dress June in yellow.

"The rest of her life," she mutters in bed.

When she wakes, she finds her hand curved around a golden apple they must have given her as a kindness, maybe because they saw that she was weaker than they knew. She cups it below her chin, against her chest, and looks out again at the wall.

1973

The dog on the farmer's porch doesn't run toward Wade like she usually does when he arrives for work. She thumps her tail, but that is all. She doesn't even lift her head.

Wade sees her from a distance, just her shape lying down on the porch. He is nineteen years old and has just parked his truck at the ranch where he's been hired to move irrigation pipes in a hay field. The dog is one he knows well, a black-and-white border collie missing her right eye. Often, she follows him as he works.

He gets out of the truck and calls to her. "Come on, come here."

She comes. She's wagging her tail and she seems okay, but it looks like there is something caught around her neck. He steps toward her, squinting into the sunlight, trying to get a better look, and then he sees.

A chicken.

A chicken?

He gets closer.

A dead chicken is tied with rope to the dog's collar, tied so tightly that the dog has trouble breathing. She pants with every labored step she takes toward Wade, the terrible weight of the dead hen pulling on her throat.

They meet each other on the dusty driveway. Wade kneels down. He knows without a doubt this dog has killed this hen. He knows without a doubt that these ropes around her neck that hold the hen in place have been tied there by his boss, the farmer, Grant. So this is Grant's idea of training. Wade has seen this kind of punishment before. Let the hen or goose or duck—whatever it is— hang there until it rots, its smell mingled up in the dog's brain with hunger and disgust and the memory of a beating. Let it pull on the dog's neck for weeks, so that the dog will learn by the weight and the smell of congealed blood the consequence of disobedience.

Wade fumbles for his pocketknife. This is not the way to teach a dog. It's true that she might not kill a hen again, but it will be a different kind of not-killing. It will be out of fear, of you.

But make a dog learn out of love, then the not-killing it learns will be out of love, too. Push its snout into the feathers once, say, "No," then let it go. It's done. The release is where it learns. The momentary weight of your hand, your heavy disappointment, then the sudden lightness, forgiveness.

In front of the farmhouse, Wade applies his blade to the rope. Tied in many places around the collar, it frays and slips away. The dead hen falls to the driveway. A puff of dust. The dog looks up at Wade, tongue hanging out, thumping her tail. He holds his hand in front of her, and she licks it gently, as if to clean a wound.

Wade quits his job without a word. He pats the seat of his truck with his hand, and the dog jumps up.

She is the only good thing that has happened to him since his dad died months ago. Watching the funny little dog snap in the wrong direction at flies, watching her bark at the field mice through the window, he feels for the first time since that terrible day that his life might go on.

He names her Rose, like a compass rose, because in the evenings he sits beside her and looks out the window of his childhood home on the Camas Prairie, looks north, at the mountains. Her black nose points in that direction.

He gets another job on another field. Mint, this time. While he's at work, the dog stays home with Wade's mother, Sarah. All day, he looks forward to the glad bark of approval, of continued surprise at the keeping of any promise. Rose waits for him on the porch for most of the day. She sleeps on top of his covers, her head on his arm. She mopes around at night not with boredom or sadness but with the weight of such hungry obedience. She loves so much and doesn't know, even when Wade is right there, where to put all of that loyalty. She raises both eyebrows when she looks at him, even though one has no eye beneath it to shine out her simple questions.

For months, he teaches her the things it seems she begs, with her sad yellow eye, to know.

Then one July morning, very early on the field, when the sun has just risen but already the heat is beating down, when the pipes look like impossibly thin lines of light lain evenly across the green land, he sees the outline of a woman in the distance.

Across the field, he sees her step over the pipes he has yet to move, holding the skirt of her dress bunched up in one hand while the other hand strays outward, as if for balance. She walks in a straight line toward him.

He doesn't stop working, but he feels for an instant an awful pang of hope. He has never been with a woman before, and so his hope is unspecific, long-standing, sad, is merely her movement toward him. But in the next instant, he has another feeling about her, too, about the way she moves. It is a terrible feeling, a kind of dread that he doesn't understand. He tries to shake it, but the closer she comes, the closer he comes to understanding.

His mom. She walked that way only once, early one winter morning. He saw her from his bedroom window. She was walking toward the house, holding her arms around herself, moving toward Wade with purpose, a strange excitement, unaware that he was watching her from his window. Had he not just received a telephone call she didn't know about, a call from a neighbor who told him his dad had frozen to death in the night, Wade would have thought the strange way his mom was walking meant she was concealing some miraculous surprise. But the joy in his mother's steps, or what Wade perceived as joy, was merely the awareness in her body of those moments being suspended in time, unreal, existing nowhere, between her old life and her new life. Until she told Wade that his dad was dead, it was as if he were not.

How could she have walked like that to get to him, to tell him what he'd lost?

Now Wade sees in this woman the same composed and terrible purpose, and he doesn't understand why. Even when she is close enough he can hear her call—"Wade?"—he pretends not to see her.

Before long, she is shouting, a few feet away from him. "Hey!"

He stops. He wipes the sweat off his forehead with his shirt. "Are you Wade Mitchell?" she asks with annoyance. She is about his age. Her brown eyes hold defiance but also some fear she tries desperately to hide with the straight way she stands there in front of him. Her brown hair is held away from her face with a yellow bandanna, strands of it flying up in the hot, tea-scented wind. Her forehead is freckled and the top of it is pink and flaking with sunburn.

She drops the long cotton dress and folds her arms in front of her.

"Can I help you?" he says.

"I've been looking all over for you," she says. "You have my dog."

It is so simple, what she wants, so much less than he thought—what could he possibly have thought?—that at first he feels relieved. But in the next moment, the loss of Rose seems the worst thing of all.

"No I don't." He lifts the pipe at his feet.

"You do. You stole her from Grant Warner."

He holds the long pipe in both his hands. Water pours out either end. "Do you know what your boyfriend did to that dog?"

She looks surprised. "He's my cousin. Whatever he did he shouldn't have, because she's my dog, and I didn't give him permission to do anything."

"If she's your dog, why wasn't she with you?"

"I go to Whitman. I couldn't take her to college."

"So you're home for the summer and want her back. Then what? You go off again and leave her with him?"

She seems angry now. "I lived in the dorms, but next year I'll be in a house with a yard. Not that I need to justify myself to you."

"You don't leave a dog with a man like that," Wade says, turning away, carrying the pipe. "I don't care if she was yours, you lost your privilege when he hung a barred rock from her neck."

"I don't know anything about the rock," she says, "but if he did, he shouldn't have, I agree."

Wade laughs, unkindly. "Barred rock," he tells her, setting the pipe down. But still she doesn't understand. "A chicken," he says. "It's a type of chicken."

"A chicken?"

"A dead chicken."

She seems caught off-guard, but regains herself quickly. "I'm sorry that happened. I will tell Grant I don't appreciate it. Grant won't come near her again."

"You tell him you don't appreciate it," Wade says coldly. Then he turns his back and moves on.

"I'm going to wait for you," she calls. "At your truck. I won't take you from your work, but afterward you're taking me to my dog."

At that, she turns abruptly away so that he can't argue, and begins walking through the field toward the house.

He works later than he needs to, trying to think of how he can put her off. All along he is aware of her car parked near the farmhouse. Every now and then she starts the engine and moves the car to new shade.

The farmer's boy, Jacob, is aware of her, too, and regards her with a strange jealousy and vengeance. He is ten years old and fiercely loyal to Wade, spending his afternoons trailing behind him as he works, asking questions about dogs, and death, and most of all, with a fascination that borders on pain, about a place his teacher has mentioned that is called the Galápagos.

In the barn, Jacob tells Wade, "I hate her."

Wade sighs. "You probably shouldn't say that," he says.

"But I hate her."

"You can feel whatever you like."

So Jacob returns to the farmhouse and comes out a few minutes later, in order to throw two cinnamon rolls at her windshield.

"You did what?" laughs Wade.

"I threw them as hard as I could." Then, in a lowered voice, he says, "I think she ate one later, though."

"Off her windshield?"

The boy smiles. "No, out of the dirt."

When evening arrives and there is nothing else Wade can do, he returns to his truck. On the way, he sees her in her car, curled up in the driver's seat asleep, a book opened and splayed on the seat beside her. In the nice cool of the evening, she has covered herself with a jacket.

He gets into his truck and turns the engine on. He sees her in his rearview mirror startle awake, grip her steering wheel.

It is not a long drive to his home. She follows closely.

"Come on in," Wade says with resignation when they arrive at the house, and when he opens the front door, Rose barks joyfully.

"Oh, Peggy!" cries the girl, as if the bark is meant for her. She kneels down and pats the floor. The dog comes toward her, shyly, wagging her whole body side to side with her head down, looking up at Wade with confusion.

"She doesn't know you," Wade says.

"Yes she does," says the girl in a bright but angry voice, smiling hard at the dog. "Hey, girl," she says, "you're my dog! You're my good girl!" Then she stands. "I can pay you for taking care of her for me. I was paying Grant." She opens her purse for some money, but Wade shakes his head. She looks ashamed at his refusal, and lingers in the living room for a moment, searching the high, bare walls for something kind to say.

"Well, thank you" is what she settles on, quickly, then goes out the open door and calls to the dog. When Rose won't go, Wade steps outside, too, and then Rose follows. Once at her car, she pats the seat inside, and the dog looks at Wade, who says, "Up," and the dog jumps.

Once in her car, the girl rolls the window down. "I had the eye removed," she says, in a new voice now, pleading. "I was only fourteen, and I used my own money for it. All the money I had. It was cancerous and needed to be removed, and no one else was going to do it. I've had her all her life."

"What's your name?" Wade says to her, a little coldly, bending down to see her through the half-open window.

"Jenny."

"Well, Jenny, you don't need to convince me. She's your dog. She's in your car now, isn't she?"

She looks ahead, her face different now. Her voice has tears in it. "I didn't know about the barred rock," she insists.

175

"I know," he says, more softly.

She turns the key and the engine comes on. She looks straight ahead for a moment more, waiting for something to occur to her to say, but nothing does.

She drives away.

Wade stands in the green grass in front of his house for a long time after she is gone, and he looks out at the empty fields beyond the fence and what he feels is even worse than when his father died. A terrible thing to admit to himself. But it isn't just the loss of Rose that hurts him. What he felt the first time he saw Jenny coming toward him—what made him recall his mom's grimly cheerful walk on the day his dad died—was right: What Jenny carried with her over that field was surely news of death. What he saw in that walk was the broken promise of his life: Someday he would forget her, forget even the way the light had landed in her hair, forget her stubborn, defiant look there among the faint brown freckles on her face.

In the early fall, the farmers burn the fields. The smoke stings Wade's eyes as he works, training horses now, mostly, and preparing for winter. The loss of Rose has made him quiet, resigned, and Jacob understands this. He follows Wade in near silence, too. He assumes Wade's sadness as his own.

Wade's mom has tried to persuade him to get another dog. He tells her he's all right, because in a lot of ways, he is. The smell of burning fields is an odd comfort to him. This is the first year since he started school that he doesn't go. He breathes in with the smoke a different kind of sadness that is not so unwelcome. It is not the sharp grief he has felt for months now, but a quiet, familiar, and long-standing heartbreak that has less to do with his dad, and Rose, and more to do with the changing trees and the new chill and charred soil that mark a yearly routine that goes on in spite of everything.

One Saturday, Wade and Jacob go walking together in the burned field, picking up tools the farmer lost from the open toolbox on the back of his tractor. Wade has found only a few tools so far in the black soil. Jacob is trying to help him, scanning the ground for the unlikely glimmers of metal.

"There," says Jacob, with excitement, and runs to something shining on the ground a short distance away.

But it is only the shine of foil that is wrapped around some jerky the farmer probably kept in the open toolbox, too. Jacob unwraps the jerky, and begins to gnaw on a piece of it. He offers a piece to Wade.

But as Wade holds out his hand to accept it, he sees someone coming toward them, still far away, over Jacob's shoulder. At first he thinks it is the farmer, but then he sees, not far behind, a dog.

Jenny walks with her head down, over the black soil.

"She took your dog," shouts the boy, at the sight of her. Then, in a whisper, "Don't look at her. Don't talk to her." But Wade only stares. He feels again the hope and dread he felt before. Jacob pulls on his sleeve again, but in that moment it seems the dog has caught Wade's scent over the smell of the smoky ground, and Rose runs as fast as she can ahead of Jenny.

Wade kneels down. The dog comes right to him, right between his crouching legs, and he puts his nose into her matted fur, squeezes both her ears with both his hands. Jacob kneels down, too, runs his fingers through her fur, fascinated, and then, when the dog turns to him, offers her a bit of jerky.

But Jacob stands again, defensively, once Jenny is near. This time she wears jeans and a jacket, her hands inside her pockets. She stands with her head tilted down, her hair falling freely over her shoulders.

"I thought you might like to see her," she says.

"You're giving her back?" demands Jacob, sensing his role as ambassador.

"It's just a visit. I'm home from school for the weekend."

Wade says nothing, except, "Hello, hello," not to Jenny but to the dog. He can't think of what else to do, so he repeats this over and over again, as if he has not noticed Jenny standing there, waiting for him to respond.

"Is this your little helper?" Jenny asks, nodding to Jacob, who winces at the insult.

Wade stands, finally, Rose pawing at his leg. "You ever heard of the Galápagos?" Wade says to Jenny. Jenny laughs, confused. "You're looking at an expert. Tell her," he says, nodding at Jacob.

"Just school stuff," Jacob mumbles.

"That's where the tortoises are," she says, to encourage him.

Jacob scoffs. "Well, there's a lot more than tortoises."

"Like what?" She is trying. Jacob can see that, and he hates her more for it.

"No dogs, if that's what you're asking."

Wade is so startled, so touched by Jacob's anger, that he laughs. Jacob is startled, too, at the fact of Wade's laughter, which he believes—Wade can see in the small, hurt face—to be against him. The child looks at Wade, and then at Jenny, and he stands there beside them, hurt and angry. There are tears in his eyes. Wade reaches out his hand to apologize to Jacob, but that's when the child shoves Wade as hard as he can. Why? For having betrayed him and the dog, for having been defeated by the woman who stands in the field. It is not a hard push, but even so Wade steps forward at the surprise of Jacob's force. Then Wade watches Jacob run down the hill toward the road, where the farmer's truck is passing by.

Wade looks down briefly and sees his boots, and he sees Jenny's shoes there, too. That's when he realizes that in stepping forward at Jacob's push, he has stepped toward her. He lifts his head, and sees her there. She is facing the road, smiling sadly, looking after the running child. Then, with the same smile but somehow without the sadness any longer, she looks at Wade.

1995

At the base of Mount Loeil, in its shadow, William and Beth sit together on the edge of their bed in the evening dimness. "We should have—" he hears her say, but she doesn't finish. She is quiet for a long while, and so is he. Finally, she asks, "Can I say it? Please?"

But William, who seems to be holding Beth, is really holding with his arms her words unsaid inside of her. Two days have passed since the truck stopped on the road, and what he tries to say with his embrace is that two days is not enough.

Don't say it, please—he holds her close.

He is still wearing the shirt that he wore when he held the younger man in his arms. There, by the front flower garden William had earlier that day in a petty fit declared "ruined" to his wife because the perfect symmetry she had forced upon it had vacated it of nature—which was the point, wasn't it, of flower gardens? Nature?—there, amid the chatty voices on the radio, which carried all the way from the backyard, where his wife was painting

179

the dresser white—William and the younger man stood. Strangers.

Wade said what he said twice. He would have said it again and again if William had not told him, finally, that he understood.

Wade—that was the younger man's name.

Beth might have thought it cold the way Wade spoke—had she heard him—the simple, declarative sentences, loud but not shouted.

Not trembling.

She would have taken note of that. She would have looked for proof of suffering enough to suit her standards. She's looking for trembling? Well, here it is, here in his own body as he holds her at the edge of their bed. William knows with certainty that what his wife is asking permission to tell him is a summary of all the ways that they—or he—failed those two desperate people who came to them for help. He can see it in her face. He hears in her request the same certainty with which forty years earlier she had announced she did not want children. Why? Because she heard him yell at two little boys, heard him lose his temper over nothing. Forty years ago. He hadn't meant it, an accident, but his then-young wife decided that she had found conclusive evidence of who and what her husband was.

Close, close he holds her.

My wife has killed my daughter in the truck. My other daughter is scared. I need to get to her.

It was the great lack of ambiguity that made William stumble. There was not room for him inside those sentences. He was humbled by Wade's face, which did not allow itself to close the eyes and let the tears fall down until what needed to be done was done, and it wasn't yet, not until William understood, which he did, but was so struck by the earnest face that he could not find the words to say so.

So Wade tried again. "My wife has killed my daughter."

He was about to say it a third time when William managed a

reply. Far too late, the first of his failures. He is ashamed of it now, in his wife's arms, how long it took to find the words. "I understand. You've told me what happened."

And that is when the younger man dropped his head. Just for a moment. That is when the damp forehead touched his own, for a moment, and that is when the younger man reached out for the old man's elbows, just for a moment, to keep himself from falling to the ground.

He rubbed the crown of his head, *no no,* side to side twice against William's chest. And all William could think was, *I can't let his knees touch the ground.* That seemed then his only role, even with that truck parked in the middle of the road.

And through all of it, his wife in the backyard painting the dresser white.

I should have, I should have, I should have. His mind fills in the absence of his wife's voice with all the ways that he has failed. How has she been able to sense, their whole marriage, the shame in him that he's kept hidden, the shortcomings she seemed to know almost at first glance, nearly fifty years ago?

The younger man's knees touched the ground.

■

We should have—

But she can't say the rest of it, so strong are her husband's arms around her that she can't pretend to misunderstand what he is asking.

But Beth saw it all from inside the house. Two full days she has waited to tell him what she saw, but he spent those two days away. He spent them on that mountain their field touches, driving up and down, apart from her.

A breeze blows through the open window and chills everywhere her husband's body isn't touching. The dresser sits in the yard, strange and luminous, half painted. She hadn't really cared if the dresser was white when they hauled it out to the yard two days before. She just needed a place to put her energy for a few hours, some project that would make her feel determined.

But she had not felt determined. She had felt so tired. What he had said about the garden had hurt her. *What's next, plastic over the furniture?* He had never said such a thing, but they were getting closer and closer to that point. She had become, over the last few years, afraid. The horses, for example. She had begun to buy little horses to put around the house. Jade horses, quartz horses, ceramic horses, Swedish horses with painted flowers on their faces, wooden and embroidered stampedes. She had been a lover of horses once. At one time that was the whole of who she was. And wasn't that important? Shouldn't that be visible, somewhere? She realized one day there were no traces of the horse-loving girl any longer, and it frightened her. How was anyone to remember that she had ridden them, had loved them, if there wasn't something in the house that she could point to— See?

The result, of course, of the cheap and carefully placed clutter was the transformation of their spare and cozy house, little by little, into a house where old people lived. She realized it was stifling William, pushing him out. The ceramic pony in the bathroom, wearing mascara and lipstick and a hat falling over one eye, hooves crossed, how sickening. What was she doing bringing these things, like a spreading disease, into their house? But she couldn't stop collecting, organizing, asserting, controlling. See? See? The garden was part of it. Its strict and perfect beauty showed the world she was still making the choices of what to include, what to exclude. And look at how well she kept it alive, everything in its proper place, contained.

And that's what she was thinking of, painting the dresser in the backyard, all of these thoughts brought to the surface of her mind by her husband's offhand complaint about her garden. *Stifling out nature.* She turned up the radio because she thought she was going to cry.

Then she went into the house, her paintbrush in her hand, feeling the tears roll freely. But what she saw when she came into the living room was the front door open, and through that open door, William and the younger man.

In that rectangle of light, William held them up, the younger man and himself. She had never seen her husband hold someone that way. They had never had children. William's hand on the back of the younger man's collar. The younger man pressing the crown of his head into William's chest. It lasted so long, these men together, she felt locked in place as long as they were. Her husband's eyes were closed at first, his head bowed down to reach the back of the younger man's head, so that the old nose rested in the young brown hair, breathing it in, like father and son.

It changed her. Everything she did from that point on was in light of those moments when William held the man.

"We should have . . ." she says on the bed, her eyes filled with tears. But William, though he does not move, though he does not tighten his arms around her, resists. She has been married to him nearly fifty years. She knows his body well enough that she can decipher the meaning of even this stillness.

Two days ago, she had left the police station before William did. When she arrived at home, she unfolded a paper bag from a drawer filled to the top with other such folded bags, and she shook it open. She went through the house, room by room, slowly, carefully, and filled the bag with the horses. Jade, crystal, ceramic, cloth.

Then she went into her room, put the bag under the bed, and she lay down in the light from the window, not thinking of the murdered child, thinking instead of her husband in the yard holding the child's father. She had seen, standing in her kitchen, fifty years of another life together, another sort of love, one that she tried to be equal to on the gravel road as she held the younger woman. She held her in spite of everything, unconditionally, but only because her husband taught her to, only because her husband held the man.

Now she holds him close, presses her cheek against his, feels the sharp gray whiskers.

He has had to bear her all his life, so she will bear this for him, this not saying of what she feels. It is not regret at her mistake, but amazement to know she was mistaken, relief not to be mistaken any longer. To feel her heart open this way, so abruptly after all these years, to feel him come inside of her heart, beyond her heart, too large for it, she feels the pain of her love, the wonder of her certainty, the arrival after all this time of a better self, the only self that has ever known this man—

We should have
we should have
we should have
we should have
we should have
had a child.

2007

Ann and Wade, followed by the six hunting hounds Wade can't go anywhere without, have carried their rowboat down from the road, along a trail, to the bank of the Pend Oreille River, and they have realized, setting the rowboat down tentatively at the water's edge in the shadows and tying it to a tree, that a rowboat is not appropriate for this river, that they should have rented a canoe or else driven to the lake.

But Ann steps into the boat anyway, holding the picnic basket. She laughs. Before she can sit down, Wade pushes the boat out of the sand, and leaps in himself, splashing Ann in the commotion. They drift out as far as the rope will let them, and then there is a soft jerk as the rope pulls taut. They are both half standing in the halted rowboat, holding on to each other for balance, staring at the shore, where the dogs stand in a bewildered line, their heads lifted, sniffing. The water rushes under the boat and on either side. Slowly, the boat drifts again to the shore, as far as the rope will let it, downriver from the dogs, and they find themselves wedged in sand again, pushing away the limbs of the honeysuckle bushes that scrape against the side of the boat.

The dogs find them, come crashing through the bushes, surround the boat, put their muddy paws on its edges, and bark.

It is a hot day. Sitting on the metal seats in this secret place, they eat their sandwiches. They have left the paddles upriver, where they got in. They can't see them now. They can't see anything but the river and the bushes and the six dogs with their tongues hanging out, begging for food. Ann and Wade drink the thermos of coffee in contented silence, lift the scooped globes of watermelon with their fingers to their mouths, the juice dripping on their laps. When they are done, they wash their sticky hands in the river, and then Ann drops her feet over into the shallow, rushing water that carries them nowhere. It is when they are sitting this way—Ann facing the river, her feet in the water, Wade sitting on the metal seat, facing her—that he says, "Maybe we should have a baby."

She is so surprised that she almost laughs. He senses her laughter and looks abashed, looks away, over the water, somewhere on the opposite bank, trying to find a place to hide his hurt.

"Oh, Wade," she says. She takes his hand, and she searches her husband's face, trying to discover if this is a question he is asking from inside his illness, or if it is something he, Wade, is really asking.

She is forty-one years old; he's fifty-three. Perhaps sensing these numbers in her mind, he says, looking embarrassed, "I know there are risks at our age."

So it is Wade. Her Wade. So it is a request tempered with the admission of risk. It's not his disease at all.

She has never been so moved by anything in her life. She feels her words caught inside her, her whole life both drifting and held, a fermata, a rowboat tied to a tree.

"I'm sorry it took me so long," he says gently, taking her other hand now, too, so that she lifts her feet out of the water in order to face him in the rowboat. They study each other's faces. She feels one tear fall from each of her eyes. She smiles.

And when she smiles, something changes in his face. He smiles, too, but sadly. He has noticed something. He touches his finger gently to the scar on her lip, aware—she can tell by his expression—that this scar is one that he gave her not very long ago. This small discrepancy in her smile is, has always been, the answer to the question he is asking her now. No. No. It wouldn't be right. It wouldn't be possible.

But the answer doesn't matter. That he has asked her at all is enough.

They both feel a need to sever themselves from this question, from the depths they've just touched, and so he stands. "Let's get in," he says.

"No!" She laughs, gripping the sides of the boat.

But he gets out of the boat, stands in the shin-deep water. He pulls her in, too. She screams, but he picks her up and throws her over his shoulder. She pretends to fight him, but he just walks through the river, cutting the current at an angle, deeper and deeper, until it's up to his waist. He throws her in and she goes under. For a moment they are separated, but as they are both carried downstream, she is carried down to him. He takes her in his arms. He kisses her, their feet drifting along the rocky bottom, tripping, spinning. She tastes the river on his lips. The dogs follow close behind, slapping their large paws against the surface, struggling to catch up.

The weeks go on, and the season changes from early fall to late, and all through this strange new happiness, Wade's question is on her mind. She is touched by it. It lives inside of her, as beautiful and as dangerous as love. The possibility of a child is almost like a child itself the way she nurtures it, the way she fears it and tries to understand.

She can never look right at his disease. It is always in her periphery, pulling at the corners of her understanding. She has never been able to find the right questions, to pin down his illness in a way she can understand. The same old questions come to the surface once again: Does he know he has already brought two little girls into the world? Has fatherhood left him as wholly as his daughters have? She doesn't know. It is painful to return to this question all over again, but his own question has startled her. Sometimes she wants to shock him back into his pain, which is better, always better, than oblivion. Sometimes, for his own sake, she wants to hold down his head with her hand, push it into his love so he can see it again.

His family.

It's been twelve years since May died and June was lost. He hasn't seen a child on this land since then. A family came knocking once, shortly after Ann and Wade were married. Jehovah's Witnesses. A mom and dad and two red-haired little girls with freckled arms. They wore pale-pink dresses, matching white sun hats with bows. Wade was in his workshop when they came, but what if he had heard their car driving up? What if he came in for a drink of water? The longer she let them stay the more likely it was that he would see them, that he would have to remember what his life might have been like.

The Jehovah's Witnesses were a beautiful family. It broke her heart to tell them to go in the way that she did. "Do not come back." No doubt they'd heard it many times before, no doubt they were accustomed to mockery, doors slammed in their faces. They nodded politely at what they perceived was her disrespect. They had no way of knowing that this turning-away was any different from all the others. But how could she have let those children stay?

She wishes now she could bring them back. Not have them any older, any different at all. Those two girls holding their Bibles in front of them the way they might hold one rose each in a photograph, with adamant delicacy. Wade would open the door, and in that first glimpse of them, he would have to remember. Even disease would not be enough to diminish their meek and pretty smiles, shining out in spite of all of those terrible mountains behind them.

Together, Ann and Wade sit on the piano bench. She turns the pages, which every week grow simpler and simpler. One week, he's playing both hands together. The next week, he struggles on a children's song, with only his right hand. Slowly, as the weeks go by and the weather turns cold, she turns the pages backward. They return to the place where they met, to the place where he didn't know the names of any notes, where he showed delight inside of his struggles to learn them. He taps on his thigh, 1-2-3, 1-2-3. But even that proves difficult, eventually. Eventually, she puts the metronome away.

Ann is the only piano teacher in Ponderosa, and so her students are willing to drive up the long mountain road three quarters of the year to learn from her on the same beautiful piano that May once played, and which now Ann works hard to keep in good repair. This year, there are three students—an elderly woman, an elderly man, a young mother named Jo—who want to continue through the winter. Wade keeps the road plowed for them, even though each snowfall takes him hours to clear, and the money they make from the lessons just barely covers the cost of fuel. But the lessons have long since ceased to be about the money.

These last few years, Ann has gone along as he plows, walking with the dogs by the road. She does it to make sure that he's all right, that he doesn't have an episode and hurt himself. Everything is uncertain now, and there seem to be no clear lines between what he is capable of doing and what he isn't. His technical skills seem wholly intact, and he has no trouble with the tractor or with his trade. She trusts him with the chainsaw, the car, the grinder, the wood stove. But not the laundry, the telephone, the shower. He has lost his finesse with her body at night. He's lost everything she has taught him of herself and her pleasures, and he fumbles as he might have his very first time.

He doesn't know that the reason she follows him as he plows is to check up on him. He thinks she just wants to come along, and he is glad. The long walk always does her some good. And besides that, she is learning about the plow. She studies his work, pays close attention to how to use the tractor so that as soon as she must take over, she can. She will push away the snow herself.

At the bottom of the mountain road, once the plowing is finished, he pauses and waves her over so that she can climb into the tractor bucket. Once she's in, her legs dangling over the edge, her hands gripping behind her, he pulls the lever and the tractor lifts her up. A funny sight, she knows. Each time she looks back at Wade, he is laughing to himself about transporting his wife this way. She smiles, too. She rides all the way back to the house like this, the dogs chasing halfheartedly on either side of her, nipping playfully at her dangling shoes.

Ann, waiting for her student one winter afternoon, sings as she plays.

I hate to see the summer end

The melody is simple, but she has improvised complications. It is the song that has been caught in her life all these years, the song whose simplicity carries with it endless questions, unspoken feelings. Wade is in his workshop, so he can't hear. He hasn't heard this song since their early courtship.

Her fingers move swiftly without her, disconnected, freed. She can't think of a note or else she will lose the music from her hands, the music that is not a memory any longer, but a feeling in her fingertips, a presence inside of her that can't be watched or else it disappears.

Seems it was never here at all

She thinks of Wade.

He has lost his daughters, but he has also lost the memory of losing them. But he has not lost the loss. Pain is as present in his body as his signature is in his hand. He can sign his name perfectly, but he can't print it. *W,* he tries. But the *a* is impossible without the cursive tilt, the remembered motion of the letter before. He knows his name but can't see, can't feel, the separate parts, which are only possible from the inertia of his hand. He knows his grief, too, but its source is also lost without its movement. It is a static thing, unrecognizable, disconnected.

And so he confuses his grief for the want of something he doesn't know he's had before. A baby. He wants to know what it's like to hold his own in his arms. He wants to know what it's like to be a father. What it *is* like, not what it was. He believes he lacks the experience, as if he's simply waited too long to want a child and hasn't wanted it hard enough. He blames himself. He blames her. Though neither one of them has mentioned it since that day on the river, at times she feels his blame, a coolness. A couple of times he has mentioned how nice it would be to have a boy. But their window of time is closing, and he seems to feel the weight of his life pressing down.

There's only been a blowin' wind

When you love someone who has died, and her death disappears because you can't remember it, what you are left with is merely the pain of something unrequited. Ann knows that in his stiller moments, he searches for the source of the pain. He looks for it in Ann. He looks for it in the mountain. Somewhere, love is not returned, and it hurts him like heartbreak does. He holds Ann in his sleep, but it is not her he holds, but the phantom hope, the baby between them, never to be born, never to be lost or yearned for or forgotten and wanted again. Perhaps it would be less painful to remember his daughters than to believe he could have daughters but has waited too long to want them. Maybe it is better for him to know that he has held them before, that he has loved in the way he wants to love.

Since your picture found my wall

Someone taps Ann's shoulder.

Ann stops mid-phrase, and her hands jump from the keys.

"Sorry. Let myself in." Jo, her student, laughs. "Didn't know you sang, too."

Jo works hard at her lesson. She is cheerful and plump, in her early thirties, her face dimpled, her hair in a thick golden braid. At the back of her neck, right above the line of her sweater, is the name *Alice,* written in a child's hand, with blue ballpoint pen.

As Jo plays, Ann's eyes keep falling on those blue letters, probably written there this morning, judging from the perfect slope of the word against the slope of this particular sweater's swooped collar. Listening to the music, Ann looks up and out the window, where the sunlight breaks through a space in the snow clouds, funnels through. It is a misplaced spring light in the middle of winter, pink and yellow, glowing and softened by the dark clouds.

"Is something wrong?" Jo asks. Ann realizes then that the music has stopped, and in this small valley of silence, Ann feels a new calm. She knows what she will do. With caution, she touches her fingertip to the pen marks on Jo's back.

"You have a new tattoo," says Ann softly.

Jo laughs. "Yeah, she's pretty possessive."

"Jo," says Ann, lifting her fingertip from the pen marks, "I've been thinking about Alice. I feel bad about what happened a year ago, when I told you I couldn't give her lessons."

Jo shrugs. "Don't worry about it. You had a full schedule."

"Yes. Well . . ." says Ann. At that moment, she looks up and out the window again, whose frame Wade has just entered in the distance. "How old is she?" Ann asks.

"She's seven."

"I wonder," Ann says, still looking at Wade, who pauses to look out at the mountains in the distance, across the valley, his dogs huddling around him, "does she still want to learn to read music?"

■

On the morning of the day that Alice will come, the first thing Ann sees from her bed, through the open door of the bedroom, is the sunrise across the piano. The orange light reaches across the keys, slowly, one by one, moving up the scale as the room brightens, right up to the very last *plink* against the high knotty-pine walls. She feels already that things are different. She's not sure what will happen, but she is sure that she must do whatever she can to help Wade remember his daughters. A little girl, playing on May's piano, might be the only way to remind him. Of course, she knows that the memory will bring him pain. But she would rather the real pain than what he feels now, an unexplained emptiness in his life, a terrible regret that the world never held his children at all. She wants him to know that it did, that they are still inside of him. Somewhere.

Later, Alice holds her mother's hand in the sunny yard. She wears yellow boots, lavender gloves, a blue hat. "You must be Alice," says Ann, in the doorway.

"Why is your voice like that?" says Alice.

"I lived somewhere else for a long time. Can you guess where?"

But Alice doesn't hear her. She stomps the snow off her boots and steps inside. She goes right to the piano, still in her coat, and trails her finger slowly up every key, like the sunrise that morning.

For most of the lesson, Wade is just out of view, in the workshop Ann can see from the window above the piano. He's opened that workshop door twice already, but so far he hasn't glanced toward the house.

Jo reads in the corner of the room, sitting in a rocking chair, as Ann teaches. The child is polite. Every now and then she is distracted by Ann's accent. She studies the way Ann's mouth moves when she speaks, and Ann can see that she isn't listening at all. Alice's eyes fall on a photograph of a fawn, framed on the piano ledge.

Alice looks up at Ann. "Did you touch him?"

"Who?" says Ann.

Alice points to the photograph of the fawn.

"Oh, you're not supposed to touch a fawn," says Ann.

"But did you?"

The question, for some reason, catches Ann off guard. "Well— Here, look. Let's take this down," she says, removing the photograph to the floor so that she can lift the piano lid. "Come look." Alice gets up and stands beside her, peers into the piano to see the strings. "There's a trick," says Ann. "I'm going to hold the pedal down." She does, still standing. "See all those hammers let go? The strings are free. Now you're going to sing to them."

"Sing *to* them?"

"To the strings, yes."

"Sing what?" The girl is skeptical.

"One note, any note you want. Lean into the piano and sing it with all your might, then stop."

Alice raises her eyebrows as if this is the craziest thing she's ever heard. Ann smiles. "Take a deep breath."

The child does.

But just as her lungs fill with air, the door opens behind them, and Ann hears Wade stomp off his boots, hears the snow outside blow over itself, and she is so suddenly aware of what she's done that she can't even turn around to face her husband, whom she has been waiting for. She feels his eyes on this little girl, feels them fall on her pretty blond head, and she sees the child as he must, and feels all at once the sharpness of their tragedy.

Her foot on the pedal, she stares at the face of the little girl, who suddenly, with widened eyes, releases her breath into a high "Ohhhhh!" and leans her face deep into the piano, her head turned ever so slightly so that she can still look at Ann.

"Ohhhhhhhhhhhhh!"

And then she stops. She stands up straight.

The piano sings on for her. This is the trick, the magic. The same note, and an aura of sympathetic notes around it, sings on and on and on, quiet enough that only Ann and Alice must hear it, her very voice, caught on the strings, singing out like a ghost.

Horrified, Ann lifts her foot from the pedal and the hammers clap the sound quiet. How could she have done something so stupid and dangerous? She has risked Wade's memory not just of May herself, but of May's connection to music and therefore to Ann. And she has risked this child's safety. If, in the past, Wade's disease has made him act out in violence, what might his disease make him do now that he is so directly confronted with his loss?

She turns around to face him.

Wade is standing there with the door still open, looking at them both. She can't read on his face what he feels. He seems to be listening to the piano's stopped voice, May's sudden silencing.

"Wade," she begins, her heart racing.

But to her surprise, he smiles. He closes the door. "You must be the new student," he says.

"I'm Alice."

"Nice to meet you, Alice," says Wade. He nods politely to her, then he sits down on a chair by the door to remove his boots. Jo does not look up from her novel.

"I've been playing since I was four," the girl says.

"Four!" Wade shakes his head. "I can barely read music now and I'm an old man."

"She can't read music," says Jo, who still doesn't look up.

"Well," Wade says. The little girl looks at him again. He winks. Conspiratorial. Playful. "Well, I bet you still know more than me." He sets his boots by the door. "Nice to meet you, Alice," he says, and there's nothing more, just a polite nod before going up the stairs.

Ann feels relief, yes, but she is also shocked. She knows from the casual gestures, from the simplicity of his smile, the absence of pain, that she has inherited his family wholly now, that nothing can bring them back.

For the first time ever, she knows for certain that they live only in her.

It was only a few years ago that Ann saw the fawn. She noticed it lying behind the barn in the tall grass, barely larger than a cat, awake and unafraid. She crouched beside it, whispered hello. She watched it long enough that it settled down to sleep, its nose in the crook of its leg. She left, then came back with a camera. It woke again when it heard the flash.

Had she known, when she reached out afterward, so softly, with just one fingertip, that she could do it harm? When Wade told her later, with just a hint of scolding in his voice, Ann admitted nothing. He did not directly ask if she had touched it.

"Because when they're that small," Wade said, "they're still invisible. They don't have a smell. They're the only thing in the woods, living or nonliving, without one. So if something or someone touches it, gets their scent all over it, well."

Well. So she thought of wiping the fawn with a wet cloth. But the cloth had a smell, too, of detergent. And so there was nothing she could do. She went back several hours later and it was gone. Periodically that evening she forgot it, and then when she remembered, her fingertip tingled at the memory of that white spot, like peppermint. She thought of those woods at night. Wade had mentioned seeing a mountain lion before, not up here but down on the river, leaping right out of the water. So they were around. Coyotes, wolves. All those dark branches and dark trunks of trees and the fawn moving in the dark. Invisible except for one place, one white spot: Ann's fingerprint moving through the woods like a point of light. *Here I am!*

She takes the photograph of the fawn off the piano ledge. She puts it in the darkness of a kitchen drawer.

She never asks Wade if there is something he felt seeing the little blond girl in his house, or if he heard the piano sing back to her in a voice that was almost Alice's, but came from somewhere else, from somewhere deep beneath the debris of all the other music in their lives, a haunted, almost joyful cry caught on those old strings, glad to be called upon, to be remembered and restored.

When she gets into bed that night, there is nothing new about the way he holds her, just that same reaching for something inside of her with the pressure of his loving arms, a feeling that hums over their bodies like those strings singing on, like the sense a parent might have of a baby's waking, just before it cries.

1995

May's dress is nearly dry from her swim in the garbage can. She's sitting in the slanted pasture, where her four dolls sleep in the moist bedding of a rotting stump, the spoiled wood as soft as mush. They've been sleeping there since Saturday; they slept there through the rain. She knew the other night when the rain was falling that they were out here in the dark. She knew the rain might wreck their clothes, might make the colors of their eyes run free and drench and dye their hair and shirts. But she did nothing. Here they are. And now she barely looks at them.

Beside the stump, she holds her knees against her chest. She looks down the slope of the pasture hill. Her feet are bare.

"Rocket," she whispers, and a voice this quiet makes her think of the dolls on June's shelves, not the women, but the men you have to lean in close to June to hear, to nearly taste June's smell to know.

In the distance, barking dogs. Her father must be throwing the ball for them. He likes to throw it as far as he can down the mountain, so that even after it hits the ground somewhere deep inside the forest, somewhere far below, it rolls and rolls and leaves its scented trail through the wild grass. Then the six hunting hounds her father has raised will wait there at his side until he says, "Go on," and then, like rockets themselves, they are off.

Her father with his dogs, her mother with her horses, her sister with her books, and Rocket gone. She has glimpsed, once or twice, a kind of logic in these facts, a logic whose doors the rest of them can open and move through down easy paths. They are all leaving her behind. It hurts. The very idea of June lost in books when there is so much else, when there is so much danger all around, and they could live inside it if they wanted, she and June. It could be like it used to be, when the two of them were the same.

May. June. May comes first in the line of months, and yet it's June who's older. June who is the start of summer when May is just the spring. She closes her eyes. The warm wind blows over her hair, and there is a picture in her mind now of June looking mournfully at May. May speaks to this vision of her sister, not moving her lips, not opening her eyes. She gives her sister permission to go on, to leave her behind.

Because this is what love is. It is the smell of her, the scared dog of her, the secret that May keeps for her. It is the threat that rises in May's throat when she can hardly bear the thing she's lost. The moon-shaped bites of her fingernails. It is the terrible secret of not being the spring that follows the winter that follows the fall that follows the summer that follows June—of being instead the spring before, the spring that touched June on the other side, first, and older, and already making room.

She opens her eyes. June is nowhere in sight. May holds herself close in the pasture.

2008–2009

It's the middle of the night. Jenny hears Elizabeth in her bed up above, breathing soundly, sleeping on and on and on. A full week has passed since Elizabeth hung up her collage. There, among those scraps and magazine clippings and photographs, in the midst of that bleak and crumpled collection of longing, Jenny saw something of her own: a signature. Just her first name, penciled, smudged, scrawled in the corner of a sketch she has no memory of making.

She worries that this delusion, which is what her recognition of the signature must be, is a sign that the last bit of herself she has hold of is beginning to slip away. She feels an immense pain when she looks at the sketch, but also something new, some reaching of life from within her.

Where Wade found it, why he sent it, she doesn't know. To have something attached to his will, even falsely, even as a delusion, reminds her that there is still some part of her alive, and that part is the man whom she once loved, out there in the world still.

In the darkness now, she strains to see the faint pencil strokes of the half-drawn woman's forehead, the dark pencil tendrils of her hair. The woman's expression is timid, as if she is ashamed that her mistakes aren't well erased, that every misstep of her self is drawn along a graph. She can't hide the shapes that she's emerged from. Shaky lines, barely melded circles, her lips drawn evenly inside a box that the one who drew her was supposed to have erased.

So many questions, but the only one she managed to ask that day a week ago, staring at that concrete wall, was "Where did this come from?"

"Oh, that?" said Elizabeth—not the weeping woman of the day before, now sassy and abrupt, her sharp shoulders jerking with the laughter of a relief Jenny couldn't then or now surmise the source of. "I found that years ago, in a how-to book in the library. There was some paper at the end that someone drew on."

"And that?" asked Jenny, as casually as she could, pointing to some other scrap, trying to pretend that none stood out to her, relieved that Elizabeth did not notice the tiny signature—

"And that?"

But how hard, how nearly impossible, it had been to breathe.

There was nothing special about the book Jenny found the next day in the library, the book called *Drawing Faces*. Thick and floppy, tattered edges. Maybe she remembered it, she wasn't sure. No trace of her past inside of it. No trace, even, of the sketch ripped out from among the practice pages. This book, she thought, was never mine. I've dreamed that signature on that sketch.

But each day, that same signature comes out of her hand. It emerges on the attendance roster in class, on the equipment sign-out sheet in the utility closet. That same cursive *J*—tall loop, tiny tail—that same slanted *e,* the two *n*'s with that extra hump that half becomes the first curl of the traditional and final-looking *y:* She would see those letters together, just like that, if someone set before her her own confession.

There was a brief phase in her life, long ago, when she tried to learn to draw. She hadn't remembered this phase until the sketch appeared and opened up a memory. Her interest in drawing was short-lived, the result of desperation during that first endless winter they were trapped on the mountain. It might have all started with the wish to make something for Wade for Christmas. She almost remembers that. She wasn't able to go shopping; all she had was some paper and maybe that drawing book. Maybe. But of course, once she saw what came from her pencil, she must have given up. She must have put it away, and surely she forgot her intention. Where did the book go after that? She'll never know. Maybe there was no book at all.

Those first few years in prison, she had been so sure that Wade would come that she did not even know to fear he wouldn't or not to fear that he would. Her surety was the only thing that kept her living. Those first five years when she was living in a cell all alone, she remained alive because she was sure, each day, that he would come.

Why had she wanted him to, when she absolutely did not want him to? She had refused her own mother, after all. She couldn't bear her mother to suffer through years of painful visits. She couldn't bear her mother's recognition of her own face in her daughter's.

She closes her eyes. Both mountains are there in the darkness, Iris and Loeil. But she won't make the mistake of believing she's found something she hasn't, like some remnant of his love, some semblance of forgiveness. She won't diminish what she's done by pretending there is meaning here.

In the darkness above her, Elizabeth breathes.

Another month passes.

They begin to walk with each other in the yard. Side by side, not saying much at first. It's cold outside again. They have lived together now for nearly half a year. Sometimes Elizabeth asks questions.

"Do you remember me at all, from before?"

"I'm not sure what you mean."

"You know, before you moved in."

Jenny smiles. "I'd seen you many times."

"Doing what?"

"Lots of things. You came into the kitchen once talking about how you were going to shave your head."

Elizabeth laughs, claps her hands with delight at herself. "I completely forgot." But when she recovers from her laughter she says, her expression very serious, "Anything else, though?"

Jenny isn't sure what Elizabeth is looking for. She often saw her with Sylvia, but she wouldn't bring up something so painful now. And she remembers seeing Elizabeth study in the library. She would spread out her schoolbooks and lean way over the table as she read, her eyes moving fast, almost panicked with pleasure. "Nothing comes to mind," Jenny says.

She knows she's supposed to put something on the wall in their room, but she can't. Her sketch, her secret, is the only trace of herself that she can stand. That relic of another time, surely sent to her by Wade, a time from when he loved her, when her baby was still in her body and safe from all that was to come: Elizabeth has given this memory to her, has found and saved that one winter from all the rest that followed. She has hung it, unknowingly, on their wall.

And so they begin to sit with each other at meals, and sometimes at common hour. In the cell, there is a comfortable stillness between them. Sometimes Elizabeth turns on the television, and they watch together, Elizabeth in the bunk above, Jenny in the bunk below. Jenny doesn't pay attention to what happens on the show, but sometimes Elizabeth asks her questions about the characters, about what she thinks of them, so she learns to pay better attention, to reply as best she can.

Then one day, there is news in the prison of a suicide.

A woman named Bell, who once worked in the pig barns with

Elizabeth, has hanged herself. The news hurts Jenny. She feels a shameful longing, not because she knew Bell at all, but because she cannot help but wish that she could allow herself the same escape. Such a feeling overwhelms her with grief for her daughters, and yearning to be free of that grief. She is on her hands and knees, scrubbing the floor, feeling once again the desire to be done with her life, when she hears Elizabeth say to her old supervisor, just down the hall, "Of course. But with Bell gone and Tanner upset, I need help out there. I'd like permission to take Mitchell."

Jenny stops mid-scrub, her face hot.

"Mitchell can go—that's fine," she hears the supervisor say, indifferently. "Tell her she can work in the barns and you'll help her in the showers after. Just today. This isn't a permanent move for you. You'll go right back to laundry when Tanner's well."

"I understand," says Elizabeth.

A day together. A day outside.

Jenny is nervous about what it will do to her mind. They've tried to make her switch jobs in the past, but when she's away from these floors, the migraines return, as well as the panic and the wish for death. She can't admit this to Elizabeth, who thinks she's done Jenny a kindness. Elizabeth seems satisfied, determined, so delighted to have a day outside again. She explains Jenny's chores. Together, in silence, they scrape out the pots, haul buckets of scraps from the kitchen to the prison farm, which is attached to but separate from the prison grounds, which means they must come and go accompanied by an armed guard. The farm is fenced in, too, spools of barbed wire along the top. They are searched going in and out of the main prison each time, but only pat-downs, quick formalities. At the farm, they're given shovels, told to clean out a stall. The guards, squinting into the sunshine, stand nearby with their guns.

In the stall beside the one they're cleaning, a sow is giving birth. The hired farmer is there, delivering the piglets one by one, but there is a problem. He is saying, "Shit, shit, shit," in such a way that Elizabeth looks at Jenny as if to ask, Do you think he wants us to reply? They are not to speak to each other as they work, except about the work itself, but they are especially not to speak to the farmer unless spoken to. But Elizabeth decides to take his muttering as being directed at her, so she says, "Is there anything we can do?" He looks at her, and then at Jenny, and something occurs to him. "You," he says, nodding to Jenny. "Come here. Get down. You see this arm?" he asks, once Jenny is kneeling on the ground beside him. His sleeve is rolled up and he flexes. "There's no way this is getting in. But your arm? Let me see." She rolls up her sleeve. Her arm is lean. "Will you?" he asks.

"I wouldn't know what to do."

"I'll walk you through it. Just put your hand in. Tell me what you feel."

Slowly the farmer inserts Jenny's hand, her fingers pressed together to fit. She feels the hot blood. She feels the shuddering muscles. She glances up at Elizabeth, whose eyes are wide, excited. "Deeper," the farmer urges her. "There's not a lot of time." So, to her amazement, she puts her arm inside the sow, up to her elbow.

"What do you feel?"

She feels a thin and flexible rubber at her fingertips, stretched tight. Smooth.

"It's like a balloon," she tells him.

"That's right," he says. "That's exactly what it's like. Now pop it."

"No," she says, surprised, looking to Elizabeth for help.

"It won't take much," says the farmer. "Just with your finger. Press."

She closes her eyes, and then she pushes with her pointer finger. There is the sudden silent burst of the balloon, a hot and running rupture and relief.

"What's behind it?" he demands.

"I don't know."

"It's a stillborn. That's what it is. Do you feel its nose or its tail?"

"Nose," she says. "And hooves."

"Hold on to the hooves. And pull it out. Gently."

And that is what she does. She delivers the stillborn piglet. Its hooves in her hand when it comes out are soft and dark purple like tulips. She casts it immediately away from herself. And once the mother is free of it, four more piglets, alive, are born easily at Jenny's knees.

The farmer stands. "You saved the sow, and you saved those four," he says. "And probably since they've got a mother now, those four, too," nodding to the first ones who had come on their own.

She is happy to have saved the piglets, but she can't believe what this event does to Elizabeth. As soon as they are out of sight of the farmer, Elizabeth slaps her thighs, wide-eyed with joy. She whispers, loudly, "You delivered *piglets*!" Then, glancing over at the armed guards, gathering her boldness, she risks everything. She shouts, "We fucking delivered piglets!" Then she claps her hand over her mouth, right as one of the guards looks at her and decides to let it go.

After that day, Elizabeth is more powerful. She gets in trouble twice for talking to Jenny during work hours. Jenny returns to scrubbing, relieved to be at her isolated and peaceful work again, but Elizabeth talks about their one day on the farm together as if that same day has happened every day. Sometimes, she talks late into the night about all kinds of lighthearted things, and Jenny doesn't say much, doesn't know how to reciprocate, won't permit herself to laugh, but does permit herself to smile, down in the darkness.

A few weeks later, Jenny tapes a small scrap of paper on the wall, so close to her sketch that it overlaps it just enough to hide her signature. The paper says only, "We delivered piglets."

2009

Ann, shivering in her half-buttoned blouse, holds Wade's arm as they walk together up the steep pine-needled road. She threw the blouse on right out of the shower when she pushed the curtain away to check on Wade and saw that he was gone.

Now, beside her on the road, he stiffens. He halts. He forgets to pick up his feet, and nearly stumbles. She catches him. "Feet up, Wade," she says to him, firmly.

"I am."

"One foot at a time," she says.

She is relieved to have found him. When she got out of the shower, she stood on the porch and she could hear him calling, just down the road, "Crow! Crow!" Calling not for a crow at all, but a pet raven, whose long-ago death he has forgotten and therefore fears will soon arrive. He tells her he worries the other birds have sensed the pet's domestication and scared her away.

But the raven is buried somewhere in the pasture with the other pets he has loved over the years. She had once learned to speak, to mimic Wade's voice, calling out his daughters' names in an ironic and scolding tone as if reprimanding them for their thoughts. Wade's told Ann all of this before. And he's told her that he had to shoot the bird after his daughters were gone, because he couldn't listen anymore to the things her voice remembered. The image of him shooting his own raven, out of his unthinkable pain, has always haunted her.

"She might be too scared to be found," he says. He has stopped in his tracks to say this. He seems oddly cheerful, as if he does not believe the raven will be missing long.

"Keep walking, love. I'm cold," Ann says.

"You shouldn't be outside with your hair wet."

Wade, at fifty-five, has already outlived his father by several months, but it's been within those months that his body has begun to change. His eyes seldom hold the serenity they used to. More often than not, there is a watery fear in them, or a vacant, daydream glaze. His face is not wrinkled except right around his eyes, but there is a looseness in his jaw and a tightness in his brow, a combination that makes him look older than he is. He has begun to shuffle when he walks. She corrects him because she's afraid that it's the little things that will make him slip away. She has been warned of what can happen. Sometimes, he does not have control over the muscles of his throat. He forgets to chew his food and little bits fall down into his lungs. He has been hospitalized once already for pneumonia. They were lucky he survived it; many people with dementia don't. It's the bits of food that kill them. She blends all his food now, but it is exhausting trying to get him to drink it.

He calls again for the raven.

"Pick up your feet, Wade," Ann scolds. She will not pretend to look for the raven, but she doesn't correct him when he calls out for her. She is glad he wants to walk, glad that he seems happy. There has not been a day like this in a very long time. Most days he stays in bed, demanding that the television remain right there on the covers with him, close enough that he can touch it at all times, even when it's off, sometimes hugging it with one of his arms. If he falls asleep and his hand slips away from the TV, it leans facedown against his chest, not hard, but he wakes up screaming.

But today, she feels as if they've both awakened from a dream. It's November; the sun is shining. The hounds have found them on the road and are following them at a distance, stirring up the leaves with their adamant snouts, barking at old traces of squirrels.

"Do you want to go on a drive?" she asks, once they reach the yard.

"Yes," he says, smiling at her, taking her hand.

"We could go to the top. Maybe they're still working on the radio tower."

"Okay."

"Let me get the shampoo out of my hair first. You're going to sit and talk to me while I shower. I want your hand on the ledge of the bathtub so I can see it the whole time."

"Okay," he says.

"Feet up. Pick them up all the way up."

■

Ann drives slowly up the long switchbacks, Wade in the passenger seat beside her. The aspen leaves have fallen since she last drove this mountain road two weeks ago; they shimmer in the icy mud in intermittent patches. Mostly along the road, the trees are evergreens.

Any day now, the snow will fall. When it does, Ann will have to take Wade away from here. He doesn't know this yet. If she told him, she doesn't think he'd understand. But they can't spend another winter on the mountain. If they were snowed in, and something happened to him— She can't do it. Last year, she plowed the whole road herself twice, having learned to operate the tractor by watching without his knowing how closely she watched. But she is afraid of what might go wrong. When the first snow falls, she will check him into the hospital, where he will live until she can get them settled somewhere in town, Coeur d'Alene or maybe Hayden. She feels a darkness approaching in him, getting closer.

But not today. Today is one of the rare days that Wade seems to remember something vital, or, if not remember it, then sense that it is there. He seems calm, acquainted with this road, accustomed to the bumps and potholes, cheerful in the cold fall air. He smiles faintly as they drive through the straight, tall shadows of the lodgepole pines. The smile is distant and absentminded, but very real, not pretending.

All six hunting hounds are crammed in the small car at Wade's insistence, five in back, one, named Roo, in the front, with his head on Wade's lap. The crowded car smells of their wet coats and their breath. Ann rolls down the window and the cold air brushes the side of her face.

"What if the cat wants in when we're gone?" he asks. There is no cat, like there is no raven, like there is no one-eyed dog. But she knows the right answer.

"You carved him a door."

"Where?"

"Everywhere."

His disease is a mystery. He has never once forgotten her name, but when she brushes his teeth for him and the foam drips down from his mouth, when she unbuckles his belt for him in front of the toilet even after it's too late, when she screams at him to stop screaming at her to find the flashlight batteries even as the light is on in his hand, the beam thrashing against the dark walls in the middle of the night, she wonders how she can go on.

But then, every so often, at his most vulnerable, most undignified moments, she will sense suddenly that the events of his life are not wholly lost, that inside of him, filling him up, is still that singular afternoon he can't recall. It's the texture of his memories, not the feeling, that is gone. A slow melding, blurring of lines, premise without impression. But still there is a center, there is a date and time around which all indistinctions constellate. Sometimes, he knows it all. He knows May and June's names. He knows about the firewood and the truck. Sometimes the memory, like a sudden blade itself, is so sharp and present he believes it happened yesterday. Then she is faced with the confusing task of comforting him with the fact that his daughters are long gone, that there is nothing he can do, that there is nowhere left to look for June. Those days are the hardest, and on those days she feels, too, the suddenness of that hatchet, the total shock of it, more strongly than she has ever felt it before.

On the windowsill by their bed he keeps a knife handle that he never got a chance to make the blade for. It is beautiful. Copper trim, Honduras redwood, cut and polished to fit his hand. He seems to know this object is important to him and he seems, as she is, fascinated by its perfection, but he doesn't know what it is for. He holds the smooth, polished chunk of wood in his fist, fitting palm and thumb into the subtle grooves he once carved there. In this wood is the memory of his hand, the anticipation of it. This wood seems to know him, and that disturbs him. She finds him rubbing the wood against the windowsill edge to try to change its shape, to get rid of its knowledge of his hand.

All this rubbing has damaged the windowsill. There is a rough, splintered groove in the knotty pine now, but she doesn't tell him to stop rubbing the handle there. It seems to calm him down. He does it while he watches television. Then in the evenings, when he is sleeping, she lies beside him, touches the damage to the windowsill while she reads all she can about what else she should expect. "There may come a day when your loved one does not remember who you are."

Loved one. She has read these words many times in such books, even in very scientific books not seeking to comfort but to inform. Ann is always moved by the tender ambiguity. Loved one, the faceless, sexless, helpless focus of her heart: A loved one is the person you will lose.

Beside him in the car, she glances over at his face, and she sees how those two words describe the peculiar absence of everything but the fact of her love, which is the only reliable fact, ordinary but complete.

They are nearing the top of Mount Iris.

2009

Not now—then. He's thirty-two. The baby sleeps, in these fields, in this shadow of the mountains, cheek on Wade's shoulder. He feels the heat and heaviness of her sleep. He feels the weight of her baby breath. Her breathing is a part of the work itself, a part of the rhythm. As are other things: the warmth and wetness of her open mouth sucking on his shoulder; the graze of her hat against his cheek when he crouches down to lift the pipe; the dampness that grows in the cloths between them, the cotton of his shirt and the nylon of the backpack, the sweat of his work working its way through, to her.

But he sees nothing of her, except the swinging shadows of her little feet. Sometimes he holds on to these feet. He feels the sticky vinyl bumps of the thin white soles. She never cries during working hours. These are the rhythms she knows. Down to the ground, then up again, the muscles pressing and softening, against her, for her, the rushing of the water pouring out either end of the thirty-foot pipe he holds, the distant sound of other sprinklers, waiting to be moved by her mom and dad.

This is the Rathdrum Prairie, where they work. Every weekend, the three of them wake up early, drive down the mountain road in predawn darkness to do the kind of work that Wade did when he was a teenager. Twenty minutes away from the base of Mount Iris, they park the car, put the baby in a backpack, and look out at the bluegrass fields, which pay twenty-five cents per irrigation pipe moved. They stand at the edge of the darkly golden field in the shadows of the mountains they live in. Jenny makes the baby comfortable on Wade's back by securing the little head in place with blankets stuffed on either side of her, blankets of oily softness whose bulges Wade feels against the muscles of his back. He can smell in these blankets from their bed the baby's sleep and Jenny's, too, so that the night is with them all the time; the beautiful nights on their own land—as in daylight they move over someone else's—are wrapped around their June, are holding her in place.

What these summer fields mean to Jenny and Wade is the pushing away of mountain snow. Five thousand dollars to buy a tractor and its blade. And they will earn it; at the end of the summer, they will earn their winter clearings.

June is three months old, but her name is only one week old. Lily has vanished from her face, a runaway, a dream. She is restless when she isn't in the fields on their backs. On her worst nights, when she cries for hours and gulps and chokes on her sobs, they put her in the backpack again, and go outside into the darkness. Jenny and Wade, with the baby on Wade's back, walk through the mountain woods, up and down the steepness of their land, singing softly to the baby that these are the fields, that this is the prairie they are walking on, the prairie she seems to love. And slowly, slowly, the infant settles down. She recognizes her life again. She falls into a sleep that is the lifting and setting down of pipes. Back and forth Jenny and Wade walk together under the ragged pine trees in the darkness, and sometimes Wade crouches to the ground

as if to lift a pipe but instead he grips the rocky soil of his own in-
fertile, perfect land.

■

August, but he doesn't know what year. He knows only that it's an
Ann summer, and therefore an after-summer, and that the smell of
cooling sap and drying earth makes him long for something that
feels like Ann but isn't, because here she is beside him, with him,
and yet something—Ann? Ann?—is gone, and he feels her absence deeply, feels the warmth of her damp palm at his elbow as
she leads him across the empty parking lot, toward the post office
door.

It is night. As they walk, he can smell the murkiness of the
nearby pond, the haze of cooling pavement. Children at the
house across the dirt street sit in a yard oblivious to them, sucking
Otter Pops in porch light, murmuring their laughter, sibling
laughter—he can hear it—not the laughter of school friends or
neighbors or cousins. Something secret in that laughter, private,
edged with meanness and devotion, a fear of the knowledge each
has of the other. He has heard it before, up in his office some summer night like this, a window open, and that same forgiving and
secret and frank and unforgiving laughter down in the yard below,
the moving of dolls in the dark grass, dolls with girls' voices, trying
out disgusting words they wouldn't speak in daytime.

Ann pushes open the post office door. It's cool in here. Empty.
He's aware of the sound of his shoes on the tile. The metal divider
has been pulled down over the counter and locked. Ann takes his
hand, leads him to the bulletin board.

"There," she says softly, nodding at the board, where there is a
painting of his daughter. Twenty-one years old, and his daughter's
eyes so green, made greener by the college grass she's left him for.
He wishes he knew which college it is, so he could go there, meet
her friends, listen to her talk about her studies.

But they've had a falling-out. She doesn't want him to come.

215

She wears a yellow bandanna tied prettily in her hair, its two tails falling over her shoulder. She smiles with flirtation, and he wonders who is holding the camera, what young man has fallen in love with her. On her wrist, a loose charm bracelet. Bug bites on her pretty legs.

■

July, a distant year. He's on his way home after a long drive alone, following a fight with Jenny. He has not gone far, but he's driven slowly, partway down the other side of the mountain, where he found, at the base of a tree, a baby raven. She was hurt and didn't have the strength to hop away. He caught her, wrapped her in a towel, and now she's on the seat beside him, her head covered, only her bill poking out, opening and closing as if she lacks the strength to caw. As he drives, he speaks to her in the same voice with which he speaks to May when she is crying, which is what she was doing when he left. He feels worse about that than the fight itself, leaving right when the baby woke and began screaming. May is eighteen months old and fighting off a mild fever. And Jenny's there at home, still mad, but having to sing to the little one, having to smile. Why should he have his escape and she not? The raven he has saved for her own sake, of course, but also his. He knows a hurt bird in a towel will distract them all from the bad feelings of the day, that even Jenny will forget her anger, and he'll become the unspoken hero of the afternoon, having brought this raven into their lives. Jenny will transfer May over to his arms, and Jenny will follow through with her instantaneous devotion to the wounded creature: tweezers pinching raw meat, a little dish of water, a box, a better towel, a heat lamp. As if because she is a mother of two daughters, she is part-mother of all living things.

That is what he pictures as he drives. And it's more or less what happens when he's home, only May isn't in Jenny's arms, but sleeping in his and Jenny's bed. June, four years old, is sleeping beside her, not sick at all, but acting with such solidarity, for the sake of getting her share of Popsicles and movies, that she believes herself sick, fatigued by so much pretending.

When May wakes, Wade is sitting on the edge of the bed, watching her. He takes her in his arms, carries her to the kitchen, then kneels down with her, her head resting on his shoulder. There is the raven, breathing hard in the afternoon sunlight, on a folded towel.

"Look, May," he says.

So she looks. She points at the raven. She says, "Crow."

"What did you say?" says Jenny, who comes quickly from the kitchen and kneels down beside them both.

"Crow."

How could this word be a part of May's vocabulary if neither one ever taught her? Just like that, she has deepened. Beneath her blond-white hair are these two new eyes that see what he can't guess. She is capable of withholding, then revealing. How has she learned to be this new thing that she is? He cups his hand to the back of her head, and holds her close, feeling already that all of it will pass too soon, that she is already becoming her own self, composed of secret knowledge.

Crow. Crow.

Late fall, maybe November, standing here with Ann, below the radio tower. He knows the names of all those mountains he can see, every name of every mountain except the one he's standing on. The clouds are soft and gray, the thin, cold breeze touches his neck. The windows of cabins glare silver in the distance, far over the valley, out in the trees on the opposite mountains. The grass up here is blue. Tall, harsh blades his dogs break tunnels through with their bodies. The boulders hold water in their gouges, lichen, like tide-pool creatures, spreading out in the dim sunlight. Down below, the crows fly back and forth between the tops of the cedars. There are only small trees up here, their roots struggling over the rocks. He turns his back to the radio tower. Strands of Ann's hair reach past her face toward the mountains across from them.

Those mountains in the distance are scales of music—he knows those, too. Up and down. A rest in the valleys. Up and down again.

Hold my hand, Ann. Lace your fingers through mine.

"I am, I'm here," she says. She shows him that they're holding hands. And maybe that's enough, to feel her rough skin, to see that it touches his own. The lines on a palm form an *M*. Their sign. Two mountain peaks, sudden slopes. One mountain so far behind the other, across a valley, but how can that be visible on a palm? Instead, the two mountains seem to touch, the distance between them diminished into two-dimensional space. This singular evening, one. This singular evening, the other.

The curtains are closed in the hospital room, and it snows up in those hills the curtains hide, those hills they are still standing in. Up there, in those hills, beyond that curtain, he presses his *M* on hers, as if to say, Here we are, we are Mitchell.

The dogs disperse in the nearly frozen grass.

But why so sad the snow is falling, Ann?

Falling on the blue grass, on the boulders, on their heads. Falling down from the radio tower they've turned their backs to.

He laughs.

"But you hate the snow," she says.

"I don't," he tells her. "I never have."

He knows the name of the moment to come, like the baby knew the name of the crow.

To die is to simply remember how to die.

"It will trap us," Ann says. She means the snow. "Not up here, but down there."

Standing on their mountaintop, she lifts their entwined hands to indicate this valley.

He laughs, gently. "Oh, Ann, you're always thinking so far ahead."

1973

Adam walks in the night through the snow. There is nothing to see yet, just the woods on either side of the white road, but he can remember the details of the approaching houses as if he has passed them every day of his life, and he has. There are five houses, separated from one another by their modest fields. One of them holds his sleeping wife Sarah, his sleeping son Wade. One of them has a door that he's allowed to open.

But he doesn't know which one it is.

He stops for a moment to catch his breath, his throat raw from the cold. He pictures the light of the first barn one mile away. He can picture the way the light lands on the snow building up on the tops of the fence posts. He can see this scene as clearly as if he were passing it now—or more clearly, since those posts and that light he has seen so many times they have become a composite of light and post that is so basic it forms less a scene than a feeling, one that is as familiar to his body as hunger, a predictable and pressing and hollow space.

Standing still in the road, he closes his eyes.

Sometimes he lets too many things become familiar. He lets the landscape of his life settle down in him so that he can't see it at all; he just feels it move through him, past him, acre by acre, each beat of his heart. There is an impression of empty space inside of him, but also outside, as if something actual is missing from the scene, as if a post has fallen over or the barn light has blown its bulb, only it isn't those things—what's missing is his own mind from them. And all he's got to do now is separate those posts and that barn from the light they both stand in. He's got to draw them out of that empty space until they are actual again.

He has had to do this more and more. It occurs to him that he doesn't know what he's doing on this road. Maybe his car has broken down. Maybe. But part of him feels, suddenly, like his being here is a lie that he's caught in. Suddenly he has the sensation in his arms of having held some woman, not his wife.

And now the sensation on his cold lips of having kissed her. A tingling of heat.

He feels guilty for this feeling. He tries to shake her warmth away.

Someone else has walked this road not long ago. There are footprints, in the other direction, half filled with snow. Someone else is out here in the night. So many secrets; he feels those secrets trading houses. Not a sound except the thud of the snow dropping from branches, deep into more snow. He walks slowly. He pictures Sarah, her slack sleep-face. He can see her perfectly in his mind, but he can't see the bed that holds her, the room that holds the bed, the house that holds his room. Has she turned over in the bed and found him missing? Often he's found her missing even when she's there, her warm body a stranger. But she's not a stranger now. He knows her name and face. But the other woman he suspects he might have held tonight, her face is missing now, her name too like a frozen breath, always half gone. Which house is hers, why has he gone there? It doesn't seem like him to leave his wife, to sneak away. Even his footprints, when he looks behind him, are foreign, having as little to do with him as the stranger's footsteps going the other way.

Too much for anyone to keep straight, let alone a man losing his mind, as he knows he is.

On the east side of the road, the woods stop. A snowy field opens. He must get the heat off his hands before he's home. He remembers, again, that home is what he can't remember.

This is what he knows for sure: The third farm along this road has a sign over the driveway announcing the last names of the family who live there. Reddle, Redline. Something like that. He doesn't quite remember what it is, but he knows it isn't Mitchell. So he knows the third farm isn't his. Besides, there is a girl who lives there, not a boy, not Wade. He's seen her throw rocks at the blue jays that bother her pigs.

And the fifth farm. He's seen a little girl there, too, jumping off a porch. So he knows that house is not his, either. The third and fifth, their little girls.

He crosses them out of his mind.

But then there is the first farm, those posts and that light. He can feel Sarah looking out the window at the snow. But this vision means nothing without his son in that house, too. It's the fourth house, not the first, where he can picture Wade, nineteen years old, sleeping up there in his room, oblivious. His dirty hair has soiled his pillow faintly gold. Adam has looked into that room some afternoons when his son's not there, and has seen the way the sunlight through the window catches the oval of dust collected in the oil on that pillowcase, in the perfect shape of his boy's head.

Upstairs. An upstairs room. The pillowcase in the upstairs room. That means the second house, an A-frame with the single story, the roof so low a girl scrapes the leaves out of the gutters with her hands, could not possibly be his because it could not possibly contain the stairs leading to his sleeping son.

Not the second, not the third or fifth.

But the first and the fourth houses. Either one could be his own. His wife in the first, looking out; his son in the fourth, asleep.

Either one feels right to him. Either one he believes.

A deer in the road lifts her head. She does not startle when she sees him, but walks slowly away, with the confidence of an animal in her element of night. She steps over the fence as if there is no fence, with no change in the rhythm of her walk. He tries to move faster. His hands are so hot inside his gloves. The snow builds up and up. His legs are rigid, his feet move as if each is stuck in a pail of mud. A hot sleepiness in his arms now where he held some woman not his wife, his arms that remember what he can't.

But who are all those little girls? What are the chances that each house but his own has one, and why, in his memory, does each little girl look the same? Why does it seem those houses hold only her and no one else?

Something is wrong with his memory of her, but he can't think about it, not now. Once he sees his house in front of him, he will know what it is. He will get into the warm bed, inside the walls of his wife's smell, and he will never leave her again.

And if it happens that he passes his house and walks up the wrong driveway, and comes up to the wrong door, there is always his fatigue to blame; there is always a lie to be told, if some other wife answers, about his truck not starting in this cold, about him walking to the nearest house for help.

He would have to knock, of course—he could not just go inside. People around here keep rifles by their beds. But the risk of knocking on his own door is almost greater than that: If he knocked on his own door, each hollow sound would expose him. Sarah would know what it meant.

Why are you knocking on your own door?

He could tell her the door would not open in the cold; he could say he had been trying; he could say the lock was frozen shut. Do you know it's ten below? He could accuse her of not knowing that.

But she would know even before she tested the door herself,

which she would do because that was the kind of woman she was. She would try the knob herself from the outside, and then she would look up at his face and through him, and she would see what he's become.

He realizes that he is on his knees now. He's lost a glove. But that doesn't matter so much, either, because he doesn't even want the glove he still has on, his hand hot and itching inside of it. He tears it off with his teeth, crawls over it, feels its softness under his knee, feels it catch on his dragging boot.

His yard will be brighter than the others because of the light of the barn, which is on even now, shining on the posts of the first house, where the curtains are drawn in the upstairs room to shield his son's closed eyelids from the light.

Which means—his heart races, sudden joy, he laughs aloud— his son is no longer in the fourth house, but in the first, where his wife has been the whole time. The pillowcase with its oil stain is in the upstairs room across the hall from Sarah's bed. Both of them in the first house now.

And suddenly those posts and that light are separate things, are entities of their own, and he knows them to be posts he's put in the ground himself, knows that light to be one that he has deemed worth the cost of keeping on, even in the winter, when the electricity bills are running high.

He tries to stand. It's not the cold that makes him fall back down; it's the hot sleepiness in his legs. But it doesn't matter; he can crawl. If it's the first house, that means it can't be far away. That means it must be just ahead. He's been walking, what, an hour now? If he just follows this road, this road—

This road has begun to hover in his periphery, to rise up from where it was to someplace level with his eyes, and then above him, the crown of his head just grazing it. A heavy road, chilled light that feels nice, cool in his hair, on his sweating scalp. He crawls to the trunk of a tree beside the road, to rest for just a while; he crawls beneath its snowy branches, into a warm cave of boughs and ground. He's growing tired. He knows he should feel the cold more than he does. He feels its weight, its density, but no pain. This warmth is moving inward. He feels for the first time in his life *inside* of his life; he feels that he has arrived at its center. And here, in this center, in the soft blaze of certainty that is the first house, that wholly remembered, perfect house—a room.

Not his and his wife's. Not his son's.

Another room.

Most of his body is this still, indifferent night, but his chest is this warm room that wanted only to be found. He had to lose his house in order to find this room inside of it.

And inside this room, his little girl.

He's been looking for her, yes. He's been looking a long time. But she must be home now. He feels her there, and he feels an incredible calm. There is only the first house now, somewhere close by, somewhere where he can nearly see it. And inside of it, his wife and both his children sleep. His little girl no longer hidden away, no longer a secret jumping off the fifth farm's porch, throwing rocks at the blue jays in the pigpen of the third house, scraping leaves from the gutters of the second. No. She's there, here, in the first house. June, his little daughter, the missing piece. And her secret mother (whose warmth won't leave his arms, whose warmth is spreading to his hair, impossible, it's filling up this quiet cave like a sun rising only here), her mother must be gone, some long ago mistake he's been long ago forgiven for, because there isn't another house, not one that he can think of, not one in all the world but the first.

2010–2011

January 2, 2010

   I write with a very heavy heart to inform you of Wade's death on December 27, 2009. He died in the Bonner General Hospital at the age of fifty-five, his dignity and kindness untouched by the disease that took his memory. In the end, he didn't remember anything from his life, but he seemed peaceful. I am sorry to be the one to inform you. He was buried beside his father in Grangeville, Idaho.

■

The letter is typed. Only the envelope is handwritten, but the sender's name does not appear there, either. It is the first letter Jenny has ever received in prison, and seeing the return address, her old address, *7846 Forest Service Road, Ponderosa,* written in a woman's hand, she knew right away the news the letter would deliver. She read it only once. There are no more tears left in her, not because she's hardened, or has sealed herself off, but because there simply aren't any left. She feels, though, that she honors him by admitting with her absence of tears that he does not belong to her, that he is not hers to mourn.

But she does feel the need to cry. She feels it deeply. She feels in fact that Wade's death is the very end of her heart. It is strange to arrive here at the end after all this time, and also strange to realize she hasn't been here before.

The letter wakes in her the numbed memories of their early days together, which strangely do not bring her pain, but a tranquillity separate from her grief, as if their courtship could be removed from all the suffering that followed it. She has never felt this way before, and allows herself this brief peace. Dusty summer days on the prairie: Wade mowed the thistles on her parents' land and she, nearby, fed and brushed the horses. On their anniversary, they carried river rocks in their shirts to pile on the grave of their one-eyed dog, Peggy Rose. Wade brought a bucket of water, too, to make the dry river stones pretty again. He trickled it down slowly, loveliness renewed, and they wished out loud for a baby, wished on those river stones.

And then there were those fall nights in the loft of the mountain barn shortly after she found out she was pregnant. Sometimes she would wake up and hear him boiling water on the campfire in the early morning, the fizzing of pine needles on fire, almost a watery sound. She does not let herself give voices to these moments, or even visions of his shape. She instead feels that he *is* that dust and those thistles and those rocks and that early-morning fire, a force that holds her up.

For weeks, she feels her grief like this. But she can also see through her grief, and what she sees is the end of their time on earth. It is finally over; it died with him. In a few years, the whole world—the dust of it, the thistles, rocks, and fire—will recover itself from that brief time when the Mitchells lived and when she destroyed them. How could such a rupture, of time and earth and the human heart, ever heal from that August day, when all things separated, broke into parts that lost one another in an instant?

And yet it will. She feels this process begin without her.

The sketch hangs there on the wall, but the half-drawn woman means nothing now. She means even less than the other scraps in the collage. The woman in the sketch was, once, a kind of window into Jenny's past and into Wade's present. But now there is no one behind it. The man who sent it is gone. Before now, she allowed the sketch to tell her that there was still a part of her that wasn't dead.

With Wade gone, she feels the world begin to close its eyes on her, and though she knows it's wrong, she feels relieved.

She says nothing to Elizabeth about Wade's death, and at times she feels guilty about keeping it to herself, since Elizabeth shares so much of who she is, shares it all the time. Still, they sit together on the bottom bunk in the evening and read aloud to each other from novels, and still, Jenny listens to the stories, feels invested in the plights of the heroines. But in this new, dazed state, she finds it difficult to talk about anything at all, and she feels fatigued in the deepest part of herself, a fatigue that is close enough to death that it seems futile to do anything but welcome it.

Nearly a full year passes by. The days are easy to bear, somehow, floating days, meaningless as clouds, spent alongside her friend. Sometimes she even teases Elizabeth, when it seems Elizabeth wants her to. But some of the things Jenny finds herself saying make her tongue feel dry and rotten, not because they are lies, but because they are all dead feelings that her friend doesn't know are dead. The prison is so small, and she is so small inside of it. Sometimes she has the feeling that her death won't matter enough to happen, that she might live forever in this state.

She scrubs the shower floor, and the fumes make her light-headed and sometimes sick. She is bothered, but doesn't change her habits, doesn't dilute the cleaning formula like Elizabeth says to. Somehow, her feet carry her to a European history class every

Thursday, where she takes notes for Elizabeth. Her hand takes dictation, separate from her.

Sometimes a woman plays the piano during common hour, and even those notes now hit her dully, as painless as thunder. She passes through that music on her way to class, and it doesn't hurt her like it used to. She follows the yellow line to the classroom, where, without feeling, she spreads out her papers on the desk.

One Thursday evening, though, about a year after the letter arrived, she finds it again, among those school papers. She has no idea how it got there. She stored it in the box with her pictures, so either she opened the box in a dream or, when her box fell during the last search, she failed to pick up the letter when she picked up her photographs, and Elizabeth swept it up instead with the school papers, not noticing it was something different.

Without realizing what she is doing, she reads the letter for the second time.

I am sorry to be the one to inform you.

She is struck right away by the simple fact that there are things written in this letter that she didn't see before. It's as if it's a different letter from the one she read a year ago. The revelation slaps her awake, and she moves with surprise in her seat. The teachers look at her, expectant. She looks down, away from them. She shakes her head no.

It isn't hard to explain to herself later what happened. Over the course of those Thursdays spent in a classroom on behalf of someone else, she has accidentally learned to read the way that Elizabeth can. That year of poetry has awakened in her only now, and she sees, plainly, that there is a new language available to her, which is the language between words. The first time she read the letter, it had seemed to her one copy of many sent out to distant relatives and friends, a public announcement of loss. But it is clear now that this is a letter to only her, that every sentence in it was chosen, so carefully, for her. She sees that the writer took great pains not to say too much, and at the same time said more than she believed was permitted.

In the end, he didn't remember anything from his life . . .

Jenny can now sense the woman behind that statement. She can hear the strain in her voice, her struggle to say what is not hers to say, her struggle to be heard behind the words:

Wade died without any knowledge of what you did. He died without any hatred for you in his heart. If this can be of comfort to you, then let it.

It is a forgiveness that they both know is not for his wife to give. Jenny feels moved by the woman's attempt to reach into her heart this way, to urge her to let go even just a little.

Why is the woman doing this?

He was buried beside his father in Grangeville, Idaho.

In that sentence, Jenny—mystified and even frightened of her ability to see into a few words such amazing depths, a well of feeling, a breaking voice—reads this:

He was buried beside his daughter in Grangeville, Idaho.

Jenny had never been told where May was buried; she knew only that she was. Every day she tried to imagine where. She knew all along that wherever May was, Wade would put himself there, too. If Wade was on the prairie beside his father, he was on the prairie beside his daughter. He would never let himself be separated from her.

Now Jenny can see her daughter's grave clearly, that quiet, peaceful prairie land of Jenny's childhood. She dropped flowers in that graveyard long ago, when she was young and went to visit Wade's father's gravestone. She remembers the shape of the stone. She remembers the white fence and the maple trees. There was space around Wade's father's grave, and Jenny walked on that space, which now holds her husband and child. Her bare feet, in a much happier time, touched that grass.

And because she has been there before, to the exact place of her daughter's grave, she can go there again and again; she can go all the rest of her life. With her closed eyelids, she can drop petals on her child. The writer of the letter has given her this.

Wade's wife could have told Jenny all of this plainly, but perhaps it would have felt cruel to write May's name; perhaps she felt it wasn't hers to write. The omission was meant to spare Jenny without sparing her, to let her know that they were in the ground together, father and daughter, without ever having to say May's name.

Even though Jenny wanted her name said: May, May. A name that asked permission, a permission that is not Jenny's to give, but which, if it were, she would like to grant to anyone who asked for it.

Now, in her cell, she feels pain again. The music down the hall strikes her sharply. The sketch on the wall has a voice again, and that voice is telling her there is still someone behind it. Not Wade— his wife.

"Elizabeth," Jenny says. She hears Elizabeth shift on her mattress above her. Then she sees those bare, dirty feet touch the ladder. She sees those feet move down rung by rung, sees the legs, the torso, and now the hands. And in a moment, Elizabeth's face, expectant. Still holding on to the ladder rungs, standing on the bottom one, she peers through at Jenny.

"My husband, Wade, has passed away," Jenny says. She does not clarify that it was nearly a year ago that it happened.

"Oh," says Elizabeth, her face pained not just with sympathy but with the momentary anguish of not knowing an adequate response.

Jenny answers the anguish. "Come sit beside me," she says.

Elizabeth does, and Jenny can see that she is grateful for this request. Elizabeth puts her arm around her friend's shoulders. They say nothing. Jenny leans her head on Elizabeth's shoulder, as they both stare at the wall.

2009

Sometimes Eliot dreams about the dock he fell through.

The dream is hardly different from a memory, not made any stranger nor any clearer in the landscape of sleep. The only difference from the way it happened is that even before he falls through the dock, his right leg is prosthetic. Walking down to the dock where he will hurt his leg enough to lose it, he walks as he has for years now, his leg already lost: slowly, with care, not feeling the muddy water soak through his right shoe, feeling it only in his left.

But the rest of the dream is just as it happened. He is fifteen again, looking for his backpack, which has been taken from its rightful place on the floor against his locker, which is too full of garbage and books and old changes of clothes to hold the backpack, too. He has stayed late for a make-up exam, and he wouldn't mind so much about the backpack except that he thinks he failed and he wants to go home.

The school is empty. Outside, the late-afternoon sky is a sudden gray. There is no wind, just a dark stillness. The sidewalk already smells like rain even though no rain has fallen yet. The young janitor, Sonny, has already swept up the commons, folded up the chairs. Eliot had planned to stay the night with his friend Justin, but Justin seems not to have realized this. Justin has left. Or maybe he's waiting at the lake; that might be.

It's October, but still warm. Before going to the lake to see if Justin is there, Eliot looks near the portable classrooms for his backpack. The only other people he sees are four grade-school girls sitting side by side at a picnic table in the weeds, waiting for their rides, working on homework, checking the sky every now and then for rain. They smile at him, but do not call out, do not raise their hands to wave. So he sings out their names in an operatic way, as if the fact he knows their names is a gift he feels compelled to give. Grateful, suspicious, they do not answer. They sink deeper down into their books, but underneath the table—he can't see, but the change of their postures seems to suggest it—one girl momentarily grips another girl's hand to acknowledge what has happened.

Feeling good about this, about being the thing that has happened, he suddenly doesn't mind so much about the exam; he feels charitable and fine. There is the sound of an approaching car. The girls hear it and gather up their things, making a show of not looking his way. He smiles. As he walks in search of his backpack, he is thinking of his girlfriend, a long-legged, short-haired girl named Alyssa whose golden midriff he has rubbed his lips across on three occasions. She is a year older than he is and doesn't go to this school, goes to Coeur d'Alene High. Alyssa is not a part of this dream, but, unlike the prosthetic leg, she is a fact of it, something he carries with him down to the water in a vague and trembly awareness, a haze of light.

He is fifteen years old, and Alyssa is a secret. Her midriff is a secret. The taste of her golden skin is a secret. And he keeps these secrets to be kind, in order not to break the hearts of all those little girls, second graders they must be, girls in his brother's class, who come up to him almost every day in threes and fours, just for a few seconds to shock themselves by saying to him what they have dared one another to say. He can never quite hear them, never quite see them, because there is always so much giggling, and hiding behind hands. Spurts of boldness followed by swift embarrassments.

Guess what she said?

I did not!

He has reached the half-sunken dock, which has an orange cone at the start of it, and a sign taped to the cone, written in the janitor's careful but shaky penmanship. Such signs are all over the school grounds, prohibiting entry. He likes that a dock can be entered like a building, as if it has walls and a ceiling. Things are possible on docks that aren't possible even in the sand right there in front of them, things that can be said and forgiven, all kinds of lines that can be crossed with older girls lost in summer laziness who lie on their backs with their feet in the water and hardly notice, hardly care about a drifting hand, as if here on the dock they are hidden, enclosed, inside of a room. As if summertime is still walled in right there in the fall, walled in by the new kind of air rising up infinitely to the ceiling sky from all the splintered edges of the dock and of the dream.

And there is his backpack on the dry end of it, open.

He wakes. He remembers that there is a woman in bed with him. Julia. Still thinking of the dock, he turns around, drapes his arm over her waist. She is thirty-one like he is, has long bleached hair she wears unbrushed and piled up on the top of her head, held by an invisible band. He holds her close, breathing on her bare shoulders. She doesn't wake.

But he is not holding her to hold her, but to prove something to himself, to shed the feeling of the water. He doesn't like what he is capable of. Already he has left her. Twice. Once in the apartment of a social worker named Allie, whom he met at a party, and once right here, alone, three days ago, when he dialed Ivy's number.

Though, if he's going to count Ivy, then he would have to admit that he's left Julia a great deal more than twice. He's left her twenty times a day, or more. He's left her even as he's still inside her body. He's left her every time he's closed his eyes.

In the hospital after his leg was gone, when he lay on the bed looking out the window by looking through the jar that sat in front of it—the jar that held the dark, slick spears of dock wood and nails that had ripped through the muscles of his leg—he remembered, through the fog of his pain and painkillers, the backpack he was headed toward.

"Mom," he said. She was sleeping in the chair beside him and woke in a panic, gripping his hand. His brother, Gary, was there, too, slouched against the hospital wall, playing Fifteens solitaire again and again. "Did anyone get my backpack from the dock?"

"Why?" his mother asked.

"I want it."

But no one had. The backpack had waited on the dock the past three days in a haze of anesthetic and the damp October light rising off his induced and fitful dreams. He felt pain in both his legs somehow. The one that wasn't there and the one that was, both these pains a mystery, because the one that remained wasn't hurt at all. The numbness of the other throbbed, the air shivered and ached in the shape of his leg. His absent foot was hot and drenched and heavy like a mud-soaked shoe.

The janitor got the backpack for him, after his mother called the school. He waded out in his jeans alongside the dock. A group of children were watching; Eliot heard about it from his friends. The janitor, Sonny, picked up the backpack from the end of the dock, cradled it in both his arms, and waded back. He brought it to the hospital himself, soaking wet up to his large belly, his clothes filling the hospital room with the smell of lake weed and sand.

"You put a cone up," Eliot managed, through his fatigue and nausea and real and phantom pains, feeling responsible for the janitor's hovering guilt. "I read your cone."

But it was clear from the janitor's face that he felt a cone was not enough. "I should have ripped the dock out a long time ago," he said. He touched Eliot's forehead like Eliot was his own son and Eliot, as sympathetic as he was, felt impatient with the burden of adequately expressing his forgiveness.

So he feigned sleep.

And when he was left alone, he struggled to sit up. He opened the backpack.

Inside was a science book, a four-day-old half-sandwich, and a piece of paper folded elaborately into a compact triangle. He opened these folds, and smoothed out the paper on his covers.

Across the top of the page were tick marks. He counted them. Twelve. Below these tick marks were several lists of items belonging to different categories: Husband, Jobs, Family, Pets, Husband's Jobs. At the bottom of the paper, in block letters, the letters MASH, the M and the A and the S crossed out. The H circled several times.

One item from every category was circled this way, the others crossed out so vigorously he could hardly read what had been written there at all. He touched his fingertips to his own name, circled only once, but boldly, emphatically.

He knew it was a fortune-telling game. He asked a nurse if she knew more. She was young still. She smiled. She touched her finger to each of the letters as she announced what they stood for. "Mansion," pressing the M with her fingertip, "Apartment, Shack, House."

"And what about these?" He pointed to the tick marks at the top.

"Those," she said, considering them, taking the paper into her hands and studying it. "So strange," she said, her voice far away, "I almost remember what those are. I almost do."

He met Ivy after he moved back to Idaho, on a frozen lake a few days after Christmas, when he was twenty-four and she was twenty-two. It was early morning and she was skating circles around the ice fishermen, who pretended not to notice her as they hunched on

235

their bucket seats over the dark holes in the white ice. Eliot saw her from a distance. He was walking on the shoreline trail alone. She wore white skates and black tights and a long, ratty, tan coat. Her hair hung over her shoulder in a long, dark braid.

He wore his leg that day.

She was skating close to the shore, looking for someone. Then she waved across the ice, and he waved, too. She skated toward him. He made his way carefully to the edge of the ice.

"Are you one of Mark's friends?" she asked.

"No," he said.

"You're not here to fish?"

"Just out walking."

"You don't know me at all?" she asked.

"No," he said, laughing. "Who are you?"

"Ivy," she said, distracted, looking over her shoulder. He saw that the coat hood was attached with safety pins, and that the coat was torn in little cotton circles where the snaps had been. "I'm waiting for people. They probably slept in."

It seemed to him then that she had nothing more to say. She sighed, turned away. So he said, to keep her there, "I have thirty dollars in my pocket. Do you want to make a bet?"

She was surprised. "What kind of bet?"

He pointed to an abandoned ice hole. "If you can keep your right leg in that water longer than I can, I'll give you thirty dollars."

She laughed. "Why the right leg?"

"Because."

"What if I can't? What do you win?"

He shrugged. "I don't win anything at all."

He has been with a lot of women in the year since he left Ivy—grad students, a poet, a vocalist in a band, a bookstore clerk, all of them alike somehow, united in a cold and academic beauty. All of these women have regarded him with a sleepy, almost stoned amusement from the ratty plaid couch in his apartment, where they sit, smoking or reading novels, with irony all over their faces. One, a diamond stud in the curve of her nostril. One, a splattered purple birthmark on the top of her sandaled foot. One, blue side bangs that curl right into her eye, so that she is always blinking them away. One—Julia—with a chip in her front tooth, which now, to wake her, he runs his tongue across.

He and Ivy were together for six years, from the time he was twenty-four to thirty. Through their whole relationship, she never seemed to notice his struggles to keep up with her. She almost always walked a step or two ahead, talking to him over her shoulder, sometimes swinging around momentarily to assess his expression. He liked that she didn't notice. He liked that, at the end of the day, she couldn't figure out why her neck was so sore. "All the craning," he told her. She only laughed. She was always tripping, lost and in the lead. Oblivious; a step ahead. This, like nearly everything about her—the ugly tan jacket she wore even on summer days, the brown frizz that escaped her braid—exasperated and excited him.

When he was thirty, they moved in together in a little duplex in Post Falls, Idaho, not far from the street where he grew up. When they were unpacking, she found the jar of dock slivers.

"Can I hold them?" she asked.

"You want to?"

"Can I?"

He opened the jar, and she reached her hand inside. The spear of wood she brought out with her fingertips was about six inches long and an inch thick, jagged and sharp and brownish green.

"Does it look this way from your blood?" she asked.

"Partially, I guess."

She nodded. Then he watched her store away whatever it was this old piece of dock revealed to her. It did reveal something; he could see it on her face. He watched her store it away, without telling him what it was. She seemed in fact for a moment to leave him there, alone.

This had happened many times before. The first time was the day he met her. She lifted her red foot out of the freezing water, and wrapped it up in her coat, and said to him, smugly, proudly, "Your turn." Then, when he put his own leg in the water, she saw suddenly the way the water made his jeans cling to the mechanism they covered. She looked up at him, amazed. He divined on her face a special kind of awareness of him that he had never seen in anyone.

So there on the bed, as on the ice, he watched, transfixed, for Ivy to return. And when she did, after a moment, she sighed and put the sliver back into the jar. "You don't remember when they cut you out?" she asked, screwing on the lid.

"I don't even remember the sound of a chainsaw."

He had told her all of this before, but she seemed to think, without ever saying so, that what happened to him was a great mystery, that it all added up to something that only she could see, and only sometimes. She often asked him to retell the story, but this time she did not ask.

He told it to her anyway, leaning in close to her, stroking her hand with his thumb.

"I didn't know how hurt I was when I first fell through. I could see the spears of wood digging into me, but not enough to lose my leg. If someone had heard me, there would be scars right here." With the hand not holding hers, he brushed the air where his leg should have been. "But it was late. So I was down there, my whole leg through the dock, calling for help. The more I tried to pull myself up, the more the dock and nails cut into me. It cut me so close that I couldn't see the water except when it rose up through the cracks, and then I saw my blood in it."

"I know," she said, softly. "That's terrible."

He could hear some polite hesitation in her voice, and he knew she wasn't in the mood for the story right now. He knew he should stop talking, but for some reason, he couldn't. He decided to pretend he didn't notice her hint, and began, once again, to describe the school and then the dock, which was a short walk down the hill on a small inlet called False Mouth Bay, whose opening to the larger lake was just a channel. The nearly full circle of trees, broken only at that channel, insulated the bay.

"Which is why nobody heard me," he told her. "Even though I screamed myself hoarse."

He described trying to break the wood with his hand. He tried to lie back, exhausted, but he couldn't do that, either, without the wood cutting into him even more. His other leg, bent on top of the dock, not at all wounded, was cramping. He remembered that the cramps in the safe leg hurt more than the cuts in the leg in the water, which must have already begun losing its feeling.

So night fell. His mother thought he was with a friend; his friend didn't know Eliot had planned to come over. He couldn't see the stars, just the hovering black clouds. He understood the storm was coming long before it did. An electricity in the air. A nervousness in the ferns and nettles.

Then, all of a sudden, the wind.

Each wave that rocked the dock rocked the spears of wood deeper into him. When a wave passed, the dock would fall, and the spears would come halfway out of his leg, and he would struggle to free himself, before another wave rocked the agony back into him. The last thing he remembered was the water splashing up through the hole in the dock. He remembered the way his blood darkened the wood all around the hole. He remembered thinking, for the first time, *This is a real thing happening right now.* It was almost laughable. In his shock and his pain, he felt like laughing at the strangeness of being a part of something that was simultaneously so horrifying and so casual. Even as the rain poured down and the dock ripped into his muscles and he was in such excruciating pain that he could hardly feel it because he could hardly comprehend it—even then he was more astonished at the realness than the pain.

The rest of what he knew, he told Ivy, he'd heard from others. The janitor found him early the next morning, fallen forward over himself at a strange angle, unconscious, his forehead on the dock just in front of the hole, so close to his eviscerated leg that there was blood in his hair. The janitor had splashed out into the water, reaching across the dock to touch him to see if he was still alive. And when he found out that he was, he got the chainsaw, and cut his way to the middle of the dock, freeing the leg. Eliot didn't wake up in the hospital for nearly a full day, and then he saw the blanket flat on the bed where his leg should have been.

Eliot paused in his telling. He looked over at Ivy. She nodded, but it seemed to him that this was not enough for her; it seemed to him the shard of the dock had meant more in her hand than all these words he'd just spoken. It bothered him that she had some kind of control over his story that he didn't have. Usually, he could reveal something new to her when he told the story. But she didn't seem surprised or captivated. She was not disappointed, exactly, but she wasn't involved. She remained right there, beside him.

"Something else," he said, trying. "Do you remember I told you there was a group of little girls?"

"Who loved you. Yes."

"I think I found something of theirs in my backpack."

"What?"

"A fortune-telling game. My name was circled."

And there it was. The look on her face. Sitting right beside him, she was suddenly far away, and he knew she was there on the dock. He felt the excitement again, the terror and relief. Her lips were parted slightly and she studied his face only because his face was there in front of her.

"What are you thinking?" he asked with more urgency in his

voice than he meant to reveal. She stood up then, set the jar on the nightstand. "Ivy, tell me what it is."

"Nothing," she said. Then she laughed with surprise.

"Please tell me."

She shrugged. "I just had the thought one of those little girls did it on purpose."

"What do you mean?"

"She set the backpack out there, knowing you'd fall through. But she was so light, the dock held her."

He was confused. "But they loved me. All of them did. Why would they do that?"

Ivy stood, tossed her braid over her shoulder, checked her face in the mirror. She seemed suddenly tired, already too far ahead of him to wait much longer for him to catch up. She said indifferently, "I don't know why. To cripple you, I guess."

This revision of his past, which she took lightly, which she might very well have forgotten by that evening, disturbed him. He stayed away from it for a long time, nearly a month, not knowing what to do with it. It was the first month they lived together. She worked at the front desk of a storage facility, and he fixed furnaces. In the evenings, she fed lettuce to the rabbits in the hutch against the house. He stood by, watching her.

What changed between them in that month was invisible. For the most part, he could ignore it. But it emerged in his happiest moments as a taste in his mouth. It hovered in the peripheries of his pleasure. But Ivy seemed completely unaware of the change at all.

The loss of his leg had seemed for so long the start of his life, of who he was. The leg was secondary to his story; it was something he was happy to give up if it meant these things existed: the janitor, the chainsaw, the dock, the shy little girls at the picnic table whose names he sang out. They were important. They occurred because there is something about him. Something that intensity follows.

But with a casual shrug of her shoulders, Ivy had changed his story. She changed the people in it. The intensity had not followed him—he followed it. Predictably. Down to the water, where someone else, some second-grade girl, had already set everything up for him. He had become a passive player in the opening scene of his life.

And if Ivy could make him feel that in one careless instant, what else was she capable of taking away?

She must have been in shock when she came home and found his things were gone. On the table, held down by the jar with the dock splinters inside, he left her a check for six months' rent and a note. They wanted different things, it wasn't her, the love was still there, and so forth.

Because coldness was better than exposure, cruelty preferable to cowardice.

But in the year since they broke up, he has felt something even stronger than his fear. He has felt, like a phantom limb, her presence close by, knowing the things that she knows, not saying the things she doesn't say.

He reaches for her. He looks for her. That is what these memories are for, conjuring not his own self, but her. As if she has something to do with that water, something to do with the spikes in his leg. The leg means nothing anymore. The dock is nothing. It's her. The start of his life has been pushed up ahead, a different lake. A different season. A different kind of exposure. The ice he couldn't feel.

He loves her.

Now, instead, he holds Julia. He tries to sleep. He tries to get back into the old dream, the one in which he walks down to the dock on two legs, the one in which he has something to lose.

But he can't. He smells this other woman's hair.

And Ivy will not answer. Ivy will not write. Likely she has thrown the jar away.

2012

It's been two years since Wade died, but still his absence is every-where. Ann feels the weight of his past even more than when he was alive because he is not here to bear it with her, to hold in his body the potential of the absolution she knew she'd never seek but that was a comfort to know might exist inside of him. *It wasn't our song, Ann. She was singing something else. This had nothing to do with you and me.*

But now, the story is as complete as it ever will be. The details of his past are both powerful and stale. Too many, not enough. The song, the beautiful song they sang early in their love, feels now like the certain cause of his daughter's death. It becomes overbearing. Sometimes it's enough to keep Ann in bed.

But she is searching all the time for another way to go on. She knows her habits are becoming strange, that she's beginning to shut herself away, and she wants to stop. When she feels the terrible weight of what her love has caused, she makes herself go outside. She trudges through the snow or through the heat. Ever since Wade died, this is the only peace she's found, wandering outside, searching for a trace of a different past. She's been doing this since a week after his funeral, when, sick with her loneliness, she drove to the museum in Sandpoint to look through the archives. Turning those brittle pages that had nothing at all to do with her loss, the January rain pouring outside and melting the snow, she had felt that the museum was the only place that she could bear. She learned that there was a history to the mountain that came before the history that she inherited. The early settlers came for a brief time in the late 1800s. They didn't stay long on the nameless mountain. Their flowers, supposedly, did. It was the flowers, in fact, that stayed long enough to give the mountain a name: Iris. Deep in the woods even now, she read, there are patches of domestic irises that bloom year after year.

The day she learned about the settlers, that rainy day a week after she buried Wade, she felt the layers of the mountain's history in the very air she breathed. She felt the waves of her grief collide with the waves of other griefs felt no longer by anyone alive, but carried on the breezes that smelled the same as they had to the people who had suffered those griefs a century ago. She felt small as she went walking with Wade's dog Roo through the rain, and the smallness was a thing she sought. She found solace only in searching for some trace of that other past that would absolve her, or so she thought, by offering some proof of her insignificance.

But her walks through the woods over the past two years have revealed nothing new. She has found no irises or wagon axles. The only special thing she has found is joy in her companionship with Roo, Wade's favorite of the six dogs and the only one she decided not to find another home for. Going up the mountain on their walks, Roo disappears down the gulches, then reappears every ten minutes or so to check in with her. Sometimes when he returns, he's dragging a deer leg or a spine or some other unfathomable treat he seems annoyed at having to carry so far, as if he is obeying some long-standing order and not his own desires.

Ann loves Roo. She loves even the tired sadness with which he looks at her because she is not Wade and because she feels it equally toward him, *You are not Wade.* Theirs is a devotion that is possible only because of their equal disappointments in each other and the knowledge they share that at one time, to the one who mattered, they were each separately enough.

But this is their shared loneliness: She does not know how to train him, though he begs for it, dropping at her feet the old skins Wade once used to test him. He seems to miss the challenges Wade posed, the elaborate hunting games they played. When Roo comes to Ann with a rabbit in his jaws, she kicks dirt at him and cries, "No, no!" and takes the dead rabbit away. Even though she knows that's what he was trained to do. Hunt. The muscles in Roo's legs are the memories of Wade's voice.

Ever since Wade died, Ann has struggled to read the only language he left behind for her—an animal's love. Still, the dog knows what Wade would have wanted. Still, the dog refrains from digging where he shouldn't, refrains from killing what he shouldn't. And here I am, thinks Ann, married to him thirteen years and at a total loss for where to go and what to do, for who I am.

They never talked about it. None of it. Even when she understood what was to come. At a certain point, it was too late to ask. Could she have believed what he told her to do? Could she have believed it was really Wade saying the things he might have said?

But to the dogs, Wade was constant. Even on his worst days, he had trained them from the same permanent place, from the same store of untouchable knowledge that Ann sometimes finds herself falling into when she plays certain songs on the piano, songs she has not played since childhood and thinks that she's forgotten, until the melodies come right out of her fingers. She knows that place, where the dogs are, and the music of childhood. A lock of memory that disease does not tamper with.

If June is alive, she is twenty-six years old.

It's September now, a dusty late afternoon, the brown pine needles already fallen in a hot, honey-smelling thatch beneath the trees. Ann is sitting on the bench in front of the post office in Ponderosa, where she has just opened a manila envelope she has been expecting.

Inside, there is no note from Tom Clark; there never is. Just several copies of a painting of June.

June, at twenty-six, is sitting on a bench like Ann is, but at a bus stop. Tom has put her in a store uniform, a name tag pinned to her striped white-and-yellow shirt. She seems to be just off work, talking on her cellphone, laughing, looking up at a swallow's nest in the eaves of the bus shelter. Four chicks in that cone of mud, their mouths open wide in the shape of diamonds. There is a bustle implied all around her, people with shopping bags, checking their watches. And yet June looks up, notices only those swallows. Her hair is short, dark brown, dyed purple-red at the tips.

Holding the painting in her hands, Ann looks up and across the street at this town, where she has lived now for sixteen years. She has driven only partway here in order to walk the prettiest two miles. Maybe it will be dark by the time she gets back to her car, but she's not afraid of those woods anymore, not even at night, even though she is more aware than she's ever been of her isolation up here, of the fact there is not one door around that she could knock on, not one door that would be answered by someone like this woman whose image she holds in her hands. A sweet-looking city girl who seems to have shed this mountain, this town, entirely from her face.

Ann stands, leaves the rest of the mail on the bench, and she goes inside to hang up the flyer. The postwoman is in the back, sorting mail. Ann can hear her humming. Roo, who has come inside, too, follows Ann to the bulletin board, where she hangs Tom's painting of June beside the official photograph already hanging there, and then steps back to see them both.

But in the post office now, seeing the official flyer from the National Center for Missing & Exploited Children there beside the new painting she has just hung up, she is surprised to discover that her feelings about it have changed.

For years, the government-issued, computer-generated photographs have disappointed her, unsettled her. They had seemed, to both her and Wade, to depict the aging not of a girl but of a tired ghost, which is why Ann and Wade turned to Tom for help. But now, for the first time, the twenty-six-year-old face seems not at all like it belongs to a ghost, but rather to a woman whom Ann has never known.

It seems suddenly that there are two Junes now, one who is that painting, one who is that photograph. The painting has filled in June's life with detail. It has given her a time and place. It has been painted out of pain. But the photograph, computerized, serene and almost indifferent, is merely a glimpse, a flash, seen out of the corner of an eye, out the window of a moving car. There is no backdrop to her life. The projected photograph is like the momentary vision a child has of her own self years from now, a new self empty of the current one; the blank eyes are not those of death but of a future not wholly imagined. Because that is what the real June wanted: to enter into the beautiful, blank state of adulthood, that dream she was forever stepping toward, where she was absolved of her childhood, herself. That is what she wants and has wanted all along—to grow, to be outgrown.

How can Ann ever leave this place? How can she ever stay?

Tears in her eyes, she turns away from the bulletin board and goes outside, where she collects the little pile of advertisements and bills she has left on the bench.

But on top of this stack of envelopes is something new, something she hadn't noticed when she first got the mail, a real person's writing.

The envelope is addressed to Wade.

In the upper left corner, the name June.

2012

Aug. 4

Dear Wade,

   I want you to know I'm grateful to your father, Adam Mitchell, whom I remember from my childhood but not very well. The fact that I have very little recollection of our friendship can only mean he never did anything cruel to me. Perhaps that is an unkind way to begin this letter, but I am at a loss about how else to do it. I want you to know that I am thankful to him for what was generosity so consistent it could be taken for granted and then forgotten and then afterward be the form taken on by his senility. Kindness that is nothing special is the rarest and most honest.

   I have no doubt that you've thought of me as a criminal. It is true in some respects, but in others, it isn't. I've wanted to write to you a long time about the money your father sent. I've wanted you to know I didn't care who it came from or why, I just cared that it came. I was never given things that other people are given to ease their lives. I never married, but I have a daughter, Bailey. She is a few years older than you, and was sixteen when the first check came, the largest check. That was in 1968. I was working as a maid in Ketchum, and I opened your father's check on one of my breaks. There was a note. I don't remember what it said exactly, but I gathered he thought I was his daughter. I knew even from the penmanship that his mind was gone. I do remember he mentioned my fourteenth birthday, and you might be moved to know with everything he got wrong, he had my birthday right. Only I was turning fifty-one that week and not fourteen.

I deposited the check within the hour, out of fear of someone discovering your father's mistake. There was a three-day hold on a check that large. It was the most oppressive and hideous three days of my life. As soon as the hold was lifted, I had Bailey excused out of her high school class in the middle of the morning and I took her to get a consultation and X-rays for braces. Before we left, I paid for the braces in advance. There was a school across town called Friedman, if you don't know of it, and it was a very respected vocational school for girls that had just opened that year. Even though she was anxious from all the confusion, I made her tell the principal at Friedman's what she wanted out of life and then, as I had done with the braces, I paid one year's tuition in full. The principal brought us to the classroom where she was to be and even though there was only a half hour left of the school day, I made her sit down and listen to the teacher while I waited outside for the bell to ring. I hope this helps you understand some. She was upset at me for making her switch schools but I made the best decision I could at the time, because I was right that someone would come for the money.

That same year, two more checks came, and the year after that, five more of lesser, varying amounts. Each check was spent on Bailey's improvement. The money came within the span of two years, then stopped. It was nearly sixteen years later that I received another envelope, only that time what was inside was a letter from you.

There is no other way to explain without sounding to you, as I must sound now, unkind. Each of your father's checks presented me with a choice, either to return the money or to invest it into my daughter. I assured myself that if your father had enough money to send to me without you noticing it was gone, then you must be doing well. I didn't think, until I got your many letters, that you had missed it. I made peace with your letters insofar as I agreed to accept whatever consequences came. What I had given to my daughter outweighed anything anybody could have said.

I am including here a photograph of Bailey's daughter's children, my great-grandson and -daughter, because I want you to see them and see how I have given them this chance, by taking my own chances in regards to your father's checks. I believe that even Bailey's marriage is a direct result of your father's generosity.

Though I do not regret what I have done, I would be remiss if I didn't confess my relief to you. I am more relieved than I can say to be returning your father's money. His money, I want you to know, has been the whole of my life. It has never been apart from me. It has never left my mind, in thanks and in fear.

Included with this letter is money that I have saved slowly over the years. Your father's generosity amounted to a total of $9,200, and since I have taken interest into account, you *will find here a check for $10,872.65. I do not include the 65 cents to be sarcastic, rather to be thorough.*

Please consider my debt to you paid. I will add that I am very old and that this letter has taken nearly three full days to write.

Sincerely yours,
June Bailey Roe

2012–2024

Ann puts down the letter.

She has never heard of June Bailey Roe, but what hurts her most isn't the content of the letter but the name of its author. The wrong June. What the letter says is secondary to this first and unforgivable betrayal: June's name in the corner of that envelope calls out in her clear, high voice, *I am alive!* But it's the wrong silence that's been broken.

The letter itself hurts Ann, too, because it reveals a pain that Wade endured long before the real pain ever began. At the sight of those great-grandchildren in the photograph, Ann feels a surprising rage, as if those two children have stolen their lives right out of the hearts of May and June. Does this woman really think she could trace her great-grandchildren's pretty smiles back to her sin of many years before, when she took advantage of a man with dementia? Does she really believe that from that isolated evil, she has forged these two happy children? Reading this response to Wade's letters is a way of reading Wade, his letters sent long ago, his fear, his demands, possibly his threats. His equal and opposing love for his two little girls not yet born, his two little girls now gone.

She shoves the letter and the photograph in a kitchen drawer, and deposits the money the following day.

She puts it all out of her mind.

But as the months go by, she feels that something is different. Not simply her anger at the old woman. Something else.

It is as if, out of her closed life, has come a different voice, and it ruptures Ann's illusion that the story is over. She feels her life open again, for the first time since Wade's death. But she doesn't know what this opening means until one day she sits down at the piano. She begins with the same old song, the source, the melody that troubles her but which she also returns to as a way of returning to Wade, "Take Your Picture Off the Wall." The melody moves into something Ann doesn't expect, something unrecognizable and all its own. She has never composed a song before, and it is nothing like she's imagined. It is neither tedious nor divine. It comes without the drama of creation, without even the joy of it. The song is simply a brief perfection of feeling, nothing more and nothing less. A distilled evening laid under her hands that needed only to be pressed in order to be found.

Deep chords in the bass clef. The brush and dust, a dissonance.

It is all here in her hands.

That original song hovers over her, barely upheld. But breaking through these terrible chords, the high intervals of the right hand trip over the rocks in streams, recover themselves, and struggle, running in a breathless scale, up.

A pause. A rest. A breath that is the stillness of Ann's hands on the piano. A half-note eternity.

The missing.

Softly at first, then crescendoed, leaping out of that missing, the hounds.

Their paws on the ground, pedaled half-steps, eerie, a soft and dampened thunder. She hears her husband in those woods, an overtone, his hands slicing the air with his determination, soprano chords rolling downward. The melody is in the bass now, barely decipherable. And now it isn't bloodhounds he follows, but the playful low and ostinato notes of Roo, dipping down the gulches of a sweet melodic road all the way to May's school, where Ann hears the mournful candles at the vigil held there, the twinkling the clear, high trill of minor thirds, and a twin vigil at June's school— Ann's—a vigil she did not attend for reasons she has never explained to herself but which she watched from the window of her classroom and which emerges from her fingers now, lights in the small schoolyard in the summer, carried by chromatic silhouettes she can hardly hear, down a trail to the lake, where the twinkling is softened by the pedal, the gauzy chords of their light.

The dock creaks: rolling, broken chords. Then, quick spasms of melody, her tense, almost jumping hands. June Bailey Roe's great-grandchildren grow louder, louder, a kind of rage. The quick staccato snaps of clothespins springing from a line in a rainy yard, tiny teacups shattered for the thrill of it, the buckled rhythms of their dancing shoes. Slowly, they part, one in the right hand moving east, one in the left, west, and the music shifts again and they are gone. An ether. An echo here of earlier measures, the first refrain.

And in this eerie haze of music, the melody carries Ann into her own woods not very long ago, when she surprised herself by getting lost. It was a month ago, maybe, and she was out with Roo, and when she turned around to orient herself, she saw the two signs she had never seen before nailed to two trees.

She realized suddenly that the land they marked was her own, but being lost, she turned a new way and faced it as if she were a stranger, arriving.

She hears herself now look into that land, past those signs. She leans into the piano; the music is expectant. The dripping pines are in her moving fingers. The mulchy ground is a major key. And this is the only place that she hears lyrics, the words of the two signs themselves: KEEP OFF, says one, loud and distinct amid the trees. And the other—slow and smooth, four gentle notes that dissolve into those trees like a veil of webs—CHILDREN AT PLAY.

A full measure of silence.

It stopped her, that sign. Here, in her resting hands, she holds those three words, which do not disturb her like the other relics of Jenny's time. For a moment at least, standing at the edge of her own woods a month ago, her left hand on a tree and her right on her heart, both hands now on the piano, she feels mysteriously absolved. At peace.

Because what the sign says is true, somehow. The music starts again, quietly, but it is no longer Ann's music, but the simple song that she began with, only in a different key. The sign's declaration over these woods, over this song, is a state of being or an atmosphere, separate and distinct from the people who live here. CHILDREN AT PLAY. It does not even matter who, which children, Wade and Jenny's, or June Bailey Roe's great-grandchildren. It is something in the rocks and soil and the smells of the trees, a reaching arm, a trailing hand. It is something beyond all of their lives; it is in fact the border of their lives. It marks the edge of all that has come to be Ann's. And so Ann steps over it, into it, home.

It takes her three days to transcribe the music on paper. The moment she is finished, she looks up at the living room and sees that her house is different. It is softer, pleasantly faded. She sees the arc of the sun's daily passage across the cloth furnishings. She's never noticed that before. She stands up from the piano, looks around. Her body feels light. Her coffee, sitting on the piano ledge, is cold, so she crosses the room and opens the door, pours it out into the grass.

A lot of things happen in the years that follow. She applies for a teaching job at a small school called Idaho Hill, and soon she finds herself surrounded by the rural children of the next town. She is surprised by the joy she feels at the chaos inside of those perfectly patterned years of Christmas concerts and spring recitals. She turns fifty. She is confided in by a teacher friend. She plows the roads in the winter, grows gardens in the spring. She mourns Roo. She begins to write to her dad again, even to talk to him on the phone. On one of these phone calls, she tells him, for the first time, the whole story of her marriage, when in the past she obscured the timeline, left out some crucial pieces not because she felt, early on, that he would try to stop her, but because she wanted there to exist a realm in which she led a more straightforward life.

But that is what she lives now. She stays on this mountain because she chooses to, not because Wade's past has anchored her here. It's the writing of music—or the rewriting of it—that has given her this. Her ability to compose. Each day begins with the first few notes of "Take Your Picture Off the Wall," but by the time she's risen out of bed, the melody has already shifted, has already become her own.

Sometimes she's surprised at what she feels when she looks at the photograph June Bailey Roe sent. She still feels pain on Wade's behalf, but she also acknowledges that June Bailey Roe made what she could of a deformed love by cashing his father's checks. There is no regret in June's words, even if there is an apology, a payment for a quality of life wrongly borrowed and returned too late.

But not too late at all. Just in time. Ann turns fifty-seven, fifty-eight. The children stand on the risers in the choir room, and she raises her hands in the air, holds up their many voices in a fermata.

And then, when she feels them drifting, closes her hands abruptly and lets their voices go.

They're off the risers. They're all around her. They're running their hands up and down the piano, smearing out scales; they're clapping the dry-erase erasers; they're swinging their jackets; they're calling, "Thank you, Mrs. Mitchell, thank you, goodbye!"

"You're welcome, you're welcome, goodbye."

■

But when she returns to the mountain every evening, after school, the past returns to her. The past returns in the summers, too, when school is out and that same old song breaks through the hundreds of voices of the rest of the year. Right at the start of summer: *I hate to see the summer end / Seems it was never here at all . . .*

But when it happens, when the darkness and her doubt and guilt return, she sits down at the piano and she plays. She finds peace there. It's so natural now to move the song beyond itself, to reshape it, let it go. Two mountains five octaves apart, but both of them D's, Iris the high D that pricks her ear with surprising vulnerability, and Loeil low, resonant. Each time, the song brings forth something new, frees her of its original accusations. Sometimes she writes the music down. Sometimes she stands up from the piano immediately after playing, and she opens up the window as if to let the music out. This is what saves her, her ability to transform that first song into the feelings that she knows and understands, not the feelings of anyone else, not speculation or fear. Her own loss. Her own life. It is a peace like she has never known. She can take a note of that original song and place it in the snow Wade's father died in, and watch that note crystallize, spring its own shatters of ice, sparkling and rigid and terrifying music that, once it's out of her and written down, she can set aside, or play again, or put into the fire.

1995

May is drawing cats.

Rocket, with his blazing orange stripes, high up in a tree. Rocket chasing bluebirds. Rocket curled up asleep in the wild grass, a circle inside a circle, triangle ears, hard dashes the tight-shut eyes, whiskers straight as nails.

But she has stopped, the marker in her hand. She is sitting on her knees below the window in her room. She had intended only to pretend to draw, and so is amazed to find the lost cats across her paper. She thinks perhaps she'll cry. She waits to see. She is looking up at the pines and the late-afternoon sky, a dry white-blue. Her father plays the piano downstairs. The blurred music of the pedal pushed down reminds her of being underwater in the blue garbage can, of June's dark fingertips tapping the outside of the garbage can while May holds her breath inside, forcing her eyes open.

It has been hours since her swim inside the clean blue can. Hours since she stared into the eyes of the girl on June's book. Hours and hours and yet—

Downstairs, her father practices the piano. The earthquake chords, the pedal tones, the fingertips, again. The words her father never gets to because his giant hands can't make it there. His hands are climbing up a mountain in the music. They are dragging his stumbling voice along, over the boulders loose in the dirt. His hands are slipping down, then reaching up, pulling at the branches and the long, tough weeds.

He sings so softly. Almost a whisper. Not like her father at all. Like the voices they give to the dolls, the men.

There is a knock on May's door.

May does not look right away; she's too startled. She stares intently out her window as if with reverence for this moment. Her door isn't closed; it never has been. No one has ever knocked on it.

Slowly, she turns her head.

There is June, standing in the doorway, asking, with her old June eyes, to come in.

■

June says, "Close your eyes and tell me when to stop."

They are sitting together on their knees in the warm wild grass on the slope of a hill, hidden from the view of the house. They have wandered a long way together, looking for Rocket. It is late afternoon, the katydids click. May isn't thinking of Rocket any longer, though now and then she calls out Rocket's name in sudden bursts of recollection.

But everything is so far from her mind except for June. June sitting before her on her knees. The golden grass makes harsh crosses on their bare legs and the palms of their hands. They have brought some paper and pencils, and also some bread that bakes inside of May's Indian pouch. They eat it in little squished crumbles pinched between their fingertips.

This place they call "The Cliffs," though there are no cliffs, just a steep slope covered in pine needles so slippery you have to hold on to the trees so that you don't slide down. They have not been here in a very long time, not since "The Cliffs" had seemed to them an accurate description of the landscape.

June laughs. "I said close them."

May laughs, too. She thought she had.

But now that her eyes are really closed, now that she can feel the summer breeze on her face, can hear the scratches of June's pencil on the page, can smell June as June leans forward over the paper on her lap, the shampoo and the sun-dried water and the dust of the barn and the secret scared dog, she feels herself leaning in, too, waiting for her certainty to strike her.

"Stop?" asks June. She pauses, holds her pencil just above the page.

"No," whispers May, the sun on her eyelids, bright, the brightness swimming. "Keep going." June's pencil draws more lines, and May listens; May feels the scratches on the page.

Her heart is beating, a fist on her own closed door.

"Stop!" May says, suddenly overcome with the certainty she's been waiting for. She opens her eyes to see what number she has chosen for their game of MASH. There are a lot of marks across the top of the page. June, without a word, begins to count them. When she is finished, she announces, like a doctor would a diagnosis, the number twenty-three.

May settles down. Her heart stops racing. There is nothing to do now but wait. She lies in the grass and turns over on her side, tearing apart a seed pod but watching her sister count to twenty-three again and again, crossing off whatever item the number lands on. She taps the tip of the pencil first over the names of boys, RYAN, ROSS, CHAD, TIM, counting. Then she taps her pencil over all the different combinations of children, 4 GIRLS 1 BOY, 3 GIRLS 0 BOYS, 0 GIRLS 7 BOYS. Then, still counting, she touches her pencil to all the jobs that May could have, all the pets, then all the places she could live. MANSION, APARTMENT, SHACK, HOUSE.

Minutes pass, and between the minutes, June is slashing out the possibilities. She is narrowing her sister's life down to its essentials.

The first to go is the vet's office where May might have worked, which is a loss, but the next to go is the mansion that May has been inside of in her dreams, a terrible, vast, cold place where the pictures are old and of other families. And so it is a relief to see it go, slashed out, burned to the ground with the hot friction of June's pencil. Then there is the loss of all possible sons, which is a tremendous relief, and then the crossing out of husbands, one by one, save one.

On and on her sister counts, sometimes laughing with surprise at what remains, sometimes pretending to be scandalized. May watches, wishing this counting down could last forever. Her sister moves excitedly, her sunburned shoulders jerking beneath her matted hair. She is so familiar, so real again. The dirty dress. The white and crooked teeth. The smell of everything she's scared of. The blades of grass press identically into the skin of their legs.

"Are you ready? You won't believe this."

"I'm ready," says May.

June takes a deep breath, widens her eyes. "You're going to have three children, all girls. You'll have two geese and one cat. You're going to own a movie store. You're going to live in a shack." She lifts her eyebrows, allowing for some suspense. "And you're going to marry Chad."

As proof of this prediction, June offers May the paper. May looks at it and nods. "Once you get the one you want," says June, "you can never play again. Let's play again," she says, tearing out another piece of paper.

June writes "MASH" across the top.

"But we can't," says May.

June looks up from the page. "What do you mean?"

"This is the one I choose." And as soon as May says it, she is certain. They look at each other, and for a moment, it seems that there is someone else there between them. On June's face is something familiar, a hint not unlike the hint of the smell, of another person about to emerge on her sunburned face. New June: *You want to marry Chad? You want to live in a shack? You're crazy.*

But then it's gone. It is still the old June, and the old June doesn't think May's crazy at all. "I can't play, either" is all she says. "I got mine two years ago."

"Where do you live?" asks May.

"An apartment."

"How many kids?"

"None."

"What are you?"

"A scientist."

"Who married you?"

June laughs.

June's dark hair has dried in matted swirls so that her sunburned forehead shines. She holds her arms around her legs. She leans forward to brush an ant off the top of May's foot, and when she does, May sees, for an instant, over her sister's shoulder, a flash in the trees.

Rocket.

2024

When Elizabeth was first in prison, thirty-two years ago, she found a piece of tin at the bottom of a pig trough, down in the water. The tin had once been part of the trough, but it had rusted and become so brittle that a pig, putting pressure there to get a drink, had broken it right off. As soon as she saw the broken tin there in the water, brown and coppery and sharp, she felt something that she can only describe to herself now as the force of her life. Without any hesitation, and without knowing why, she reached into that dirty water and she grabbed the tin. Standing there in the open on a board over manure, the pigs turning over the mud with their noses, the winter sun falling on the fence posts and water, she examined the tin with awe. Its value had nothing to do with the possibility of ever using it as a weapon. What mattered was the idea that she could have something that was hers that she should not have.

It was difficult, but at some point she managed to sneak it into the kitchen, where she peeled up a vinyl mat on a plastic shelf, put the tin beneath it, then stacked the pots on top again.

Nearly sixteen years after that, when it occurred to her that she would stab Sylvia, she remembered the metal. It flickered in her mind periodically as she planned. She was afraid that it was not there under the mat any longer; she was afraid that it was. Each time that she gathered her courage to sneak into the kitchen and look, she felt overcome with something like grief, for herself.

But the metal also made her sure of what she planned to do. She came to believe it wasn't really herself who picked the tin out of the water all those years ago, but someone else, someone who was nearly gone. Her childhood self running through the sprinkler. It was as if with her last strength, that little girl thrust Elizabeth's hand into the water, knowing what Elizabeth did not, that someday Sylvia would try to take her away, and someday Elizabeth would need this tin, of all things, to save her, to save herself.

The tin would have been a terrible idea. Sometimes laughing with Jenny, making gifts for her, Elizabeth goes cold with the thought of what might have happened had she not thought Sylvia's stabbing through, had she used the tin instead of the mirror. She could have poisoned her blood with the rusty metal. Sylvia might have died. And the friendship Elizabeth was capable of later on, with Jenny, would never have been possible.

But her childhood self was right about everything else. She was right that Elizabeth was losing her to Sylvia. If that friendship had continued, the little girl inside Elizabeth would have grown up to become a cruel person. This would have happened had Elizabeth used the tin, or it would have happened had she done nothing at all.

But the little girl is safe. She will grow up fine, in part because of the mirror, in part because of Jenny. A woman who once murdered her own little girl has made possible a kind of love that has kept another little girl alive. A kind of love Elizabeth did not know she was capable of giving or allowing. And though Elizabeth works in the kitchen once again, she does not look beneath the vinyl. What protects her now is the knowledge that she will never need it, even though she knows in her heart the tin is still there.

Elizabeth turned fifty-four last week, the very day that Jenny, now seventy, collapsed right after she stood up from cleaning the shower.

Her fall came as a shock to Elizabeth, who has somehow never noticed until now that her friend is so old. Jenny has been in prison for twenty-nine years. Her hair is mostly white. She wears it short, to the middle of her neck, and she has thick bangs, which look a little unusual with such white hair, but also pretty. It makes the brightness of her eyes stand out, to have the white above them.

Jenny spent two days in the infirmary recovering from her fall, even though she told the nurses she was fine. Elizabeth was allowed in the infirmary in the evenings during common hour. She sat on the edge of Jenny's bed with her legs crossed.

They talked about a lot of things while Jenny recovered. A few times, Elizabeth asked her questions about the kind of life she would choose if she were free.

"I don't want to be free of anything," Jenny said.

"I mean if you had to be," said Elizabeth, annoyed. "What would you do for a living?"

They had never spoken this way before, in all the years of their friendship, and she could tell that Jenny didn't like it. But still Elizabeth pressed her.

Finally, Jenny said, "I don't mind scrubbing." Elizabeth laughed. But Jenny was sincere. "It's very peaceful."

"Tell that to your cough and the bump on your head."

The bruise on Jenny's head was deep lilac in the center, edged with olive green.

But Jenny had declined job reassignment at least a dozen times in the prison, so maybe it was true she preferred scrubbing the showers to anything else. Or maybe she was afraid of trying something new.

"I have something for you," Elizabeth told her.

"What?" Jenny asked.

But Elizabeth controlled herself. "A surprise."

"Oh, please. Don't do that."

"Don't tell me what to do."

Jenny laughed.

In the thirty-two years that Elizabeth has been in prison, she's done exactly four jobs, each of them for long periods of uninterrupted time, separated by long periods of other uninterrupted time, and then repeated. Pigs, two years. Laundry, four years. Scrubbing, two. Kitchen, three. Pigs, five. Laundry, six. Scrubbing, one. Kitchen, nine—and counting.

Such rotations distort time. The pigs seem to her like one long unbroken year, the laundry another, the kitchen another still. She connects the eras to one another. She is always moving forward or back in time, becoming the person she had been the last time she did that job, picking up where she left off. There is no sequence (as it might seem) of pigs-laundry-scrubbing-kitchen, pigs-laundry-scrubbing-kitchen. There is just: Pigs. Laundry. Scrubbing. Kitchen. Death. In any order. Four long years have aged her from twenty-two to fifty-four. There is the scrubbing year, which is a faint and awful memory for her, brief but never-ending—like junior high—watery eyes and bad skin. Give her that job again, and that is who she'll be, fifty-four or not, pubescent and weepy and demeaned. Or the laundry year—old age—squinting through boredom. Stale, artificial air, infirmary sheets that smell like sickness mixed up with all the smells of prior years (kitchen rags, pig-soiled shirts, blood on bathroom towels), memories of other times corrupted and made worse by their fermenting proximity to one another. A heap of dirty cloth is a constant, teeming reminder of other, blending times, a dementia of smells, and the washing machines so loud you don't hear them at all, like static, the background music of tedious dreams that leave her cold and sweaty. It was like that even when she was young and strong. In laundry, she was living in old age, a mere place then, which she could leave once reassignment came.

Or the kitchen year—adulthood—tedious but also lively, busy, the oppressive buildup of mean-spirited gossip, and careless orders thrown around, lemon bubbles and long, slimy ribbons of burned soup, oppressive jocularity that is a kind of disguise under the gaze of guards, who stand around and wait for you to try to cut yourself on the plastic dishes you could never possibly break.

And then there are the pigs. The pigs are her favorite. She associates them with the brief time she was allowed to go to the prison school herself, and she associates them with that one perfect day that Jenny delivered the piglets. The smells were awful, and the work was hard, but the pigs are a place she yearns to return to, though there is no chance of that, at her age. It is now an era past. She thinks of it like childhood. And if prison is an afterlife, then the pig farm is the childhood of the afterlife. Fresh air. An awareness of seasons. A misguided sense of purpose. A variety of minor catastrophes. There were pig matters of life and death, traumas and triumphs that in the grand scheme of things meant very little—they raised the pigs to eat, after all—but at the time carried a sort of secret meaning that got her through the day. Like the errors, the victories, of youth.

Put her back on that farm, hand her a bucket, and she will feel it again. The earliness of her own life buzzing through her veins like power. The weird, chaotic joy of a catastrophe or else its occasional and just as shocking avoidance.

The distortion of time, made possible by periodic reassignment, is something she is grateful for. It is a kind of distraction that renders chronology idiotic. And that is what she needs to go on living. That is how she copes with what she's done. The events that got her here exist inside another year, a distant year, a year that she's not living, and never will again.

But Jenny works in a straight line toward the end of her life. The backdrop is the same: water—headache-blue—sponges, tile, drain, and walls. These are the sterile witnesses. And her body aches and ages before them, visibly, to them and to herself. Maybe she thinks that what she did all those years ago is a point in time that only a straight line can someday render too far in the distance to see clearly.

Elizabeth is Jenny's only friend. Elizabeth loves her. Inside this life she didn't choose, she has found the friend she would have chosen and she has led a life with her, a chosen life. Jenny. Her face is now immune to the tragedies of music. Her brown eyes are always sad but never filled with tears. She is tortured by the popcorn strung through the hallway at Christmastime, and she is tickled by the swallows that make their nests in the eaves of the recreation shed. Her arthritic hands have braided Elizabeth's hair, have tossed down playing cards with mock defiance. How pretty she would look, with her brown eyes and her white-and-brown hair, in a blue sweater and pearls, some academic-looking blazer. She's the longest-standing student at Sage Hill, but in all these years she hasn't noticed that she's a student at all. She believes herself a note-taker; once again, she's reduced herself to her own hand.

They have never talked about what they did to get here, never. But Elizabeth knows that nearly thirty years ago, at Jenny's sentencing, the straightforward brevity of which was due to her adamant plea of guilt—that word spoken with the same dim-eyed passion someone else (Elizabeth) might use in her impossible denial—her husband didn't look at her, not once.

Elizabeth has heard from others, in here, who heard from others out there, that what Jenny said at her sentencing, when asked to plead for her life, was this:

"I wish that you would kill me. But I should never again be granted anything close to what I wish."

Elizabeth doubts that Jenny would have said something so composed or direct. But she does believe that Jenny does not wish for anything. Or if she does, then she wipes out her own wish with a soaking blue rag, and waits there for whatever else will happen to her against her will, like (or so Elizabeth hopes), the mysterious arrival of her freedom.

Nothing is for sure, of course, but there's a chance. Jenny's thirty-year mark is approaching soon. There will be a hearing if she wants one. If anyone is a good candidate for parole, it's her. Never a single transgression in prison. Never a single snide word to a guard. She is the only person to have taken classes consistently each term, never to have lost the right or interest. The teachers love her. If only she didn't guard herself against what she has learned, if only she allowed herself to be more than a vessel for Elizabeth. But no one else will know, no one except the chaplain, who's gone now, that she hasn't been doing the schoolwork for herself. It will look on paper as if she's been actively pursuing her own humanity through education all these years. The committee will like that. They will see an old woman sitting at that table, and they will not be able to imagine that she has ever done anything that wasn't gentle and composed.

But if it's up to Jenny, she'll waive the right to the hearing. There's no question about that. The idea of forgiveness repulses her. She won't even believe in God because she can't believe in anyone who would forgive her for what she did. She has said as much before.

Fine. Well, that's fine. Let her go on in her long-suffering devotion to that moment long ago, that one moment in all her life that she was not herself. But let her do it somewhere else. Not here. Not where Elizabeth has to watch her waste her life on this endless regret.

Elizabeth will apply for her. That's the great surprise; that's her great sacrifice; that's what will be, in Jenny's eyes, her great betrayal. Elizabeth will fill out the parole application. She will do as she has done all these years: She'll write as if she's Jenny. Not a poem this time, though, not a history paper. A statement of rehabilitation. She will forge Jenny's signature on the bottom of the page.

In the dark of the night, she has practiced. She has written a hundred different paragraphs, memorized her better lines, destroyed them all for fear of Jenny discovering them. How to talk about what happened all those years ago, when she can't understand, when she doesn't in fact see the need to understand? This impossible task is her one opportunity to make use of what she's learned. Language, history, poetry, art. The form on which she'll forge this paragraph will be the culmination of it all, her farewell to the world, her one good thing in all her life, including her life before.

Trying to write in Jenny's words about who she was then and who she is now, trying to force upon these terrible, stale mysteries the kind of language and summary that a parole hearing requires, has forced Elizabeth to consider, for the first time since she's been locked up, what she herself once did. She shot her boyfriend. When she tried to get away and her neighbor saw, she shot him, too.

She was given two life sentences, back to back, and that seems right to her. That seems just. But it was really only the first murder that she committed. The second was something that happened to her; it was an extension of the violence that had just occurred, an act committed by her hand and nothing more. Terror not at her neighbor at all, not at being caught, but at the new thing that she was. The moment she shot her boyfriend, nothing else mattered. It felt in her body that nothing ever would again. Not even the very same act, committed just moments later. It, too, could not compare, could not hope to matter against that first and terrible act.

Unlike Jenny, Elizabeth had planned to do what she did. It

wasn't in her mind for very long, a few hours, maybe, but still it was in her mind. But even though she planned it, she doesn't understand why. He was mean to her sometimes, and sometimes he was very mean. But never violent; no, he never hit her. She remembers perfectly the argument that led her to the gun, but the argument can't be a reason. How could it all be reduced to that? Why would anyone choose to believe a thing so ugly as an equal sign? Even to say that she was "led" to the gun at all, that she was "brought" to a point within herself, is language that doesn't really feel true to her. Almost true. But somewhere in there is a lie. She didn't know, the moment after it happened, why it had. When compared to all that blood, when compared to that new, swimming dimension ripped into the world by her act, intention is nothing. It is diminished to the point of nonexistence. Even stabbing Sylvia, an act that she had planned and planned. There was reason, cunning, intention, strategy, knowledge of consequence, *intention* of consequence, aforethought. All of that is true. But even so, Sylvia's stabbing, the logic of it, was derived from the non-logic of that very first killing. Access. A door she opened only once.

She has studied Jenny's handwriting all these years. Tiny blue trails in the margins of her schoolbooks and photocopies. Hours and hours in the dank but friendly classroom captured by Jenny's hand, for Elizabeth, like a gift of pretty insects in a jar. Thank you—but what to do with this now but give it back?

One time, years ago, Jenny talked in her sleep.

"She saw a fish up in the stream."

That's what Jenny said once, in the deep of the night. There was something about her voice, something so trusting and relieved. It was Elizabeth she was talking to in her dream. It had to be. It was as if Elizabeth could see herself in Jenny's mind, could see the two of them sitting on the floor together, talking about what they'd never spoken of before. That's why it felt okay, in that moment, to speak back, to permit herself this one trespass upon her best friend's mind.

"She did?" was all Elizabeth said, gently.

"She wanted me to come and see it."

"Who?" Careful, careful.

"May."

"Where were you?"

"I was too busy. There was so much work to do."

"I know," said Elizabeth. "A lot of wood, right?"

"I made her wear long pants because of all the brush."

"That was good of you."

"Scratched and sunburned. Snakes, too."

"You wanted to protect her."

Very calmly, "Yes. Yes." Then, with a hint of panic, "Who?"

"May," Elizabeth said.

"May?" An ache in Jenny's voice. "May? May?"

Elizabeth, her heart racing, knocked her fist on the wall until she heard Jenny wake up and catch her breath. Then she heard Jenny turn over, and fall asleep once more.

Long pants out in the brush. Long pants under the sun. Jenny had worried about her child getting snakebitten or sunburned the very day she killed her. Whatever brought that hatchet down was not a thought or an intention. No, the hatchet caught on the inertia of a feeling already gone. This will be something Elizabeth will mention at the parole hearing, if it comes to that, if she herself is called upon as a witness, and she might be, because it's her own name that she's writing down on the form in Jenny's handwriting, as someone to call upon to speak.

How to say it? How to forge a statement of it all?

This being my first opportunity for parole, I apply humbly and with no expectation. What I did all those years ago can't be forgiven, not by you, not by myself or by God or by anyone alive or dead

Except Elizabeth.

Elizabeth forgives me

Elizabeth is letting me go

Beautiful Eliz

She has torn up that one, too.

Jenny could stop her, of course. Jenny could tell the parole committee that she didn't apply for parole, that Elizabeth has done it all. She could say that she knows herself to be a threat to society and they'd better not let her out. There is nothing she wants less than to be let go.

But that's why Jenny won't resist. Because she believes she should never again be granted anything close to what she wishes, and what she wishes is to die in here. Jenny will see leaving this prison as the worst punishment possible and therefore the punishment she deserves.

But it's Elizabeth who will die in here when Jenny's gone. She knows that. She'll live for a while for Jenny's letters, and for a photograph or two, but then she will ask for a transfer to laundry. And on Sundays, when the new girl sits down to play the piano, she will listen to its kindness, to its painful chords, and she will fall asleep on Jenny's behalf, fold her soul up like someone else's sheet fresh out of the dryer, and she will not wake up.

Whether the judge all those years ago agreed that Jenny had no right to what she wished, or whether her plainspoken grief, which she shouted out in silence from her eyes, moved him, or disturbed him, or confused him, doesn't matter. He whispered, "Life." And so she lived. Is living still. Will go on living, to the end of that whisper.

May 2025

There was a time long ago that Ann tried to find out what *Idaho* meant. There wasn't an easy answer, the history was so intricate and poorly recorded. It seemed at first to be the Shoshoni word for the way the rising sun moves downward along the edge of a mountain. But reading deeper into the history, she found out that was a lie; there was no word like *Idaho* in any native language. It did not mean, as so many sources claimed, "gem of the mountains."

The real story seemed instead to be about a miner, a delegate to Congress. He was playing with a little girl in the House chamber of the nation's capitol. She was the daughter of a friend of his. A little girl named Ida. She wasn't supposed to be there in the House chamber, but she was, playing with this man, a stranger to her, while discussions went on around them about the name of a proposed state. When suddenly she ran away from him, toward the door that led into the halls of Congress, he called out to her, *Ida! Ho! Come back to me!*

Come back to me.

When the other delegates heard his exclamation, they asked him where he learned such a beautiful word. They did not understand his shout was meant for a little girl no longer there, a little girl they hadn't noticed. They thought that he had been overcome with inspiration for a name. A sentimental man, he replied that it was the only word worthy of such a rugged land, and in an instant he made up a story. He told them he had heard the Shoshoni chant the word at dawn. He told them it was how the Shoshoni described the rising sun—the gem of the mountains.

Congress was moved.

By a landslide vote, the territory was to become, with Denver at its center, the state of Idaho.

But just before statehood was official, the man's lie was found out. Disappointed and embarrassed at having nearly named a state after nothing—after a little girl—Congress swiftly changed the name to Colorado.

But *Idaho* did not die. The miner brought it into the mines with him. He repeated the word and its false meaning again and again. The sound was so magnetic, it took hold. People began to believe they themselves had heard the Shoshoni's chant. The word moved north; it moved west. It appeared on the side of a steamboat traveling down the Columbia River. The vision of this steamer, with the Shoshoni word painted in white on its side, caught on the hearts of the people on the shore. They remembered it. A trail of impressions, followed through like a line of unconscious music.

It is no wonder someone thought to give this meaningful name to a child.

Because, before long, another little girl was born, named for what her parents thought was the Shoshoni word for the rising sun, but was really just the name of another little girl, a child by now long forgotten. It was this second child's aunt, an important woman, who brought the word to Congress and requested a territory—a new territory—be named for her newborn niece, a little girl named Idaho.

So. A state named after a little girl named after another little girl. Follow the trail and that's what you find. A girl, a lie, a steamboat. Then another little girl. And then this land.

Come back to me.

Meaning is like music; it catches and is carried. It returns. Refrains, phrases, the names of passing boats. Stuck in my head, it's stuck in my head. The way stories fasten themselves to words, words fasten themselves to vulnerable rhythms, impressionable tunes. Ann is skilled in the archaeology of carried music. It holds on like fear, like love.

> *Take your picture off the wall*
> *And carry it away*
> *Dye your hair the shades of fall*
> *Don't let time turn it to gray*

In a few hours, someone will come to tow the truck away. In a few months, Ann will leave Idaho forever.

The Idaho she'd once forgotten.

The Idaho for which she'd longed.

■

Come back to me.

The space around the woodshed hasn't changed much since Ann first saw it nearly thirty years ago. There are still the crumbling bricks overtaken by grass, the spindles of wire. The two ropes that had once been a swing still hang from the same larch tree, though they are rotted at the ends and frayed. They sway in unison with each other, though there is hardly a breeze.

Ann is fifty-nine years old. The last time she came up here was a March day twenty-one years ago. She came up here and the truck exhaust clung to her hair. Wade had smelled it; he had known without knowing; he had held her face down in the fallen blades, had cut her lip, and she had sworn to herself that night that she would never hurt him by coming here again. This day is that very same day, but aged like her, the air an older air, keener, but the same. A two-decade-old day emerged from its confinement.

The truck is spotted with rust in the dent in the hood where the water stands. Ann opens the passenger side door. There is a slightly moldy smell inside the truck, though not unpleasant, like a barn of old hay. There are mice droppings on the floor. She buckles herself in, brushes her hand over the dashboard, then looks at the orange pollen on her palm. She thinks, with amazement, even though this knowledge is not new to her: I have lived here longer than anyone.

It's been sixteen years that Wade's been gone. He lived on Mount Iris for twenty-four years, Jenny and June for nine, May for only six. Ann has lived here for twenty-nine. She has lived here for half her life.

The call from the prison came a month ago. The man on the phone spoke of Jenny's parole as if Ann had known about it already. He seemed to believe that they were sisters. She could not find the words to correct him. In her shock, she's found focus. She's reduced her possessions to six cardboard boxes and a suitcase of clothes. She has quit her job. She has sold her things. And she has sold this land.

She has not had time to comprehend the severity of this goodbye.

In the truck, dust and cobwebs hang on the dyed, dangling feathers of the dream catcher thrown around the mirror. Ann rolls the window down, lets the faint breeze touch her face as she stares at the empty woodshed. She looks over her shoulder at the two backseats, not used in nearly thirty years, the right seat a brighter shade of blue than the left, but both faded from the sun.

The song that breaks through now is the one she taught Wade many years ago, a song whose significance was not clear to her until that evening in the woods, when she remembered Wade's first declaration of love: a love brought to life by music, by those hesitant early days in the classroom before—when—all of this began.

That first song, crystal clear, is all its own again. The words shatter the peace of the last dozen years.

> *Take your picture off the wall*
> *So I won't have to see your eyes*
> *And maybe soon I won't recall*
> *The painful things that once were nice*

Ann must do better. She must go further. This can't be the best that she can do. How self-centered that her fear has not changed in all these years, has grown only in detail, not in likelihood. But she can't imagine beyond what has already become the only explanation she is capable of—the explanation that there is an explanation, that all of this has a source. She angles the rearview mirror sharply toward herself. She looks at her nearly sixty-year-old face. Behind her, the empty seat.

> *Love is but a blowin' breeze*
> *That sweeps us all into the fall*
> *Now you're leaving like the leaves*
> *Take your picture off my wall*

Wade hums this melody, standing on his boulder, looking at the valley they have dipped into and out of again, down one mountain, up another.

He hums it and his fingers in his deerskin glove absentmindedly tap his thigh, middle finger C, ring finger D, pinky finger E, ring finger D. *Take your pic-ture.* He's unaware of what he's revealing by bringing her music here.

But the melody is Ann. It is a way of holding her, up on this mountain where she will never go. He loves her. He loves her.

And May has heard. She doesn't know why, doesn't understand

what it is. But she has carried the music around, allowing everything around her to keep it alive. The buzzing flies, the summer melancholy, the few words of the song that are true to her: *I hate to see the summer end. Seems it was never here at all.* The rest of the lines are ornamental, hanging on that central sentiment of summer's end, that one terribly true admission that is a joy to sing, a pleasure to get right.

And so she sings it. Inside the truck, behind Ann. There, in that small, contained space behind her seat, the child sings. Jenny turns around. Ann feels the horror of what's to come; she feels sick; she feels fear of the melody so present in her now, so present in May, then.

And Jenny hears it, too.

Take your picture off the wall
And carry it away
Dye your hair the shades of fall
Don't let time turn it to gray

It is the same melody Jenny heard Wade humming just moments ago. The same melody she's heard in her periphery, brought up the mountain road by her husband from somewhere else, a melody she could not place but that now her child has given words to. No longer just a hum. The child's lips have parted, and in doing so have broken the buzzing line that before was just a thread of many threads of sound. The mere vibration is suddenly given shape by that open mouth that once had closed around her breast; words used elsewhere every day are different when caught along this singular thread. What is the only force except for death strong enough to make your body not your own? *Love, love, I have loved you since I first saw you— Don't say it, please don't— in the classroom.*
Jenny hears.

It is a thought and it's not a thought. It is the tense rubbing and shifting of elements: the heat, the crackle of the brush, the fatigue of her arms, the endless drive over potholes, the gouged dirt road that shakes them all open little by little against the windows of the truck, fissures they can't feel, the slamming of logs in a truck bed, the spiderwebs and spiderweb-thin cuts on legs, the drops of sweat stinging their open pores, the pinprick bites of flies, the thinning of the air between her and her child in the backseat, a thought and not a thought: How easily we come apart. How quickly someone else's life can enter through the cracks we don't know are there until this foreign thing is inside of us. We are more porous than we know.

Ann's hand hangs out the open door, limp. She holds, miraculously, the key to the ignition. Where has it come from? The kitchen drawer. She hardly remembers opening it. But her hand remembered. It acted on impulse, on knowledge inside of Ann. And now, it tenses around what it has found without her.

A song caught in three different minds. Caught—like a piece of a soul trapped between a cup and palm, buzzing, buzzing: someone else. Caught—like a sleeve on barbed stems, snagged on this child's mind. And inside of Jenny's child now, this other voice will live. Ann's voice has taken root, casually, has altered May's whole body. It moves her eyebrows with the sincerity of those lyrics she's too young to understand. It nods her head with its rhythms. It alters her breath. It opens and closes her mouth. How much her daughter seems to have become this thing that's caught inside of her, this fragment of an English childhood a continent away, the slant of light on a harbor.

Every second syllable of the song is emphasized with a slap of her small bare hands on bare legs.

Jenny moves—

1995

Afterward.

No sound. A dream.

The dust on the windshield makes the trees behind it real. The trees describe the sky; the sky, the clouds. All of this in front of her, forever and forever, deep beyond that forest that is real and she can see.

But behind her where she does not look—that is where this second really passes.

Blot of silent earth across the moment. Blot of shivered moment across the silent earth. Forever Jenny's hand.

1995

The loose skin of a bloodhound is meant to hold the ground. The ears that drag along the forest floor send the scent up to the skin, where, trapped within the wrinkles and folds, it reminds the hound what the trail is even when the trail is lost. The smell of the trail becomes the smell of himself, trapped between the wrinkles of the neck and all around the eyes, which require an effort to raise under all that skin. Head down, whatever the dog follows he follows blind; gravity heaps the forehead down to the top of the snout, so that the scent between the wrinkles is more of a means of seeing than the eyes the wrinkles cover. The heavy ears flopping forward at all times create the walls of the trail, a kind of tunnel and tunnel vision, the tips of the ears stirring up the particles on the ground for the wrinkles to gather and hold.

Off-duty, head up, the bloodhound is a different dog. The wrinkles fall open. The forehead is smoothed, the scent let go.

This is how a dog forgets. This is how a dog moves on.

He lifts his head.

There are footsteps in the water, carried down, down, but the water isn't deep and the footsteps are caught between exposed stones, and caught downstream on the wet bark of a fallen branch, over which the water runs but not—not—completely, not between the flakes of bark, where a single fragment of a footstep is trapped and saved for him, collected by him, held by him, and stored away. His snout down in the water. He can breathe it, between it.

Hints.

And the footprints are like that other time he remembers only in flecks and traces, before he was old enough to wander out of the barn, when he was still in his mother's skin, collapsed and condensed there, her trail himself, there in her forehead. And the smell of her milk—the only trail he followed but did not need to follow because it surrounded him at all times, and he was too weak to stray from it. His eyes were swollen shut, closed not from the cascades of wrinkles yet but from the earliness of his life. The fragments of footsteps years later are like a gathering up of that earliness, that other time, the sweet and terrible confusions of morning, which he catches whiffs of only sometimes, a hint above the water, when the trails fall heavily down over his eyes and the ground rises to his snout, and he merely senses what is not yet a smell, but the trace of a trace of a memory.

But there are so many. Footsteps. People. Everywhere the people are calling out the name of the trail and he can hear the name even with his ears closed. It is dark. He knows that much at least, though it is dark always under the heaviness of his forehead. He smells the darkness in the men's sharp breaths as they go calling, not for him, but for whatever he is after, the smell inside a glove, the smell that is a thousand smells, of leather, mice, and water, fires, hands, and feet, and the confusion of other dogs that ran this trail hours before, the heat of rubber tires, engines stopped, clothing, boots, mud that is not from a forest caked and carried in the traction of the people's shoes from other places, farms, sidewalks, mowed grass, and the fresh deer pellets that get stuck, too, the smells crushed open, ruptured between the rubber and the ground.

He bores this tunnel through the thicket of smells, the bear a week ago, musk trapped in the mats of his fur broken open by the trunk he rubbed against, the pine whose bark a day ago was peeled off by sour teeth smelling of digested grass and fear and even stone, thrown fragments of foam from being startled, rabbits, too; he smells the newborn rabbits underground, where the afterbirth has dried in the eroded dirty fur, some just born, some old enough to have returned wounded, the blood already licked up off the pine needles by coyote tongues rancid and smelling of starvation, or other dogs, not on a hunt, but with hay in their fur and the insides of houses, digging halfheartedly with their pungent snouts in piles of scat sweetened and bittered by post-frost elderberries the bears eat to sizzle and slime the tapeworms out of their intestines.

And the soil itself, dry, splattered here and there with urine, human and animal, and the stream shaken out of fur or off fingertips gummed with mud and sweat and something sickly artificial. And at times the undercurrent of exhaust, trucks, a chainsaw nearly gone now, antlers clashed against one another, a dull, shredded smell, small flies, their crushed brains on human skin and under weeds, men's fear and cortisone, batteries shaken inside the lights they hold, a muted metallic buzz in his nose, tree bark cooling and crystallizing sap like honeycomb, honeycomb itself, beetles stirred, rubbing, bushes of spoiled flowers, cooling weeds, a cat's breath on claws licked clean.

And one man smells harder than the rest, the smell is a kind of staggering, dangerous, other people on his clothes, and the dog won't go near that man, though the man is trying hard to follow him closely, his desperation teeming, the smells of his anger and need waterfalling over his shoulders, over his hands, out of his mouth, calling out its sour-hot odors. The man has been inside that glove. The glove that they've held over his snout, the warmth of the glove, the sweat inside, the deer it was once the skin of. Inside that glove is the truck, which smelled like blood but other things, too, carried out on dirty, perfumed hair, on skin lashed open in cuts no thicker than threads, candied breath hot with salt and near-vomit, but almost gone, evaporated, the bright zing smell of seeds burst open from pods grazed by a child's fingertips, or else by the leashes, whiskers, snouts of other hounds, whose heads so very long ago, hours maybe, have lifted, moved on to other trails.

July 2025

Night. The lights are off. The mountain's gone.

Ann's suitcase rests against the wall. Six cardboard boxes, holding all of her possessions, are stored in her car, parked on the street. She sleeps on an air mattress on the living room floor, not in the bed, not in those sheets that no one's ever touched.

A broom, a chair, a bucket of paint. She surveys her work in the dark. She has hardly slept in days.

It took her a long time to find a street without children in this town. She stayed three days in a bed-and-breakfast nearby before she agreed to rent this place. She waited to see if any children in residence made themselves known, and they didn't. There were families in passing, child visitors to the houses. But none of them lived there. Ann made sure. Only when she was sure did she sign the lease.

The building, which holds three apartments, is on the slope of a hill in Moscow, not too far from the University of Idaho campus, on a dead-end street that touches a leafy forest. It has a brick face with dry brown ivy around the door. In the apartment, there are large windows on three sides, which look out on the street, and one that looks right into the branches of a maple tree at the edge of the forest. Sometimes, in the morning, a deer comes out of the forest to eat the grass in front of the building.

In the kitchen, there is pale-yellow linoleum, a small gas stove, a shallow sink, and just enough space for a table and two chairs. Just off the kitchen is a four-foot balcony where Ann has hung a basket of geraniums. These she waters every day with the old-fashioned watering can she purchased not for the flowers at first—they came later—but in order to place it on the railing as a sort of declaration, an assertion of a larger life, a real life, lived behind these windows.

On the wooden shelves in the small bathroom, she has folded new white towels. She has scrubbed the rust from the drains.

There are no pictures on the walls, no patterns on the kitchen towels, no birds or flowers on the shower curtain or on the valance she has hung from the kitchen window or on the new comforter, which is a smooth off-white. Even the mugs are simple: They say nothing, speckled pink. No sign of Ann in this home, anywhere.

The next morning, in town, she buys a bus pass and a magnet to hold the bus pass to the refrigerator door. She purchases a toolbox, then returns to the apartment to replace a faucet. She leaves again. At a yard sale in the next neighborhood, she buys a bookcase and a large cherrywood desk. In its top drawer, she leaves a map of the town.

Afterward, she walks the long way to the English building on campus. It's warm and windy. Even with the darkening sky, there are summer-term students lying under trees with their arms crossed over their open books and their faces down on their arms. These students turn their heads to gaze at the mallards or at the other students walking by with their take-out containers smelling of the dining hall.

She has never been to the English building before, and it takes her a while to find it. When she does, she goes up the wide concrete steps and through the door, and then stands there in the hallway. A few students pass by, thinking surely: Poor, confused old lady looking at her past, reminiscing. But what she's looking at is the carpeted floor. She's imagining this place at night, the moon through the window, the radio brought from home and the volume turned up, and an old lady, not herself, pushing as slowly as she likes, a vacuum down the hallway.

She sets up a bank account in both her name and Jenny's, and deposits almost eleven thousand dollars, the money June Bailey Roe sent, plus interest it would have gathered over the past forty-four years. As soon as Jenny can go to the bank in person, she can have Ann's name removed from the account. Usually, the teller required both account holders to be there to set one up. But she made an exception because they shared a last name.

She assumed that they were family.

It is her last night in Moscow. Before bed, she stands in the middle of the living room and tries to see the apartment with impartial eyes.

The feeling she gets from the apartment is a nice enough feeling. Melancholy and lonely, yes, but the loneliness is softened by the sashes of streetlight thrown by the maple tree's moving branches, and by the comforting sound through the open window of someone riding a bike swiftly down the street. It is an old apartment, friendly, a little run-down in all the right ways. When Jenny opens this door the day after tomorrow, the room that will greet her will be a gentle one, filled with no feelings but its own. No children here, none of their sounds, to remind her.

Of course, Ann has not spoken to Jenny about their plan. A social worker, who, like the teller, assumed Ann was a relation, passed pieces of information between the two women as if he thought they both already knew the main ideas, as if they must have been speaking to each other every week for thirty years. Because Jenny did not tell him otherwise, Ann didn't, either. She followed Jenny's lead, participated in this silence, and in that way came closer to communicating with her than she ever had. Ann, on her end, gleaned what she could from the social worker's remarks, and she never let on she didn't know anything about the plans he assumed that she had made. In assuming those plans, he allowed her to make them.

Ann turns out the light, lies down on the air mattress.

The night is warm.

■

She rises early, just before six. She makes a cup of coffee, heats a piece of apple bread in the oven. She lets the air out of the mattress. She waters the geraniums outside.

She will leave this morning.

But for now, she pours herself some coffee, and removes the bread from the oven. She takes it to the living room and sits at the desk in front of the window. The sun is just beginning to rise. All the windows in the other houses are still dark. She feels that she's the only one awake for miles. Then, in the early light, out on the street, she sees the deer, and this time a fawn, too. It follows its mother slowly, tearing at dandelions in the sidewalk cracks.

Ann thinks of what Wade told her years ago, about fawns being invisible to the noses of predators. She watches the fawn walk, nibbling the grass, and she thinks: It leaves no trail. It is safe from the danger of its history.

The fawn disappears into the trees, behind its mother. She feels surprised to discover that she has clasped her hands on her lap.

"If you are there." She whispers this aloud, as if to explain to the quiet apartment what she means by bowing her head, by closing her eyes. She has never said a prayer before, and it fills her before she knows that's what it is.

If you are there, June. If you're alive. I hope you've found a way to forget. I hope you hold on to whatever good you may have found.

Whatever good you may have made.

She opens her eyes. She looks around at the apartment. Then she opens up the window.

1995

Rocket is not used to being chased.

May and June know this. They know the only reason he is running is that they are running, too; they know the only reason he's afraid is that he senses his fear is their intention, and it is—it is—how can it be? But they can't stop. They can't slow down. They can't quiet his name leaping out of their throats.

"Rocket!"

They are slipping down the wooded slope, down the streams not of water but of pinecones. Their cheeks burn hot. And it is joy. August. Everywhere hanging in the crevices of the weeds is the white froth the insects suck and foster out of stems, a froth to live inside of, to grow in. May's legs and June's legs are smeared with this spit from running through it, tearing at the grasses as they go. The weeds lash at their legs, deposit the noxious juice in their abrasions, but what do they care? What do they care? They are laughing! They are shouting! They are running down the slope; they are falling down it; sliding. Their hands are burned from grasping at branches they are moving too fast to think to let go of.

Several times up ahead the cat stops his fleeing abruptly and latches himself to the low part of a tree trunk, ears back, and does not move. He gives them the chance to stop, to approach him like they have before, to become what they have always been, to peel him off, gently, one claw at a time.

But they don't take his chances; they take their own. They scare him. On purpose now. They don't stop, even when it seems possible that they could catch him if they did. And so he leaps away. His tail spiked, his spine caught fire. They shout his name like it's a threat, even though what they want, the reason they are running, is to get him back.

Since he was lost.

They have forgotten that. It means nothing.

They chase him because they are already chasing him. Because it is the thing that they are doing, now, together.

He leaps. High. High off the back of an armchair, into the branches of a tree.

—An armchair.

They stop.

Their hearts calm first at this sudden halt, at Rocket's ending of their game. But then, in an instant, their hearts deepen. They do not move, but lean in close to each other, as if to hear the other's thoughts.

They don't know where they are. They look around, breathing hard.

"A dump," says June.

"We found a dump," says May.

"Look at all this stuff," says June.

"A whole lot of junk," says May.

But it is just three things. A wooden picture frame without any glass. A crushed lampshade painted with roses and black, spotted mold. And a large cushioned chair. Blue. Badly faded from sun and rain but not so bad they can't make out each faint yellow fleur-de-lis. At the top of this chair, torn perhaps by Rocket's claws, are three slashes out of which the stuffing bursts like the white of a hardboiled egg through a crack in its shell.

"May," says June, about to laugh, "do you know what this is?"

"What?" asks May.

"It's your *shack*!"

And May slaps her thighs with her hands she's so surprised. She laughs out loud. "It is!"

"We'll fix it up a little," says June, swiping the pine needles off the cushion of the chair. "You and Chad can sleep on this."

May's laughter.

"Really," says June. "He's little. He'll fit." She fixes the lampshade by punching its dent. "We should come back. We should put a rug down. We'll put that frame up on that tree. We'll bring down a nail and hammer. Do you have a picture of him?"

"Chad!" May laughs. "Chad! I'm going to marry *Chad*!" May, still laughing, throws herself backward on the chair.

"This is disgusting," says June, but even so, she is crawling onto the chair to sit beside her sister.

"How about tomorrow?" asks May.

"We can put that lampshade on a stick in the ground," says June. "A welcome mat! You've got to put down a welcome mat! Where will your movie store be?"

"We can break up a plate, and eat off it!"

"We don't even need a nail," says June, getting up from the chair. The back of her striped cotton dress is damp from the cushion. She picks up the frame from the ground, and dusts it off with her hand. A few pill bugs fall away. May watches June carry the frame toward the tree. June puts her foot on a low knot, and lifts herself up as high as she can, and hooks the frame onto a short limb. Then she comes down, examines what she's done.

"Nice," says May. "Now come back here."

"We could put a skylight up there," says June, pointing at the sky. She returns to the chair. She huddles up inside the chair with her sister.

There is the sound then of nothing at all. They pause here together in this sudden hush, which is one of sound and also light, a coppery evening light that does not fall on them, but approaches them openly from the side, in wide, slanted rays between the trees. This light catches the soft brown hairs of June's temples, the hairs at the edges of her cheeks. Even, May sees, when June turns her head a little, the tiny hairs running down the slope of June's nose. Amazing they have been there all along. Amazing in a moment they'll be gone again. She reaches up her hand to touch them with her fingertip, but June, looking deep into this quiet, too, bats her hand away, and then they both are still again.

It is too hot for crickets, but the nightjars and bats have already begun their hunt for the early mosquitoes. The silence makes it possible to hear the buzzing air between the wings of the free-falling birds folded into torpedoes. And then there is the firework sigh of reversed, recovered wind. Open wings. They're flying. One less mosquito in the sky. One less pitch to hear, woven, threaded through the hum that's rising now, they feel it, rising like a feeling from the ground.

May feels tired. Happy, and tired. She feels for this brief moment, June so close beside her, and the scared-dog smell of June invisible beneath the smell of the wet cushion and the cooling trees, that she could fall asleep here on her sister's shoulder. She could fall asleep right now and not wake up until morning. And maybe tomorrow June won't be so nice. Maybe she'll want to read her books. Maybe she'll want to go out exploring on her own. Realizing this possibility, May decides not to sleep, to stay right here for now, to make it last. She fights to stay awake by looking at each thing she has before her. The giant fans of the thimbleberry leaves are wrinkled in their centers, browned at the edges as if touched by fire. The achillea grow serenely in their own little paths; they follow themselves on trails not one of them will find the end of, trails made by standing still but in proximity with the rest of their kind. Silvery-green stems and tiny white flowers already hardened the moment they bloom, easily crushed into a powder if rubbed between two palms, then blown away.

She begins to do what she often does just before her eyes close. She decides to forget things. She picks up all the parts of the day that are lying around in her mind, so that she can set them aside and out of her way, maybe on the shelves inside a closet, whose door she can close for a while.

And so, looking out at the grass, with June in the corner of her eye looking out, too, she forgets the face on the book, forgets her mother's hat on June's head, the pinecone petals in the blue water. She forgets their plans for tomorrow, the trip to the other mountain for wood, the possibility of June's meanness there. She forgets the dolls asleep inside the stump. The piano downstairs. Her father, playing a song. The scratches of the pencil. Rocket.

And the very moment he's forgotten, the cat calls out. Calls out in his round, mournful, chastened, and forgiving tones.

They both look up to see him looking down.

"Oh, Rocket," says May, exasperated. "Come *here*."

August 2025

There is still the smell of detergent, the smell from another life inside this cardboard box. Jeans, a dark sweatshirt, nothing else. This is all that she left for herself when they asked her thirty years ago to put something in this box if the time should ever come she'd be let go.

The clothes of a much younger woman. The ghosts of her fingertips in the folds.

Alone in this changing room, a room just off the main hallway of the free part of the prison, she pulls this sweatshirt over her head. These jeans, loose and too long, she pulls on, too. She never thought she'd see these things again. She had hoped with all her heart that she would not.

There is a glass mirror in this room. It's behind her; she saw it when she first came in, but she has been careful not to face it. She hasn't looked at herself in a glass mirror in thirty years. From the stainless-steel mirrors in the bathroom, she has received only hints of her appearance. But now, as she turns around and makes herself look in the glass, she is suddenly given the literal truth of her face that those thirty years of muddled hints implied.

The face she sees is unrecognizable. A face completely different from her own. Even her brown eyes are foreign on this clear face, this face of a person. A human being. An elderly woman.

She looks away.

She does not know how she will bear the hours, the years to come.

But her leaving is an act of kindness, on Elizabeth's part, and on her own. She's accepted what Elizabeth has given because Elizabeth will never rest until she's given all she has. And so Jenny will take this one last and devastating gift, if it will bring Elizabeth her rest. Perhaps it's what both their hearts have been wanting all along—to be broken. In order to know that they are whole enough to break.

"I have something for you, too," Jenny said yesterday. "It's something on our wall."

"Where?"

"One of only two things I ever put up there."

"But you only put up one. The piglet note."

"Beside it. Look beside it."

"But nothing's new—"

The quiet monotony and the still years and the comfort of nothing new. Yes. That is what their friendship is, that is what she's leaving. Years and years of trapped kindnesses, isolated love. Two fans of playing cards facedown and side by side on a concrete floor, to be returned to after this or that mundane chore; trust made out of the slow movement of light and the sharing of any rare thing. A new book in the library. A television show. A piece of candy. Old hands examined by older hands. A sharing of a temple on a shoulder.

The sketch on the wall.

Elizabeth touched the smudged signature.

"I drew it before I ever came here," Jenny told her when, yesterday, she saw Elizabeth on the brink of understanding. "Years and years before, when my husband and I were trapped on a mountain in the winter. It was going to be a gift for him." Then she saw the question flash across Elizabeth's face, and she took Elizabeth's hand. "There's no answer," she said, sparing her friend from a hope she herself studied for years, only to surrender it. "It just came. I didn't tell you because I didn't want you to search it for meaning. There is no meaning except that you found it. You brought me into your life before either of us ever knew."

Elizabeth took the drawing down from the wall, and sat on the bed beside Jenny. She set the paper down gently on her thighs. She looked at it a long time without saying a word. Then she put it back onto the wall.

Each, their sacrifice to the other. Giving and giving at the expense, only, of happiness.

They have been in each other's lives much longer than they knew.

They will be in each other's lives forever.

Dressed now in her old clothes, alone in this room where she's never been, she looks at the door, which is unlike any other door she has known for the past thirty years. This one serves only her privacy. It is a kindness that she can hardly bear, and she wants to take this room back into her cell, this perfect thing smuggled back in from the outside, and give it to Elizabeth.

But there is no going back inside. Jenny is, in fact, already free.

She wishes there were something in her arms. Something she could carry with her. She searches the small room for something she can hold, but the room is vacant except for the cardboard box with her prison clothes inside of it.

But maybe she is lingering here too long. She has been free for hardly a moment and already that old sensation returns: a desperate desire not to keep another person waiting.

She pulls her sweatshirt over her head. She bunches it up, and holds it to her chest.

She steps out of the changing room. The guard who brought her here has left. But the exit is just down the hall. She moves toward it. An ordinary door to the outside, unmarked.

She opens it.

The sky pours into her. It is a dizzying sensation, but she does not close her eyes. She forces herself to feel the sky's incredible weight inside of her. The smell of wildflowers is deeper on this side of the fence. The early-morning shadows of cars are long and dark on the pavement. Still propping the door open with her body, she squeezes her sweatshirt tight against her. There doesn't seem to be anyone waiting for her here, but she doesn't know where to look. Finally, though her body feels strange and heavy, she takes a step, and the door shuts behind her.

It's at the sound of the door closing that a woman in the distance turns her head, and so Jenny sees her suddenly. She must have been standing there all along, facing the wrong door, the front door, waiting. Now she leans forward a little, as if straining to see. She is slight, not very tall. Her hair is gray and blond. She lifts her hand from the back of the car where it was resting, then holds it up to shield the sunlight from her eyes.

There is nothing left to do but cross this parking lot. Nothing left to do but go to her.

Jenny holds her sweatshirt close, looks at the ground as she walks. At first, she hears only her own footsteps, but then, as if having crossed a threshold, she hears the other woman's, too. In a moment, they both stop walking and look up. They stand only a few feet apart.

It seems for an instant that they will shake hands. A reaching out, a quick, almost accidental embrace.

But they don't.

"Jenny?"

Ann has a gentle and worried face. It flickers with pained wonder about whether she should smile.

"Ann."

"Do you have anything you need to be carried out?" Ann asks, and she sounds almost frightened.

"No," says Jenny, quietly. "But thank you."

What to say to this person standing before her, this frightened woman waiting with the wide eyes of a child? Waiting for what?

"You're sure you don't mind?" It's all that Jenny can think to say.

"I don't mind at all." Ann's expression opens. "Do you?"

Jenny is surprised that the question has been returned. "I'm very grateful," she manages.

Then Ann does smile. It is a sad smile, an honest smile. And it opens up the possibility of moving on. So they begin to walk, side by side, toward Ann's car. Each step is a step in a dream.

When they reach the car, Ann goes to the driver's side. She opens the door, but doesn't get in. She pauses. Jenny touches the silver handle of the passenger door. "Ann," Jenny says. She says this over the roof of the car. They face each other. The hood shimmers, sparkling between them, a hazy plane of blue. "What will happen after?" Jenny asks.

"You'll live in Moscow," Ann says. But Jenny does not want to clarify. There isn't a way to put the question, a selfish question. She wants to know if the mountain is still Ann's home. She feels she must know before she gets into the car. But what difference does it make? Why would it be so hard to know— "And I'll live in Scotland," Ann says, to Jenny's surprise and relief. Relief not only at the answer, but that she didn't have to ask the question.

"So far away from home?" she says to Ann.

"I grew up in England. I used to have an accent, but it's gone now."

Suddenly, across the bright roof of the car, Jenny sees something new on Ann's face. A shadow of something like shame that Jenny can't understand.

The mountain, maybe.

Maybe she's ashamed of having called so carelessly to mind the place where her accent was lost.

Jenny has the feeling suddenly of Elizabeth watching her, though of course she's in the cell and the window doesn't face this way. She looks at the prison. At the thought of her friend, she feels that she will cry for the first time since the sound of the piano trailed down the hallways of the prison all those years ago.

"I think I do hear it a little," she says.

■ ■ ■

Over the hood of the car, Ann studies Jenny. But after thirty years of imagining this person, she can hardly see her now; all she can see is herself through Jenny's eyes. This has never happened before. She feels the early-morning light frame her own face. She has become a picture of herself, in this parking lot edged with cacti blooming in the gravel. She is overcome with this vision, with its sudden clarity, its closeness, and she feels the need to sit down in her car, where Jenny won't, for a moment, be able to see her.

But Jenny gets in, too.

Shutting their doors, sitting so close—it is a strange severance from the closeness they approached just a moment ago, over the roof of the car.

They face the windshield. They see the chain-link fence that surrounds the lot, the field beyond it. Ann starts the car.

For the first part of the drive, Ann feels glad for the distraction of navigating the roads of this little town. But once they're on the freeway, the silence between them becomes its own dimension, a single point of time inside of which they drive on and on and on, the landscape moving by.

Interstate 84 cuts through the wide open country of the Snake River Plain. It is a flat and vast place, carved by volcanic eruptions, marked by scrub sage and dark rocks, jackrabbits and deer. The farmland is intermittent, only where the irrigation reaches. Sugar beets and alfalfa. Sheep. The green borders of these farms are straight lines against the reddish, cratered land they have been coaxed from. Some of these craters hold standing water, surprising sheens of silver-blue amid the otherwise endless brown.

It is a landscape unlike any that Ann has ever seen before, since she passed this land the night before in darkness. She was in Grangeville, once, long ago, but her memory holds no distinct impression of that place, except for the cemetery where she buried Wade. She is shocked by the difference of this Idaho from her own, and at times she feels like this difference might be a thing to say aloud.

But Jenny, who has seen nothing of the earth but a fenced-in yard and a parking lot for thirty years, is quiet, regards the landscape out her window with calm acceptance, a warm, interested gaze.

So Ann says nothing of her own surprise. For once, she is unable to imagine anything more than what is right before her. She feels aware of her hands and face. Now and then she looks over at Jenny, but Jenny does not look back at her.

The old letter from June Bailey Roe is in the glove compartment, still in its torn envelope. At some point in the next few hours, Ann will have to tell Jenny that it's there. She will tell her about the money she put into the bank account in Moscow. But right now, she can't even offer Jenny the apple bread she has baked for the long drive, stored in a paper bag in the glove compartment, too. Ann is afraid of Jenny's gratitude, afraid of Jenny's misunderstanding her reasons for being here at all. At one time, Ann might have been carried here by guilt, by a desperate need for Jenny's forgiveness. At another time, earlier still, by curiosity, a question.

But that isn't how it is anymore. Ann is getting older, too. The mountain is gone. The love of her life is gone. She has her father and her uncle. But there is no one else in the world that she knows.

No one but the woman in the seat beside her.

The Snake River is only visible at rare points along the freeway, and only then by looking deep down into the canyon it has cut. It is the river that feels like something she could say. She points out the view to Jenny.

"Yes," Jenny says, kindly, getting very close to the window and looking at the silver water. "It's so open, isn't it?"

Does she mean here to make a reference to what she was denied inside those walls? Is it a polite response to Ann's pointing out the river, or is it some way of talking about their lives?

"Very open," agrees Ann.

On either side, the dry, strange land.

It is an eight-hour drive from Sage Hill to Moscow. It is understood that this drive is the only time they will ever share together. They will never hear from each other after this. In a few days, Ann will fly to Edinburgh, where she has bought a house just down the street from the house where her uncle and father live. Inside the house already is the piano she played as a little girl.

She never found out why Jenny chose Moscow. She doesn't ask.

And so the silence between them all these years continues in this car.

"Do whatever you want with the radio," says Ann. Jenny nods her thanks. The radio stays off.

Up ahead, the morning sky.

A running herd of antelope change direction, leap over a fallen fence. Jackrabbits as large as dogs scatter in the distance, terrified at all times of the pursuit of horizons, of their own alarming shadows on the dry, ragged ground.

Ann points none of this out, but there is the sense—Ann feels it—that something will happen, that something is possible.

In a few hours, the landscape will change. Once they make the turn north, they will go through the mountains. Ann is uneasy moving toward them, aware even now that the canyon this highway follows is cut by their water; the farms they pass now are fed by their highest snows. Even in this flat, endless space, she feels a premonition of their echoes. She feels that what must be said must be said before those mountains.

Up ahead, she sees a turnout off the highway. She sees a large brown sign, like the kind she and Wade used to stop and read on road trips. Perhaps from that point, a view of the river.

"Do you want to stop?" Ann asks.

"Where?"

"Up ahead."

"Okay," says Jenny.

So Ann pulls over.

She is right that they can see the river, not far below. The brown sign explains its history. The two women stand beside each other, reading it in silence. The major events of the river are marked along a timeline. Ann reads without really reading. The volcanic hotspot under Yellowstone. The spawning salmon so important to the Nez Perce. Lewis and Clark crossing the Rockies. Horses from Europe. Fur traders on steamboats. Hydroelectricity, dams and reservoirs. The decline of the salmon.

Ann sees there is an easy trail down to the river. "Would you like to go down?" she asks.

"To the water?"

"We could dip our feet in."

"That would be nice," says Jenny.

So they make their way slowly down the trail through the blue grass as tall as their waists. The frogs, which had been singing loudly, go silent along the edges of the trail, but continue singing about ten feet out on either side. The hundreds of stilled frog voices form a pathway much wider than the narrow dirt one, a pathway of quiet the two women both follow and create.

It is not difficult going down, and after a minute or so, they are standing by each other in the muddy clearing in the knee-high weeds, just in front of the river, which rushes smoothly by. In the mud are the tracks of small birds.

"Strange" is all that Ann can think to say. Then they both are quiet for a long time. The wind blows and Ann sees some dark hair hidden among all of Jenny's white. For an instant, Ann feels that she is standing next to June, that they have found the girl here, after all this time. All those portraits, all those years—this is the face they've been approaching.

Jenny says, "On a different part of this river, I saw a mountain lion leap up, right out of the water. It was the only time I ever saw one."

"I know that story," Ann says. "I didn't know you were there, too. Wade told me."

"He did?" Jenny smiles, surprised. "What else did he tell you?"

Ann isn't sure what Jenny means. Jenny seems not to be sure, either. She laughs a little, for the first time.

Acknowledgments

My sincere gratitude to Jin Auh, for her support, wisdom, and generosity. And to Kate Medina and Anna Pitoniak, for their vision, enthusiasm, and patience.

My heartfelt thanks to Mark Mayer, for his careful editing of numerous drafts and for seeing in my novel a better version of itself, and to Becky Hardie, Robin Duchnowski, and Amy Edelman, for their many wise suggestions.

Thank you to Catherine Jackson Dale, for her wonderful friendship, and for being such an inspiration to me since we were very young.

A sincere thank you also to Kari Trogen, Chinelo Okparanta, Steven Kenneven, Mark and Molly McPhee, Annette Ruskovich, PJ Terry, my grandparents Larry and Mardell Williams, and my neighbors Mike and Debbie Mann of Idaho Knife Works.

In addition, I'd like to thank the University of Iowa Writers' Workshop, the Wylie Agency, the James C. McCreight fellowship and the English Department at the University of Wisconsin, the sponsors of the Taylor-Chehak Prize, and my friends and colleagues at the University of Colorado Denver.

I am very indebted to the many wonderful writing teachers I have had throughout my life, especially Marilynne Robinson, Ethan Canin, Lan Samantha Chang, Michelle Huneven, John Ball, Deirdre McNamer, Judy Blunt, Jeremy Smith, Bill Proser, Bruce Baker, and Cindy Clabby, all of whom have touched my life profoundly.

In addition to these teachers, I feel deeply indebted to Alice Munro, whose stories will continue to teach me, and inspire me, and move me, the rest of my life.

And my most heartfelt thanks to my family.

Mindy, thank you for your support and love. Matt, thank you for your encouragement. And Mary and Rory, thank you for reading the manuscript over and over again and for helping me remember our childhoods. Your kindness has been invaluable to me.

My dear parents, thank you for building the "hovel" where I wrote most of this book, for reading and editing every single draft, and for all those beautiful years on Hoo Doo Mountain. Dad, thank you for your song "Take Your Picture Off the Wall."

And Sam McPhee, my husband, who read this novel more times than anyone, who wrote beside me every day, I want to thank you not only for your love and kindness and insight and hard work, but also for your perfect imagination, which has guided me and challenged me and—if I have been so lucky—has found its way into these pages.